Ab

Brenda Jackson is a *New York Times* bestselling author of more than one hundred romance titles. Brenda lives in Jacksonville, Florida, and divides her time between family, writing and travelling. Email Brenda at authorbrendajackson@gmail.com or visit her on her website at brendajackson.net

Debra Webb is the award-winning, *USA Today* bestselling author of more than 150 novels, including reader favourites the *Faces of Evil*, the *Colby Agency*, and the *Shades of Death* series. With more than four million books sold in numerous languages and countries, Debra's love of storytelling goes back to her childhood on a farm in Alabama. Visit Debra at www.DebraWebb.com or write to her at PO Box 176, Madison, AL 35758.

Sandra Marton is a *USA Today* bestselling author. A four-time finalist for the RITA®, the coveted award given by Romance Writers of America, she's also won eight Romantic Times Reviewers' Choice Awards, the Holt Medallion, and Romantic Times' Career Achievement Award. Sandra's heroes are powerful, sexy, take-charge men who think they have it all – until that one special woman comes along. Stand back, because together they're bound to set the world on fire.

Hot Heroes

May 2020
Protection Detail

June 2020
Armed and Dangerous

December 2020
The Rules of Her Rescue

January 2021
Surrender Your Heart

February 2021
Undercover Temptation

March 2021
Tough Love

Hot Heroes: Undercover Temptation

BRENDA JACKSON

DEBRA WEBB

SANDRA MARTON

MILLS & BOON

First Published in Great Britain 2021
by Mills & Boon, an imprint of HarperCollins*Publishers* Ltd,
1 London Bridge Street, London, SE1 9GF

www.harpercollins.co.uk

HarperCollins*Publishers*
1st Floor, Watermarque Building,
Ringsend Road, Dublin 4, Ireland

ISBN: 978-0-263-28211-5

MIX
Paper from responsible sources
FSC™ C007454

This book is produced from independently certified FSC™ paper to ensure responsible forest management.

For more information visit: www.harpercollins.co.uk/green

Printed and bound in Spain
by CPI, Barcelona

AN HONOURABLE SEDUCTION

BRENDA JACKSON

To the man who will forever be the love of my life,
Gerald Jackson, Sr.

To all of my readers who asked for Flipper's story.
This one is for you!

To the Brenda Jackson Book Club/Facebook fans.
Over 4,000 strong and after fourteen years, you
guys still rock!

Many waters cannot quench love; rivers cannot
sweep it away.
—Song of Solomon 8:7

Prologue

The Naval Amphibious Base
Coronado, San Diego, California

"What kind of trouble have you gotten into?"

David Holloway, known to his Navy SEAL teammates as Flipper, glanced at the four men surrounding him. They were like brothers to him. More than once they'd risked their lives for each other and they would continue to have each other's backs, on duty or off. That bond was what accounted for the concerned looks on their faces. He wondered how they'd known he'd been summoned to the admiral's office.

"Let's hope I'm not in any trouble, Mac," Flipper said, rubbing a hand down his face.

He had to admit he was wondering what was going on, just like they were. Usually, you were only summoned to a meeting with the admiral when you were getting reprimanded for some reason, and he never got into trouble. At least he *rarely* did. As the son of a retired SEALs commanding officer and the youngest of five brothers—all Navy SEALs—he knew better.

"Maybe there's an event on the base and he wants you to escort his daughter now that you're the single one among us," Coop said, grinning.

Flipper didn't grin back. They'd seen Georgianna Martin, the admiral's twenty-three-year-old daughter. She was beautiful, but they'd heard the horror stories from other teammates who'd been ordered to take her out on dates. According to them, those evenings had been the dates from hell. The young woman was spoiled rotten, selfish as sin and had an attitude that sucked. That's why Flipper didn't find Coop's comment at all amusing. He hoped that wasn't why the admiral wanted to see him.

It didn't surprise Flipper that it was Mac who'd asked if Flipper had gotten into trouble. Thurston McRoy—code name Mac—was older than the other four men on the team, who had all started their careers as SEALs around the same time. Mac had been a SEAL five years before the rest of them. Mac seemed to like to think he was the big brother looking out for them, almost like he figured they couldn't take care of themselves. He was forevcr giving them advice—even when they didn't ask for it.

In addition to Mac and Flipper, their SEAL team included Brisbane Westmoreland, code name Bane; Gavin Blake, whose code name was Viper; and Laramie Cooper, whose code name was Coop.

Flipper checked his watch. "Since I have a couple of hours to spare before meeting with the admiral, let's grab something to eat," he suggested.

"Sounds good to me," Bane said.

Less than an hour later, Flipper and his four teammates shared burgers, fries and milkshakes at one of the most popular eating places on base. They decided to sit outside at one of the café tables in the front instead of inside where it was crowded since it was such a beautiful May day.

No one brought up his meeting with the admiral again or the notion of him taking the admiral's daughter on a date. He was glad. Instead, the guys had more important things to talk about, namely their families.

Bane's wife, Crystal, had given birth to triplets last year and he had new photos to share, so they passed Bane's cell phone around.

Viper's wife, Layla, was expecting with only a few months to go before Gavin Blake IV would be born. Viper was excited about becoming a father, of course.

Like Bane, Mac had plenty of photos to share; he was married and the father of four.

And Coop had a two-year-old son he hadn't known about until he'd run into his old girlfriend about six months ago. They'd reconnected, gotten married and were now a happy family.

Earlier in the week, the teammates had gotten word from their commanding officer that next week was the start of a four-month leave. For Flipper, that meant heading home to Dallas and he couldn't wait. His mother had a birthday coming up and he was glad he would be home to celebrate.

"I don't care what plans you all are making for your leave, just as long as you remember my mom's birthday celebration. I understand you not showing up, Viper, with a baby on the way. The rest of you guys, no excuses."

"We hear you," Bane said, grinning. "And we will be there."

When Viper ordered another hamburger, everyone teased him about being the one to eat for two instead of his wife. And then everyone talked about what they planned to do with their four months off.

It was two hours later when Flipper walked into the admiral's office. He was surprised to find Commanding Officer Shields there as well. Flipper saluted both men.

"At ease. Please have a seat, Lieutenant Holloway."

"Thank you, sir," he said, sitting down. He was used to being under his commanding officer's intense scrutiny, but there was something in the sharp green eyes of Admiral Norris Martin that was making him feel uncomfortable.

"You come highly recommended by your commanding officer here, Lieutenant Holloway. And the reason I asked to meet with you is that we need you. Your country needs you."

Flipper was happy to step up. He was a Navy SEAL, and the reason he'd enlisted, like his father and brothers, was to protect his country. "And what am I needed to do, sir?" he asked.

"Our investigators have provided intelligence and a preliminary report that says acts of espionage are happening in Key West. Someone is trading valuable government secrets to China."

Flipper didn't respond immediately.

The one thing he hated was a traitor, but he'd discovered that for the right price, a number of American citizens would perform acts of treason. He understood that. However, what he didn't understand was why he'd been singled out for this meeting. He was part of a SEAL team. He didn't work in naval intelligence.

Confusion must have shown on his face because Admiral Martin continued, "The report was given to me, but I don't believe it."

Flipper raised a brow. "You don't believe a report that classified documents are being traded in Key West, sir?"

"Oh, I believe all that, but what I refuse to believe is that this suspect is guilty of anything."

"Is there a reason why, sir?"

"Here is the information," said Commanding Officer Shields, speaking for the first time as he handed Flipper a folder.

Flipper opened it to find a picture of a very beautiful woman. She looked to be around twenty-four, with dark, sultry eyes and full, shapely lips. Then there was her mass of copper-brown spiral curls that flowed to her shoulders, crowning a cocoa-colored face. A pair of dangling gold earrings hung from her ears and a golden pendant necklace hung around her neck.

He knew he was spending too much time studying her features, but it couldn't be helped. The woman was strikingly beautiful.

Reluctantly he moved his gaze away from her face to check out the background of the photo. From the tropical vegetation captured by the photographer, she seemed to be on an island somewhere. She stood near a body of water that showed in the corner of the eight-by-ten photo. Scribbled across the bottom were the words:

Miss you, Godpop 1

Love, Swan

Swan? It was an unusual name, but it fit.

He moved to the next document in the file. Attached to it was a small family photo that showed a tall Caucasian man with sandy-brown hair and brown eyes standing beside a beautiful woman who closely resembled Swan. Her mother. In front of the couple was a beautiful little girl who looked to be around eight.

Flipper studied the child's face and knew that child had grown up to be the gorgeous woman in the first photo. The shape of her face was the same, as were her eyes. Even as a child, she'd had long curly hair.

The family photo was clipped to a profile of the young woman. As he'd guessed, she was twenty-four. Her name was Swan Jamison. She was an American, born in Key West. Presently, she owned a jewelry store on the island. That was all the information the document provided.

Flipper lifted his gaze to find his commanding officer and the admiral staring at him. "I assume this is the person naval intelligence believes is the traitor."

"Yes," Admiral Martin said. "She's my goddaughter. I am Godpop 1."

"She's my goddaughter as well," added Commanding Officer Shields. "I am Godpop 2."

Flipper's gaze moved from one man to the other. "I see, sirs."

Admiral Martin nodded. "Her father was part of our SEAL team and our best friend. His name was Andrew Jamison."

Flipper had heard that Commanding Officer Shields and Admiral Martin were part of the same SEAL team a number of years ago.

"Andrew was the best. He lost his life saving ours," said Commanding Officer Shields. "He didn't die immediately, and before he died, he made us promise to look after his wife, Leigh, and his daughter, Swan." The man paused and then said, "Over twenty-eight years ago, when we were taking some R & R in Jamaica, Andrew met Leigh, who was a Jamaican model. They married a year later, and he moved her to Key West, where our team was stationed. After Andrew was killed, Leigh returned to Jamaica. When Swan graduated from high school, she returned to the Keys and moved into her parents' home."

"How old was she when her father was killed?" Flipper asked.

"She was fifteen," Admiral Martin said. "Swan was close to her dad. Leigh was so broken up over Andrew's death that she didn't want to live in the States without him, which was why she returned to Jamaica. She passed away two years ago."

Flipper's commanding officer then took up the tale. "Leigh sent for us before she died of stomach cancer, asking us to look out for Swan after she was gone. We would have done that anyway, since we always kept in touch with both Leigh and Swan. In fact, Swan rotated summers with us and our families even after Leigh returned to Jamaica. We took our roles as godfathers seriously. We were even there when Swan graduated from high school and college."

"Did Swan have any American grandparents?" Flipper asked.

He saw both men's lips tighten into frowns. "Yes. However, her paternal grandparents didn't approve of their son's marriage to Leigh," said Commanding Officer Shields.

"So they never accepted their granddaughter." It was more of a statement than a question.

"No, they never did," Admiral Martin confirmed. As if it was a topic he'd rather change, the man added, "We've been given some time to find out the truth, but not much. Luckily, Swan's Godpop 3 has a high-level position at naval intelligence. Otherwise, we wouldn't know about the investigation. We have thirty days to prove Swan is not a traitor and identify the person who is. That's where we need your help. Instead of releasing you to go home as we're doing for the other members of your team, we are assigning you to a special mission, Lieutenant Holloway. You are being sent to Key West."

One

Key West, Florida

Swan Jamison was beside herself with excitement as she opened the huge box on her desk. Although it contained only her jewelry-making supplies, the package served as affirmation that while rebuilding was still taking place in certain areas, the majority of the island had recovered from the hurricane that had hit eight months ago.

"Anything for me?" Rafe asked, sticking his head through the office door.

Her shop was in a very trendy area so she could capitalize on the tourists visiting the island. To help with high operating costs, she leased out one of the large rooms in the back. Rafe was her tenant, who'd converted the back room into a tattoo shop. On some days, he got more customers than she did.

"Nothing for you, Rafe, just supplies for me." She

checked her watch. "You're early today." Usually he didn't open up until noon.

"I have a special appointment at ten thirty and I need to ready my ink." And then he was gone. Rafe didn't say a whole lot except to his customers.

The door chime alerted her that *she* had a customer. Jamila, who worked part-time and usually only in the mornings, had taken time off for a day of beauty—hair, nails, pedicure, bikini wax, the works. Her boyfriend worked on a cruise ship that was due in port tomorrow. Swan was happy for Jamila and happy for herself as well. The cruise ships always brought in tourists who wanted to purchase authentic handmade jewelry.

She walked out of her office as a man perused her jewelry display case near the door. That was good. While he checked out her jewelry, she would check him out.

He had a nice profile. Tall, broad shoulders that looked good in a T-shirt and a pair of muscular thighs that fit well in his jeans. He had diamond-blond hair that was neatly trimmed and his hands were the right size for his body.

There was something about the way he stood, straight and tall, that all but spelled out *military man*. And the way his legs were braced apart, as if he had to maintain his balance even on land, spelled out *navy*.

Too bad. She didn't do military men. In all honesty, lately she hadn't done men at all. Too busy.

And then there was the issue of Candy's divorce. Swan knew she shouldn't let what had happened to her best friend darken her own view, but Swan was known to claim whatever excuse suited her and that one did at the moment.

And speaking of the moment, she had looked her

fill. She needed to make her first sale of the day. "May I help you?"

He turned and looked at her, and every cell in her body jolted to attention.

Wow! She'd seen blue eyes before, but his were a shade she'd never seen. They were laser blue; the intense sharpness of the pupils captured her within their scope. And his features… Lordy! The man had such gorgeous bone structure! There was no way a woman had ever passed by him and not taken a second look. Even a third, while wiping away drool.

"Yes, you can help me."

And why did he have to sound so good, too? The sound of his voice—a deep, husky tone—made her throat go dry.

"All right," she said, walking over to him. She knew she had to get a grip. Her store had been closed for two months due to the hurricane, and now that the tourists were returning, she needed to catch up on sales.

"And how can I help you?" She didn't miss the way he was looking at her. She saw interest in his eyes. There was nothing wrong with that. She took pride in her appearance because she had been raised to do so. Leigh Rutledge Jamison, who'd been a Jamaican model, had taught her daughter that your appearance was everything.

Pain settled in Swan's heart. She missed her mom so much.

"I'm looking for a gift for someone."

Swan nodded as she came to stand beside him. Not only did he look good and sound good, but he smelled good as well. She glanced down at his hand and didn't see a wedding ring. He was probably buying a gift for his girlfriend or soon-to-be fiancée.

"What do you have in mind?"

"What do you suggest?" he asked her.

"Well, it depends," she said, looking into those gorgeous eyes.

"On what?"

"What the person likes. I make jewelry from stones, but as you can see, there are a number of them, in various shades, colors and styles."

He smiled and Swan felt a tingling in the pit of her stomach when a dimple appeared in one of his cheeks. "I honestly don't know what she likes. Her tastes change from year to year. It's hard to keep up."

Swan nodded. "Oh. Sounds like the two of you have known each other for a while."

His smile widened even more. "We have. I would have to say I've known Mom all my life."

"Your mom?"

"Yes. Her birthday is next month. I was passing by your shop and thought I would drop in to see what you had."

A racing heart for starters, Swan thought. So the woman he was thinking about buying jewelry for was his mother. "Well, I'm glad you came in. Let me show you what I have."

"All right. There looks to be a lot of nice pieces."

She appreciated the compliment. "Thanks. I made most of them myself."

"Really? Which ones?"

She led him to the area set aside for Swan Exclusives. "These. Most of the stones come from India, Argentina and Africa."

He leaned in to look. "You did an excellent job."

Whoever said flattery, especially coming from a

good-looking man, would get you anywhere knew just what they were talking about. "Thank you."

"I'm David, by the way. David Holloway." He offered her his hand.

She took it and tried to ignore the sensations that suddenly flowed through her from the contact. "Nice to meet you, David." She quickly released his hand. "And I'm Swan."

"The name of the shop."

"Yes."

"It's a unique name."

"Yes, my parents thought so. On their first date, my father flew Mom from Jamaica to New York to see *Swan Lake*."

"Some date."

"Yes, he was trying to impress her."

"I take it he did."

Swan chuckled. "Yes, because he actually flew them there. He had his pilot's license."

"Now I'm impressed."

She didn't like bragging about her father but there were times when she just couldn't help it. "He served in the air force—that's where he learned to fly. And then he went into the navy after deciding he wanted to be a SEAL. That's when he met Mom, while he was a SEAL. She hadn't known about his stint in the air force until the night he rented a plane to fly them to New York."

Why was she telling him all this? Usually she wasn't chatty. "What about this one?" she asked as they moved to another glass case. "I call this piece *Enchantment*."

"Why?"

"Look at it," she suggested, leaning closer to the glass. He followed suit. "This is one of my favorite pieces because the teardrop gemstone necklace is pretty similar to my very first piece." No need to tell him that she'd made that one for her own mother.

"It is beautiful."

Something in his tone made her glance over at him, and she found him staring at her and not at the jewelry in the case. His eyes held her captive and their gazes met for a minute too long before she broke eye contact with him.

She swallowed. "So are you interested…in this piece?" She wanted to ignore the way her stomach seemed to be filled with all kinds of sensations, but she could not.

"I'm interested in a lot of pieces, Swan, but I'll start with this one."

Swan Jamison was even more beautiful than the photograph he'd seen last week.

The photographer hadn't fully captured the rich creaminess of her skin. And the shade of red lipstick she wore today seemed to make her lips plumper, more well-defined. Luscious.

He had read the dossier on her. He knew his commanding officer and Admiral Martin were operating based on a personal connection with her. He was not. If Miss Jamison was guilty of any wrongdoing, he would find out. And if she wasn't the one handing out classified data to China, then he would discover who was.

"So you want to buy this particular piece?"

Her question brought his thoughts back to the present. "Yes."

"Wonderful. I think your mother will like it."

"I'm sure she will. What about earrings?"

She lifted a brow. "Earrings?"

"Yes. Do earrings come with the necklace?"

"No, but I can make you some."

He'd been hoping she'd say that. "When?"

"It will take me a couple of days. The cruise ship docks tomorrow, so the shop will be busy. Two days from now will work for me, unless you need them sooner."

"No, I can wait. My mother's birthday is next month."

He would have an excuse to return to her shop.

Flipper watched her open the case and pull out the necklace. He knew his mother was going to love it.

"If you don't mind, please complete this ticket," she said. "And I will need full payment for the earrings before I make them."

"That's no problem," he said, taking the document from her.

After he completed the form, he handed it back to her. She glanced at it. "So you're from Texas?"

"Yes. Dallas. Ever been there?"

"Yes, once. I thought it was a nice city."

"It is. I was born and raised there."

"And what brought you to Key West?" she asked him.

"Work, at least for the next thirty days." That wasn't a total lie.

"Hurricane relief?"

"Something like that."

"You're military?"

"At one point but not now." He would let her think he was no longer military.

"I knew immediately."

He lifted a brow. "How?"

She shrugged. "Military men are easily recognized, at least by me."

"Because your dad is military?"

"He *was* military. Dad died years ago in the line of duty."

"I'm sorry." Flipper was always sorry whenever a fellow soldier lost their life.

"Thank you. Your package will be ready in two days, David. Your mobile number is on the form you completed. If I get to it sooner, I will call you."

"Two days is fine. I'll be back."

"'Bye, David."

"'Bye, Swan." He then turned and walked out of the shop.

As much as he wanted to invite her out to lunch today, he knew he couldn't rush things. He needed to earn her trust, even though he had less than thirty days to prove her innocence and determine who had no qualms about making her look guilty.

Swan was cheerful that night as she let herself into her home. Sales today had been better than normal. A tour group from New York had converged on the island and they'd come to spend money. She'd been happy to oblige.

Opening a jewelry shop had been a risky business move, but one that had paid off. She'd earned a degree in business management from the University of Miami and returned to the island after college to work as a manager at one of the elite hotels on the island. She'd enjoyed her job but had felt something was missing in her life. She hadn't been using her jewelry-making talent.

She'd promised her mother on her deathbed that she would find a way to use that talent.

Even after taking care of all her mother's funeral expenses, there had been more than enough money left to buy a little storefront. It had been a good investment because of its location. Some days were busier than others. This had been one of those busy days.

Now she was ready to wind down for the evening. She pulled her hair back in a ponytail and eased her feet into her favorite flats before heading to the kitchen for a glass of wine. As she did so, she couldn't help but think about her first customer of the day.

David Holloway.

He was a cutie, she had to give him that. And the memory of those eyes had stayed with her most of the day.

David Holloway had come into her shop to buy a birthday gift for his mother. How sweet. His mother was lucky. A lot of men didn't even remember their mothers' birthdays. She'd dated quite a few of those men and never developed lasting relationships with any of them. She figured if a man didn't treat his mother right, then there was no hope for a girlfriend.

As she opened the French doors to step out on the patio, she again remembered those blue eyes and how she'd felt whenever she'd looked into them. No man's eyes had ever made her feel that way before.

The effect was unsettling.

Okay, so what was wrong with her? Cutie or no cutie, she normally didn't get caught up over a man. She dated when it suited her, but she would admit that no one had suited her lately. At least not since her best friend, Candy, had left Key West to go live in Boston. Candy had refused to live on the island with her ex and his new wife—the one he'd married before the ink had even dried on the divorce papers.

Refusing to dwell on how shabbily Donald Knoll had treated Candy, Swan looked out at the water. It was calm tonight. When she had evacuated due to the hurricane, she hadn't known what to expect when she returned. Between her home and her shop, there had been some damage, but not as much as she'd feared.

The thought of losing her home had been devastating. This was where her father had brought her mom after they'd married. This home held so many childhood memories—of her father leaving on his missions as a Navy SEAL, of how happy she and her mother would be whenever he returned.

But then he hadn't returned.

Swan felt a knot in her throat as she recalled that day. She'd never seen that sparkle in her mother's eyes again. Swan recalled her mother telling her once that when you met a man who could put that sparkle in your eyes, then you knew he was a keeper.

Swan often wondered if she would ever find her keeper.

She had plenty of time. Besides, she needed to rethink her opinion about men first. If what Don had done to Candy wasn't enough to keep her single, all Swan had to do was remember William Connors, the businessman she had met whilc working at the hotel.

At the time, he had convinced her he was a bachelor without a care in the world but claimed that he wanted to make her Mrs. William Connors one day.

For some reason, Candy hadn't trusted him. She had a friend who worked for a private investigator check him out. Swan had been devastated when the investigation revealed there was already a Mrs. William Connors, along with three Connors children.

William had been playing her. He had been a lesson well learned. Her only regret was that she'd shared her body with him. She'd been young, naive and impressionable. He had been her first and he should not have been.

She was not naive now and she went into relationships with caution and even a little mistrust. Her mother once told her that being mistrustful wasn't a good thing. Swan knew she would have to learn how to trust again.

She took another sip of wine. Unfortunately, she hadn't gotten there yet.

"So how did things go, Flipper?"

"Have you met her yet?"

"Does she have a traitorous face or just a pretty one?"

"Do you think you'll be able to prove she's innocent?"

Flipper heard the questions coming at him nearly all at once. While unpacking, he had placed his mobile call on speaker to engage in a five-way conversation with his SEAL teammates.

"I think things went rather well, Mac. And yes, I met Swan Jamison today, Viper. I went into her jewelry store to purchase Mom a birthday gift."

Flipper eased open the dresser drawers to place his T-shirts inside. "She doesn't have a traitorous face or just a pretty one, Coop. The woman is simply gorgeous. Beautiful beyond belief. And yes, I hope to prove she's innocent, Bane, because Commanding Officer Shields and Admiral Martin truly believe she is."

"What do you believe?" Viper asked.

Flipper leaned against the dresser for a minute and thought about Viper's question. "Too early to tell."

"Did you ask her out on a date?" Coop wanted to know. They could hear Coop's two-year-old son, Laramie, chattering in the background.

"No, not yet." Flipper's attraction to her had been instant. He'd felt it the moment he looked into her face. Discussing her now wasn't helping matters. All it did was force him to recall what a beautiful woman she was—a woman he would have to spend time with in order to discover the truth.

"Then how do you plan to see her again if you don't ask her out?" Mac wanted to know, interrupting Flipper's thoughts.

"I ordered a pair of earrings to go with the necklace I bought for Mom. She has to make the earrings and I'll make my move when I pick up my purchases in two days."

"And if she turns you down?" Viper asked.

"Not an option. I now have less than thirty days to get this all straightened out."

"We should be there with you, watching your back," Bane said.

"No, you guys are just where you need to be, which is home with your families. I've got this."

"Well, some of our families don't appreciate us being home," Mac grumbled.

Flipper rolled his eyes. They'd all heard the complaints from Mac before. After every extended mission, their teammate went home to an adjustment period, where he would have to get to know his wife all over again and reclaim his position as head of the house. Sometimes the adjustment didn't go over well. Mac had a strong personality and so did Mac's wife, Teri. "Do we have to send both you and Teri into the time-out corners?"

"Hell, I didn't do anything," Mac exclaimed.

Flipper chuckled. "Yeah, right. You better get your act together, Mac. No other woman is going to put up with your BS."

"Whatever. So what did you notice about the place today?"

Mac was changing the subject and Flipper decided to let him. "Everything matched the architectural report I was given. Even with the repairs due to the hurricane, there were no major changes. Front door. Back door. High windows. Glass storefront. No video cameras outside. There are several rooms in back. One is being used as a tattoo parlor. I didn't see the person who runs it. I think I'll go out tonight and do a little more investigating," he said, sliding into a black T-shirt.

"Be careful, Flipper," Viper said. "Although you might not have seen any video cameras, that doesn't mean there aren't any."

"I know. That's why I'm wearing my Pilf gear."

Everybody knew how much Flipper liked digital technology. In addition to all the futuristic developments the military used, Flipper had created a few of his own high-tech gadgets behind the scenes. Some had been so impressive the federal government had patented them as Pilf gear to be used by the military. Pilf was the name Flip spelled backward. On more than one occasion, Flipper had been offered a position with the Department of Defense's Research and Development Department and had turned down each offer, saying he loved being a Navy SEAL more.

"We don't give a damn if you plan to parade around naked tonight, Flipper. Be careful."

He knew Mac was in his big-brother mode. "Okay, Mac. I hear you and I will be careful."

"Call to check in when you get back to the hotel tonight," Bane said.

"It will be late and I wouldn't want to wake up any babies, kids or a pregnant woman. I'll text everyone."

A short while later, wearing undetectable military gear under his clothing, Flipper left his hotel using the stairs.

Two

Two days later, Swan didn't leave the shop for lunch. Instead she accepted Jamila's offer to bring her something back from the sandwich shop on the corner. Although she'd tried convincing herself her decision to hang around had nothing to do with the fact that David Holloway would be returning today to pick up his items, she knew it did.

And her anticipation was so bad that every time the door chimed, her heartbeat would kick up a notch, only to slow back down when someone other than him walked in. She checked her watch. The shop would be closing in an hour. What if he didn't make it before closing time? What if…?

The door chimed, and her heart nearly stopped when David Holloway walked in.

She'd told herself the man hadn't *really* looked as good as she remembered from that first day, but now she saw that he did. In fact, today he looked even better than she remembered. Maybe it had something to do with the unshaven look. Men with a day-old beard had sex appeal. But it could also be his tan, which indicated he'd probably spent the last couple of days lying in the sun.

If he'd been at the beach, there was a good chance he hadn't been there alone. But didn't he say he was in the Keys working?

Why did she care?

She quickly dismissed all those questions from her mind as she continued to watch him walk toward her in a strut that had blood rushing through her veins. His blond hair and blue eyes seemed brighter against his tanned skin. He was deliciousness with a capital *D*.

But then that capital *D* could also stand for *dangerous* if she wasn't careful. Or it could stand for *delusional* if she didn't get control of her senses. Right now, she would play it safe and claim the capital *D* stood for *David*. She couldn't allow herself to think any other way for now, no matter how tempting.

She smiled. "Hello, David."

"Hi, Swan."

"Your tan looks nice."

He chuckled. "So does yours."

She grinned. "Yes, but mine's permanent."

"I know and I like it."

She didn't say anything to that because she understood what he was implying. He was letting her know he had no problem with interracial dating. She didn't have a problem with it either. Neither had her father, although his family had had conniptions about his marriage to Swan's mother. She pushed that thought to the back of her mind, refusing to dwell on an extended family that had never accepted her or her mother.

She reached behind the counter and retrieved a box. "I hope you like the way the earrings came out." She opened it to show him the final earrings.

"Wow!" He ran his finger over the stone that came closest to matching the color of his eyes. "You're very gifted."

"Thank you, and I believe your mother will love them."

"I'm sure she will. I think I've outdone my brothers this time."

She closed the box and placed it, along with the one containing the necklace, into a shopping bag. "You have brothers?"

"Yes, four of them. I'm the youngest."

"My goodness. Any sisters?"

"Not a one. Three of my four brothers are married, so I have sisters-in-law. They are the best."

"And the fourth brother is still single?"

"He's divorced but has a beautiful little girl. And she's my parents' only granddaughter. They have six grandsons."

"Sounds like a nice family. Is your father still alive?"

"Yes, Dad is still alive. He and Mom own a medical supply store."

She nodded as she offered him the bag. "Here you are, David. Thanks again for your business."

He accepted the bag. "Thanks. Now that this is taken care of, there's something I want to ask you, Swan."

She lifted a brow. "What?"

"Would you go out to dinner with me tonight?"

Normally Flipper was good at reading people, but he was having a hard time reading Swan. He definitely needed to remedy that. Although both Commanding Officer Shields and Admiral Martin were convinced of her innocence, the jury was still out for him. He had to remain impartial and deal with the facts, not speculations.

For two nights, he'd searched the area around her shop. Getting inside without triggering her alarm hadn't been easy, but he'd done it. Once he'd picked up the location of the interior security cameras, it was a small matter to make sure he stayed out of their range and within a certain perimeter until he could deactivate them and do what he needed to.

"Go to dinner with you?"

"Yes."

She was apparently mulling over his invitation in her mind and he would give her time to do that. He had no problems studying her while he waited for her answer. Today she looked even prettier than the other day. He figured it had to be the lighting in this place.

"Yes, David. I'll go to dinner with you. You name the restaurant and I'll meet you there."

She wasn't going to give him her address and he had no problem with her being cautious. Little did she know he already knew where she lived and had visited yesterday while she'd been here at her shop. She had a beautiful home on the ocean. Inside it was as neat as a pin with no clutter. She'd even made up her bed before leaving.

"I noticed a restaurant off the pier. Summer Moon. I've heard only good things about it since I've been here." And he knew the place was within walking distance from her home.

"Everything you've heard is true. Summer Moon is fabulous and one of my favorite eating places. I'd love to join you there. What time?"

"What about seven? Will that be a good time for

you?" He figured since it didn't get dark until close to nine, he wouldn't have to worry about her walking to the restaurant in the dark. After dinner, he would walk her home or put her in a cab regardless of the fact that she lived only a few blocks away.

"Seven is perfect."

"Good. I'll see you then."

Swan watched him walk out of the shop.

David had the kind of tush that made a woman want to squeeze it…after doing all kinds of other things with it.

She jumped when fingers snapped in her face. Frowning, she looked at Jamila. "What did you do that for?"

"To keep you from having an orgasm in the middle of your shop."

Swan rolled her eyes. Jamila, the attractive twenty-two-year-old green-eyed blonde, evidently thought reaching a climactic state was that easy. "It would take more than ogling a man for that to happen, Jamila."

"I don't know. Your eyes were about to pop out of their sockets and your breathing sounded funny."

"You're imagining things."

"Denial can be good for the soul, I guess. So who is he?"

Swan and Jamila had more than an employer-and-employee relationship. Their friendship had started when Jamila first moved to the island a couple of years ago and patronized Swan's. It didn't take long to discover that Jamila liked nice things and decided Swan's was one of her favorite places to shop. Last year, Jamila had been looking for work after she lost her job as a day cruise ship captain.

As far as Swan was concerned, it hadn't been Jamila's fault when an intoxicated customer had tried coming on to her and she'd kicked him in the balls. Surgery had to be performed and the man had sued the ship company. They'd settled out of court but not before firing Jamila for all the trouble she'd caused.

Jamila had gotten an attorney herself so she could not only sue her former employer for an unfair firing but also sue the intoxicated customer. To avoid negative publicity, her former employer wanted to settle out of court with her as well. The intoxicated customer was also trying to settle since the woman he'd been with on the ship hadn't been his wife. If things worked out in Jamila's favor, she wouldn't need a job at Swan's much longer.

"He is a customer who came into the shop a couple of days ago to buy a gift for his mother."

"His mother and not his wife?"

"He says his mother."

Jamila snorted. "Men lie all the time."

How well she knew, Swan thought. Then she wondered why Jamila was men-bashing today. This wasn't the first comment of that type she'd made since arriving to work. Her boyfriend had come to town a couple of days ago with the cruise ship, right? So what was going on?

Swan decided not to ask. She didn't want to hear another sad story about a man that would ruin her date tonight with David. It was a date she was definitely looking forward to. She figured going out to dinner with him wouldn't be risky as long as she kept things in perspective.

She knew what could happen if she let her guard down when it came to a man.

* * *

Flipper deliberately arrived at Summer Moon early so he could see when Swan arrived. His stomach felt floaty the moment she turned the corner from the street where she lived.

Be still, my...everything.

She was wearing a printed sundress and a pair of high-heeled sandals, but what caught his attention—and was still holding it tight—were her long shapely legs that seemed to go on forever. He would love to see where they stopped under that dress. He forced that thought to the back of his mind.

But the closer she got, the more that thought wiggled back to the forefront. He shouldn't let it. He was on assignment and she was the subject of an investigation. He shouldn't see her as temptation. Letting his guard down around her could be a dangerous and costly mistake. He had to keep his head screwed on straight, no matter how innocent she seemed and how beautiful she was, and she was definitely one gorgeous woman.

Men, even some with female companions, were giving Swan second looks, and Flipper tried to downplay his anger. He had no right to be upset about other men checking her out when he was checking her out himself. The best thing to do to control his crazy reaction was to stop looking at her, so he glanced down at his bottle of beer and thought about the reports he'd finished reading a short while ago on her employee and her tenant.

Jamila Fairchild had worked for Swan for a year. He knew all about her former job as a captain of a day cruise ship, why she'd gotten fired and her litigation against not only her former employer but also the man who'd caused the ruckus in the first place. Naval intelligence hadn't left any stone unturned in Ms. Fairchild's report and she'd come up clean. Flipper would verify that she was.

Then there was Rafe Duggers, the tattoo artist. Although his parlor was located inside Swan's shop, there was a back door for his customers to use without entering through the jewelry shop. Flipper hadn't gotten a chance to look around the tattoo parlor and he intended to do another visit in a few days. Rafe was too squeaky-clean to be true.

No wonder naval intelligence was trying to point the finger at Swan. After all, it was her shop and they had somehow traced activity as originating there. But how? When? He hadn't found anything.

He had searched Swan's office, the small kitchen in the back, the bathrooms and another room that she used as a workshop where she made her jewelry. He'd come up with nothing, even after checking out her computer. So what were the grounds for accusing her?

Flipper's mind flicked back to Swan and he stood when the waiter escorted her to his table. "Hello, Swan. You look nice."

"Thanks and so do you. I was trying to be early and you still beat me here," she said, sitting down across from him.

"I was thirsty," he said, sitting back down and indicating the beer. Now that she was here and sitting directly across from him, he was more than thirsty. If he wasn't careful, he could have a full-fledged attack of desire. She had a pair of beautiful shoulders and her skin appeared soft and smooth to the touch.

Then his mind drifted to wanting her and he quickly snatched it back. "You walked here. Does that mean you live close by?" he asked, deciding it was best to keep the conversation moving.

"Yes, not too far," she said. He knew she was deliberately being evasive.

The waiter handed him another beer and gave them both menus. "What would like to drink, miss?" the waiter asked her.

"A glass of Moscato please."

When the waiter left, she glanced over at Flipper before picking up her menu. "You're not working so hard that you're not enjoying the Keys, are you?"

"I'm doing a bit of both. I admit the ocean is beautiful tonight."

She smiled. "I think it's beautiful every night."

He nodded as he took another sip of his beer, straight from the bottle. "So are you a native or a transplant?"

"A native. I was born and raised right here on the island in the same house I live in now. My mother never made it to the hospital before I was born."

He raised a brow. "She didn't?"

"No. Mom came from a part of Jamaica where the belief was that when it comes to delivering a baby, a midwife is better than a medical doctor. My father promised to find her a midwife here. Otherwise she would have insisted that I be born in Jamaica and he didn't want that. He wanted me born in America."

"So he was able to find a midwife?"

"Yes, but I was born a few weeks early and the midwife wasn't here."

"So who delivered you?"

"My dad, with the help of three of his closest military friends. They were stationed at the base here and were visiting, watching a football game at the time. Needless to say, over the years I've gotten four different versions of what happened that night. My mother didn't remember a thing other than it took four men to deliver me. Although Godpop 1 claims my father passed out trying to cut the umbilical cord."

Flipper laughed. He then asked, "Godpop 1?"

"Yes, my father's three closest friends, the ones who assisted that night, became my godfathers. That's how I distinguish them. Godpop 1, Godpop 2 and Godpop 3."

Flipper nodded. No wonder the three men felt such strong ties to her. "You're lucky to have three godfathers. I don't have a one."

"Yes, I'm lucky," she said, after the waiter set the glass of wine in front of her. "They were my and Mom's rocks after we lost Dad, especially when my grandparents showed up at the funeral trying to cause problems."

Then, as if she realized she might have shared too much, she asked, "So what do you plan to order?"

Swan thought David had picked the right place for them to have dinner. When he asked for recommendations on what to order, she suggested Summer Moon's crab cakes and, as usual, they were delicious. The mango salad was superb, and after dinner they enjoyed listening to the live band.

When the band played their last song, she glanced over at David to discover him staring at her. The intensity in his gaze nearly scorched her and she took a sip of her wine. "Thanks for dinner, David."

"Thank you for accepting my invitation. The place is about to close. Are you ready to go?" he asked her.

"Yes." Because she knew he would suggest that he walk her home, she added, "If you still have a little bit of energy, I'd like to treat you to something."

He lifted a brow. "What?"

"A laser show that officially kicks off the summer season. It's a short walk from here." Since it was in the opposite direction from where she lived, she would have no problem catching a cab back later—alone.

He smiled as he beckoned for the waiter to bring their check. "Then by all means, let's go."

Once the show began, it didn't take Swan long to decide that David was wonderful company. She could tell he was enjoying the laser lights as much as she was.

She attended the event every year and it seemed the displays only got better and better. Each year, they honored a different state and tonight that state was New York. The New Yorkers in the crowd showed their happiness with whistles and shouting. And when a huge display of the Statue of Liberty flashed across the sky in a brilliant variety of colors, Swan caught her breath.

After that, the showrunners took the time to honor the servicemen in attendance with a flag salute. She couldn't hold back her tears as she remembered how much her father had loved his country and how, in the end, he'd given his life for it and for her.

David must have detected her weepy state. He pulled her closer to his side.

"Sorry," she said. "I get all emotional about our servicemen and servicewomen, especially those who sacrifice their lives."

"You sound very patriotic."

She pulled back and looked up at him. "Of course I'm patriotic. Aren't you? You did say you used to be in the military, right?"

"Yes, I'm very patriotic," he said, wrapping his arms around her. She wished she didn't think the arms around her felt so strong and powerful.

"I thought you would be, but you said I sounded patriotic as if you thought that perhaps I wasn't."

"I apologize. I didn't mean it that way. I'm glad you're so patriotic."

She nodded, accepting his apology. Scanning the area around them, she said, "They are serving complimentary wine coolers over there. Let's go grab a couple."

"Sure thing." He placed his hand on the small of her back.

The contact sent a rush of desire through her that was so strong she had to force herself to breathe. Swan quickly glanced up at him and noticed he'd been affected by the feeling as well. However, he hadn't removed his hand.

Instead, he pressed his hand more firmly into her back and she felt him urging her away from the crowd and toward a cluster of low-hanging palm trees. Once they stood in the shadows, he turned her in his arms, stared down at her for a long moment and then lowered his mouth to hers.

The moment their lips touched, he slid his tongue inside her mouth, and she recalled her thoughts from earlier that day. He was delicious—and dangerous—with a capital *D*. And it wasn't just because he tasted of the beer he'd consumed at Summer Moon, but because he tasted like a hot-blooded man. All the sexiness she'd seen in him was reflected in his kiss.

When she began kissing him back, he wrapped his arms around her and deepened the exchange by crushing his mouth to hers.

She didn't mind his eagerness. In fact, she welcomed the pleasure of his hunger, his taste, which was getting more provocative with every stroke of his tongue. It had been a while since she'd been kissed, and certain parts of her were reminding her of just how long it had been. Not only that, those certain parts were goading her to keep up with the forceful demands of his mouth. She hadn't been kissed so thoroughly or possessively before in her life. Or so passionately.

Swan wasn't sure how long they stood there kissing. It wasn't until they heard the sound of fireworks that they disengaged their mouths. She glanced up as more fireworks exploded in the sky. Instead of looking up, David trailed his tongue along her neck and collarbone with wet licks.

"Say you'll go out with me again, Swan."

There was no way she wouldn't say it. She looked at him and saw deep desire in the eyes looking back at her. "Yes, I'll go out with you again."

"Good."

And then he lowered his head and kissed her again.

Flipper had tried everything possible to get to sleep. He'd counted sheep, counted backward, rolled his eyes for a full thirty minutes and had even tried hypnotizing himself. None of those things helped.

He couldn't remember ever feeling this tight with need. So here he was, close to four in the morning, and still wide awake. Nothing he did could erase the taste of Swan from his mouth and the act of kissing her from his mind.

The kiss would complicate his mission, but it hadn't been an act. It had been the most real thing he'd done in a long time. He had wanted that kiss. Needed it. It had been inevitable.

Sitting across from her at dinner and watching the movement of her mouth had caused a throbbing need to erupt in his gut, making him rock hard. There had been no way to ignore the delicious heat of carnal attraction spiking between them.

And the patriotism he'd seen in her eyes when she'd gotten teary-eyed in support of servicemen, and then when she'd told him about her work with the city to find lodging for homeless vets, hadn't helped. Neither had the fact that she'd looked stunning and had smelled irresistibly hot tonight.

Kissing her had made his entire body feel alive. Had revved up his passion to a degree that his libido had him tied in knots and had his pulse tripping. He could feel himself riding the fine edge of intense desire heightened by more sexual energy than he'd felt in a long time.

While kissing her, he hadn't cared that they could have been seen in spite of the low-hanging trees. He'd been beyond the point of caring. He'd been tempted to drag her to the ground right there.

Damn. How was he going to clear her of anything when the only thing he'd wanted to clear her of was her clothes?

He had access to women whenever he needed them. There were always women who went bonkers for men in uniform and he had no problem engaging in one-night stands. Those types of relationships had always been the way to go for him. He liked being single, coming and going as he pleased, with no one to worry about but himself.

It had been a long time since any woman had kept him up at night and that wasn't cool.

Grabbing his phone he texted the message: If anyone is awake. Call me.

Within seconds, his phone rang. It was Bane. "What's going on, Flipper?"

"Why are you up?" Flipper asked his friend.

"Feeding time. Crystal and I rotate."

"Oh? You're breastfeeding now?"

"No, smart-ass. The trio are on bottles now. What are you doing up?"

Flipper stretched out across the bed. "I couldn't sleep. I tried everything. I even tried to hypnotize myself."

Bane chuckled. "I guess it didn't work."

"No, it didn't work."

"So why can't you sleep, Flip?"

He wasn't one to kiss and tell, no matter who the listener was, so he said, "I still haven't figured out anything about the situation down here and the CO and the admiral are depending on me."

"Maybe they're going to have to accept naval intelligence's report that she's guilty."

"I don't think so." Flipper paused. "She cried tonight."

"What do you mean, she cried?"

"Today was the first day of summer and there's an annual laser show to commemorate the change in season. One of the laser displays was a salute to New York, where they did an awesome light replica of the Statue of Liberty and American soldiers. She got emotional and cried. Dammit, Bane, a person who is betraying their country doesn't cry for those in the service. Call me a sucker for tears but I don't believe she has a traitorous bone in her body."

"Then it's up to you to prove it. What about those two people who hang around her shop?"

"The woman who works for her and the tattoo guy? Both seem clean. But I will dig further. I have to."

"Okay, but make sure while you're digging for answers that you're not burrowing yourself into something you can't handle."

"What do you mean?"

"I think you know what I mean, Flip. You were sent there to prove her innocence—not to prove she has a passionate side. Remember that. Good night."

Flipper clicked off the phone and rubbed a hand down his face. Little did Bane know that after the kiss with Swan tonight, Flipper was driven to do more than prove her innocence, or her passion.

He wanted to possess Swan completely.

And he had a feeling the desire wasn't one-sided. He'd seen the look in her eyes during dinner. He'd felt how her body had responded to his touch. He was certain the same sensations that rushed through him had affected her, too. Kissing her had been inevitable, something they both wanted and needed.

The genie called desire was out of the bottle and Flipper honestly didn't know how to get it back inside.

Three

Swan pushed away from her desk and took another huge gulp of ice-cold lemonade. It had been that way for her all day. Instead of concentrating on the online orders she needed to fill and ship out, her mind was wrapped around that kiss from last night.

All she had to do was close her eyes to remember every single detail, specifically every sensuous lick of his tongue inside her mouth. Even now, the memory sent multiple sensations coursing through her body, causing pleasure the likes of which she'd never encountered before.

She looked up at the sound of a knock on her door. "Yes?"

Jamila stuck her head in. "Mr. Make-you-have-an-instant-orgasm is back."

Swan didn't need to ask Jamila what she meant or who she was talking about. "Any reason you can't wait on him?"

Jamila smiled naughtily. "I could use the pleasure but he specifically asked for you."

Swan nodded. "I'll be out in a minute."

"Okay, I will let him know."

Swan reached over and took another gulp of her lemonade. She didn't want to admit it, but after that kiss last night, David could become an addiction. Besides putting down a gallon of lemonade, she'd been twitching in her seat most of the day, thinking that if his tongue could do that to her mouth, then Lordy…she could only imagine what else he would be able to do…

She quickly stood, refusing to go there even as a naughty part of her mind wished that he would. Leaving her office, she rounded the corner and stopped.

David stood in the middle of her shop wearing a pair of khaki shorts and a muscle shirt. The sight of his muscled abs and strong legs made Swan bite back a groan. Just when she thought he couldn't get any sexier, he'd proved her wrong.

He must have heard the sound of her footsteps because he turned and smiled.

As if on cue, she smiled back. "Hello, David, you came to make more purchases?" Hopefully he would take the hint that she didn't expect him to just drop by without a reason.

"Yes. I'm buying jewelry for my three sisters-in-law and would love for you to offer suggestions."

Swan couldn't help but smile since she liked making sales. What store owner wouldn't? "I'd love to help you pick out pieces of jewelry for them."

An hour later, Swan stood at the cash register to ring up all of David's purchases. With her assistance, he'd selected some really nice pieces, with a number of the stones chosen specifically because that's what he'd said they would like. Then he wanted earrings to complement the necklaces, which he paid for in advance. They decided to select stones for the earrings tomorrow since they'd spent a lot of time on the necklaces today and her shop would be closing in less than an hour.

From their conversation, she knew the Holloways were a close-knit family. He'd even pulled out his phone to show her pictures of his young niece and nephews.

"No pressure for you to marry?" she asked when he tucked his phone back into the pocket of his shorts.

"None. My parents have been married for more than forty years and are still very much in love. They make sure their kids and grandkids know that. They believe we will know when it's time for us to marry without any pressure from them. We'll be the ones to have to live with the people we choose. They just want all their children to be happy."

She nodded. "I like the way your parents think. I want to believe that, had my parents lived, they would have a similar philosophy. Dad used to tell me all the time that he wanted me to grow up and be whatever I wanted to be and do whatever I wanted to do, and that he and Mom would always have my back."

She suddenly felt a deep sense of loss. "Appreciate your parents, David. You never know how truly great they are until they're gone. But in all honesty, I think I've always known I had great parents."

At that moment, he did something she wouldn't have expected from him—he reached out and took her hand. "They sound great and I know they're proud of your accomplishments."

"Thanks." That was a nice thing for him to say. To avoid thinking about just how nice he was, she slid the bag with his purchases toward him and gave him the credit card slip. He signed it and gave it back to her.

"How would you like to go to happy hour at Danica's with me?"

After talking about her parents and missing them like crazy, she could use more than just an hour of happiness. She would love to be able to have a lifetime of that feeling.

It wasn't that she was *unhappy*, because she wasn't, but there were times when she wondered if maybe there was more out there for her than what was currently in her life. Perhaps she was shortchanging herself on some things. What those things were, she had no idea.

"I would love to go but good luck getting a table at Danica's. They have the best hot wings and are always crowded, *especially* for happy hour. I think the entire island heads over there at five."

"Since I know you don't close your shop until five, how about if we meet over there at five-thirty? I guarantee we'll have a place to sit."

"Um, sounds like you might have connections, David Holloway."

"We'll see." He took the bag and turned to leave, and just like before, she watched his movements until he was no longer in sight.

"Wow. You do have connections, don't you?" Swan said, sliding into a stool at the bar. "I've been here a number of times and the best seat I've ever gotten is at one of those tables outside."

Flipper smiled. Like at Summer Moon, he'd arrived early and was waiting for her. He liked seeing her stroll down the sidewalk looking as beautiful as ever.

Today she was wearing a pair of shorts and a pretty

top. Her legs were long and shapely and he could imagine them wrapped around him while…

Whoa, he didn't need to go there. Ever since that kiss, he'd been trying *not* to go there—no matter how tempted he was to do so. Quickly, he changed the direction of his thoughts.

"I know Danica personally," he said, trying hard to keep his naughty thoughts in check.

She lifted a brow. "Really? How?"

There was no way he would tell her the whole story. Danica was the godmother of former SEAL team member Nick Stover. Nick had given up being a SEAL a few years ago to take a job with Homeland Security after his wife had triplets. Instead of the whole history, Flipper gave her a modified version. "Her godson and I used to work together."

"Oh." The bartender chose that moment to take their drink order.

"I know you used to be in the military at one point but what do you do now?" she asked once the bartender had walked away.

Flipper had expected that question sooner or later and had a prepared answer. "I travel a lot and my job deals with ocean marine work. I guess you can say I'm a specialist in that area."

"Sounds interesting."

He chuckled. "Trust me, it is."

The bartender set their beers in front of them along with a huge plate of hot wings. They dug in.

"Your assistant at the store seems nice," Flipper commented. "I hope she didn't get offended when I asked specifically for you."

"No, very little offends Jamila, trust me."

"You've known her a long time?"

If his question seemed odd, she didn't mention it. "We met a couple of years ago when she moved to the island. The first time she came into my shop she nearly bought out the place. Like you, she has a huge family living up north and wanted to buy holiday gifts for everyone. Thanks to her, I made my month's quota in that one day. She earned a friend for life."

Flipper took a long swig of his beer. What Swan had just told him was interesting. Based on the naval intelligence report he'd read, Jamila didn't have any family. No parents, siblings, aunts, uncles or cousins. She'd been adopted and her adopted parents had been killed in a car accident in her last year of high school. And they hadn't lived in the north but out west in California.

Why had Jamila lied?

"So you hired her that day?" he asked, grinning, trying to make a joke of what she'd told him.

"No, she had a job as a ship captain at one of the day cruise companies in town. When things didn't work out for her there, I hired her on part-time."

He'd read the report and knew why Jamila had been let go and knew about her pending lawsuits. There was a big chance both cases would be settled out of court in her favor. "Is the reason she's part-time because she's a student?"

"Sort of. She saw how much money Rafe makes and—"

"Rafe?" He knew who Rafe was, but Swan didn't know that.

"Yes, Rafe. He rents space in my shop where he operates a tattoo parlor. He's good and always has a steady stream of customers. Some are so pleased with his work that they recommend him to others. I've known people to fly in just to use his services."

She took a sip of her beer, grinned and added, "Jamila decided to give him some real competition by becoming a tattoo artist as well. I have to admit she's pretty good. But Rafe doesn't seem worried. He even allows her to assist him sometimes. I guess you can say he's taken her under his wing. I think that's nice of him."

Flipper took another swig of his beer. "Yes, that is nice of him. Real nice."

Later that night, as they waited for a car at the taxi stand, Swan turned to face David. "I had a wonderful time this evening."

Once again, she had enjoyed his company and hated that their time together was about to end. It didn't come as a surprise to her that the sexual chemistry between them was more explosive than ever. The kiss they'd shared the night before had ignited something within her. From the way she'd noticed him looking at her, she believed something had ignited within him as well.

More than once, her smooth bare legs had brushed against his hairy ones. The sensual contact had sent a gush of desire through her.

The first few times it happened, she'd pulled away. But finally, she'd decided not to pull her legs back and he'd given her one of those *I know you did that on purpose* looks and she had smiled innocently and sipped her beer.

He had initiated the next physical contact and she could envision his mind at work trying to decide how to push her sensual buttons. She doubted he could push them more than he was already.

"I'm glad I got to meet Ms. Danica. After all the years I've been living here, this was my first time meeting her. She's nice."

"Yes, she is."

"And I definitely appreciate this," she said, holding up the bag of hot wings the older woman had given Swan to take home.

"I think she appreciated how much you enjoyed them."

She chuckled. "You're probably right."

"What do you have planned for later?" he asked in a deep, husky tone that seemed to have dropped a purposeful octave.

He had taken her hand when they left Danica's to walk to the taxi stand. The feel of his fingers entwined with hers had stirred something within her, something that grew with every step they took. She was aware of every detail about him as they walked together. Because of his long legs, more than once he had to slow his pace so she could keep up with him.

Swan could have walked home but figured he would suggest walking there with her. She was still cautious about letting him know where she lived. When she left Jamaica to begin living on her own, her mother had drilled into her the danger of letting a man know where you lived too soon. In her heart, Swan felt David was safe, but still…

"It's near the end of the month and I need to work on the books for my accountant." No need to mention she had tried doing that very thing today at work and hadn't been able to concentrate for remembering their kiss from last night.

"How about dinner tomorrow night?" he asked her.

She didn't answer right away. Instead, she broke eye contact with him and glanced down at the sidewalk. Hadn't they seen each other enough these last few days?

Where was this leading? Wasn't he leaving the Keys in less than a month?

She glanced back at him. "Why? We've gone out twice already. I wouldn't want to dominate your time."

"You're not. And the reason I want to take you out again is because I enjoy your company."

She certainly enjoyed his. "Can I ask you something, David?"

He nodded. "Yes?" Considering her history with William, it was something she probably should have asked David before going out on their first date. She'd discovered the hard way that a man not wearing a wedding ring didn't mean anything these days.

"What do you want to ask me, Swan?"

She met his gaze and hoped she would be able to see the truth in his eyes. "Do you have a wife or a significant other?"

Instead of guilt flashing in his eyes, she saw surprise. "No. I'm not married and I've never been married. I dated a woman for years but because of my frequent travels, she decided to end things. That was over six years ago." He then leaned against a light post and asked, "What about you, Swan? Have you ever been married or is there a significant other?"

"Of course not."

He nodded slowly. "Then I assume there is a reason you thought that maybe I was in a relationship?"

"I needed to be sure."

He didn't say anything. Instead, he looked at her as if tumbling her answer around in his head. "But like I said, I assume there is a reason you needed to know."

"Yes." However, she didn't intend to go into any details.

"Well, rest assured there is not a Mrs. David Holloway out there anywhere. Nor is there any woman wearing my ring. Satisfied?"

"Yes."

At that moment, a taxi pulled up. "Thanks for dinner again." She was about to move toward the taxi when he reached out, took hold of her hand and tugged her to him. He lowered his mouth to hers and kissed her quickly but soundly on the lips.

"I'll see you tomorrow," he said, his words a soft whisper against her wet lips.

"Tomorrow?" she asked in a daze from his kiss.

"Yes, we're supposed to go over designs for the earrings, remember?"

It was hard to remember anything after a kiss like that. "Yes, I remember," she said.

"Then I'll see you tomorrow."

She nodded, and when he opened the door for her, she quickly got into the taxi and headed home alone.

The moment Flipper entered his hotel room he went to the small refrigerator beneath the wet bar and pulled out a beer. Just then it didn't matter that he'd already drank a couple at Danica's. He needed another. There was just something about Swan that was getting to him, touching him on a level he wasn't used to when it came to women. He had truly enjoyed her company tonight.

He and his SEAL teammates had just returned from a two-month mission in South Africa and more than anything he had needed to unwind. He would be home in Texas doing just that had he not been summoned to the admiral's office.

So here he was, and although he was in Key West on official military business and he was supposed to be investigating Swan, he loved spending time with her.

Tonight, when she'd met Danica, it had been priceless. You would have thought Swan had met a Hollywood celebrity. He had sat there while the two women conversed, immediately as comfortable as old friends.

The sound of Swan's voice had been maddeningly sexy with a tinge of sweetness that had stroked his senses. For the first time since returning to the States, he had allowed himself to uncoil, to loosen up and relax while appreciating the richness of her personality. Her persona was uniquely hers and the sensuality of her very being called to him in a primitive way.

And that wasn't good.

Taking a huge swig of his beer, he switched his thoughts to what he should be focused on—what she'd told him about Jamila and Rafe. Remembering what she'd said, he pulled his phone out of the pocket of his shorts and with one click he connected to his friend Nick Stover.

"This better be good, Flipper. Natalie is taking an art class at the university tonight and I have babysitting duties."

Flipper couldn't help but smile. Like Bane, Nick had triplets and from the sound of the noise in the background, the triplets had him. "Stop whining. Taking care of a trio of three-year-olds can't be too bad."

"Then you come do it."

"Sorry, I'm on assignment."

"So I hear. In the Keys, right?"

He figured for Nick to know that much meant he'd either talked to Bane, Viper, Mac or Coop. "Yes, I'm in Key West."

"While you're there, be sure to stop by Danica's. Give her a hug for me."

"I did that already. Tonight, in fact."

"Good."

"I think she has more photos of the triplets than you do."

"I wouldn't doubt it. So if you can't be a backup babysitter, why are you calling?"

"When you arrive at your cushy job at Homeland Security tomorrow, there are two people I need you to check out for me. I've read naval intelligence reports on them, but something isn't adding up. Call me a suspicious bastard, but after that situation with Bane, when those traitors within the agencies were exposed, I'm not taking any chances."

He then told Nick about the discrepancies between what the reports said and what Swan had told him. "Somebody is lying. Either Jamila lied to Swan or someone falsified the report, and I want to know which it is."

Four

"He's *baaack*," Jamila said.

Swan pushed away from her desk. She didn't have to ask who Jamila was talking about. "I was expecting him," she said in what she hoped was a professional tone. "He needs to look at designs for earrings."

"If you say so. I'll send him in here."

Swan was about to tell Jamila they could use the computer out front, but Jamila was gone after closing the door behind her.

Standing, Swan inhaled deeply. How she had finished the books last night, she wasn't sure. Thoughts of David had been stronger than ever after their night out. When she'd gone to bed, she had dreamed about him. Okay, she'd dreamed about him before, but the dreams last night had been so hot it was a wonder they hadn't burned her sheets. She had been tempted to do something she hadn't done in a long time, reactivate her vibrator.

She drew in a deep breath when she heard the knock on her door. "Come in."

And in walked David, looking sexier than he had the other times she'd seen him. Last night, to stay focused, she had come up with every reason she could think of for why she shouldn't be attracted to him and why a relationship with him wouldn't work.

She'd even thrown in the race card. But of course that was thrown out when she remembered her parents and how happy they had been together. Yet she also couldn't forget how her father's family had ostracized him for his choice in love. Would David's family be the same way? There was no reason to think they wouldn't. And wasn't she getting ahead of herself for even throwing love in the mix?

"Hello, David."

"Swan." He glanced at her desk, taking in all the folders spread across it. "You're busy."

"That's fine. Besides, I need to get those earrings ready for you."

Now that he'd seen her desk, it would make perfect sense for her to suggest they use the computer out front to design the earrings. But now that she had him behind closed doors, she liked it.

Not that she planned on doing anything about having him here.

"Please have a seat while I clear off my desk." Today he was wearing jeans and she couldn't help but watch how fluidly his body eased into the chair. How the denim stretched across a pair of muscular thighs. She quickly switched her gaze before he caught her looking.

"Nice office."

"Thanks." She closed the folders and placed them in her inbox tray. She then glanced over at him and caught him looking at her. She followed his gaze and soon figured out why he was staring.

She was wearing a skirt with a V-neck blouse, and when she'd leaned over to place the folders in the tray, her shirt had shown a portion of her cleavage. Instead of calling him out for trying to cop a view of her breasts, the fact that he was interested sparked a distinct warmth between her legs.

She quickly sat down. "Now if you would roll that chair over here, I am ready." Too late, she realized how that sounded and quickly added, "To look at designs."

He smiled. "I know what you meant."

He rolled his chair behind her desk to place it right next to hers. When he sat down, their legs touched. Moving away would be pretty obvious so she let the denim of his jeans rub against her bare legs.

"Now, then," she said, trying not to notice how good he smelled. "What do you think of these?" she asked, bringing up a few designs on the computer screen.

When he didn't answer, she glanced over at him and found him staring at her. Sitting so close to him, she could look directly into his laser-blue eyes. It was as if his gaze was deliberately doing something to her, causing a surge in her breath and arousal to coil in her core. She saw the dark heat in his eyes and desire clawed at her even more.

"May I make a suggestion?" he asked in a voice that seemed to wobble in a sexual way.

"It depends on what that suggestion is," she heard herself say.

He leaned in a little closer and whispered, "I want to kiss you again. Only problem is that I don't want to stop until I get enough. And I'm not sure I would."

She had been staring at his lips, watching how they

moved while he talked. She slowly dragged her gaze back up to his eyes. She saw need flare in his gaze at the same time that anticipation for his kiss thickened the air flowing in and out of her lungs.

"I don't know what to say."

"Don't say anything, Swan. Just bring your mouth closer to mine."

She knew she shouldn't, but she found herself doing it anyway.

Flipper drew in a deep breath when Swan's lips were almost touching his. He flicked out his tongue and she gave a sharp intake of breath when he began licking her lips from corner to corner with the tip of his tongue.

"What are you doing?" she asked on a wobbly breath.

"Since you asked..." He captured her mouth and when she closed her eyes on a moan, he reached up and cradled her face in his hands while he kissed her with a greed he didn't know was in him.

What was there about her that made him accept the primitive part of himself that wouldn't be satisfied until he made love to her? Was it because she crept into his dreams at night and into his every waking thought? Or was it because an arrow of liquid heat shot straight to his groin whenever he saw her? Or could he blame it on the fact that whenever she touched him, he burned? She made him edgy and aroused him as no other woman could.

It was all of those things and more.

Right now, he didn't know how to back away. So he didn't. Instead he accepted the stream of heat in his gut and the crackle of energy passing between them.

Their lips were copulating in a way that sent blood coursing through his veins like a raging river. It was raw, hot and explosive, causing a hot ache to erupt in his gut. It wouldn't take much to lose control and take her here on her desk. At that moment, his entire body was tight with need, totally entranced by everything about her.

The phone rang and they quickly broke off the kiss, drawing in deep breaths of air. He watched as she reached across her desk to press the speaker button. "Thank you for calling Swan's."

At first, no one said anything and then a deep male voice said, "Swan? Are you okay? You sound out of breath."

He watched as she pulled in another deep breath before a smile touched her lips. "I'm fine, Godpop 1. How are you?"

Knowing who she was talking to on the phone was like a pail of cold water drenching Flipper. He was quickly reminded why he'd been sent to Key West. His admiral would have him court-martialed if he knew what Flipper had just done with his goddaughter. If the man had any idea how many times Flipper had kissed her already and how each time he'd wished they had gone even further…

She turned off the speaker so he heard only one side of the conversation, and from the sound of her voice, he knew she was happy about receiving the call.

Feeling a tightness in his crotch from his still-aroused body, he got up from the chair and walked to the window. If she could have this sort of effect on him just from a kiss, he didn't want to think about what would happen if he were to make love to her. Just the thought of easing his body into hers had his stomach churning and caused an ache low in his gut.

Knowing he needed to think of something else, he

glanced up into the sky. It was a beautiful day. Monday was Memorial Day and he wondered if Swan had made any plans to celebrate. He'd heard there would be a parade and unlike some places in the States, where stores remained open on Memorial Day, the laid-back businesses in the Keys closed up for one big party.

He liked the Keys. When he retired from being a SEAL, he could see himself moving here to live out the rest of his days. The island was surrounded by the ocean and they didn't call him Flipper for nothing. He loved water. Being in it and being a part of it. Living this close to the sea would certainly be a plus for him. But then there was the question of how he would deal with Swan if he chose to retire here. Even if he could prove she was not guilty of espionage, there was always that possibility she would hate his guts regardless of the outcome, because he had not been truthful with her.

"Sorry about that, David."

He turned, not caring that she could see his still-hard erection. It was something he couldn't hide even if he had tried. Was she sorry they'd been interrupted or was she regretting that they'd kissed in the first place? He hoped it was the former because he doubted he could ever regret kissing her. "I take it that was one of your godfathers?" he asked, knowing it had been.

She was staring at him below the waist, but after his question, her gaze slowly moved upward to his face. "Ah, yes, that was one of my godfathers. The other two will be calling sometime today as well. It always works out that they all call within twenty-four hours of each other."

He nodded and slowly walked back over to his chair to sit down. "I know you're busy so let's look at the designs."

Had he just seen a flash of disappointment in her eyes? Did she want them to continue what they'd been doing before she'd gotten that call? Didn't she know how close they'd both been to going off the edge and falling into waters too deep to swim out of? Even for him, a SEAL master swimmer.

Somehow they got through the next half hour looking at earring designs. Just as each one of the necklaces were different, he wanted the earrings to be different as well and reflect each one of his sisters-in-law's personalities.

When he was satisfied with his choices, he stood, convinced he needed to rush back to the hotel and take a cold shower. Sitting beside Swan and inhaling her scent without touching her was one of the most difficult things he'd had to do in a long time.

She was so female that the maleness in him couldn't help responding to everything about her. A part of him felt drugged by her scent and the intense physical awareness of her. Even now, desire was racing through his bloodstream.

"I owe you additional monies, right?" he asked. A couple of the designs he'd selected cost more than what she'd originally estimated.

"Yes. I'll let you know the difference after I finish designing them, when you pick up everything."

He hadn't missed the fact that when he stood her gaze had immediately latched on to his crotch once again. Was she still hoping to see him with a hard-on? If that was true, then she wasn't disappointed. He could get aroused just from looking at her.

And why did she choose that moment to lick her lips? She had no idea that seeing her do such a thing sent the pulse beating in his throat and desire hammering against his ribs.

On unstable legs and with an erection the size of which should be outlawed, he moved around her desk and looked at her. "Yesterday I asked you to go to dinner with me again, but you never gave me an answer."

He figured that seeing how aroused he was, she probably wouldn't give him an answer now either. She surprised him when she said, "Yes, we can dine together this evening."

He nodded. "Okay, you get to pick the place."

She took a slip of paper off her desk, wrote something on it and handed it to him. He looked at it and he must have stared at it too long, because she said, "It's my address, David. I'm inviting you to dine with me this evening at my home."

He broke eye contact with her to glance back down at the paper she'd given him. He looked back at her while trying to downplay the heat rumbling around in his gut.

"Do you need me to bring anything?" he asked her.

"No, just yourself."

Swan glanced around her home and felt the knots beginning to twist in her stomach. She hoped she hadn't made a mistake inviting David here.

Today marked a week since they'd met and if she was going to continue to see him while he was on the island, she couldn't take advantage of his thoughtfulness and expect him to invite her out without ever returning the kindness. However, more than anything else, she needed to keep things in perspective. She needed to remember he was someone she could have a good time with and that's it.

She didn't want anything more than that.

One day, she would be ready to explore her options and consider a future with a man, but that time wasn't now. She liked being single and responsible only for herself.

She knew from Candy that a serious relationship was hard work. And on top of all that hard work, you could assume you had the right person in your life only to discover you didn't. By then, you would have opened yourself up to hurt and pain in the worst possible way.

The thought that a man had caused her best friend that kind of agony bothered Swan whenever she thought about it. Candy loved Key West as much as Swan did, and for a man to be the reason she had moved away was disheartening.

Swan tried telling herself that not all men were like Candy's ex, Don, or like William. On days when Swan wanted to think all men were dogs, all she had to do was remember her dad.

Andrew Jamison was the yardstick she used to measure a good man. She'd watched how he had treated her mother, had seen the vibrant and sincere love between them. She had not only seen it, but she'd felt it as well. Both her parents had been demonstrative individuals and Swan had often interrupted them sharing a passionate kiss or embrace.

She still felt it here, within the walls of her house and in the very floor she walked on. All the love that had surrounded her while growing up was in this house she now called home.

She was glad her mother hadn't sold it after her father died, when Leigh had made the decision to move back home to Jamaica. Instead, she had kept the house, knowing one day Swan would want to return. It was almost too spacious for one person but Swan knew she would never sell it or move away. This house had everything she needed.

She could see the water from any room, and at night, whenever she slept with the window open, the scent of the ocean would calm her.

Her favorite room in the house was her parents' old bedroom, even though she had not moved into it. It had floor-to-ceiling windows and a balcony she liked sitting on while enjoying her coffee each morning. A couple of years ago, she'd had the balcony screened in to keep the birds from flying into her house, although she loved waking up to the sound of them chirping every morning.

Although neither one of her parents would tell her the full story, Swan knew her father had come from a wealthy family. And she knew he had been disowned by them when he had fallen in love with her mother and refused to give her up. Before dying, Leigh had given Swan a beautiful leather-bound diary to read after her death. That's what had helped keep Swan sane, reading the daily account of her mother's life and love for her father and believing they were now back together.

For weeks following her mother's death, Swan had wanted to be alone to wallow in her pity and read about what she thought was the most beautiful love story that could exist between two people. Her mother had always been expressive with the written word and Swan enjoyed reading what she'd written.

It had made Swan long for such a man, such a love. Maybe that's why she had been so quick to believe in William and why, once she'd found out about his duplicity, she'd been so reluctant to get serious with a man since.

From her mother's diary, Swan discovered her mother's appreciation for her husband's agreement to make Key West their home. The people on the island embraced diversity and tolerated different lifestyles.

Swan had read the account of when her father had been stationed at a naval base in Virginia and had sent for her mother to join him there. In the diary, her mother had written about the hateful stares they would receive whenever they went out together. The unaccepting and disapproving looks. The cruel words some people had wanted them to hear.

Her father hadn't tolerated any of it and hadn't minded confronting anyone who didn't accept his wife. But to avoid trouble, Leigh had preferred to live in Key West, where people's issues with an interracial marriage were practically nonexistent.

However, people's attitudes never kept Leigh from leaving the island to join Andrew whenever he would send for her. Oftentimes, Leigh would take Swan along and they would both join Andrew in different places for weeks at a time.

When she heard the sound of the doorbell, Swan drew in a deep breath. The time for memories was over. The only plans she had for *this* evening were for her and David to enjoy the meal she'd prepared and later enjoy each other's company.

She had no problem with them deciding what the latter entailed when that time came.

"Hello, David. Welcome to my home."

Flipper pushed from his mind the thought of how Swan would feel if she knew this wasn't his first time here. How she would react if she knew he had invaded her space without her knowledge. If she ever found out the truth, would she understand it had been done with the best of intentions? Namely, to keep her from wasting away in a federal prison after being falsely accused of a crime?

He forced those thoughts to the back of his mind as he smiled down at her. She looked absolutely stunning in a wraparound skirt and yellow blouse. “Hi. I know you said I didn’t have to bring anything, but I wanted to give you these,” he said, handing her both a bottle of wine and a bouquet of flowers.

He had decided on the wine early on, but the flowers had been a spur of the moment thing when he’d seen them at one of those sidewalk florist shops. Their beauty and freshness had immediately reminded him of Swan.

“Thank you. The flowers are beautiful and this is my favorite wine,” she said, stepping aside to let him in.

He chuckled. “I know. I remember from the other night.” There was no way he would also mention having seen several bottles of Moscato in the wine rack the time he had checked out her house.

He glanced around, pretending to see her home for the first time. “Nice place.”

“Thanks. I thought we would enjoy a glass of wine and some of my mouthwatering crab balls out on the patio before dinner.”

“Mouthwatering crab balls?”

“Yes, from my mom’s secret recipe. You won’t be disappointed,” she said, leading him through a set of French doors. The first thought that came to his mind when he stepped out on her patio, which overlooked the Atlantic Ocean, was that it was a beautiful and breathtaking view. This had to be the best spot on the island to view the ocean in all its splendor.

He recalled how, as a boy, he would visit his cousins in California and dream of one day living near the beach. Over the years, being stationed in San Diego had been the next best thing. He owned an apartment close to base that was within walking distance of the beach.

However, his view was nothing like this. All she had to do was walk out her back door and step onto the sand. It was right there at her door. If he lived here, he would go swimming every day.

He glanced over at her. "The view from here is beautiful."

"I love this house and appreciate my mother for not selling it when she decided to move back to Jamaica after Dad died. She got a lot of offers for it, believe me. So have I. Mom said being here without Dad was too painful, but she knew I'd feel differently. For me, it was just the opposite. Being here and recalling all the memories of when the three of us shared this place makes me happy."

Hearing how the loss of her parents affected her made Flipper appreciate his own parents even more. Colin and Lenora Holloway had always been their sons' staunch supporters. Their close and loving relationships had been the reason none of their sons had had any qualms about settling down and marrying. All the marriages had worked out, seemingly made in heaven, except for his brother Liam's.

When Bonnie had gotten pregnant, Liam had done the honorable thing by marrying her. Bonnie had always been a party girl and didn't intend to let marriage or being a mommy slow her down. While Liam was somewhere protecting his country as a Navy SEAL, Bonnie was conveniently forgetting she had a husband.

No one, not even Liam, had been surprised when he returned from an assignment one year and she asked for a divorce. Liam had given it to her without blinking an eye. Since then, Bonnie had remarried, which had introduced another set of issues for Liam. He was constantly taking Bonnie to court to enforce visitation rights to see his daughter because the man Bonnie married didn't like Liam coming around.

Flipper had no qualms about marriage himself, but he had too much going on right now. Namely, resisting the temptation of Swan while he continued his investigation. That was his biggest challenge. The more he was around Swan the more he liked her and the more he wanted to prove her innocence. It was hard staying objective.

"Here you are," she said, handing him a cold bottle of beer. "I figured you would like this instead of the wine."

He smiled. Like he had picked up on her drinking preferences, she had done the same with him. "Thanks. I've never been a wine man."

She chuckled. "Neither was my dad. That's how I knew when it was time for him to come home because Mom would have his favorite beer in the fridge."

He opened the bottle, took a sip and noticed her watching him. He licked his lips, liking the taste of the beer, which was the brand he'd chosen the other night at Summer Moon. When he took another sip and she continued to watch him, he lifted a brow. "Is anything wrong?"

She smiled. "No, nothing is wrong. I just love to watch how you drink your beer."

He chuckled. That was a first. No woman had ever told him that before. "And how do I drink it?"

"First there's the way your mouth fits on the beer bottle. I find it very sensuous."

He tried ignoring the quiver that surged through his veins at the tone in her voice. "Do you?"

"Yes. And then there's the way you drink it like you're enjoying every drop."

"I am."

"I can tell." Then, as if she thought perhaps she'd said too much, she took a step back. "I'll go get those crab balls for you to try."

When she turned to leave, he reached out and touched her arm. He couldn't help it. The air all but crackled with the sexual energy between them. "Come here a minute before you go," he said, setting his beer bottle aside. "Although I do enjoy drinking beer, I've discovered I enjoy feasting on your mouth even more."

And then he lowered his mouth to hers.

Perfect timing, Swan thought, because she needed this. She'd wanted it the moment he tilted his beer bottle to his mouth and she'd watched him do so. And now he was doing her. Showing her that he was enjoying her mouth more than he'd enjoyed the beer. Just like he'd said.

There was a certain precision and meticulousness in how he mastered the art of kissing. First, as soon as his tongue would enter her mouth, he would unerringly find her tongue, capture it with his own and begin gently sucking in a way that made the muscles between her legs tighten. Then he would do other things she didn't have a name for. Things that made desire flow through her like sweet wine, kindling heated pleasure and burning passion within her.

He rocked his thighs against her and she felt him pressed against her. His arousal was massive. Instinctively, she moved her hips closer, wanting to feel him right there, at the juncture of her thighs.

When he finally pulled his mouth away, she released

a deep, satisfied breath. Her mouth was still throbbing and there was an intense ache in her limbs. Right now, their heavy breathing was the only sound audible, and the laser-blue eyes staring down at her sent a tremor to her core.

She licked her lips when she took a step back. “Ready for a few crab balls?”

“Yes,” he said, after licking his own lips. “For now.”

Five

He wanted her.

Flipper knew he shouldn't, but he did. All through the delicious dinner Swan had prepared and while engaging in great conversation with her, the thought of just how much he wanted her simmered to the back of his mind. Now with dinner coming to an end, desire was inching back to the forefront. Images of her naked tried to dominate his mind, the thoughts made him shift in his chair to relieve the ache at his crotch.

"Ready for dessert, David? I made key lime pie."

Right now, another kind of dessert was still teasing his taste buds. "Yes, I would love a slice, and dinner was amazing by the way. You're a good cook. My mother would absolutely love you."

Too late, he wondered why he'd said such a thing. From the look on her face, she was wondering the same thing. So he decided to clean up his mess by adding, "She admires other women who can cook."

Swan smiled. "You don't have to do that, David."

"Do what?"

"Try to retract the implications of what you said so I won't get any ideas."

He *had* done that, but not for the reason she thought. He'd done so because it wasn't right for either of them to think something was seriously developing between them. More than likely, she would hate his guts when she learned why he was really in Key West, when she discovered she was his assignment and nothing more. He couldn't tell her the truth, but he could certainly set her straight on what the future held for them.

"And what ideas do you think I wanted to retract?"

"The ones where I would think we were starting something here, the ones that meant I would be someone you'd take home to meet your mother."

He sat down his glass of ice tea, which she had served with dinner. "Any reason why I wouldn't want to take you home to meet my mother *if* we shared that kind of a relationship, Swan?" Although he didn't think he needed to let her know—again—that they didn't share that kind of relationship, he did so anyway.

"Honestly, David, do I really have to answer that?"

"Yes, I think you do."

She stared at him for a minute. "I'm well aware when it comes to interracial relationships that not all families are accepting."

He chuckled. "My family isn't one of them, trust me. Interracial or international, we couldn't care less. My brother Brad met his wife, Sela, while working in Seoul, South Korea, and my brother Michael met Gardenia in Spain. Like I told you, my parents would accept anyone who makes us happy, regardless of race, creed, religion, nationality or color."

She didn't say anything to that. Then she broke eye contact with him to glance down into her glass of tea. Moments later, she raised her gaze back to him.

"My father's parents didn't. They threatened him with what they would do if he married Mom and they kept their word. They disowned him. Still, my mother reached out to them when Dad died to let them know he'd passed. They came to his funeral but had no qualms about letting Mom know they still would not accept her. They would only tolerate me since I was biracial. They even tried forcing Mom to let me go back with them. That's when my godfathers stepped in."

Flipper shook his head, feeling the pain she refused to acknowledge, the pain she'd obviously felt because of her grandparents' actions. But he'd heard it in her voice nonetheless.

"It's sad that some people can be such bigots. At the risk of this sounding like a cliché, some of my closest friends are black," he added, immediately thinking of Bane, Viper and Coop. Like her, Mac was of mixed heritage and had a white mother and black father.

"I'm sure some of your closest friends are, David."

He wondered if she believed him. One day, she would see the truth in his words. Then it suddenly occurred to him—no, she would not. There would be no reason for her to ever meet the four guys who were just as close to him as his biological brothers.

"I'll be back in a minute with the pie," she said. Then she stood and left the room.

Flipper watched her leave, feeling that he hadn't fully eradicated her doubts the way he'd wanted to do. That bothered him. He didn't want her to think he was one of those prejudiced asses who believed one race of people was better than another. What her grandparents had done to her father and mother, as well as to her, was unforgivable. Regardless of how she'd tried to come across as if their actions hadn't hurt her, as if they still didn't hurt her, he knew better.

She needed a hug right now.

He pushed back his chair and left the dining room to enter her kitchen. Instead of getting the pie like she'd said she would do, she was standing with her back to him, looking out the kitchen window at the ocean. And he could tell from the movement of her shoulders that she was crying.

"Swan?"

She quickly turned, swiping at her tears. "I'm sorry to take so long, I just had one of those miss-my-daddy-and-mommy moments."

He crossed the room to her, knowing that her tears were about more than that. He knew it and he intended for her to know he knew it. "Not wanting to get to know you—that was your grandparents' loss, Swan."

She gazed into his eyes and nodded. "I know, David, but their actions hurt Dad, although he never said it did. I knew. Mom knew, too. I think that's one of the reasons she loved him so much, because of all the sacrifices he'd made for her. That's why she did anything she could to make him happy so he would never regret choosing her. But it wasn't fair. He was a good man. Mom was a good woman. They deserved each other and should have been allowed to love freely and without restrictions, reservations or censure. It just wasn't fair, David."

And then she buried her face in his chest and cried in earnest. Wrapping his arms around her, he held her, leaning down to whisper in her ear that things would be all right. That her parents had had a special love, one she should be proud of, one the naysayers had envied.

Emotions Flipper hadn't counted on flowed through him as he continued to stroke her hair and whisper soothing words next to her ear. Inwardly, he screamed at the injustice of trying to keep someone from loving the person they truly wanted to love. It was something he'd never understood and figured he never would. And never would he accept such a way of thinking from anyone.

Swan knew she should pull out of David's arms, but found she couldn't do it. Being held by him felt good. His fingers, the ones that were stroking through the strands of her hair, seemed to electrify her scalp. They sent comforting sensations all through her—and something else as well. A need that he was stroking to fruition. As a result, instead of pulling out of his arms, she closed her eyes and enjoyed being held by him while inhaling his masculine scent.

She wasn't sure how long they stood there, but it didn't take long for her to notice his breathing had changed. But then so had hers. His touch had shifted from comforting to passionate. He was using the same strokes, but now the feelings within her were beginning to build to an insurmountable degree of desire.

Opening her eyes, she lifted her head to stare up at him. The minute she did, she caught her breath at the intense yearning she saw in his gaze. That yearning reached out to her, jolted her with a level of throbbing need she hadn't known existed. She'd heard of raw, make-you-lose-your-senses passion, but she had never experienced it for herself.

Until now.

"David..." She said his name as something burst to life in the pit of her stomach. It made a quivering sensation rise at the back of her neck. He implored her with his eyes to follow this passion, as if letting her know he understood what she was experiencing even if she didn't.

"Tell me what you want, Swan," he said in a deep voice while gently caressing the side of her face. "Tell me."

The intensity in his eyes was burning her, scorching her with the sexual hunger that was coming to life inside her. She wanted more than his erection pressing hard against the apex of her thighs. She wanted him on top of her. She wanted him to slide into her body and begin thrusting in and out. She needed to lose herself in more than just his arms.

Suddenly, she felt emboldened to tell him just what she wanted. "I want you, David. In my bed."

Flipper wanted to be in her bed as well. Lord knows he shouldn't want it, but he did. He would have to deal with the consequences later. He felt too tight and hot to try to fight the demands his body was making. Sweeping her into his arms, he quickly walked out of the kitchen and headed toward her bedroom.

"You think you know where you're going, David?"

He slowed his pace, remembering that she had no idea that he knew the layout of her home. Not only did he know where her bedroom was located, he knew the blueprint of the plumbing underneath her floor. He looked down and met her gaze, grateful she wasn't suspicious. "I figured you would stop me if I went in the wrong direction."

"Yes, I would have stopped you, but you're going the right way."

"Good." When he resumed his swift pace, it didn't take him long to reach her bedroom.

Swan had gotten next to him in a way he hadn't counted on happening. Seducing her had not been part of the plan and he should not have allowed things to get this far. He didn't want to think of the major complications involved, and not just because she was the goddaughter of three top naval officers.

But something was happening that he hadn't counted on. His mind and body were in sync and a rare sexual aura was overtaking him. He could no more stop making love to her than he could stop being a SEAL. For him to even make such a comparison was pretty damn serious.

Instead of placing Swan on the bed, he eased her to her feet, loving the feel of her soft body sliding down his hard one. "If you're having second thoughts about this, Swan, now's the time to say so."

She shook her head and then in a wobbly voice, she said, "No second thoughts, David."

Hearing her affirmation spoken with such certainty, Flipper released a low, throaty groan as he lowered his mouth to kiss her again, needing the connection of her lips to his as much as he needed to breathe. Wrapping his arms around her waist, he pulled her body closer to him as he deepened the kiss, wanting her to feel his erection, the hard evidence of his need for her.

He had never wanted a woman with this much intensity in his life, and he had no idea why Swan was having this kind of an effect on him.

Why she, and no other woman before her, had tempted him to cross a line during a mission. His mind didn't function that way. He had yet to prove her innocence, so technically, she was still naval intelligence's prime suspect, but at the moment that didn't matter. For all he knew, he could be about to sleep with the enemy.

But right now, that didn't matter either because deep down, a part of him believed she was innocent.

What was happening between them was definitely out of the realm of normal for him. He'd known he would have to get close to her, but he hadn't counted on this—his intense desire to do inappropriate, erotic and mind-blowing things to Swan Jamison.

But he wanted her and there would be no regrets. At least not for him, and based on what she'd just said, there would be no regrets for her either.

The moment he ended the kiss, his hands were busy removing her skirt, followed by her blouse, and when she stood in front of him in her lacy panties and bra, he couldn't help but growl his satisfaction. She looked sexy as hell and the rose-colored ensemble against the darkness of her skin was stunningly beautiful. *She* was beautiful.

He reached up and traced a finger along the material of her boxer-cut panties. This style on a woman had never done anything for him. Until now.

"You should have been a model," he said in a deep, throaty voice, filled with profound need and deep appreciation. She had such a gorgeously shaped body.

"My mother used to be a model. I was satisfied with being a model's daughter."

"And a strikingly beautiful one at that," he said, lowering to his knees to rid her of her panties. He couldn't wait to touch her, taste her and do all those erotic things to her he had dreamed of doing over the past few nights.

He breathed in deeply, getting more aroused by the second while easing her panties down a pair of long, beautiful legs.

After tossing her panties aside, he leaned back on his haunches and gazed at her, seeing her naked from the waist down. Her small waist, her stomach, the shape of her thighs and longs legs were perfect. She was perfect.

After looking his fill, he leaned forward and rested his forehead against her stomach, inhaling her luscious scent. He loved the way it flowed through his nostrils, opening his pores and causing his body to become even more erect.

And then he did something he'd wanted to do since their first kiss. He used the tip of his tongue to kiss her stomach, loving the indention around her naval and tracing a path around the area. Then he shifted his mouth lower, licking his way down and enjoying the sound of her moans.

When he came to the very essence of her, he licked around her womanly folds before leaning in to plant a heated kiss right there. It was as if sampling her special taste was as essential to him as breathing. His hands held firm to her thighs when he slid his tongue inside of her, loving the sound of his name from her lips.

Then he went deeper, using his tongue to taste her, claim her and brand her. The latter gave him pause but not enough to stop what he was doing. He'd never claimed a woman as his own and had never thought about doing so. But with Swan, it seemed such a thing wasn't just desired but was required.

And he didn't want it any other way. She was the first woman he wanted to claim. Forcefully, he pushed to the back of his mind what it could mean to make any woman his and decided he would dwell on that aspect of things at a later time. For now, he wanted to focus on the delicious, succulent, enjoyable taste that was Swan.

He took his time, wanting her to know just how much he loved doing this to her. He wanted her to feel the connection his tongue was making with her flesh. However, he wanted her to do more than feel it, he wanted this connection absorbed into her senses, into her mind, into every part of her body.

Moments later, Flipper knew he'd achieved his goal when he felt her fingers dig into his shoulder blades, followed by the quivering of her thighs. Tightening his hold on her hips, he knew what would be next and he was ready.

She screamed his name when she was thrown into an orgasmic state. Her fingernails dug deeper into his skin, but he didn't feel the pain because knowing he was giving her pleasure made him immune to it. What he felt was a desire to take things to the next level, to slide into her body and go so deep it would be impossible to detect where his body ended and hers began.

He finally pulled his mouth away and looked up at her, saw the glazed look in her eyes. Without saying a word, he traced his fingers around the womanly mound he'd just kissed before inserting his finger inside of her. She was ultra-wet and mega-hot and he had every intention of capitalizing on both. The orgasm she'd just experienced would be small in comparison to the one he intended to give her.

Pulling his finger from her, he licked it clean, knowing she was watching his every move. "Sweet," he said softly, holding her gaze.

He slowly eased to his feet and reached behind her to

remove her bra. When she stood totally naked in front of him, he feasted his gaze on her. "And I'm about to show you just how sweet I think you are, Swan."

Six

Swan was having difficulty breathing and the blue eyes staring at her made getting air to flow through her lungs even more difficult. Never had she felt this energized from a sexual act. And when David got to his feet and leaned in to kiss her, letting her taste herself on his lips, she felt weak in the knees. But he held her around the waist, holding her up as he kissed her more deeply, making her wish thc kiss could last forever.

She released a low disappointed groan in her throat when he pulled his mouth away.

"Don't worry, there's more coming."

He swept her off her feet and carried her over to the bed, placed her on it and joined her there.

"You still have clothes on," she said, reaching out to touch his shirt.

"I know and they will be coming off. Right now, I just want to lie here with you and hold you in my arms."

She smiled at him. “You’re not going to fall asleep on me, are you?”

Chuckling, he said, “Asleep? With you lying beside me without a stitch of clothes on? Sleep is the last thing I’d be able to do, trust me.”

He’d already pleasured her with his mouth, so she couldn’t help wondering what was next. She soon discovered his intent when he reached over and cupped her breasts.

“You are perfect,” he said in a deep husky voice.

The words triggered a memory of overhearing her father whisper the same compliment to her mother, after she surprised him with a special dinner after he returned home from one of his missions.

Swan knew she was far from perfect. Those were just words David was speaking. But still, hearing them filled her with joy. Maybe she shouldn’t let them, but they did.

Then any further thoughts dissolved from her mind when David eased a nipple between his lips. She moaned at the pleasure she felt all the way to her toes. Just when she thought she couldn’t stand anymore, he began torturing her other nipple.

When he finally eased away, she opened her eyes to watch him undress. When he removed his shirt, she saw the tattoos covering his tanned skin on both of his upper arms—huge dolphins emerging from beautiful blue ocean waters. Another tattoo of even more dolphins was painted across his back in beautiful vivid colors. She’d never been into tattoos but she thought his were stunning.

“I like your tattoos,” she said.

He glanced over at her and smiled. “Thanks.”

When he lowered his shorts, her gaze moved to the area between a pair of masculine thighs. His shaft was massive and marvelously formed. Just the thought of him easing that part of himself inside of her sent her pulse skyrocketing.

"You okay?"

She lifted her gaze to his. She wasn't sure if she was okay. A thickness had settled in her throat when she saw how he was looking at her. Not only did he intend to join his body with hers, she had a feeling he planned to keep them connected for a while.

"Yes, I'm okay."

Swan continued to check him out, thinking he had a mighty fine physique. His body was all muscle and it was obvious that he worked out regularly. A man didn't get those kinds of abs if he didn't.

She watched as he pulled a condom from his wallet and sheathed himself in a way that was so erotic, she felt herself getting wetter between the legs just watching him. Then he was strolling back toward the bed. To her.

"I'm about to make sure you feel more than okay," he said, reaching down and easing her up to rest her chest against his. Her breasts were still sensitive from his mouth and rubbing them against his chest caused a multitude of arousing sensations to swamp her.

"What are you doing to me?" she asked in a ragged breath, barely able to get the words out.

"Anything you can imagine," he whispered, lowering her back on the mattress and then straddling her. He stared down at her as he gently moved her legs apart. She felt him, that part of him, lightly touch her feminine folds and then he was rubbing back and forth across them, sending even more sensations racing through her bloodstream.

"Trying to torture me, David?"

"No, trying to pleasure you. Ready for me?"

The movement of his manhood against her was making it impossible for her to concentrate. "What do you think?"

"You're wet and hot, so I think you're ready." And then he entered her in one deep thrust.

She gasped at the fullness and was glad he'd gone still for a minute. This gave her the chance to feel him fully embedded deep within her. It had been a long time for her and her inner muscles were greedily clamping on to him, tightening their hold.

"You're big," she whispered.

"You're tight," was his response. "But we're making this work."

And he did. First he began moving again, gently sliding in and out of her. That only lasted a few seconds before he picked up the pace and began thrusting harder.

She responded by wrapping her legs around his waist. Then he lifted her hips to receive more of him. When he established a slow and deep rhythm, touching areas in her body that hadn't been touched in a long time, or ever, she fought back a scream. She grabbed hold of his hair and pulled it, but he didn't seem to mind.

"Rule number one, Swan. Don't hold back."

Was he kidding? It wasn't a matter of holding back. It was more like she was trying to keep her sanity. David was so powerfully male that he was pushing her over the edge with every deep stroke. Every cell within her vibrated in response to his precise thrusts.

"Hold on, baby. Things are about to get wild."

Flipper had given Swan fair warning. When he began pounding harder, making strokes he'd never attempted with another woman—going deep, pulling out and then going deep again—he felt a quivering sensation start at the base of his testicles and move toward her womb with each and every thrust. He had to hold on tight to her to keep them on the bed. He was determined to show her wild.

Simultaneously, he leaned down to have his way with her mouth, licking it corner to corner and then inserting his tongue inside with the same rhythm he was using below.

What he was feeling right now was more than off the charts, it was out of the atmosphere. When she finally let go and screamed his name, the sound vibrated in every part of his body, especially in her inner muscles. They clamped down on him, trying to pull everything out of him while her hands tightened even more in his hair.

"David!"

She screamed his name again. The sound drove him. He wanted more of her. Wanted to go deeper. Throwing his head back, he felt the veins in his neck strain. There was pain but not enough to dim the pleasure.

And he knew at that moment Swan had gotten under his skin in a way no other woman had.

He began rocking hard into her with an intensity that made him go deeper with every thrust. Then he was the one hollering out in pleasure, saying her name as an explosion ripped through him. Then like a crazed sexual maniac, he leaned in to feast on her mouth and breasts. It was like his desire for her could not end.

"David!"

He knew she was coming again and, dammit to hell, so was he. Marveling at such a thing, he tightened his hold on her. His control had not only gotten shot to hell and back but had died an explosive death as the result of the most powerful orgasms he'd ever endured.

This was what real lovemaking was about. No holds barred. No restrictions. Every part of him felt alive, drained, renewed. The room had the scent of sex and more sex. But that wasn't all. Emotions he'd never felt before touched him and swelled his heart.

He quickly forced those emotions back, refusing to go there. Knowing he couldn't go there.

The husky sound of deep, even breathing made Swan open her eyes. She was still in bed with David. Their limbs were entangled and his head was resting on her chest as he slept.

This man had been the most giving of lovers. He didn't come until he made sure she came first. He had kissed every part of her body, some parts more than others, and he had stoked passion within her in a way that had made her reach the boiling point. No man had ever made love to her with such intensity.

He had warned her about them getting wild. As far as she was concerned, they had gotten more than wild, they had gotten uninhibited, untamed. She hadn't known she had so much passion within her. He had brought it out and made her do more than own it. He had made her so aware of it that she doubted she could undo what he'd done.

David Holloway had done more than push a few of her buttons. He had turned on all the lights.

That thought made her smile and pull him closer. Feeling exhausted, she closed her eyes and drifted into sleep.

Flipper slowly opened his eyes, taking in the sight and scent of the woman lying beside him, snuggled close to his body. He was so sexually contented, he could groan out loud. He didn't. Instead he tightened his arms around her.

Things had gotten wild. They had finally fallen asleep after four rounds of the most satisfying lovemaking possible.

While making love with Swan, he had discovered there was a vast difference in making love to her versus making love to other women. He'd known it before but she had made that point crystal clear tonight.

With other women, he'd usually had one goal in mind—seeking sexual pleasure and making sure she got hers. With Swan it had been about that, too, but it had also been about finding closeness. No other woman had made him want to stay inside her. It had only been the need to replace condoms that had forced him from Swan's side. And then he had been back inside her in a flash…like that was where he belonged. Hell, he was still thinking that way and the twitch in his aroused manhood was letting him know just what he desired.

Flipper was known to have a robust sexual appetite. When you lived your life on the edge, engaging in covert operations as his team did, then you needed a way to release.

Usually, unerringly, he found his release in some woman's bed. He made sure she knew it was one and done. Due to the nature of his occupation, he didn't have time for attachments or anything long-term. Some SEALs did; he didn't. He'd tried it once and it hadn't worked out. Now he preferred being a loner. It didn't bother him that he was the lone single guy among his close friends. To each his own.

So how could one night in Swan Jamison's bed have him thinking things he shouldn't be thinking, especially considering why he was in Key West in the first place?

It had everything to do with the woman he'd had mind-blowing sex with for the past four hours or so. Now he saw her as more than an assignment. Now she was also a woman who had the ability to match his sexual needs one-on-one, something he found invigorating and energizing on all levels. He was a totally physical male and Swan Jamison was wholly, utterly female. Almost to the point that she'd blown his ever-loving mind.

Now she was sleeping peacefully while he was lying here thinking, knowing his honor was being tested. As a military man, he always did what was honorable. On top of that, his mother had drilled into all five of her sons that honor was not just for their country but extended to humans just as much, especially women. Why had that thought settled deep into his mind now?

One reason might be that he'd read the report on her. He knew about those elderly people residing at the senior living complex that she visited on her weekends off and how she'd championed so hard for the homeless. She was working with the mayor to help find funding to build a housing complex for them.

She was a caring person. He'd witnessed her love for her country, for her father, that night at the fireworks and the more he was around her, the more he believed in her innocence.

She made a sound now and he glanced down and met beautiful brown eyes staring at him. Immediately his senses connected with those eyes. She trusted him. He could see it in the gaze staring back at him. Otherwise he would not be here in her bed.

What would she think when she learned the truth? Would she still trust him? He pushed the thought to the back of his mind.

She gave him a beautiful, sleepy smile that melted

his insides. Made him wish he had come here to the Keys for a real vacation, a much-needed one. He wished he had entered her shop with no ulterior motive but to do as he claimed, which was to buy his mother a birthday gift. He would still have tried his hand at seducing her, but things would have been different. Specifically, he wouldn't feel as if his honor was being compromised.

"You didn't try my key lime pie," she whispered.

"We can get up and eat some now if you want," he said.

"No, I like being just where I am. We can always eat some later…or even for breakfast."

He leaned down and brushed a kiss across her lips. "Um, breakfast sounds nice. Is that an invitation to stay the night?"

"Only if you want to."

He wanted to. And when he brushed another kiss across her lips, he slid his tongue inside her mouth to kiss her deeply and let her know how much he wanted to stay.

He knew at that moment that his commanding officer and the admiral weren't the only ones with a personal interest in Swan Jamison. He now had a personal interest in her as well.

Seven

The next morning, Swan woke up to bright sunlight flowing in through her window and a powerfully male body sleeping beside her.

Last night was rated right up there with *Ripley's Believe It or Not.* It had been just that spectacular. They'd made love a couple more times before getting up after midnight to eat the pie she'd prepared for dessert. After clearing off the table and loading the dishes into the dishwasher, he'd suggested they walk on the beach.

So at one in the morning, they had strolled hand in hand along the water's edge. It had been a beautiful night with a full moon in the sky. The breeze off the ocean had provided the perfect reason for him to pull her close while walking barefoot in the sand. He told her more about his family; namely about his parents' medical supply company.

Then at some point, they began talking about her

company and she found herself telling him just about everything about jewelry making. He was curious about her stones and complimented how beautiful they were and inquired how she was able to create so many pieces.

No man had ever taken an interest in her work before and she was excited that he thought what she did for a living was important. She had found herself explaining the day-to-day operations of Swan's. He couldn't believe how she found the time to handcraft a number of the items sold in her shop.

David also thought it was great that Rafe, through his connections with a huge distributor in California, was able to get some of Swan's more expensive stones at a lower cost and had even helped her save on shipping by including them in the packaging with his ink.

She glanced over at him now as he shifted in bed. He kept his arms wrapped around her while he slept. She studied his features and saw how relaxed he looked.

She drew in a deep breath, still amazed at the depth of what they had shared last night. It had been the most profound thing she'd ever experienced with a man. Making love with David had touched her in ways she hadn't thought possible. He had made her feel things she hadn't ever felt before and those things weren't just sexual in nature. While in his arms, she had felt safe and secure. Protected.

As far as she was concerned, what they'd shared last night was more compelling and meaningful than any other time she'd shared with a man, even more meaningful than the time she'd spent with William. She'd never really allowed herself to fully let go with William. Now she could admit to herself that she'd known in the back of her mind that something didn't add up with him.

Yet she'd been so desperate for companionship after

losing her mother that she had wanted to believe William was honest, even though he'd seemed too good to be true. She was glad Candy had become suspicious when he'd never wanted them to be photographed together or when he'd insisted that they spend the night at Swan's place instead of the hotel.

At the time, his requests hadn't bothered her because she hadn't wanted her employer or her coworkers to get in her business. But Candy had seen through all that and knew something in the milk wasn't clean, as she would often say. It had been Candy who'd unveiled her own husband's secret affair with a flight attendant. And once confronted, Don hadn't denied a thing. He'd said he was glad she'd found out because he wanted a divorce.

Pushing thoughts of Don's and William's betrayals to the back of her mind, Swan continued to study David. She couldn't help but recall the number of times he'd made her climax. Now that was simply amazing all by itself.

She was enjoying her time with him, even knowing it wouldn't last. Later this month, he would leave the island and she would probably not hear from him again. She knew that, accepted it. She had long ago learned to live for the now and not sweat the small stuff. Especially those things she couldn't change.

"You're awake."

She couldn't help but smile at the slumberous blue eyes staring at her. The dark shadow on his chin made him look even sexier. "Yes, I'm awake. I guess I should be a good host and prepare breakfast before you leave."

"Um, I've overstayed my welcome?"

"No, but today is Sunday and I have a lot to do."

"Maybe I can help you."

"You don't know what I'll be doing."

He reached out and pushed her hair back off her shoulders so he could completely see her face. "Then tell me."

She gazed into his eyes. "The shop is closed on Sundays and I use my day off to visit Golden Manor Senior Place. My mom used to do volunteer work there when we lived on the island years ago. I would go with her on Sundays to visit everyone. I guess you could say it's become a family tradition that I decided to continue."

"I think that's a wonderful thing you're doing. I'm sure the residents there appreciate it."

"Yes, they do, although those who knew my mom are no longer there. They've passed on. I'm establishing new relationships and friendships."

"Good for you. I'd love to join you."

"You would?" she asked, surprised.

"Yes, and don't worry about preparing breakfast. I'll go home and refresh and be back here within an hour. We can grab breakfast somewhere before heading over. Afterward, we can spend more time on the beach. I enjoyed the walk last night with you."

And she had enjoyed it, too. The thought that he wanted to spend more time with her made her feel really good inside. "Okay, that sounds wonderful."

"I'm glad you think so, and before I leave..."

"Yes?"

He leaned over to kiss her and she knew where things would lead from there. She looked forward to getting wild again with him.

Flipper clicked on his phone the minute he walked into his hotel room. He noted several missed calls since he'd deliberately cut off his phone last night. One was from the admiral, who was probably calling for an update. But first Flipper would return the call to Nick.

"Flipper, should I ask why I couldn't reach you last night?"

"No, you shouldn't," Flipper said, flopping down in the nearest chair.

"You have heard the saying that you shouldn't mix business with pleasure, right?"

Too late for that, Flipper thought, running a hand down his face. Instead of responding to Nick's comment, he said, "I hope you have something for me. There's another angle I want you to check out."

"Okay, and yes, I have something for you. I found out the initial investigation was handed off to a group of civilian investigators, which means naval intelligence didn't rank it at the top at first."

Flipper was very much aware of the part government bureaucracy played in certain investigations. If someone thought a case should be under naval intelligence's radar, then they made sure it got there. "Why?"

"Not sure yet, but first, let's talk about Jamila Fairchild."

Flipper leaned forward in his chair. "Okay, let's talk about her. What do you have?"

"Not what you obviously think. What she told Swan was the truth. She does have a huge family who lives in the north."

Flipper raised a brow. "Then who made the error in the report from naval intelligence?"

"Don't know, but it's worth checking out, although I don't think it's anything suspicious on Ms. Fairchild's end. Especially when I tell you who her family is."

"And who is her family?"

"Her mother's brother is Swan's grandfather."

A frown covered Flipper's face. "The grandfather who disowned Swan's father?"

"Yes, from what I've gathered. But I can find no record of her grandfather ever reaching out to her."

"Interesting."

"Yes, it is. I take it Swan Jamison doesn't know about the family connection."

"No, she doesn't." Flipper decided not to try to wrap his head around this bit of news just yet. Instead he asked, "What about Rafe Duggers?"

"Personally, I think something is going on with him."

Flipper lifted a brow. "What?"

"First of all, certain aspects of his info are sealed."

"Sealed?"

"Yes. I would think if naval intelligence was checking into something related to Swan and her story, they would see that sealed record for her tenant as a red flag. For them not to have flagged it raises my own suspicions about a few things."

That raised Flipper's suspicions as well. Was Rafe a double agent? Someone working undercover? Was someone in naval intelligence deliberately setting Swan up as the traitor? If so, why?

"You weren't able to find out anything about him?"

There was a husky chuckle. "I didn't say that. There are ways to find out anything you want when you know how to do it."

And Nick knew how to do it. He'd been an amazing SEAL, but as far as Flipper was concerned, Nick's natural investigative talents were better served at Homeland Security. "When will you let me know something?"

"Give me a couple of days. In the meantime, don't say anything to anyone about my suspicions about Duggers."

"Not even the CO and admiral?"

"Not even them for now. You mentioned Swan had a third godfather who was someone high up at naval intelligence. Was his identity revealed to you?"

"No, it wasn't but then I didn't ask," Flipper said.

"It wasn't hard to find out," Nick replied. "All you have to do is find out who Andrew Jamison's SEAL teammates were at the time he died and do a little research to determine where they are now."

"I take it you've done that."

"Yes, and would you believe Swan Jamison's third godfather is Director of Naval Intelligence Samuel Levart?"

Flipper would not have considered Director Levart in a million years, but it all made sense now. In order for someone to have delayed making formal charges against Swan, that person would have to be someone in power. The admiral had alluded to as much. "Swan doesn't know how favored she is to have three powerful men in her corner."

"Yes, but we both know it wouldn't matter if one of her godfathers was the President. If naval intelligence believes they have enough evidence to prosecute her, they will," Nick said.

Flipper knew that to be true. Now more than ever he had to find the person intent on framing Swan. To him, it was beginning to look like an inside job.

"So what else do you have for me to check out?" Nick asked, reclaiming Flipper's attention.

"It's about something Swan told me." He then shared with Nick the information about Rafe Duggers's association with some huge distributor in California. "I need you to check that out."

"I will. I know time is of the essence so I'll get back to you soon, Flipper."

"Thanks, I appreciate it."

"If you're so concerned about me, then why not return to the Keys and keep an eye on me, Candy?" Swan asked. She moved around her bedroom getting dressed while talking to her friend on speakerphone.

"You know why I won't return, just yet. But I did hear something that's interesting."

"What?" Swan asked as she shimmied into her skirt.

"I talked to Francola the other day and she said Marshall mentioned to her that Don is thinking about moving away from the island."

Swan paused. Francola and her husband, Marshall, had been close friends of Don and Candy's while they were married. The two couples often did things together. Personally, Swan didn't care much for Francola because the woman had been aware Don was cheating on Candy but hadn't told her friend. "I would take anything Francola says with a grain of salt these days," Swan said as she continued dressing.

"I know you still fault her for not telling me about Don and I admit I was angry with her, too, but now I understand her not doing so."

"Do you?"

"Yes. Her relationship with me is not like our relationship, Swan. You and I have been best friends since grade school and we have no secrets. You would have told me about Don had you suspected anything."

"Darn right."

"Well, Francola and I didn't have that kind of relationship. We only met through our husbands, who worked together. Besides, I'm not sure I would have believed her even had she told me. I would have been in denial." Candy paused. "Now, enough about me. Tell me more about this David Holloway."

Swan smiled while putting hoop earrings into her ears. "He's a real nice guy. Thoughtful. Considerate. Handsome as sin." She glanced over at her made-up bed. Although there were no signs of anyone sleeping in it last night, it didn't take much for her to remember all the wild action she and David had shared under the sheets. "And he's great in bed. More than great. He's fantastic."

"Just be careful, Swan. Protect your heart."

Swan slipped her feet into her sandals. "My heart? It's not like I'm falling for the guy, Candy."

"Aren't you? I can hear it in your voice. You like him a lot."

Yes, she did like him a lot. "It won't go beyond me liking him," she said, trying to convince herself of that more so than Candy.

"Can you honestly say that?"

"Yes, because I can't let it. His work brought him to the island and he'll be leaving soon. In less than thirty days."

"Doesn't matter."

Swan knew for her it *did* matter. She only wanted short-term. The last thing she wanted was to do long-term with any man.

Eight

"I enjoyed my time with you today, Swan," Flipper said, looking down at her.

They'd had brunch at Summer Moon before heading to the senior living complex where they spent the next four hours. She assisted the staff by reading to groups of people and even taking a few of the seniors for walks around the complex. Some, she'd explained, had family who rarely visited so she had become like their surrogate granddaughter.

On the flip side, considering what she'd missed out having in her life, he couldn't help but wonder if they had become her surrogate grandparents.

From the moment she walked into the facility, everyone brightened up when they saw her. It was amazing to him. She knew just what to say to elicit a smile or to get them to engage in more conversation. The majority of the seniors knew her by name and he couldn't help noticing a number of the women wearing what looked like necklaces she'd made.

When he inquired about the necklaces Swan confirmed they were her designs but she had taught the women to make them from stones she'd given them. It had taken longer than normal since a lot of the older women's hands weren't as nimble as they used to be.

After leaving the nursing home, they'd grabbed lunch at a sidewalk café before returning to her house where they'd spent the rest of the day on the beach. Later, after ordering takeout for dinner from Arness, they were back at her place.

No matter how tempting Swan was making it for him to stay longer at her place, he would leave when it got dark. The information about Rafe Duggers's sealed records bothered him and he'd decided to poke around in the tattoo parlor later that night to see what he could find.

He glanced over at Swan as she sat across the table from him eating dinner. Earlier today, when he had returned to take her to breakfast, she had opened the door looking fresh and perky and dressed simply in a pair of shorts and a tank top. Seeing her dressed that way reminded him of just what a gorgeous pair of legs she had, as well as how those same legs had wrapped around him while they'd made love that morning and the night before.

When they had gone swimming, she'd worn one of the sexiest two-piece bathing suits he'd ever seen. He had totally and completely enjoyed his day with her. They would be attending the Memorial Day festivities together tomorrow in town, which included a parade.

Because he needed some investigative time, he'd

come up with an excuse for why he couldn't see her a couple of days this week. Time was moving quickly and he had yet to find anything to clear her of wrongdoing.

Because of Nick's warning, Flipper hadn't told Admiral Martin everything when he'd called him back yesterday. Namely, he'd left out the discrepancies between what Nick had found out and the actual reports from naval intelligence. Until Flipper discovered what was going on, he would follow Nick's advice and keep that information to himself for now.

"Although I won't be seeing you for a few days because of work, will you still be on the island?" Swan asked.

It was hard not to be totally truthful about why she wouldn't be seeing him. She was the last person he wanted to be dishonest with but he had no choice. His goal had always been to prove her innocence and now that was doubly true. He would check out the tattoo shop tonight and look around in both Rafe's and Jamila's homes this week while they were here at work. Although it had been established that Jamila was Swan's relative, as far as Flipper was concerned, she was still a suspect.

"Yes, I'll still be on the island but I have to concentrate on this project I was sent here to do." No need to tell her that the project involved her.

"I understand how things are when work calls."

He reached up and caressed the side of her face. "We still have a date for the parade tomorrow, right?"

"Yes."

"What about dinner on Friday evening?" he asked her.

Her smile touched something deep within him. "I'd love that, David."

"Good. I'll swing by your shop at closing time Friday and we can go to dinner directly from there. You pick the place."

"All right."

"What time do you want me to come get you for the parade tomorrow?"

"It starts at ten in the morning and we need to get there early to get a good spot. How about if I prepare pancakes for us in the morning around eight?"

"You sure? I wouldn't want you to go to any trouble."

She waved off his words. "No problem. I told you I enjoy cooking."

After they finished dinner, he told her he needed to leave to read some reports for work, which wasn't a lie. She walked him to the door. He leaned down to kiss her, intending for it to be a light touch of their lips.

But the moment his mouth touched hers and she released a breathless sigh, it seemed the most natural thing to slide his tongue inside her mouth and deepen the kiss. Wrapping his arms around her waist, he pulled her tight against him and knew the exact moment the kiss had changed to something more.

It was no longer a *goodbye and I'll see you later* kiss. Instead it was one of those *I need to have you before I go* kind. And Swan seemed to be reciprocating those feelings as she returned the kiss with equal fervor.

The next thing Flipper knew, he was sweeping her off her feet and moving quickly toward her bedroom. When he placed her on the bed, they began stripping off their clothes.

For him, she'd become an itch he couldn't scratch and a craving that wouldn't go away. There was something about making love to her that made every part of his body ache with need. She had imprinted herself on his soul and in every bone in his body and there was nothing he could do about it but savor what they had for as long as he could.

When she was completely naked, his pulse kicked up a notch and his breathing was forced from his lungs when he looked at her. She was beautiful and perfectly made.

He pulled a condom from his wallet in the shorts she'd helped him remove and toss aside. Knowing she was watching his every move, he rolled it over his aroused manhood.

"I want to do that for you the next time."

He looked at Swan. "All right." So she was letting him know she intended there to be a next time for them. He was glad because he wanted a next time, too.

There was a big chance when she found out the truth about why he was here on the island that she wouldn't want to have anything to do with him again. But he forced the thought from his mind.

"You don't have all evening, you know," she teased.

She was right, he didn't and it was a good thing she didn't know why. He moved toward her. "Impatient?"

She smiled up at him. "Yes, you could say that."

"In that case, I can help you with that problem." He leaned in. "I've got to taste you again," was all he said just seconds before his mouth came down on hers.

Swan automatically lifted her arms around his neck the moment his lips touched hers.

Capturing her tongue, David drew it into his mouth. Blood rushed fast and furious to Swan's head, making her feel both light-headed and dazed as his tongue began mating with hers. His technique was rousing her passion to a level that electrified every part of her. Insistent need rushed up her spine, spinning her senses and mesmerizing her with his delectable taste.

He suddenly broke off the kiss and they both panted furiously, drawing deep gulps of air into their lungs.

She rested her head against his chest and inhaled his scent as she continued to catch her breath. She knew she was losing herself to passion again when she felt the hardness of his erection brushing against her thigh, energizing the area between her legs.

Then she heard him whispering erotic details of what he wanted to do to her. His words spread fire through her body and when he gently cupped the area between her legs, she moaned.

"You're torturing me, David," she said, before twisting to push him down on his back so she could straddle him. Before he could react, she lowered her head between his masculine thighs and eased his erection into her mouth.

"Ah, Swan," he growled huskily, gripping her hair. She was fully aware of him expanding and felt a sense of triumph in her ability to get him even more aroused than he already was. The feel of his hands locked in her hair sparked even more passion within her and motivated her to use her mouth in ways she'd never done before.

"Swan!"

She felt his thighs flex beneath her hands before he bucked forward. She wasn't prepared when he quickly switched their positions so that she was the one on her back. The blue eyes staring down at her flared with a passion that sent tremors through her.

Before she could whisper his name, he slid inside

her. He kept going deeper and deeper, stretching her in ways she didn't know she could be spread, inch by inch.

"Wrap your legs around me, baby," he whispered in a throaty voice.

When she did as he asked, he began thrusting hard. It was as if his total concentration was on her, intent on giving her pleasure. She felt every inch of him as he rode her hard, not letting up.

"David!"

She screamed his name as he continued to make love to her, throwing her into a euphoric state that seemed endless. He was using her legs to keep their bodies locked while relentlessly pounding into her. Her world was spinning and she couldn't control the need to moan, moan and moan some more.

She was unable to hold anything back when her body erupted into an orgasm so powerful it propelled her toward utter completeness. She screamed his name once again as a deep feeling of ecstasy ripped through her entire body.

Flipper eased off Swan to lie beside her. Pulling her into his arms, his nostrils flared as he inhaled the scent of sex. The scent of woman, this woman. A woman he still desired even now.

He was not new to lust. Been there, done that and he figured he would be doing it some more. A lot more. With Swan lying in in his arms, snuggled close to him, close to his heart, he knew something had changed between them.

Bottom line, Swan Jamison was not only intoxicating, she was addictive.

"I don't think I'll be able to move again, David."

A smile touched the corners of his lips. He definitely

knew how she felt, but he knew he had to move. He had somewhere to be tonight and as sexually drained as he was, he intended to be there.

"Then don't move. Just lie there. I'll let myself out," he said, reluctant to go, although he knew he must.

"You sure?" she asked in a lethargic voice.

"Positive. I'll be back in the morning for the parade and then we have a date on Friday."

"Yes. I'm going to need it. I'll be working late Wednesday doing inventory. I probably won't leave work until around ten."

"With your worker's help?"

"No. The cruise ship comes in Wednesday."

He released her to ease out of bed and put on his clothes. "What does a cruise ship have to do with anything?" He could feel her gaze on his body. He couldn't disguise the impact of knowing she was watching him. He was getting aroused all over again.

"Jamila dates a guy who works on the cruise ship and they only see each other whenever the ship comes to port. She always requests the day off to spend with him. I guess they made up."

He had planned to check out Jamila's house when he'd assumed she would be at work. Good thing he now knew otherwise.

"Made up?" he asked, pulling his shirt over his head.

"Yes. I got the impression they weren't on good terms last week. Not sure what happened but it's all good now since they've apparently kissed and made up."

He nodded. "How long have they been together?"

"About six months now."

Flipper didn't say anything as he continued dressing. There hadn't been any mention of a boyfriend for

Jamila Fairchild in the report he'd read. Another discrepancy. There were too many inconsistencies for his liking and he was determined to find out why. One thing was certain, he didn't like the idea of Swan being at her shop alone late at night.

He moved back to the bed, leaned down and brushed a kiss across her lips. "I'll see you in the morning."

"Looking forward to it."

He smiled down at her and then turned and left.

Later that night, Flipper, dressed all in black, moved in the shadows, careful to avoid streetlights and security cameras. He had scoped out the area and was familiar with where the cameras were located. More than once, he'd had to dart behind a shrub when people were out for a late-night stroll.

He reached the area where Swan's shop was located and when he heard voices, he darted behind a building to hide in the shadows.

Two men stood not far away. One of them was Rafe. Neither of the men saw Flipper. The other guy was a little taller and appeared to be a foreigner. Their conversation sounded like an argument and was in a language Flipper wasn't familiar with and he spoke four. Most SEALs spoke at least that many, except for Coop, who had mastered seven.

When the men lapsed into English, they lowered their voices and could barely be heard. Flipper did make out the words *ink* and *roses*. Was someone getting a tattoo of roses painted on their body? If so, did it mean anything?

Flipper was glad when the men finally moved on. More than ever, he was determined to check out the tattoo parlor. He waited a half hour to make sure the men didn't return. When he was certain they had gone, he went to work bypassing the security alarms and cameras.

Using a sort of skeleton key, he opened the back door and walked inside the tattoo parlor. Using night goggles, he glanced around.

The place looked like a typical tattoo parlor. He should know since he and his brothers had frequented a number of them. He was proud of the images on his body. Luckily, Swan hadn't asked him about them. He was glad because the last thing he wanted to do was lie about why he was into dolphins.

Pulling off the camera attached to his utility belt, he replaced the night goggles with a high-tech camera, which was his own creation. This particular piece of equipment detected objects underground and under water. Looking through the lens, he scanned the room. It wasn't long before the camera light began blinking.

He moved toward the area and aimed the camera lower, toward the floor, and the blinking increased. Evidently something was buried beneath the wooden floor, a portion covered by a rug. The architectural report he'd been given of Swan's shop had not exposed any secret rooms or closets.

Putting the camera aside, he moved the rug and felt around to find a latch. He opened the trapdoor to find a small compartment beneath the floor. He saw more containers of ink. Why? There was a supply case full of ink on the opposite side of the room. Why was this ink hidden?

The first thing he noticed was the difference in the labeling. Was there something different about this particular ink? There was only one way to find out, he thought, taking one out of the cubby. He would overnight one of the containers to Nick instead of naval intelligence.

At this stage of the game, he wasn't taking any chances about who could be trusted.

Nine

Swan had just finished the last of her inventory when she heard the knock on her shop's door. Crossing the room, she peeped through the blinds to see who it was. A smile touched her lips as she unlocked the door. "David, I didn't think I'd see you until Friday."

He glanced around her empty shop before looking back at her. "I finished work early and remembered you saying you were working late tonight doing inventory. I wanted to make sure you got home okay."

That was really nice of him. "You didn't have to do that." But she was glad he had. They had spent Monday together celebrating Memorial Day. He had arrived at her place for breakfast and then they'd walked to where the start of the parade would take place.

After the parade, they'd gone to the island festival marketplace where various vendors had lined the streets with booths and a huge Ferris wheel. They had taken one of the boat rides around the islands and had ended up eating lunch on Key Largo.

She had thought about him a lot since Monday, remembering in explicit detail how he'd made love to her before leaving.

"I know you said Jamila would be off today," David said. "What about your tattoo guy? Is the parlor closed on Wednesdays as well?"

"Yes, but Rafe dropped by earlier. He was expecting a shipment of more ink to come in today but it didn't. He wasn't happy about that."

"He wasn't?"

"No. He said there was a particular shade of blue he was expecting."

Flipper nodded and checked his watch. "Ready to go?"

"Yes, I just need to grab my purse from my office." She was about to turn to get it when there was another knock at the door.

"Expecting anyone?" David asked her.

"No. I'll see who it is."

She walked to the door and David went with her. After glancing out of the blinds, she turned back to David and smiled. "It's Jamila and Horacio."

She unlocked the door. "Jamila, hi."

"Hey, Swan. Horacio and I were in the neighborhood and I remembered you would be here late. I thought we'd drop by to say hello."

Swan smiled at the man with Jamila. "Horacio, it's good seeing you again."

"Same here, Swan," he said in a heavy accent that Swan always loved hearing.

"And this is my friend David Holloway. David, you

already know Jamila. This is her friend Horacio Jacinto," Swan said, making introductions.

The two men shook hands. Swan wondered if she'd imagined it but she thought David had tensed up when he'd seen Jamila and Horacio. "Nice meeting you, Horacio," David said. "I can't place your accent. Where are you from?"

"Portugal."

"Nice country," David said.

"Thanks."

"I hope you'll leave before it gets too late, Swan," Jamila was saying.

"I will. David came to make sure I got home okay." Usually whenever she worked late, either doing inventory or making her jewelry, she would catch a cab home even though she lived only a few blocks away. But since David was here, she would suggest they walk. It was a nice night and she would love to spend more time with him.

"We'll see you guys later," Jamila said. "We had dinner at Marty's Diner and now we're going to Summer Moon for drinks and live music."

"Okay. Enjoy. And I hope to see you again the next time the ship ports, Horacio," Swan said.

Horacio smiled. "I hope to see you as well."

After they left, Swan went to her office to get her purse. She returned and noticed David was standing in the same spot where she'd left him, staring at the door. "Are you all right?"

He turned to her. "Yes, it's just that Horacio looks familiar and I was trying to remember when I might've seen him. Maybe I've run into him before, here on the island."

She nodded. "That's possible. He's a chef on the Century Cruise Line that docks here once a week. Whenever it does, he comes ashore and meets up with Jamila. I think I mentioned that to you."

"You did, but I could have sworn I saw him a few nights ago. Sunday. After leaving your place."

Swan shook her head. "It wasn't him. The ship didn't arrive in our port until today. But you know what they say about everybody having a twin."

He chuckled. "You're probably right, but I'm sure you don't have one. I'm convinced there's not another woman anywhere who is as beautiful as you."

Swan knew better than to let such compliments go to her head, but she couldn't help the smile that spread across her lips. "You, David Holloway, can make a girl's head swell if she's inclined to believe whatever you say."

"I hope you do believe it because I spoke the truth." He took her hand in his as they headed for the door.

Flipper pulled out his phone the minute he walked into his hotel room later that night. He'd felt it vibrate in his pocket when he was walking Swan home but figured it would be a call he needed to take in private.

Swan had invited him inside but he'd declined, telling her he had a ton of paperwork waiting on him back at his hotel. That wasn't a lie. He'd begun rereading all those naval intelligence reports to see if he could determine why those investigators had failed to do their job and instead intentionally went after Swan as a scapegoat.

He checked his phone and saw Nick had called and Flipper quickly returned the call. "What do you have for me?"

"More than you counted on. All I can say is whoever handled that investigation did a botched-up job."

Or they did the job they'd been expected to do, Flipper thought. "I guess there's a reason you feel that way."

"Yes. That ink you sent to be analyzed isn't what it's supposed to be."

"It's not ink?"

"Yes, it's ink, but coded ink. When applied to the skin as a tattoo, it can be decoded by a special light. It's my guess that's how the classified information is leaving Swan Jamison's shop—with people's tattoos and not with any of her jewelry. Guess where the ink is being shipped from."

"Swan mentioned from some place in California."

"Yes, that's right and the distribution company is a few miles from the naval base in San Diego. That means someone on the base must be passing classified information that's being shipped in the ink."

Flipper frowned. "And because Rafe Duggers is conveniently including Swan's stones with each shipment, it makes sense for her to be suspect."

"Right," Nick agreed. "Someone is setting her up real good, Flipper. They are definitely making her the fall guy."

Flipper wondered who in naval intelligence had targeted Swan and why. "I have another piece of the puzzle I need you to check out."

"What?"

"The guy who was with Rafe Duggers two nights ago. The one I told you he was arguing with. I saw him today."

"You did?"

"Yes. He came into the shop when Swan was closing up. His name is Horacio Jacinto and he's Jamila Fairchild's boyfriend."

"That's interesting. I'll find out what I can about

him," Nick said. "I wonder if Ms. Fairchild knows what's going on or if she's being used as a pawn."

"I don't know, but I'm going to make sure I keep an eye on all of them."

"Be careful, Flipper."

"I will."

A few hours later, after taking a shower, Flipper was sitting at the desk in his hotel room suite when his cell phone went off. Recognizing the ringtone, he clicked on and said, "What's going on, Coop?"

"You tell us."

Us meant Bane, Viper and Mac were also on the phone. "I guess Nick called you guys."

"Yes, he called us earlier today," Bane said. "What's going on with Swan Jamison sounds pretty damn serious. Don't you think it's time to call the CO?"

Flipper ran a hand down his face. He glanced at the clock on the wall. It was close to three in the morning. "If Nick told you everything, then you know it's an inside job at the base. There's a traitor somewhere and until I know who I can trust, then—"

"You know as well as we do that you can trust our CO, Flipper," Viper said. "Once you tell Shields what you've found out, if he suspects Martin or Levart of any wrongdoing, he will know what to do."

"Yes, however, the three of them share a close friendship. What if the CO is blinded due to loyalty?"

"We're talking about our commanding officer, Flipper. Shields would turn his own mother in if he thought she was betraying our country. You know that."

Yes, he knew it. But still… "I don't know if Martin or Levart is really involved. Like Shields, they are Swan's godfathers and I would hate to think they are shady. I just know it's an inside job and right now I'm suspicious of just about everybody."

"We figured you would be, so open the damn door," Mac said.

Flipper frowned. "What?"

"We said open the door," Coop said, knocking.

Flipper heard the knock, clicked off his phone, quickly went to the door and snatched it open. There stood his four best friends.

"What are you guys doing here?"

"What does it look like?" Mac asked as the four moved passed Flipper to enter the hotel room.

"We figured ten pairs of eyes were better than two," Bane said, glancing around. "Besides, we need to keep you objective."

"But what about your families? Viper, your wife is having a baby!"

Viper chuckled. "And I plan to be there when she does. According to Layla's doctor, we still have a couple of months, so I'm good."

"And our families are good, too," Coop said. "They know we look out for each other and they agreed we should be here for you."

"Teri is glad I'm gone," Mac said, grumbling. "Maybe when I go back, she'll have a new attitude."

"Or maybe you'll have one," Bane said, frowning at Mac.

"Whatever," Mac said, picking up the hotel's restaurant menu book. "Is it too late for room service?"

Flipper closed the door and drew in a deep breath as he watched the men gather around the table, already rolling up their sleeves, ready to help him figure things out. They worked together as a team and he would admit that whenever they did so, good things happened.

"There's something all of you should know," he said, getting their attention.

They glanced over at him. "What? No room service at this hour?" Mac asked in a serious tone.

"That, too."

"What's the other thing we should know, Flipper?" Viper asked, sitting back in the chair he'd claimed as soon as he came in.

Flipper leaned against the closed door. "Investigating Swan Jamison is no longer just an assignment for me. It's become personal."

The men nodded. "And you think we don't know that, Flipper?" Coop asked in a steely tone. "That's why we're here. Someone is trying to frame your woman and we're going to help you find out who and why. But first things first. You know what you have to do, right?"

Flipper stared at the four men. Yes, he knew. Instead of answering Coop, he picked up his cell phone from the table and placed a call to his CO.

Ten

As far as Swan was concerned, Friday hadn't arrived fast enough. With every passing hour, she would glance at her shop's door expecting to see David walk in. One would think his surprise visit Wednesday would have sufficed. Unfortunately, it hadn't.

She'd had two days to think about how irrational her thoughts about David were becoming. He didn't come across as a forever sort of guy and she wasn't looking for a forever kind of relationship, so what was up with this urgency to see him?

The only reason she could give herself was that she'd been alone and without a man's attention for so long that now that she had it, she was in greedy mode, lapping it up like a desperate woman. And she had never done the desperate thing before.

The door chimed and she looked up to see that it was Rafe who walked in. Lately she'd noticed him using the front door a lot more, instead of the back door to his parlor. They had decided at the beginning of his lease that the entrance to her shop was off-limits so his customers wouldn't trounce back and forth through her shop on the days Rafe worked late.

"Did your box of ink finally arrive?"

He stopped and looked over at her. "Why would you be asking about my ink?"

Now that, she thought, was a silly question. Did the man have a short memory? "Because you came by Wednesday looking for the shipment and left in a tiff when it hadn't arrived."

"I wasn't in a tiff and yes, I did get my box of ink."

Yes, he had been in a tiff, but if he wouldn't acknowledge it, then she would leave it alone. "Good. I'm glad you got it."

She watched him walk off toward his parlor. He hadn't been in a good mood lately. But then, maybe she'd been in such an extremely good mood that she had a distorted view. In fact, come to think of it, it was pretty normal for him to be moody.

Moments later, while she worked with a customer, Swan watched as Rafe walked back through her shop and toward the front door. She decided if he did that again she would remind him of their agreement about which door he should use whenever he went in or out of his tattoo parlor.

After her customer left, she glanced at her watch. Her shop would be closing in a couple of minutes. David usually arrived early. It would be understandable if he'd gotten detained, but she hoped he hadn't been. She was so anxious to see him.

The thought of how much she was looking forward to being with him should bother her, but for some reason it didn't. Like she'd told Candy, Swan wasn't expecting anything from her relationship with David. There had been no promises made, so none would be broken. The only thing she was expecting was exactly what she was getting—a good time. He was excellent company and great in bed.

It had been almost three years since William, and during that time, although she'd dated, she hadn't allowed herself to get serious over a man. Instead she had concentrated on opening her shop and making it a success.

She had put her mind, heart and soul into Swan's. Especially her heart, deciding that if she put it into her business, she wouldn't run the risk of placing it elsewhere. Now it seemed there might be a risk after all and that risk had a name. David Holloway.

A part of her wanted to protect herself from another possible heartbreak by calling David and canceling any plans for tonight and then to stop sharing any time with him after that. He had given her his number so she could reach him. She could certainly come up with a plausible excuse. But did she really want to do that?

No, she didn't.

David would be her test. If she could handle a casual affair with him, then she would ace the test with flying colors.

The door chimed and she glanced up and there he was. She watched him lock her door and put the Closed sign in place before pulling down the blinds. Then he slowly sauntered toward her wearing a pair of khaki pants and an open white shirt and holding her within the scope of those laser-blue eyes. There was his too-sexy walk and a smile that made her heart beat rapidly.

Suddenly seeing him, when she'd been thinking of

him all day, took complete control of her senses. Without much effort, the man had turned the sensuality up more than a notch. He had his own barometer of hotness.

Finally moving her feet, she strolled across the floor to meet him halfway and walked straight into his arms. The moment he pressed his body to hers, she reached up and looped her arms around his neck. He responded by wrapping his arms around her waist, drawing her even closer so she fit against him.

"I missed you, Swan."

She shouldn't let his words affect her, but they did—to the point where she was having difficulty replying.

"I missed you, too."

And she had, although they'd seen each other Wednesday. Even when she'd tried to convince herself that missing him to such a degree meant nothing. Now, as she stood wrapped in his arms, with her body pressed tight against his, hip to hip and thigh to thigh, she knew it meant everything.

"That's good to know, sweetheart," he said in a throaty voice.

Sweetheart? The endearment left her defenseless. She was trying to summon all her senses to regroup. And it wasn't helping matters that his arousal was cradled in the apex of her thighs. Good Lord, he felt so good there.

"Ready?" she found the voice to ask him.

His gaze studied her face as if he was seeing her for the first time. As if he was trying to record her features to memory. And then a mischievous smile touched his lips. "I'm ready for whatever you have in mind, Swan."

Shivers of desire skittered down her spine and Swan

wished his words hadn't given her ideas, but they had. Ideas that were so bold, brazen and shameless she felt her cheeks staining just thinking about them. But at that moment, she didn't care. She could and would admit to wanting him.

She should wait until later to act on her desires. That would be the safe thing to do. But she knew she would be tortured during dinner whenever she looked at him. The way his mouth moved when he ate, or the way his hands—those hands that could turn her on just by looking at them—gripped his beer bottle. There were so many things about David Holloway that would do her in if she were to wait until later.

"You sure about that, David?"

"Positive. Do you want me to prove it?"

Did she? Yes, she did. "Where?"

"I will prove it anywhere you want. Right here in the middle of the floor if you like," he said. "But I suggest your office."

Flipper could tell by the way she was looking at him that she was giving his offer serious thought. He had no problems tilting the scale in his favor and he decided to do so. Lowering his head, he kissed her, trying to be gentle and finding gentleness hard to achieve. Especially when her taste made him greedy for more.

He knew she'd ceased thinking when she responded to his kiss by sinking her body farther into his embrace and tightening her arms around his neck.

Some things, he decided then and there, were just too mind-blowingly good, and kissing Swan was one of them. What they'd shared these last few days was a dimension of pleasure he hadn't felt in a long time—or maybe ever—while devouring a woman's mouth. And when his hands shifted from around her waist to cup her backside, he groaned at the feel of her body pressed tightly against his erection.

When he finally broke off the kiss, he buried his face in the curve of her neck and drew in a deep breath. This woman was almost too much. She looked good, tasted good and as he drew in another deep breath, he concluded that she smelled good, too.

"You want to come with me, Mr. Holloway?" she asked, stepping out of his arms.

"Yes." The answer was quick off his lips.

She took his hand. "Then follow me."

He had no problem following her and the minute he crossed the threshold into her office, he recalled the last time he'd been in here. Namely, when they'd shared a kiss that had nearly brought him to his knees.

"It appears dinner will have to wait."

He glanced over at her. She had stepped out of her sandals. After locking the office door, he leaned against it and watched her undress. She was wearing a burnt-orange sundress with spaghetti straps. It looked good on her and the color of the dress seemed to highlight her hair and skin tone.

He had gotten little sleep since his friends had arrived in the Keys. But then they hadn't come here to rest. They had left their families to come here and help him solve a sinister plan of espionage against the country they loved.

And to protect the woman *he* loved.

He suddenly swallowed deep when that last thought passed through his mind. As he watched Swan remove her panties, he knew without a doubt that he had fallen in love with her. He wouldn't try to figure out how it happened but just accept that it had. Now more than ever he was determined to make sure whoever was trying to screw her over didn't succeed.

"Are you going to just stand there?" she asked, standing before him completely naked.

"No, that's not my intention at all," he said, moving away from the door to stand a few feet from her in what he considered his safe zone. If he got any closer, he would be tempted to take her with his clothes on. He removed his shirt and eased both his khakis and briefs down his legs at the same time. Quick and easy.

"I love your dolphins," she said. "I meant to ask you about them a number of other times, but always got sidetracked. So I'm asking you now. Any reason you chose dolphins?"

He decided to be as truthful with her as he could. One day he would have to explain to her why he'd lied about so many things. "Like the dolphins, I love being in the water. But this isn't just any dolphin."

"It's not?"

"No. This dolphin's name is Flipper. Surely you've heard of him."

"Not as much as I know Willy from *Free Willy*."

He chuckled as he moved toward her. "Willy was a whale. Flipper was a dolphin. That's what my friends call me. Flipper."

"Flipper?"

"Yes. Like I said, I love being in the water."

"You don't look like a Flipper."

He came to a stop in front of her. "Don't tell that to my family and friends. They wouldn't agree with you."

She reached out and touched the tattoo of the dolphin on his arm. Her fingers felt like fire as she traced along the design with her fingertips. "Beautiful. Not just your tattoos but all of you, David."

"Thanks." And in one smooth sweep, he picked her up and sat her on the desk, spreading her legs in the process.

"Did I tell you how much I missed you?" he asked, running his hands over her arms.

"Yes. Just a few moments ago when you arrived here and I told you I missed you, too. You also told me that you missed me when you walked me home Wednesday night and I invited you to stay."

Flipper heard the disappointment in her voice. If only she knew how much he'd wanted to stay. But once he'd found out Jamila would be out for a while with Horacio, he needed that time to check out her place. "I couldn't, but I intend to make it up to you when we have more time."

He was letting her know this little quickie didn't count. He had something planned for her when all this was over and he could sit her down and tell her everything.

"Not here and not now? What do you call this?" she asked when he reached up and cupped her breasts in his hands, marveling at just how beautiful they were.

"This is an I-can't-wait-until-later quickie."

"Interesting."

Shifting his gaze from her breasts to her eyes, he said, "Let me show you, Swan Jamison, just how interesting it can be." He leaned forward and kissed her while placing the head of his erection against her wet opening. The contact sent heat spiraling through him.

While his tongue mated greedily with hers, he entered her in one hard stroke. Pulling his mouth from hers, he let out a guttural moan when her muscles clamped down on his throbbing erection. That made him push harder and sink deeper.

And when she moaned his name, he knew she could feel the fire of passion spreading between them as much as he could.

Swan wrapped her legs completely around Flipper, loving the feel of him moving inside her. He was giving her body one heck of a workout on her desk. She could feel the heat in his eyes as he stared at her.

He used his hands to lift her hips off the desk's surface for a deeper penetration. When his erection hit a certain part of her, she gasped and arched her back.

"David..."

She whispered his name when she felt him going deeper and deeper. The intensity of their joining sent emotions skyrocketing through her.

She needed this. She wanted this. Like him, she needed it now, not later. This was more than interesting. This was a hot, frenzied, torrid mating. More than a quickie. David was thorough, meticulously so, and not to be rushed. It was as if he intended to savor every stroke.

Suddenly, she felt herself falling. Not off the desk but out of reality when an orgasm rammed through her at the same time as he shuddered with the force of his own release.

They stared at each other, realizing something at the same time. Wanting to make sure he didn't stop, she whispered, "Pill."

It seemed that single word triggered another orgasm and she felt him flooding her insides again while his deep, guttural groan filled the room. His release sparked another within her. His name was torn from her lips when her body shattered in earth-shaking and mind-blowing ecstasy.

As the daze from Swan's orgasmic state receded, she felt David slowly withdraw from inside her. That's when she forced her eyes open to stare at him and accepted the hand he extended to help her off the desk. Once on her feet, she wrapped her arms around his waist, feeling weak in the knees.

"It's okay, baby, I got you. I won't let you fall," he whispered close to her ear as he leaned down.

Too late, she thought. She'd already fallen. Head over heels in love with him. The very thought suddenly sent her mind spinning.

Hadn't she just given herself a good talking to moments before he'd arrived? Told herself he was someone she could enjoy, both in and out of bed and nothing more? That he was someone she knew better than to give her heart to because she hadn't wanted to take the risk?

What on earth had happened?

She knew the answer as she moved closer into the comfort of his warm naked body. David Holloway had happened. As much as she hadn't meant to fall in love with him, she had.

It didn't matter that she had known him less than three weeks. Somehow he had come into her world and turned it upside down, whether that had been his intent or not. When his work on the island was finished, he would move on and not look back. But still, knowing that he would leave hadn't stopped him from winning her heart.

"Ready?"

She lifted her head and look up at him. "You know, David, that lone question will get us in trouble."

He held her gaze for a long moment and then caressed the side of her face. "Or take us to places we really want to go and inspire us to do things that we really want to do."

Then he lowered his mouth to hers and kissed her.

Eleven

"Great work finding out about that ink, Lieutenant Holloway. I knew there was no way Swan would have betrayed her country."

"Yes, sir. Those are my thoughts as well," Flipper said. He had placed his CO on speakerphone so his SEAL teammates could listen to the call. "There's no doubt in my mind the persons naval intelligence should be concentrating on are Rafe Duggers and Horacio Jacinto."

"I agree. I met with Admiral Martin and Director Levart this morning and they concur there's a mole within the organization."

"By meeting with them, sir, does that mean you feel certain they can be totally trusted as well?" Flipper felt he had to ask.

"Yes, Lieutenant Holloway. I do. I know that because of what you discovered and what went down with Lieutenant Westmoreland a few years ago involving those moles at Homeland Security, you're not sure who you can trust. I understand that. However, I assure you that you can trust the three of us to protect Swan with our lives if we have to. We knew she was innocent, which was why we sent you there to prove we were right. You have. Now it's up to us to find out who's behind this and bring them to justice."

"And in the meantime?"

"In the meantime, Lieutenant, you are free to consider this assignment completed. Go home to Texas and enjoy the remainder of your leave."

There was no way he could consider this assignment completed, although under normal circumstances it would be once the CO said so. "I think I'll hang around Key West for a while."

"Why?" Commanding Officer Shields asked. "Do you think Swan's life might be in immediate danger?"

"As long as Duggers and Jacinta don't know they're suspected of anything, then no. However..."

"However what, Lieutenant Holloway?"

Flipper had no problem being truthful to his CO. "However, Swan has come to mean a lot to me, sir."

"Oh, I see."

Flipper figured since his CO knew him so well, he did see. "In that case, Lieutenant Holloway, how you choose to spend the rest of your leave is your decision. But keep in mind, since this is an ongoing investigation, you cannot tell Swan anything, including your reason for being in the Keys in the first place. That in itself will place you in what might be perceived by her as a dishonorable situation."

"I'm aware of that, sir, but I refuse to leave her until I have to. How long do you think it will take to wrap up the investigation?"

"Not sure. We will not only be investigating the original investigators but we'll have to restart the entire case, making Duggers and Jacinta the primary suspects. If you remain in the Keys and notice anything I need to know, don't hesitate to bring it to my attention."

In other words, Commanding Officer Shields was pretty much giving Flipper the green light to do his own thing, unofficially. "Yes, sir."

When Flipper clicked off the phone, he glanced up at his friends. "So what do you guys think?"

"Personally, I think you're doing the right thing not leaving here until you're certain Miss Jamison's life is not in any danger," Bane said.

"And since we don't plan to leave until you do, it's time we figure out just who is behind this," Coop added.

"I agree with all the above," Viper tacked on.

They all looked at Mac, who rubbed his chin as if contemplating something. Then he said, "Someone needs to play devil's advocate, so I guess it has to be me."

"No surprise there," Bane said.

Mac shot Bane a glare and then glanced back at Flipper. "Think about what the CO said. You can't tell Miss Jamison anything. Once she finds out the truth, that she was nothing more than an assignment to you, she's not going to like it, no matter how noble or honorable your intentions might have been."

Flipper drew in a deep breath. He knew Mac's words to be true. Although Swan had yet to tell him anything about her affair with William Connors, it had been in the report. The man had betrayed her and there was a chance she would probably see Flipper as doing the same. "So, Mr. Know-It-All, what do you suggest I do?" he asked.

"Start drawing a line in your relationship and don't cross it. In other words, stop seducing her," Mac said.

Too late for that, Flipper thought. All he had to do was remember what they'd done yesterday in Swan's office and again when he'd taken her home after dinner. Especially when he'd sat in one of her kitchen chairs and she'd straddled his body. The memories of what had started out in that chair and ended up in her bedroom made him feel hot. He hadn't left her place until dawn this morning. There was no way he could put a freeze on his relationship with Swan like Mac was suggesting.

"That's not an option, Mac. I'm going to do what I have to do now and worry about the consequences later."

"What's this about you having a boyfriend? I can't leave you alone for one minute."

Swan smiled when she glanced up at Rosie McCall, one of her frequent customers. Rosie, an older woman in her midforties who'd been away for the past three months visiting her family in Nevada, had returned to the Keys just yesterday. "I see Jamila has been talking again."

"Doesn't matter. So tell me, who is he?"

Swan closed the jewelry case. "First of all, he's not my boyfriend. He's just someone I'm seeing while he's here on the island working, which won't be much longer."

"Um, short meaningless flings are the best kind. What's his name?"

"David. David Holloway."

"Where he is from?"

"Texas."

"You said he's here working. What does he do for a living?"

"Whoa, time-out," Swan said, using her hand for the signal. "You don't need to know all that. David's a nice guy and that's all you really need to know."

She knew how Rosie liked to play matchmaker. She'd been the one who'd introduced Jamila to Horacio. Rosie had met him at one of the nightclubs and thought he was cute, too young for her but just the right age for Swan or Jamila. Swan hadn't been interested in a blind date but Jamila had. Horacio and Jamila met, hit it off and had been an item ever since.

"You can't blame me for being curious, Swan. You seldom date."

"My choice, remember? Besides, you do it enough for the both of us." And that was the truth. After her second divorce, Rosie had made it known she would never marry again but intended to date any man who asked her out as long as they were the right age. Not too old and not too young.

Rosie smiled. "Yes, I do, don't I? But that doesn't mean you shouldn't go out and have fun every once in a while. There's more to life than this shop, Swan. I hope you're finally finding that out."

"Whatever." Swan had heard it before and all from Rosie. She liked the older woman and thought she was a fun person who had a zeal for life. There was never a dull moment around her.

At that moment, the shop's door chimed and Swan knew without looking in that direction that David had walked in. She also knew when he saw her with a customer that he would wait until she finished before approaching her.

Rosie leaned in. "Looks like you have a customer.

Let's hope he buys something since he came in a minute before closing."

Swan inwardly smiled. "We can only hope, right?"

"But then he's such a cutie. Look at him."

Swan didn't have to look at David to know what a cutie he was, but she did so anyway. He was browsing around the store wearing a pair of shorts and a sleeveless T-shirt with flip-flops on his feet. He looked laid-back and sexy as sin. "You're right, he is a cutie."

"I love those tattoos on his upper arms. Nice."

"Yes, they are." She knew Rosie was into tattoos and was one of Rafe's frequent customers. The woman had them everywhere, visible and non-visible.

"You need to go wait on him. See what he wants. If he's not sure, offer him a few things."

Swan smiled. Little did Rosie know, but she intended to offer David a lot. "I will. Come on, I'll walk you to the door. I'm officially closed now," Swan said, coming from around the counter.

"You honestly want me to leave you here with him?" Rosie whispered. "For all you know he's not safe."

Swan chuckled and decided it was time for her to come clean. "He's safe, Rosie. That's David and he's here to walk me home. I'll introduce you on your way out the door."

"You mean that gorgeous hunk is your guy?"

Swan glanced over at David again. He was definitely a gorgeous hunk but she couldn't claim him as her guy. "Yes, he's the guy I've been seeing a lot of lately."

"Smart girl."

David glanced up when they approached and gave her a huge smile. "Hi," he greeted.

"Hi, David. I'd like you to meet Rosie McCall. A friend who has been away for the past few months and just returned back to the island. Rosie, this is David Holloway."

David extended his hand. "Nice meeting you, Rosie."

"Same here, David. I like your tattoos."

"Thanks and I like yours," he responded.

"Thanks. Well, I'll be going. I hope you guys enjoy yourselves."

"We will," Swan said, smiling up at David. "I'll be back after seeing Rosie out," she told him.

He nodded. "Nice meeting you, Rosie."

"Same here."

Swan returned to David a few moments later, after putting up the Closed sign, locking the door and pulling down the shades. She turned and studied him as he stood across the room, looking so amazingly sexy. She felt a lump in her throat. She loved everything about him, especially the muscles beneath his shirt, the masculine thighs and his tanned skin.

"Got more sun today, I see."

"Yes, I had to go out on the boat today."

"One day you're going to have to explain to me in detail just what your ocean duties entail."

"I will. But for now, come here. I missed you today."

She crossed the room to walk into his arms. "I missed you, too."

"That's good to know. Rosie seems like a nice person."

"She is."

"She has a lot of tattoos."

Swan chuckled. "Yes, she does. She's one of Rafe's best customers."

"Is that right?" David asked, still smiling. "He did an awesome job."

She checked her watch. "We can leave as soon as I

grab my purse." They would be having dinner at Nathan Waterway and afterward would attend an art show. "I'll be back in a second."

Flipper watched Swan walk off toward her office while thinking of what she'd told him about Rosie McCall. He recalled what he'd overheard Rafe and Horacio arguing about that night behind this building. Ink and roses. Or had they said Rosie? Was she a part of the group? If she was, that meant she had an ulterior motive for befriending Swan.

Pulling his phone from his pocket he texted Nick. Check out Rosie McCall.

He received an immediate reply. Will do.

He then texted Bane. Excursion tonight.

The reply was quick. On it.

Most of today he and Viper had pretended to go fishing after Mac, who'd been tailing Rafe for the past two days, reported that Rafe had rented a boat and headed in the direction of another island close by. Today Flipper and Viper had also rented a boat, making sure they stayed a good distance behind Duggers.

The man had docked in Fleming Key. Bane and Cooper, who'd arrived ahead of them, picked up the tail on Rafe. It seemed the man had gone into a sports shop where he'd stayed for three hours.

Pretending to be two guys enjoying their time out on their boat, Flipper and Viper had waited at the pier and knew when Rafe had left the island to return to Key West. Mac had been there to pick up the tail and reported that the man had been carrying a package when he went inside his tattoo shop. A package Rafe had gotten from the sports shop, according to Bane and Coop.

"I'm ready."

He looked up and when Swan met his gaze, she quickly clarified, "I'm ready *for dinner*."

He placed his phone back into his pocket and smiled. "That's all?"

The smile she returned made his insides quiver in anticipation. "For now, Mr. Holloway."

Twelve

It was getting harder and harder to leave Swan's bed, Flipper thought as he and his teammates docked at Fleming Key close to two in the morning. But at least he'd left her sleeping with the most peaceful smile on her face.

Without waking her, he had brushed a kiss across her lips and whispered that he loved her, knowing she would remember neither. But he decided to tell her how he felt when he saw her later today. He couldn't hold it inside any longer. She deserved to know. He wanted her to know. And when all this was over and she knew the truth, he would do whatever he needed to do to win her forgiveness and her love.

He jumped when fingers snapped in his face. He glared at Mac, who glared back. "Stay focused. You can daydream later."

"I wasn't daydreaming," Flipper countered. He then

realized he was the only one still in the boat. The others had already gotten out.

"Then night-dreaming. Call it what you want" was Mac's reply. "Just get out of the damn boat."

Flipper didn't have to wonder why Mac was in a rotten mood. Teri had texted him earlier in the day to say the new washer and dryer had been delivered. They were new appliances Mac hadn't known they were buying.

Moments later, dressed in all black military combat gear, the five of them circled around to the back of the sports shop Rafe had frequented lately. Being ever ready and not taking any chances, Glocks were strapped to their hips and high powered tasers to their thighs. Due to Viper's hypersensitive ears—known to pick up sound over long distances away—he would stay outside as the lookout. Flipper, Bane, Cooper and Mac bypassed security cameras to enter the building.

Once inside, they used Flipper's cameras and it didn't take long to find a hidden room. Making swift use of their time, they took pictures of everything. It was obvious this was the group's operation headquarters. More tattoo ink was stored here along with several specific tattoo designs. One design Flipper quickly recalled seeing on the side of Rosie's neck.

Flipper scanned the room with his camera and then opened several drawers in the huge desk and took photos of the contents. When he came across a photo in one of the drawers, he suddenly froze. "Damn."

"What is it, Flipper?" Bane asked.

Instead of saying anything, he motioned his head to the photograph he'd found. Mac, Bane and Coop came around him to see it as well. They looked back at him and Mac said, "We've been royally screwed."

An uneasy feeling settled in the pit of Flipper's stomach. "I need to get back to Swan as soon as possible."

Swan was awakened by the knocking on her door. She glanced at the clock on her nightstand and wondered who on earth would be at her house at four in the morning. Was it David returning? She didn't recall when he'd left but knew it was the norm for him to leave her place around midnight to return to his hotel because of his work. Usually she would be awake when he left but tonight sexual exhaustion had gotten the best of her.

Pulling on her robe, she tied it around her waist as she headed for the door. Looking out the peephole, she saw it was Jamila and Horacio. What were they doing out so late and why were they at her place? She found it odd that Horacio was on the island when the cruise ship wasn't due back in port again until next week.

From the look on Jamila's face, it appeared she wasn't happy about something. In fact, from her reddened eyes, it appeared that she'd been crying. Swan wondered what on earth was wrong. Had something happened?

Suddenly filled with concern, she quickly opened the door. The minute she did so, Jamila was shoved inside, nearly knocking Swan down.

"Hey, wait a minute. What's going on?" Swan asked, fighting to regain her balance.

"Shut the hell up and don't ask questions," Horacio said, quickly coming inside and closing the door behind him.

Swan frowned. "Horacio? What do you mean, I can't ask any questions?"

"Just do what you're told," he barked.

Swan glanced over at Jamila and saw the bruise on

the side of her face. “Did he do this to you?” Swan demanded, getting enraged. At Jamila’s nod, Swan then turned to Horacio. How could he have done this when he adored Jamila? “I want you to leave now.”

“If I don’t, what are you going to do? Call the police? Or call that SEAL you’re sleeping with?”

Swan frown deepened. “I don’t know what you’re talking about. Now leave or I *will* call the police.”

“You won’t be doing anything other than what I tell you to do. When I get the word, the two of you will be coming with me.”

Swan placed her hands on her hips. “We’re not going anywhere with you.”

A cynical smile touched Horacio’s lips as he pulled out a gun from his back pocket. “This says you will.”

Swan stared at the gun, not believing Horacio had it pointed at both her and Jamila. She was about to say something when Horacio added, “I’m giving you five minutes to go into your bedroom and put on clothes. Bring me your phone first. I don’t want you to get any crazy ideas.”

Swan had no idea what was going on, but from the pleading look in Jamila’s eyes, she knew it was best to do as she was told. She went and got her cell phone and handed it to him, but not before she noticed several missed calls from David. Why had he been trying to call her? Her mind was filled with so many questions.

“You got five minutes to get dressed. If you’re not back in five minutes or try some kind of funny business, your cousin here will pay for it.”

Cousin? Why did he refer to Jamila as her cousin? At what was obviously a confused look on her face, he said, “That’s right. Secrets. There are plenty more where those came from, Swan, and you'll be finding out about them later. Now go."

Swan got dressed in less than five minutes. If she hadn't thought Horacio was serious about hurting Jamila, she would have escaped through her bedroom window. That bruise along the side of her friend's face indicated the man was serious.

Swan was walking out of her bedroom fully dressed when Horacio's phone rang. Instead of answering it, he said, "That's my signal that things are ready. We'll go out your back door to the beach. The boat is waiting."

"What boat?"

"Please don't ask him anything, Swan," Jamila pleaded, reaching out and grabbing her arm. "All of them are crazy."

Swan wondered just who were *all of them*. But she decided not to ask.

"Move!"

Following Horacio's orders, she and Jamila walked toward Swan's kitchen to go out the back door.

As soon as their boat docked, Flipper raced through the streets of Key West toward Swan's home with his teammates fast on his heels. He had tried reaching her on the phone but didn't get an answer. He immediately knew something was wrong because she kept her phone on the nightstand next to her bed and the ringing would have woken her up. He had tried several more times with no luck, which was why his heart was beating out of control and fear was gripping his insides, especially now that he knew who was involved.

They had contacted their CO and told him what they'd discovered. He was as shocked as they'd been and they knew Shields would be taking the necessary actions on his end. Flipper hadn't had to tell the man there would be hell to pay if anyone hurt one single hair on Swan's head.

When they reached her house, they found the door unlocked. Her cell phone had been tossed on a living room table and a quick search of her bedroom indicated she'd change clothes.

"Take a look at this, Flipper," Mac called out.

When he reached them in the kitchen, Mac pointed out the window. Flipper saw lights from a boat that was sitting idle in the ocean as if waiting to rendezvous with another vessel.

"I traced footprints in the sand that led to the water. A small watercraft probably took them out to that boat," Viper was saying. "There were three sets of shoe prints belonging to two women and a man. And they left around thirty minutes ago."

Flipper raced out Swan's back door and after putting on his night-vision eyewear, he stared out at the ocean.

"Intercept with our boat," he shouted over his shoulder to the others. Quickly dropping to the sand, he began removing his shoes, T-shirt and pants, leaving his body clad in a pair of swimming trunks.

"Don't try it, Flipper. The boat's too far out," Mac said. "It's too dangerous for anyone, even you."

Flipper glanced up at them while putting the waterproof military belt that contained combat gear around his waist. He then put a pair of specially designed water goggles over his eyes. "The woman I love is on that boat and I have no idea what they plan to do, so I have to try. Even if I die trying."

Without saying anything else, he raced toward the water and dived in.

* * *

Horacio had tied their hands before forcing them into a small boat, which carried them out into the ocean to a much bigger boat. Now they were sitting idle in the waves.

Swan wondered why. She glanced around and noticed that, other than the lights on the boat, there was only darkness. They were so far from land she couldn't see the lights from the homes where she lived anymore.

As if Horacio realized she was trying to figure out what was happening, he said, "I'm waiting for the rest of the gang, then we'll decide what we will do with the two of you."

What he said didn't make much sense. "Will someone please tell me what's going on?" Swan asked, getting angrier by the minute. None of this made any sense.

"I'll let your cousin go first since Jamila has a lot of explaining to do," Horacio said, grinning.

Swan turned to Jamila, who was sitting on a bench beside her. "What is he talking about? Why does he keep referring to you as my cousin?"

At first Jamila didn't say anything. In fact, it seemed she was refusing to meet Swan's gaze, but then she finally met Swan's eyes and said, "Because we are cousins, Swan. My mother is your grandfather's youngest sister."

"My grandfather?"

Jamila nodded. "Yes, Lawrence Jamison is my uncle. I knew for years that Uncle Lawrence disowned your father but I didn't know why until I was much older. Then I thought the reason was downright stupid and told the family what I thought. Everyone else in the family thought the same thing but were too afraid to stand up to Uncle Lawrence."

Swan didn't say anything. She was still trying to dissect the fact that she and Jamila were related. She'd known from her father that Lawrence had a sister and another brother. That was all she'd known.

"When I turned twenty-one and finished college, I decided to come find you. Uncle Lawrence didn't like it but I told him I didn't care. I'm one of the few who stands up to him. He said the family would disown me if I came here."

"Yet you came anyway," Swan said.

"Yes, I came anyway."

Swan glanced over at Horacio. He wasn't saying anything and didn't appear to be listening to what they were saying. Instead he stood at the bow of the ship looking through binoculars as if he was searching for someone. He'd said they were waiting for another boat with the gang and Swan couldn't help but wonder who the gang was.

She wanted to ask Jamila how much she knew and why they were being held hostage but figured that although Horacio was pretending not to listen to their conversation, he probably was.

Swan glanced over at Jamila. "Why didn't you tell me who you were when you first came into my shop that day? Why did you keep it a secret all this time?"

"Because I knew how my family had treated you and your mother. I figured the last thing you'd want was to meet a relative from that side of the family. I decided to let you accept me as a friend and then later I would tell you the truth that we were cousins."

"Now isn't that a touching story?" Horacio said, strolling back over to where they sat.

"Yes, it is touching," Swan said, defiantly lifting her chin. "Why are we here?"

He smiled. "You'll find out soon enough. And I hope you're not holding out any hope that your SEAL boyfriend will be coming to rescue you because he won't."

"Why do you keep saying David is a SEAL when he's not? He was in the military once but he was never a SEAL."

"Sounds like you've been conned by him just like your cousin here was conned by me," he said as if it was something to brag about. "Your lover boy *is* a SEAL and he was sent here to get the goods on you. Whether you know it or not, you've been his assignment."

Swan shook her head. "No, that's not true. I don't believe you."

"I don't care if you believe me or not but it's true. I only found out today what he's been doing and why he was sent here by naval intelligence."

Naval intelligence? Swan glanced over at Jamila, who said, "I don't know whether what he's saying is true or not, Swan, but he told me the same thing tonight."

"Why would naval intelligence suspect me of anything? It doesn't make sense." And more than that, she refused to believe David wasn't who and what he said he was.

At that moment, they heard the sound of a boat approaching. Horacio drew his gun and pointed the flashlight toward the oncoming boat. He put his gun back in place. "Hold on to that question, sweetheart. The person who will explain everything just arrived."

Swan kept her gaze trained on the boat that pulled up beside theirs and saw two people onboard. Both of them she knew. What in the world…?

She watched in shock as Rafe and Rosie came aboard. She was so focused on staring at them that she almost missed the third person who also came on board.

She gasped in shock when the person said, “Swan, you look well.”

Suddenly losing her voice, Swan couldn’t do anything but sit there and stare. There had to be some mistake. A very big mistake. There was no way the person standing before her was a part of this craziness.

No way.

She finally found her voice. “Georgianna? What are you doing here? What is this about?”

Thirteen

Flipper reached the boat and attached himself to the ladder on the side. Lucky for him, no one had thought to pull it up. Taking slow, deep breaths, he pulled air into his lungs while ignoring the pain in his arms and legs. He didn't want to think about just how far he'd swum, but like he'd told his friends, he'd had to try.

He quickly eased back into the water when he heard the sound of an approaching boat and was grateful the vessel pulled up on the other side from where he was hiding. He glanced at his watch. It was synchronized with the ones worn by his teammates, and he knew they would do their best to get here soon. In the meantime, there was something he had to do.

Pulling a micro audio recorder off his belt, he moved back up the ladder to peek over the railing and into the boat.

Good. Everyone's attention was on the approaching

vessel and no one saw him when he attached the audio recorder that was no bigger than a dime to the interior wall of the boat. He saw Swan and Jamila seated on a bench with their hands tied behind their backs and Horacio was standing not far away. Other than a man in the cockpit, there was no one else onboard. Flipper knew that was about to change when he heard voices.

Satisfied that the conversations would be recorded, he eased back down the ladder. When his watch began vibrating, he glanced down at the text message from Bane. On our way. Had 2 take care of a little problem 1st.

Flipper wondered what kind of problem his friends had to take care of. No matter. They were on their way and that's what counted. He listened to the conversation going on in the boat as he began pulling items from his belt. He intended to be ready to crash this little party when the time came.

He shook his head, knowing Admiral Martin would be heartbroken to discover his own daughter had sold out their country.

"I hate you," Georgianna said, glaring at Swan.

Swan was taken aback by the woman's words. "Why? What have I ever done to you? To any of you?" she asked, glancing around at the people she'd assumed were friends—Rafe, Horacio and Rosie. She hurt more at seeing Rosie than the others because she'd believed the woman had been a good friend.

"They work for me and did what they were told," Georgianna said.

"Work for you?" Swan was even more confused.

"Yes. I'm in charge of the entire operation. But I'll tell you all about that later. First, let me tell you why

I despise you so much. I've waited a long time to get this out in the open. When your father died and your mother would send you to us for the summer, my parents thought you were golden. They put you on a pedestal, especially my father. Did you know he called you his little island princess?"

Yes, Swan knew but she also knew her godfather hadn't meant anything by it. It was just a nickname he'd given her when she was born. All three of her godfathers called her that sometimes. "It was just a nickname, Georgianna."

"For you, it might only have been a nickname, but for me, it was Dad shifting his attention from me to you."

"Godpop 1 loves you. He wasn't shifting his attention to me, he was just being nice."

"Too nice, and I despised you for it. He had a daughter, yet any time your mother would call, he and Mom would drop everything and take off. Just because your father saved Dad's life—that meant nothing. They were all SEALs and your dad was doing his job when he died. But it was as if Dad blamed himself and he needed to make it up by being nice to you, like you were somebody special. So, with the help of some friends, I decided to change everyone's opinion of you."

It was hard for Swan to believe what she was hearing. She'd never known that Georgianna harbored such feelings. Granted she hadn't always been overnice and had a tendency to be moody, but Swan hadn't detected animosity like this.

"What did you do?" Swan asked her.

Georgianna smiled like she was proud of what she was about to say. "I set up an espionage operation out of your shop with the help of Rafe and Horacio. Then, with Rosie's assistance, I made it appear that the secret information being sent to China was being done through your jewelry."

"What!" Swan couldn't believe it. Her head was spinning from all the shocks she'd received tonight.

"I have to admit I put together a perfect plan. This guy I was sleeping with at the time assisted me by tipping off naval intelligence with what you were supposedly doing. They did their own investigation and my team and I made sure everything pointed at you. It should have been an open and shut case and you were to be arrested and charged with espionage."

As if she was tired of standing, Georgianna moved to sit on one of the benches. She frowned over at Swan. "Everything was going according to plan until the final thread of the investigation reached Director Levart's desk."

"Godpop 3?"

"See what I mean? You have three godfathers and I don't have a one," Georgianna said in a loud voice, pointing a finger at her. "You don't deserve such love and loyalty, and I intended to tarnish their image of you."

Flipper's watch vibrated and he glanced down at the text message. Here. N place. Coop got layout of boat.

He texted them back. 1 N cockpit. 4 others. 2 hostages.

He quickly received a reply from Viper. Eliminating cockpit.

Got 4 in scope. That particular text came from Bane, a master sniper.

Flipper knew that although everyone was in place, timing was everything. Georgianna had no idea her words were being recorded so he wanted to let her talk before making his move. Then there would be no way she could deny anything.

From listening to what the woman was saying, it was obvious she had mental issues. That could be the only reason to have such a deep hatred of Swan that Georgianna would go to such extremes. Georgianna assumed she'd had the perfect plan for Swan's downfall and Flipper was glad things hadn't turned out the way Georgianna intended.

Before inching up the ladder to listen to what else she was confessing, he texted the message: Will give signal.

Swan shook her head. It was obvious Georgianna's jealousy had blinded her senses and fueled her hatred. Didn't the others see it? Why were they following her blindly? Swan glanced over at Jamila and could tell by the look in her cousin's eyes that she was wondering the same thing.

"When Director Levart saw the report, he refused to believe you could be guilty of anything, especially betraying your country."

Thank God for that, Swan thought.

"He requested a thirty-day delay before agreeing to take any actions against you. Even after we made sure the investigation clearly spelled out your role in everything. There was no reason for you not to be charged," Georgianna said.

She paused a moment before continuing. "Unknown to me and the others, Director Levart went to your other two godfathers and they put their heads together to see what they could do to prove your innocence. They decided to send one of their top SEALs to find out what he could and to prove your innocence."

Swan drew in a deep breath. *Oh no, please don't*

let what Horacio said tonight be true. Please don't let David turn out to be someone other than what he said he was.

Georgianna's next words ripped into Swan's heart.

"The SEAL they sent was Lieutenant David Holloway. I guess you didn't know that all the time he spent with you was nothing more than an assignment. You meant nothing to him, Swan." Georgianna laughed as if she found the entire thing amusing while Swan's heart broke.

"Imagine how amused I was to find out just how taken you were with him, while not knowing the true purpose as to why he showed up here on the island. You were played, Swan," Georgianna was saying in between laughter. "But don't worry. I sent some other members of my group to take care of him for you. I think he's dead by now."

Suddenly a deep voice at the back of the boat said, "As you can see, I'm very much alive."

Swan gasped just as the others did. Standing with legs braced apart and wearing only a pair of swim trunks with a utility combat belt around his waist, David looked like a mad badass. It was obvious everyone was shocked to see him, especially Georgianna, who had assumed he was dead.

"Drop your gun," he ordered Horacio, who was still holding his weapon on Swan and Jamila.

"How the hell did you get here?" Horacio asked, enraged.

"I swam from Swan's home."

"That's impossible!"

"Not if you're a SEAL master swimmer," David said. "Now, do like I said and put your gun down."

"And if I don't? It will be a shame if I kill Swan or Jamila before you can get to anything on that belt you're wearing," Horacio sneered.

"Don't try it, Horacio. One of my team members who's a master sniper has all four of you within his scope. Before you could get off the first shot, you'd be dead."

"I don't believe you. There's no one else out here," Horacio said. When he lifted his gun to take aim at Swan, a shot rang out, hitting the man in the chest. The impact toppled him to the floor.

Jamila screamed and Swan understood. Jamila had fallen in love with a man who'd betrayed her and then gotten shot right before her eyes.

Suddenly, Rafe dived for the gun that had dropped from Horacio's hand. Before he could reach it, another shot rang out that hit him in the side. He fell to the floor as well.

"Either of you ladies want to join them?" Flipper asked Georgianna and Rosie.

Rosie looked like she was in shock and ready to pass out.

However, Georgianna looked furious. "You won't get away with this. No matter what you tell my father, he will never believe you over me," she said with absolute certainty. "I'll tell him that you decided to team up with Swan and she turned you against your country."

"I figured you would lie. That's why I've recorded your little confession to Swan detailing everything. I can't wait for your father to listen to it."

Suddenly the boat was surrounded by several naval vessels and sharp beams of light shined on them. A voice through a foghorn said, "Lieutenant Holloway, we are coming aboard."

A dozen men wearing SEAL gear rushed on board with their guns drawn, immediately taking Georgianna and Rosie into custody. Bane, Viper, Coop and Mac boarded the boat as well. Mac rushed over to check Horacio and Rafe. There really was no need since they were both dead.

Flipper rushed over to Swan and Jamila to untie their hands. More than anything, he wanted to pull Swan into his arms and tell her he loved her. He wanted her to put out of her mind what Georgianna had said about him until she'd heard his side of things. However, he knew when she pulled away from him to give her cousin a hug that she didn't want to give him a chance to explain.

He didn't intend to let her walk away.

"We need to talk, Swan," he said, looking down at her.

She glared up at him. "We have nothing to say to each other. Your assignment is over, Lieutenant Holloway. Now leave me alone."

Fourteen

Two weeks later

"How long are you planning to be mad at the world, Swan?"

Swan glanced over at Candy. Her best friend had returned to the Keys after hearing about what happened and she'd decided to stay. Swan was glad Candy had returned home but she was saddened by what had brought her back.

"I am not mad at the world," Swan said, taking a sip of her orange juice.

"But you are still mad at one particular man," Candy said, coming to sit beside Swan on the sofa.

Swan couldn't deny that was true so she didn't. "And what if I am?"

"He had a job to do, Swan. He was given orders. Surely you understand that."

Swan glared at Candy. “I’m sure none of my godfathers’ orders included sleeping with me.”

“I’m sure they didn’t but David didn’t force himself on you.”

“No, but he deceived me.”

“So did the others.”

Did Candy have to remind her? “And I’m not talking to them either.”

That wasn’t totally true since Swan had reached out to Georgianna where she was being held at a federal prison in Orlando. The woman had refused to see her. Swan knew Georgianna was undergoing psychiatric evaluations to see if she was fit to stand trial.

Swan’s godparents were heartbroken and she understood how they felt. Like her, they’d had no idea Georgianna harbored such hatred toward Swan, enough to do what she’d done. With both Rafe and Horacio dead, it was Rosie who was singing like a bird, telling everything she knew for a lessened sentence.

According to Rosie, Georgianna had manipulated a number of the men at naval intelligence into doing whatever she wanted them to do. When you were the admiral’s daughter, you could wield that kind of power. She had even threatened a few with blackmail. She’d deliberately recorded several of the men having sex with her and then threatened to give the tape to her father and accuse them of rape.

Some of the men were not only married but a number were high-ranking military officers. Fearful of court-martial, the men had done whatever Georgianna asked, including falsifying records. So far, more than twelve men had been named in the scandal.

“I take it David hasn’t called.”

Swan drew in a deep breath. She had seen him last

week when they'd had to show up at the naval station to give statements. "Yes, he's called. Several times. But I refuse to answer. Like I told him, we have nothing to say to each other. His assignment is over."

"And do you honestly think that's all you were to him, Swan?"

"Yes, but it doesn't matter."

"I think it does," Candy countered.

"And you think too much," Swan said, easing off the sofa.

The first week after the incident on the boat, she had closed her shop while naval investigators did a thorough search of Rafe's tattoo parlor. She had used that time to take care of Jamila, who was still broken up over Horacio. Jamila had loved him and in a single night had seen him become an abusive monster, a man she hadn't known. Then in the end, Jamila had watched him die before her eyes.

Swan knew Jamila was going through something that only time could heal. That's why when Swan had reopened the shop this week and Jamila had asked for extra work hours, Swan had given them to her.

"So what are you going to do?" Candy asked her.

Swan glanced over at her. "About life? Work?"

"No, about David."

Swan just couldn't understand why Candy couldn't accept that David was no longer in the equation. "I'm a survivor, Candy. Although it was hard, I made do after my parents' deaths and I will make do now." She glanced at her watch. "I'm getting dressed to go into the shop today. The cruise ship comes into port tomorrow, so business will pick up. I want to make sure most of my new pieces are on display."

Another thing they had found out was that Horacio

had been fired from the cruise ship months ago but hadn't told Jamila. He had moved into Rosie's place while the woman had been gone. The duplicity of the people she'd thought she knew simply amazed Swan.

"And I need to be on my way," Candy said. "I promised my folks we would go out to dinner tonight. You can join us if you like."

"Thanks for the invite, but I'll pass. I just want to have a relaxing evening here tonight. I might go swimming on the beach later."

Swan had called Jamila and told her she would bring lunch from their favorite sandwich café. However, there were no clients in her shop when Swan got there, so she decided to do something she usually didn't do, which was close for lunch.

Normally, the shop remained open and she and Jamila would alternate lunch duties. But today she wanted to check on Jamila, talk to her to see how she was faring. Although Swan had been there for Jamila last week, they hadn't had a real honest-to-goodness talk since Jamila had admitted to being her cousin.

"What are you doing?" Jamila asked when Swan put up the Closed sign and pulled down the blinds.

Swan smiled over at her. "New store policy. From here on out, we will close at noon for lunch."

"What about the sales you'll lose?"

Swan shrugged. "Sales aren't everything. Besides, it's just for an hour. Come join me in my office."

"All right, let me grab some sodas out of the refrigerator."

A few minutes later, she and Jamila were enjoying their lunch when Swan gave Jamila a long look. "How are you doing?"

Jamila shrugged. "Okay, I guess. Trying to move on.

I loved Horacio so much only to find out he wasn't the man I thought he was."

"I know the feeling."

"No, you don't."

Swan snatched her head up, frowning. "Excuse me?"

"I said you don't know the feeling, Swan. David Holloway was nothing like Horacio. David intended to save you and Horacio would have killed me if that woman had ordered him to do so. Big difference."

"But like you, I was betrayed."

"How?" Jamila countered. "Your godfathers sent David Holloway here to prove your innocence and he did."

Jamila put her soda can down and then added, "And another thing. What man takes a chance and swims across the ocean to save a woman? Do you know how far from land we were? Think about that."

Swan had news for her—she *had* thought about it. She could never forget how David had appeared seemingly out of nowhere on that boat, looking tough and ready to kick asses while wearing nothing more than an outlandishly tight pair of swim trunks with a military belt around his waist. Even when she'd been in what seemed like a dire situation, that hadn't stopped the woman in her from noticing how dangerously sexy he'd looked at that particular moment.

"When I mentioned what an astounding feat he'd accomplished to his friends," Jamila said, reclaiming Swan's attention, "they said that's why they call him Flipper. Did you know that's his code name as a SEAL?"

Swan wiped her mouth with a napkin. "Yes, I knew he was called Flipper. But no, I didn't know it had anything to do with him being a SEAL because I didn't know he was one. I assumed Flipper was his nickname."

Swan forced from her mind the day she'd asked him about those dolphin tattoos. He'd told her then they represented Flipper. That had been the day they'd made love in this office. Right here on this desk.

She wished she wasn't thinking so hard about that now.

She looked over at Jamila. "Why are we talking about me instead of you?"

"Because I think you should and because I think I should," Jamila continued. "Talking about your situation actually helps me believe that not all men are jerks and that there are some who still possess real honor, Swan. Whether you want to admit it or not, David Holloway is an honorable man. He couldn't help being attracted to you any more than you could help being attracted to him."

Swan stuffed the wrappings from her sandwich into the empty bag. "Now you sound like Candy."

"Maybe there's a reason why I do," Jamila said, stuffing her own wrappings into a bag. "It might be because Candy and I can see things that you refuse to see. I often think about what could have happened to us had David and his friends not shown up when they did. Do you ever think of that?"

Swan drew in a deep breath. "I try not to."

"I think you should," Jamila said, standing. "Thanks for bringing lunch. It will be my treat the next time." She then walked out of the office.

Swan stayed in her office after Jamila left, trying to put their conversation out of her mind. She was working on her computer, verifying inventory, when her office phone rang. "Thank you for calling Swan's. How may I help you?"

"Hello, island princess."

She smiled upon hearing her godfather's voice. "Godpop 2. How are you?"

"I'm fine. I just wanted to check on you. So much has happened and I wanted to make sure you're okay."

She had spoken to each of her godfathers and had thanked them for believing in her. They had taken a risk with their individual careers to do that. "I'm fine. How is Godpop 3?"

"He's fine but as the director of naval intelligence, he has his hands full with the investigation. It seems that more names are popping up in this scandal each day."

"And how are Godpop 1 and Barbara?"

"They are as well as can be expected under the circumstances. Learning about Georgianna was a shocker for all of us. We had no idea. When we decided to send Lt. Holloway to prove your innocence, the three of us weren't sure just what he would uncover. The only thing we knew for certain was that you weren't guilty of anything."

"Thanks for believing in me."

"You have Andrew's blood in your veins. You could no more be a traitor to your country than he could. Considering all that happened, I'm glad Holloway remained in Key West when he could have left."

Swan sat up straight. "Wasn't David on assignment?"

"Not the entire time. His assignment officially ended when he sent that ink in to be analyzed and we discovered it was tainted. I told him that he no longer had to stay in the Keys since by then we knew you weren't involved and we would take over the investigation from there."

"Then why did he stay?"

"To protect you."

"He told you that?" she asked.

"Yes. I remember the conversation like it was yesterday. I told him he could consider his job assignment complete and go home to Texas and enjoy the remainder of his leave. But he said he wanted to hang around Key West for a while."

Her godfather paused. "I asked him if the reason he wanted to stay was because he thought your life might be in danger. He said he felt that as long as Duggers and Jacinto didn't know they were suspects, then no, your life wasn't in any immediate danger. He informed me that the reason he wanted to stay was because you had come to mean a lot to him. I told him in that case how he spent the rest of his leave was his decision. And, Swan?"

She drew in a deep breath. "Yes?"

"As his commanding officer, I felt the need to remind him that although he was no longer on assignment, since the issue that had started with you was an ongoing investigation, he could not tell you anything."

When Swan didn't reply, her godfather asked, "You're still there, Swan?"

"Yes, Godpop 2, I'm still here."

"Did you not know how Holloway felt about you?"

"No. I thought I was just an assignment."

"You were at first and I'm glad you were. Otherwise you would be in jail wrongly accused of a crime you hadn't committed. But on the flip side, I'm also glad that when you stopped being an assignment, Holloway had the insight to stay and look out for you because he cared for you."

Long after her telephone conversation with her godfather ended, Swan remained seated at her desk, leaning back in her chair and sitting in silence while thinking about what Candy, Jamila and her godfather had said.

Some people never got betrayed, but she had been,

a lot. William, Rafe, Horacio, Rosie, Georgianna and even Jamila. No one had been who she'd thought.

She remembered David and replayed in her mind all the time she'd spent with him since that day he'd first walked into her shop.

Was anything he'd told her true? Did he really come from a huge family? Was his mother even celebrating a birthday? Did he honestly have three sisters-in-law?

One thing was for certain, both Candy and Jamila were right. David hadn't pushed her into sleeping with him. In fact, Swan was the one who'd invited him to dinner at her place with the full intent of having sex with him.

She got up from her desk and walked over to the window. She knew from Jamila that David had left the island with his friends after that first week, after he'd completed all the questioning by naval intelligence. Was he back home in Texas? Did his parents really own a medical supply company? What parts of what he'd told her were true and what parts were fabricated for his assignment?

And why did she still love him so much it hurt... even when she didn't want to love him? Even when she didn't know how he felt about her? He might have told her godfather he cared for her but David hadn't told her anything. Shouldn't he have? But then, had she given him a chance to do so?

The answer to that flashed in her mind quickly. No, she hadn't.

He had saved her life that night, swam across the ocean to do so, and then she'd told him she didn't want to talk to him. And he had honored her wishes...for that one night. Then he had called her almost every single day since, and yet she had refused to take his calls.

He hadn't called today.

Did that mean he'd given up and wouldn't try contacting her again? Was she ready to put her heart on the line and contact him?

She wasn't sure. But what she *was* certain of was that they needed to do what they hadn't done before. They needed to get to know each other. She needed to know which parts of what he'd told her about himself were true and which were false.

She wanted to get to know the real David Holloway.

Then what?

Hadn't she convinced herself she wanted no part of a man in the military? And what about her decision to never to get seriously involved in an interracial relationship like her parents had? Why did all of that no longer matter to her when she thought about her and David deciding to have a future together?

Maybe that's how love worked. It made you see the possible instead of the impossible. It made you want things you told yourself were not good for you because you were afraid to reach beyond your comfort zone.

Taking a deep a cleansing breath, she decided to call David tonight before going to bed. She had no idea what she would say to him but the words would come.

She doubted he would want to come back to the Keys anytime soon, so she would let him know she would come to him if he still wanted to talk. She would see what he said before asking Jamila if she could take care of the shop while Swan was gone. David might very well tell her that it was too late, that they had nothing to talk about. But there was a chance he would embrace her words. Embrace her.

Her mood suddenly lightened, knowing that was a possibility.

* * *

Flipper entered the hotel room and tossed his luggage on the bed. Different hotel but same city. He had given Swan two weeks and now he was back. They needed to talk and clear up some things. She hadn't accepted his calls, but now he was here and he wouldn't be ignored.

He shook his head when his cell phone rang. "Yes, Coop?"

"Have you seen her yet?"

"No, I just got here. In fact, I walked into my hotel room less than five minutes ago."

"Okay. And there's another reason I called. Bristol is pregnant."

"Wow, man. Congratulations. I didn't know you guys were trying."

Coop laughed. "We're always trying. But seriously, we figured it was time Laramie had a playmate."

"Sounds good to me."

"I hope things work out with you and Swan, Flipper."

"I hope so, too."

"And do me a favor."

"What?"

"For once, open up. Tell her how you feel. Don't beat around the bush. You have a tendency to do that. Women love a man to get straight to the point and share their feelings. I hate to say it, bro, but you're not good at doing that."

Coop was right, he wasn't. "I never had to do that before. I've never truly loved a woman before Swan."

"I understand. But you do love her, so make sure she knows it. A woman has to believe she's loved."

Flipper chuckled.

"What's so funny?" Coop asked him.

"You're giving relationship advice. Do you know how much like Mac you sound?"

Coop chuckled as well. "You would have to point that out. I guess it comes with loving a woman."

"I guess so."

"No guess in it, remember it. Know it. Feel it. Take care and good luck."

After ending the call with Coop, it wasn't long before Flipper got calls from Bane, Viper and Mac as well, all letting him know they hoped things worked out for Flipper and Swan. All giving him advice. They were married men who had the women they loved and they wanted him to have the woman he loved as well.

He appreciated good friends who not only watched his back but who also cared about the condition of his heart. They knew about the pain he had lodged there and it got worse every day he and Swan were apart.

Flipper glanced at his watch. Swan's store would be closing in less than an hour. He would give her time to get home and relax before paying her a visit. He refused to let her put things off any longer. They needed to talk.

He loved her and it was damn time she knew it.

Fifteen

Swan had just poured a glass of wine to enjoy while sitting on the patio when she heard the knock at her door.

She knew Candy had gone out to dinner with her family and Jamila had mentioned she would just stay in tonight and chill. Swan had invited Jamila to join her so maybe her cousin had changed her mind.

Her cousin.

That was taking a lot of getting used to but Swan knew her parents would want a family connection for them. Jamila was the only family Swan had and she appreciated their friendship more than ever.

She reached the door and glanced through the peephole. Her heart nearly stopped.

Was it really David? She blinked and looked again and saw it was really him. Back in Key West. And he was standing in front of her door looking like he always did, sexy as hell.

Drawing in a deep breath, she removed the security lock and opened the door. "David? I thought you'd left the island."

"I had but I returned today. May I come in?"

She nodded and stepped aside. The moment he passed her, she caught a whiff of his masculine scent, the same one she was convinced still lingered in her bedroom.

Swan closed the door and stood to face him. He was standing in the middle of her living room wearing a pair of shorts and a sleeveless shirt with a huge picture of a dolphin. *Flipper*. Her gaze moved beyond the shirt to his face to find his laser-blue eyes staring at her.

She cleared her throat. "I was about to sit out back and drink a glass of wine while enjoying the view. Would you like to have a beer and join me?"

She could tell he was surprised by her invitation. She hadn't bothered to ask why he was there.

"Yes, I'd like that."

Moments later, they were sitting side by side on a bench that overlooked the beach. They had been sipping their drinks for a few moments when he said, "I told you that night two weeks ago that we needed to talk, Swan. I think we still do."

Yes, they did. She would let him go first. "Okay, I'm listening."

"I want you to do more than just listen, Swan. I want you to engage by asking questions, giving me feedback, and I would like to be able to do the same with you."

"Okay, that seems fair because I do have some questions for you."

"Ask away."

She took another sip of her drink. "You didn't tell me you were a SEAL and I'd—"

"I couldn't tell you I was a SEAL, Swan," he interrupted to say. "That's why I lied and said I was no longer in the military."

"Yes, I know that now. I want to tell you, because of what happened to my father, I had made up my mind never to get serious about a military man…especially not a SEAL."

"Oh, I see."

She wouldn't tell him yet that she'd changed her mind about that. "Is your mother's birthday really next month and do you have four brothers?"

"Yes. Everything I told you about my family is true. I never lied to you about anything pertaining to them. I just omitted some details and couldn't elaborate on certain things."

She then put her wineglass down and turned toward him. "Why did you sleep with me, David, when I was just an assignment to you?"

Flipper knew this was the time of reckoning and what he told her would have an impact on their relationship for the rest of their days. He needed her to understand.

"You were supposed to be an assignment, Swan. But honestly, I don't think you ever were. From the moment I walked into your shop and saw you, a part of me knew I had to fight hard to be objective and do the job I'd been sent here to do."

He paused. "I tried to keep my attraction to you out of the picture but found it harder and harder to do. Each time I saw you while getting to know you, I fell deeper under your spell. It was hard pretending with you."

He decided to be totally honest with her. "Just so you know, that day you invited me to your place for dinner wasn't my first time there. I'd been to your home without you knowing anything about it. But at the time, it was just a house I was checking out as part of an investigation. The day you invited me to dinner, I saw it through another pair of eyes. Yours. And for me, it then became your home."

She drew in a deep breath. "You invaded my privacy by letting yourself into my home, but that's not why I'm upset. I accept that you had a job to do and I was your assignment but…"

"But what?"

"You still haven't fully answered my question, David. Why did you make love to me?"

David frowned, realizing that he *hadn't* answered her question. His teammates often teased him about beating around the bush, sometimes providing too much context instead of just sticking with the facts.

"The reason I made love to you, Swan, was because I desired you. Everything about you turned me on. Your looks, your scent, your walk…and then after our first kiss, it was your taste. Fighting my desire for you was no longer an option, although I tried being honorable enough not to seduce you."

"But then I seduced you," she said quietly.

He smiled. "No, I think that night we seduced each other. Everything we did was mutual."

"Yes, it was." She took another sip of her wine. "I spoke with Godpop 2 today and he told me your assignment ended but you decided to stay. Why?"

Okay, no beating around the bush this time, Flipper decided. "The reason is that by then I had fallen in love with you. In all honesty, in my heart you stopped being an assignment the first time I made love to you. I crossed the line of what was honorable, and I knew why. Because I felt you here, Swan," he said, pointing to his heart. "I felt you here in a way I've never felt before. No woman has ever been here, Swan. But during the one time you shouldn't have, you got there anyway."

"And now? How do you feel now?"

He placed his beer bottle aside and turned toward her. "Now you are still in my heart. Even more so. I love you so much I ache on the inside when I'm not with you. I love you so much I think of you even at times I shouldn't."

He reached out and took her hand in his. "Now I need to know, Swan, just how you feel about me."

Swan felt the gentle tug on her hand and, surprising even herself, she moved to sit in his lap.

When he wrapped his arms around her, she felt comfort flow through her. She turned in his lap to look down at him. He'd given her answers to all her questions, now she intended to give him answers to his.

"I love you, David. I fought it at first. I didn't know about you being present-day military, but I also had a problem…not with interracial dating…but with allowing anything to come of it. I saw how others saw my parents at times. Not as a beautiful couple in love but as an interracial couple in love. There should not have been a difference. I never wanted to deal with what they had to deal with in the name of love."

She paused. "But then I moved beyond thinking that way after I fell in love with you. Then I realized how my parents must have felt, believing nothing mattered but their love. Even if the world was against them, as long as they had each other, that's what truly counted."

"So you do love me?" he asked her as if for clarity.

Swan didn't have a problem clarifying anything for

him or anyone else. "Yes, I love you, David Flipper Holloway." And then she lowered her mouth to his.

Shivers of profound pleasure shot through every part of Swan's body when David slid his tongue into her mouth. Sensations bombarded her as she concentrated on his taste, his scent and the way he pulled her tongue into his mouth to mate with his. And when she felt his hands inch upward and slide beneath her top, his touch made her purr.

Both his taste and his touch were awakening parts of her, making her feel alive in a way she hadn't felt since the last time they'd been together. Here at her house. In her bed.

When his fingers touched her bare breasts, using his fingertips to draw circles around her nipples, she oozed deeper into the kiss, almost feeling like melted butter in his arms.

He slowly pulled his mouth from hers and looked at her. His blue eyes were sharp and filled with the same desire she felt. "Any reason why we can't take this inside?"

She wrapped her arms around his waist. "No, there's no reason."

"Good."

And then standing with her in his arms, he carried her into the house.

"Just so you know, David, I didn't ask you all my questions," Swan said when he placed her on the bed.

David glanced down at her. "You didn't?"

"No, but I can wait. None are more earth-shattering than this is going to be. And I need this."

He caressed the side of her face with his finger. "I need this, too. I know why I need it, tell me why you do."

She met his gaze and held it while she said, "I love the feel of you inside of me. I've never felt anything so right before. So pleasurable." She smiled. "Do you know I retired my sex toy?"

He chuckled. "That's good to know."

"Um, not too much information?"

"No. Nice to know what used to be my competition," he said as he began removing her clothes. Lucky for him, she wasn't wearing much. Just a top, shorts and a thong. Flipper had discovered outside earlier that she wasn't wearing a bra. He'd noticed more than once that she liked her breasts being free and so did he.

She reached out and tugged at his T-shirt and he assisted by removing his own shorts. Then he rejoined her on the bed. Reaching out, he lifted her by the waist.

"Wrap your legs around me, Swan. I'm about to join our bodies, to make us one."

As soon as her legs were settled around his waist, his shaft touched her core. She was wet and ready. Tilting her hips, he whispered the words, "I love you," before thrusting hard into her.

"David!"

Arching her back off the bed, she provided the prefect position for his penetration to go deeper. They were a perfect fit. They always would be. Not just in lovemaking but in everything they did from here on out. They had become a team.

He began moving, slowly at first and then harder and deeper, over and over again. The only constant sounds in the room were their breathing and flesh slapping against flesh. The air surrounding them was filled with the aroma of sex.

He felt on fire, like his entire body was burning and the flames fueled his need, his desire and his love. She was looking up at him, holding his gaze, and he hoped Swan saw the depth of love in his eyes.

He clenched his jaw when he felt it, the stirring of pleasure in his groin. The feeling was slowly spreading through his body and when Swan gripped his shoulders and dug her fingers into his skin, he continued to thrust inside of her like his life depended on it.

And when she screamed out his name, he knew the same sensations that were taking him were taking her.

He drew in a sharp breath only moments before calling out her name. Multiple sensations tore into him, causing an explosion inside of him that had him bucking his body in an all-consuming orgasm. The sensations kept coming until he let go and his release shot deep inside of her.

He knew right then that he wanted her to have his baby. If not this time, another time. One day, he intended to make it happen.

Moments later, he slumped down beside her and wrapped his arms around her as he tried to get his breathing under control. After recovering from his explosive orgasm, when he was able to talk, he said, "I feel like I've been burned to a crisp."

"Hmm, speaking of burning, do you know what I thought was hot?" she asked, drawing in deep breaths of air into her lungs.

"No, what?"

"You on that boat wearing nothing but swim trunks and that military belt around your waist. Now, that was hot."

He grinned. "You liked that, huh?"

She smirked up at him when he straddled her body again. "I liked it." Then her features became serious. "I still can't believe you swam all that way to save me."

He leaned in and brushed a kiss across her lips. "Believe it."

He then pulled back and looked down at her. His expression was serious. "I'm a damn good swimmer. I'm known to be able to hold my breath underwater for long periods of time. Longer than what most would consider normal. But I wasn't sure I was going to make it to the boat, Swan. I told my friends I had to try even if I died trying because the woman I love was on that boat. That's what kept me going. That's what fueled every stroke I made into the ocean waters. And when my body felt tired, like I couldn't possibly swim another lap, I would think of a life without you and for me that was unacceptable."

He drew in a sharp breath. For a quick minute, he relived the feel of the cold water as he swam nonstop to the boat to save her, not knowing if he would make it in time. "I had to save you."

"And then I rebuffed you. I refused to have that talk you wanted."

"I understood. I had been listening to what Georgianna Martin was saying, the picture she painted. I told myself that once I talked to you and told you the truth that you would believe me. I was just giving you time to think about everything. I figured you would realize that I did care for you."

She reached up and caressed the side of his face. "You never told me you cared."

"I did. Our last night together, when you were asleep, I told you before I left that I loved you. I had planned to tell you the next day when we were together but that's when you were taken."

"And you came back," she said.

"That was always my plan, Swan. I never intended to

let you go. I love you that much. And just so you know, my entire family is rooting for me. I told them about you and they can't wait to meet you. My brothers and I are giving Mom a party for her birthday next week. Will you go to Texas with me?"

When she hesitated, he added, "What I told you about them is true. My parents accept people for who they are and not how they look. Will you trust me about that?"

She met his gaze and nodded. "Yes, I will trust you and yes, I will go."

A huge smile spread across his face. "I can't wait to introduce you to everyone. And I've got the perfect thing for you to wear." He quickly eased off the bed.

She pulled herself up. "What's going on? You plan on dressing me that night?"

He glanced over his shoulder, chuckling as he pulled a small white box out of his shorts. "Something like that."

He returned to the bed and pulled her up to stand her on her feet beside the bed. Then he got down on one knee and looked up at her. "I love you, Swan. I know we have a lot of things we still need to overcome. But I believe we will do so together. Forever. Will you marry me?"

He saw tears form in her eyes when she nodded. "Yes, I will marry you."

He slid the ring on her finger and at that moment Flipper knew he was halfway to having his world complete.

He would get the other half the day she became his wife.

Sixteen

Swan glanced down at the ring David had put on her finger last week. Seeing it gave her strength and she definitely needed strength now, she thought as she entered a huge ballroom on his arm. It was his mother's sixtieth birthday party.

They had flown into Dallas last night so this would be the first time she met his family. Nervous jitters had tried taking over her stomach but a smile from David was keeping most of them at bay. He was convinced his family would love her and he had told her over and over that she was worrying for nothing. She was the woman he wanted and his family would love his choice.

"There's Mom and Dad," he said, with his arms around her shoulders as she carried his mother's gift. The same gift he'd purchased that first day he'd come into her shop.

A man she knew had to be one of David's brothers whispered something to the older couple and they turned with huge smiles on their faces.

At that moment, Swan knew David had inherited his father's eyes and that the smiles on the couple's faces were genuine. She could actually feel their warmth. David's mom was beautiful and did not look like she was sixty or that she had five grown sons.

When they reached his parents, David made the introduction. "Mom. Dad. I want you to meet the woman who has agreed to be my wife, Swan Jamison."

"It's an honor to meet you," Swan said, extending her hand to his mother.

Instead of taking it, the older woman engulfed Swan in a huge hug. "It's wonderful meeting you as well, Swan, and welcome to the family."

"Thank you. Here's your gift. Happy birthday."

"Thank you."

She received a hug from David's father as well. Then suddenly she was surrounded and a laughing David made introductions. All his brothers had those same blue eyes and like David, they were very handsome men. She could see why when she looked at the older Holloways; they were a beautiful couple. And Swan could tell from the way Mr. Holloway looked at his wife and the way Mrs. Holloway would look back at him that the couple was still very much in love.

A few nights ago, David had shared the fact that because his mother had been married to a Navy SEAL for over forty years and had five sons who were SEALs, she counseled a number of SEAL wives who had difficulties with the frequency and longevity of their spouses' missions. Swan had been glad to hear that since she would become a SEAL's wife soon.

Because David would be leaving in less than four

months on anther mission, they hoped to marry within a year. Surprisingly, David wanted a big wedding. She agreed as long as the wedding took place in the Keys.

The logistics of having a big wedding were enormous, given he had four brothers who were SEALs on different teams. Not to mention his closest four friends were SEALs as well. That meant Swan and David had to make sure everyone would be on leave in the States at the same time.

David also introduced Swan to her future sisters-in-law and they loved her engagement ring. The three were friendly and she liked them immediately. She was also introduced to other members of David's family—his grandparents, his niece, nephews, cousins, aunts, uncles—it was obvious the Holloway family was a huge one.

"Now I want to reintroduce you to four guys who are just as close to me as brothers. As you know, they came to the Keys to assist me in proving your innocence. And even when my assignment with you ended, they didn't leave. They stayed."

She had met his four friends that night after the incident on the boat, when they'd had to give statements. She had thanked them for their help but they hadn't been officially introduced.

"Did I tell you how beautiful you look tonight, sweetheart?"

She smiled up at him as they walked across the ballroom floor to the four men and their wives. "Yes, you told me. Thank you." She, Candy and Jamila had gone shopping in Miami. She'd known this was the perfect dress when she'd seen it on a store mannequin.

Within a few minutes, she had been introduced to Brisbane "Bane" Westmoreland and his wife, Crystal; Gavin "Viper" Blake and his very pregnant wife,

Layla; Laramie "Coop" Cooper and his wife, Bristol; and Thurston "Mac" McRoy and his wife, Teri.

After spending time with the couples, Swan felt that just like her future sisters-in-law, the four women were genuinely friendly and Swan looked forward to getting to know them better. They loved her engagement ring as well and told David he'd done a great job in picking it out.

"So what do you think?" David leaned down to ask, taking her hand in his and leading her to where his parents, siblings and their spouses were getting ready to take a group picture.

She grinned up at him. "Um, for starters, I think I need to start calling you Flipper, since everyone else does. And then, *Flipper*, I think I am one of the luckiest women in the world right now. I love you."

He chuckled as he pulled her to the side of the room and wrapped his arms around her waist. "And I, Swan Jamison, think I'm the luckiest man in the world, and I love you."

"A very wise woman, my mother, once told me that when you meet a man who puts that sparkle in your eyes then you'd know he was a keeper. You, Flipper, are a keeper."

He smiled. "You, my beautiful Swan, are a keeper as well."

Flipper then lowered his mouth to hers.

Epilogue

A year later in June

Bane Westmoreland leaned close and whispered to Flipper, "Don't get nervous now. You wanted a big wedding and you got it."

Flipper couldn't say anything because Bane was right. He stood flanked by his father, who was his best man, and twelve groomsmen—namely his brothers, best friends and cousins.

Only his SEAL teammates knew Flipper had a tendency to tap his finger against his thigh when he was nervous. He stopped tapping but not because he noticed that Viper, Mac and Coop were grinning over at him. But then he figured both Viper and Coop had reasons to grin since they'd both become fathers this year. Viper was the proud father of a son, Gavin IV, and Coop had a beautiful daughter they'd named Paris, since that was where he'd first met his wife.

It was a beautiful day for a beach wedding and so far everything was perfect and going according to plan. Swan had hired one of the local wedding planners and the woman had done an awesome job. She had thought of everything, including the super yacht that could hold their five hundred guests that they'd be using for the wedding reception. It was anchored in the ocean near Swan's beachfront home. A fleet of passenger boats had been chartered to transport the wedding guests out to the yacht.

A ten-piece orchestra sat beneath towering balustrades draped from top to bottom in thin white netting. Chairs were set up on the beach, auditorium style, facing the decorative stage where Flipper and the men in the wedding party stood waiting.

Suddenly, the music began and all the ladies strolled down the beach and up the steps.

Swan had chosen her wedding colors of purple and yellow and Flipper had to admit the combination was striking. It took all twelve women long enough to do their stroll. His niece was a flower girl and Coop's son and one of Flipper's nephews were the ring bearers.

Flipper almost held his breath when what looked like a huge forty-foot golden swan was rolled onto the beach. When the orchestra changed their tune for the "Wedding March," the swan opened and his Swan appeared in a beautiful, dazzling white gown. She looked beautiful, stunning and breathtaking all rolled into one.

Flipper stared at the woman who would be his wife and felt so much love in his heart. He hadn't known until now just how much he could feel for one woman. They had spent the past year deepening their friendship and their love. He looked forward to returning from his covert operations, knowing she would be there waiting on him.

He watched as she slowly strolled toward him. All three of her godfathers participated in walking her up the aisle, passing her off to the other so many feet along the way. Then all three of them gave her away. When Swan reached his side and extended her hand to him, he accepted it while thinking she was *his* Swan.

His beautiful Swan.

The wedding ceremony began. What Flipper would remember most when he looked back was when the minister announced them husband and wife and told him he could kiss his bride.

Flipper pulled Swan into his arms and lowered his mouth to hers. She was his and he intended to keep her happy for the rest of his days. They would be flying to Dubai for a two-week honeymoon and then return to the Keys where they planned to make their permanent home.

When David released Swan's mouth, the minister said, "I present to everyone David and Swan Holloway."

Flipper knew they were supposed to exit by walking down the golden steps that led to the boat that would transport them to the yacht. But at that moment, he couldn't deny himself another kiss and lowered his mouth to his wife's again.

* * * * *

STILL WATERS

DEBRA WEBB

I feel so blessed to be surrounded by wonderful, supportive friends. Among those many amazing friends are the members of my incredible Street Team. Thank you for all you do and for simply being you.

Chapter One

Fourth Avenue North
Birmingham, Alabama
Monday, October 17, 9:30 a.m.

Jess Harris Burnett had just poured her third cup of decaf when the jingle of the bell over the door sounded. As she walked toward the lobby, she heard receptionist Rebecca Scott welcoming the visitor to B&C Investigations. The office had been open almost a whole month now. Jess and her lifelong friend Buddy Corlew had made a good decision going into business together. With a nineteen-month-old daughter and a son due in a mere six weeks—Jess rubbed her enormous belly—stepping away from her position as deputy chief of Birmingham's major crimes team had been the right move.

The memory of being held prisoner by Ted Holmes attempted to bully into her thoughts, and Jess pushed it away. Holmes, like the many serial killers before him she had helped track down, was history now. Still, Jess was well aware that there would always be a new face of evil just around the next corner. She intended to leave tracking down the killers to the Birmingham PD. Her goal now was to concentrate on the victims. With B&C Investigations, she was accomplishing that goal.

"I'll let Mrs. Burnett know you're here, Ms. Coleman," Rebecca said as Jess came into the lobby.

"Gina, what brings you here this morning?" Jess flashed a smile for the receptionist. "Thank you, Rebecca. We'll be in my office."

Gina Coleman, Birmingham's beloved and award-winning television journalist, gave Jess a hug. "You look great!"

"You're the one who looks great," Jess countered. "Married life agrees with you."

Gina smiled and gave Jess another quick hug. On the way to her office, Jess grabbed her coffee and offered her friend a cup.

"No, thanks. I've had way too much already this morning."

When they were settled in Jess's office, Gina surveyed the small space. "You've done a wonderful job of making this place comfortable."

Jess was proud of how their offices had turned out. The downtown location was good for business even if the building was a very old one. In Jess's opinion, the exposed brick walls gave the place character. It was a good fit. Anyone who knew them would say that she and Buddy had more than a little character.

"Thanks." Jess sipped her decaf and smiled. "You really do seem happy." Gina looked amazing, as always. Her long brunette hair and runway-model looks had ensured her a position in the world of television news, but it was her incredible ability to find the story that had made her a highly sought-after journalist. Her personal bravery, too, inspired Jess. Gina had taken some fire when she'd announced she was gay and married the woman she loved. Standing firm, Gina had weathered the storm.

"I am very happy." Gina stared at her hands a moment. When she met Jess's gaze once more, her face was cluttered with worry. "Barb and I need your help."

"What can I do? Name it." Jess set her coffee aside.

"A couple of hours ago Barb's younger sister, Amber, was called into the BPD about a murder."

A frown lined Jess's brow, reminding her that by the time this baby was in high school she would look like his grandmother rather than his mother. She spotted a new wrinkle every time she looked in the mirror. *Don't even go there.*

"I hadn't heard. There was a homicide last night?" This time a few months ago and Jess would have known the persons of interest and the prime suspects in every homicide long before an arrest was made in the city of Birmingham. Not anymore. Dan made it a point not to discuss work when he came home. Though she could still nudge him for details when the need arose, it was one of the perks of being married to the chief of police. A sense of well-being warmed her when she thought of her husband. He was a genuinely good man.

"Dan explained as much as he was at liberty to share. He assured me it was routine questioning, but I'm worried. I told him I was coming to you." Gina sighed. "I don't think he was very happy about my decision. He obviously prefers to keep murder and mayhem away from the mother of his children."

Two years ago Jess would have been jealous at hearing Gina had spoken to Dan. The two had once been an on-again, off-again item. Now she counted Gina as a good friend. "Don't worry about Dan." Jess shook her head. "I've warned him time and again that just because I'm no longer a cop doesn't mean I won't be investigating murders."

"If he had his way, you'd retire," Gina teased. "We both know how he feels about keeping you safe."

Jess had been cursed with more than her fair share of obsessed killers during her career first as an FBI profiler and then as a deputy chief in the Birmingham PD. Dan's concern was understandable if unwarranted. Just because she was a mother now didn't mean she couldn't take care of herself. Admittedly, she had grown considerably more cautious.

"Tell me about the case." Considering it was a murder case, she could get the details from Lieutenant Chet Harper or Sergeant Lori Wells. Chet had recently been named acting chief of the small major crimes team—SPU, Special Problems Unit—Jess had started. Lori was reassigned to Crimes Against Persons. One or the other would be investigating the homicide case. Jess hoped the case was with Harper. She counted Lori as her best friend, but the new chief of the Crimes Against Persons Division, Captain Vanessa Aldridge, was brash and obstinate, and carried the biggest chip on her shoulder Jess had ever encountered.

Though they'd only met once or twice, Jess was familiar with Barbara's younger sister. Amber Roberts was a reporter at the same station, Channel Six, as Gina. She was young, beautiful and talented. Her and Barbara's parents were from old money, but Gina would be the first to attest to the fact that a sparkling pedigree didn't exempt one from murder. Gina's own sister had paid the price for her part in a long-ago tragedy.

"Kyle Adler's body was found in his home yesterday. He'd been stabbed repeatedly. Amber hardly knew the man. The very notion is ludicrous." Gina held up a hand. "I know you're probably thinking that

I felt the same way about Julie, but this is different. Amber had nothing to do with this man's murder."

As much as Jess sympathized with Gina, Amber would not have been questioned if the police hadn't found some sort of connection between her and the victim. "The police have something," she reminded her friend. "You know this. What about the murder weapon—was it found?"

"They haven't found the murder weapon." Gina shook her head. "The whole thing is insane. Amber swears the only time she ever saw this guy was when he made a delivery to her or someone at the station. Apparently he made a living delivering for various shops around town. But the cops claim they found evidence indicating she'd been in his house. Unless someone is framing her, it simply isn't possible."

Jess chewed her bottom lip a moment. "It's conceivable someone may have wanted Adler dead and set it up to look as though another person, like Amber, committed the act."

"If that's true—" Gina leaned forward "—not only do we need help finding the actual murderer that the police may not even try to find, we also need to protect Amber. She could be in danger from the real killer."

Jess sent a text to Harper. "Let's see who's working the case first. Then we'll know whether or not we have to worry about finding the truth. As for the other, I agree. If Amber is being framed, it's quite possible she could be in danger. Personal security would be a wise step until we know what we're dealing with."

"Buddy said you do protective services as well as private investigations."

"We do," Jess agreed. "Right now the only investigator we have available is Sean Douglas."

Gina's gaze narrowed. "I'm sensing some hesitation. Do you have reservations as to whether he can handle the job?"

Jess considered how to answer the question. "He spent the past five years as a bodyguard to various celebrities in Hollywood." She shrugged. "Based on our research into his background, he was very, very good at his job. For two years prior to that he was a cop with the LAPD. He's had all the right training, and his references are impeccable."

Gina said, "There's a *but* coming."

"His last assignment was Lacy James."

Gina sat back in her chair. "Damn."

Lacy James had been a rising pop star. The rumors about drug abuse had followed her from singing in the church choir in her hometown of Memphis all the way to her Grammy nomination in LA last year.

"Her agent hired Douglas to keep an eye on her," Jess explained. "According to Douglas, she had been straight for a while and her agent wanted to ensure she stayed that way. Six months into the assignment, she died of an overdose."

Gina pressed her hands to her face, then took a

breath. “Do you think what happened was in some way his fault?”

Jess shook her head. “Responsibility for what happened to Lacy James lies with her agent and her other handlers. They cared more about her career than they did her health and welfare. My only hesitation is that Douglas is a little too cocky for his own good. I think he uses attitude to cover the pain and guilt he feels about James’s death.” Jess paused to weigh her words. “I’m concerned his need to prove himself again might be an issue, but as for his ability to protect a client, he’s more than capable.”

Gina’s expression brightened. “Trust me—whatever this guy’s attitude, Amber can handle it. You don’t rise as rapidly in my business as she has without a tough skin and a little attitude. I’m desperate, Jess. I promised Barb I would take care of this.”

Jess felt confident Gina was right about Amber. Putting herself in front of the camera every day was hard work, and it wasn’t for the faint of heart. “Why don’t I learn all I can from the BPD and then I’ll brief Douglas. I’ll arrange a meeting with Amber, and we’ll go from there.”

“I will be forever in your debt.”

“We’ll take care of Amber,” Jess assured her friend.

Gina stood. Jess did the same, albeit a little less gracefully.

“I’m aware that we don’t always know a person as well as we believe—even the people closest to us,”

Gina confessed. "But I would wager all I own that Amber had nothing to do with this man's death."

Jess nodded resolutely. "Then all we need to do is ensure she stays safe until the BPD can find the killer."

Chapter Two

Forest Brook Drive, Homewood, 12:32 p.m.

Amber Roberts entered the necessary code to stop the infernal beeping of her security system, tossed her keys on the table by the door and then kicked off her heels. This had been the longest morning of her life. She closed her eyes and reminded herself to breathe as the man assigned to keep an eye on her rushed past her to have a look before she went any farther into the house.

Forcing her mind and body to focus on her normal routine, she locked the front door and set the alarm. Without waiting to hear the all-clear signal, she grabbed her shoes and headed for her bedroom. This was her home. The alarm had still been set, for God's sake. If anyone was in her house, he or she had been there since Amber left that morning. Otherwise the alarm would have gone off, right? She closed her eyes for a moment. At this point she wasn't sure of anything.

Her stomach knotted at the memory of the police showing up just as her early morning news broadcast ended. Everyone had watched as the detective explained she was needed downtown and then escorted her from the station. She didn't have to look to know her face would be plastered all over the evening papers as well as the internet and television broadcasts.

The damage control had to start now. She'd already tweeted and posted on Instagram and Facebook. The station had backed her up, as well. If the reaction didn't make her sound petty and paranoid, she would swear Gerard Stevens from the station's primary competitor had set her up.

Amber walked into her closet and shoved her shoes into their slots. Her head spun as she dragged off the dress that would forever remind her of the interview room where she'd endured a relentless interrogation by one of the BPD's finest. She tossed the dress into the dry-cleaning hamper and reached for a pair of sweatpants and a tee. Worst of all, a man was dead. Though she only knew him in passing, she felt bad about his murder. He was someone's son. Probably someone's brother and significant other. She pulled on the sweatpants. Most people had a life—unlike her. Gina and Barb warned her repeatedly that she was going to be sorry for allowing her life to fly by while she was totally absorbed by work.

Who had time for a social life? Gina should know

better than anyone. Amber was fairly confident her mentor was saying what Barb expected her to say. It didn't matter either way. Amber was twenty-eight; her top priority was her career. She still had decades for falling in love and building a family.

Even if her narrow focus on her career did get lonely sometimes.

She yanked on the tee and kicked the thought aside. The police believed she was somehow involved in a man's murder. Her love life, or lack thereof, was the least of her worries.

How the hell the police could think she was involved was the million-dollar question. Why in the world would she hurt this man, much less kill him? She scarcely knew him. He had made a few deliveries to her house. He was always pleasant, but they never exchanged more than a dozen words. None of what she'd been told by the police so far made the slightest bit of sense.

"The house is clear."

Amber jumped, slamming her elbow into the wall. Frowning at the broad-shouldered man filling the doorway to her closet, she rubbed her funny bone.

"Thank you," she said even though she didn't quite feel thankful. She did not want a babysitter. She hadn't killed anyone, and there was no reason for a soul to want to harm her. Reporting the news for the past six-plus years had given her certain insights into situations like this one, and hiring a bodyguard this early in the investigation was overreacting. There could only be two potential explanations for her current dilemma: mistaken identity or a frame job. Both happened. As hard as she tried, she could come up with no other explanation.

Her bodyguard's gaze roamed from her face all the way to her toes and back with a couple of unnecessary pauses in between. Now that annoyed her. He was here to keep her safe—supposedly. He had no business looking at her as if she was the next conquest on his radar. Though she suspected Mr. Sexy-as-Hell usually didn't have to work very hard to get what he wanted. The man was gorgeous. Tall, with those broad shoulders that narrowed into a lean waist. Thick blond hair just the right length for threading your fingers through and deep blue eyes. His muscular build attested to his dedicated workout ethics. With every extra thump of her pulse she understood that beneath his smooth, tanned skin was an ego large enough for the Vulcan iron man that watched over the city of Birmingham from high atop Red Mountain.

Sean Douglas was hot, and he damn well knew it.

As if he agreed wholeheartedly with her assessment, he gifted her with a nod and disappeared.

Amber sighed. She should pull herself together. Her attorney was on the way over with whatever details the police had shared with him. They'd done nothing but ask questions this morning. Each time her attorney had asked about the evidence, the detective had evaded the question. Still, she hadn't needed a lawyer to tell her that she wouldn't have been called in and so thoroughly questioned had there been no evidence. Friends, colleagues and people acquainted with the victim were questioned in their homes or workplaces. Only the ones about to be named a person of interest—or, worse, a suspect—were hauled to the station and interviewed. The police had wanted her off balance—which was not a good thing.

How the hell was this possible?

She needed a couple of cocktails and a good night's sleep. Maybe she'd wake up in the morning and discover this had all been just one big old bad nightmare.

Finding Sean Douglas kicked back on the sofa in her living room reminded her that the situation was all too real.

"I put on a pot of coffee." He leaned forward and braced his forearms on his knees. "I figured some caffeine would be useful the next few hours."

She would have preferred a caramel latte, but she'd been too emotional to think of dropping by her favorite coffee shop after leaving the police department. Her parents were beside themselves. They were in a remote part of Africa on a medical aid mission and couldn't get back for days. She and Barbara had insisted they stay and do the important work they'd gone there to do. This entire business was nothing more than a mistake. Surely it would be cleared up in a day or two.

Belatedly she remembered to say, "Thank you." Her attorney, Frank Teller, was a coffee drinker. Vaguely she wondered how Douglas had known this or if he was a coffee guy, too.

"I can call in some lunch for delivery. I'm guessing you didn't take time for breakfast this morning."

She appreciated the offer but said, "I had a protein smoothie. I'm fine."

He dismissed her response with a wave of his hand. "How about a pizza or a burger? Your choice."

She couldn't possibly eat. "I'm not hungry. Feel free to raid my kitchen or order something for yourself."

His mouth eased into a lopsided grin. "Already done that. You're fresh out of real food."

A frown furrowed her brow. He'd prowled through her kitchen? What kind of bodyguard checked the fridge?

"Why don't you tell me about yourself," he suggested with a pat of the sofa cushion next to him.

Amber felt sure that inviting pat worked well for him under normal circumstances, but those blue eyes and that hopeful smile did little more than annoy her at the moment. "Weren't you briefed on my case?"

The need for personal security was entirely new to her, but instinct told her a man assigned to protect her would certainly have been briefed about the situation. Small talk was the furthest thing from her mind. He needed to find a way to entertain himself if he was bored. She had no desire to chat.

"I was." He clasped his hands between his spread thighs.

"What else do you need to know?" She gave herself a mental pat on the back for not sounding as snippy as she felt.

"Until this situation is resolved," he began, tracking her movements with those blue eyes as she settled in a chair a few feet away, "we'll be spending a lot of time together. It's helpful to know a little more than the facts of the case. What time do you like to get up in the mornings? What's your usual bedtime? Do you watch television or read or just relax in the evenings? Should I expect company? Is there a boyfriend to accommodate?" He shrugged. "Things like that are good to know."

For the love of Mike. Amber shook off the frustration. His request had merit. *No need to be unreasonable.* "I'm up at six unless I'm called to a scene earlier or I host the morning news the way I did this morning. I go to bed right after the ten o'clock news assuming I haven't been called out to a scene. I usually leave the television turned on all night." She glanced at the dark screen hanging on the wall above her fireplace. She imagined that every channel was running stories about her and the murder. "I might be taking a break from that habit for a few days."

"Understandable." He cocked an eyebrow. "What about a boyfriend?"

"There is no boyfriend." Somehow saying it out loud sounded far worse than simply knowing it. She hadn't been in a serious relationship in more than a year. Maybe there wouldn't be another one. Who had time? More important, who cared? She had everything she needed. *If that's so, why the sudden need to justify your status?*

He made a knowing sound as something like surprise flashed across his face. "A girlfriend then?"

"No girlfriend."

He made one of those male grunts that could convey surprise as easily as indifference. Either way, the sound got on her already-frazzled nerves.

"Your degree is in mass communications," he said, changing the subject. "When did you decide you preferred working in front of the camera versus behind it?"

"I didn't decide. The journalist I assisted during my first assignment was in a car accident. Everyone was on the scene except her and the cameraman told me to get in front of the camera and do the job.

The audience responded well to me, so that's where the powers that be decided I should be—on-screen."

"But you had aspirations?"

Amber nodded. "I had my heart set on hosting one of the big entertainment news shows." She laughed, remembering the horror on her parents' faces when she'd told them. "It wasn't exactly the career my family had hoped for."

He smiled. It was nice. Really nice. *Too nice, damn it.* "Your parents and your sister are all doctors."

"Yes. I'm the black sheep." The realization that her words had never been truer stole the air from her lungs. Now she was a potential suspect in a homicide.

The doorbell saved her from going down that pity path. She stood to go to the door, but Douglas moved ahead of her and checked the security viewfinder.

"It's Mr. Teller."

Douglas opened the door, and Teller came inside. He'd already been introduced to the man who would be keeping watch over her. There was just something wrong with calling him a bodyguard. Particularly since she continued to have a bit of trouble keeping her attention off *his* body. The foolish reaction had to be about sex. She hadn't been intimate with anyone since she and Josh had ended their relationship.

Her gaze drifted to the man assigned to protect her. *Don't even go there.*

"We should speak privately," Frank Teller announced before saying hello. He looked from Amber to Douglas and back.

"I'd like him to stay," Amber countered. Douglas and his boss would need to be kept up to speed anyway.

When Teller relented, Douglas insisted on serving the coffee. Amber was happy to let him do the honors. Her knees were feeling a little weak as she sank back into a chair. Maybe it was the grim expression Teller wore.

He placed his briefcase on the coffee table and opened it. "The news is not good."

Amber's stomach did the sinking now. "What sort of evidence could they possibly have? I don't even know this man! He…he made deliveries to my house and the station a couple of times." Maybe more than a couple of times. Still, the whole thing was incredible.

"Amber." Teller closed his briefcase and placed the folder he'd removed atop it. "I've known your family for most of my life. Your father is my father's personal physician. Your mother was my pediatrician. I, of all people, know this is wrong. You couldn't possibly have harmed this man. Yet the evidence is enough to make even me have second thoughts."

The trembling she had experienced that morning after the initial shock that no one was playing a joke on her started anew. The police had mentioned evidence without providing the details. "What evidence? I don't know how they could find evidence that leads back to me in a home where I've never been...on a body I've never touched."

"They found a teacup with your prints on it."

"What?" The situation had just gone from unbelievable to incomprehensible. "If there is anything in that poor man's house that either belonged to me or bore my prints, someone—besides me—put it there."

Before Teller could respond, Douglas returned with the coffee. He'd gone to the trouble to find her grandmother's serving tray and to dig out the china cups and saucers rather than the stoneware mugs. He'd even prepared the creamer and sugar servers. Her disbelief was temporarily sidelined by the idea that he would think to go to so much trouble.

Douglas placed the tray on the coffee table, and she noted there were only two cups. "If you need me for anything—" he hitched his thumb toward the rear of the house "—I'll be outside checking the perimeter."

"Thank you." Amber suddenly didn't want anyone else to hear these incredible lies—at least not until she had heard them.

When Douglas was gone, Teller said, "Amber, I realize this is shocking."

He'd certainly nailed her feelings with that statement. "I don't understand how any of this happened." She shook her head, overwhelmed and confused and, honestly, terrified. "You see it on television or in the movies, but this is real life. *My* life."

"Do you drink a tea called Paradise Peach?"

Something cold and dark welled inside her. She moistened her lips and cleared her throat. "Yes. It's my favorite. There's a specialty shop downtown that stocks it."

"A can of Paradise Peach tea was found in the victim's home. Your prints were on the can."

Worry furrowed her brow and bumped her pulse rate to a faster rhythm. "Maybe he shopped there, too. He may have picked up a can after I did." Hope knotted in her chest, but it was short-lived. How did a person prove a theory as full of circumstantial holes as the one she'd just suggested?

"Certainly," he agreed. "Bear in mind that the burden of proof is not ours. It will be up to the BPD to make their case. For that they need evidence, which brings us to the cup that also bore your prints."

The rationale she had attempted to use earlier vanished. Dear Lord she felt as if she had just awakened in the middle of a horror film and she was the next victim. All she had to do now was scream.

"Take a look at these crime scene photos." He opened the folder and removed two eight-by-ten photographs. He scooted his briefcase and the serving platter to the far side of the table and placed the photographs in front of her. "These are copies, so they're not the best quality."

The first one showed the victim lying on the floor next to the dining table in what she presumed was his kitchen. Blood had soaked his shirt. He appeared to have multiple stab wounds to the chest. *Poor man.* She swallowed back the lump of emotion that rose in her throat and moved on to the second one. The second was a wider-angle view showing more of the room. Definitely the kitchen. Her attention zeroed in on the table. The table was set for two. Teacups sat in matching saucers, each flanked by a spoon and linen napkin. She squinted at the pattern on the cups. A floral pattern for sure, but difficult to distinguish.

"He was having tea with someone." She lifted her gaze to Teller's. "Whoever that person was, he or she is likely the one who killed him. Based on the prints found at the scene, the police believe that person was you."

Hands shaking, she pressed her fingers to her mouth to hold back the cry of outrage. "The medical examiner is certain about the time of death?"

Teller nodded. "Last Friday night, around eight. It'll be a while before we have the autopsy results, which will tell us what he had for dinner and various other details that may or may not help our case."

Amber made a face.

"Knowing what and where he ate might help us," Teller explained. "The police might be able to track down the restaurant—if he ate out—and someone there might remember if he was alone."

Sounded like a long shot to her. The detectives had pressed her over and over about her whereabouts on Friday night. It was the one time she'd come home early and hit the sack. She hadn't spent any time doing research at the station, she hadn't spoken to anyone and she'd had no company. None of her neighbors could confirm she was home. She hadn't done any work on her home computer, which might have confirmed her whereabouts. Bottom line, she had no alibi.

Disgusted, she shook her head. "Single people all over the world should be terrified of spending a quiet evening at home alone." If she were married or involved in a relationship, she might have spent time or at least spoken to her plus one that evening.

"There's more."

His somber tone caused her heart to skip a beat.

"A pair of panties were found in his bed. There was trace evidence. A pubic hair and a much longer hair…" He touched his head. "They want you to agree to a DNA test."

The heart that had stumbled a moment ago slammed against her ribs now. "Do you think I should?" Considering her fingerprints were there, she couldn't help but feel somewhat tentative as to how to proceed. "I know I haven't been in his house or his bed, so I have nothing to hide, but my fingerprints were there." She pressed a hand to her throat. "If someone is setting me up…"

He reached into his folder and removed another photograph. "Do you recognize these?"

The red panties in the photograph stole her ability to draw in air. She shot to her feet and rushed to her bedroom. Opening drawer after drawer, she rifled through her things and then slammed each door closed in turn. Her pulse pounding, she moved to the laundry hamper.

The panties weren't there.

Teller stood at her bedroom door, worry lining his face. "Lots of women have red panties. My wife has red panties. How can you be sure you recognize these?"

Her lungs finally filled with air. "The little bows." She paused to release the big breath she'd managed to draw in. "There should be a little satin red bow on each side. One is missing. It annoys me every time I see it. I've meant to throw them away..."

Of course any woman with red panties that sported little red bows could be missing a bow. In her gut, Amber knew better than to believe it was a mere coincidence. Her red one-bowed panties were missing. There was a teacup in the man's house, for God's sake, with her prints on it. She didn't need a DNA test to prove a damned thing. The hair and any other trace evidence would be hers, as well. Whoever wanted her to appear guilty had done a bang-up job.

Douglas appeared behind Teller. "Is everything okay?"

No. Everything was not okay. In fact, nothing was okay.

"I'll do the DNA test," Amber said to the man representing her.

Teller gave her a resigned nod. "I'll set it up."

Dear God. She was in serious trouble here.

Chapter Three

The mouthpiece hung around awhile longer, asking more questions and making Amber even more upset. Sean had heard of the guy. All the rich folks in Jefferson County used him. Teller didn't need billboards or commercials with catchy jingles. The family name got him all the business he would ever need. It didn't hurt that he had a reputation for being the best damn attorney in town.

Sean turned his attention back to assessing Amber's place. If the items found in the victim's residence were Amber's and she hadn't put them there, someone had been in her home. The reality likely hadn't sunk in for her just yet. It would hit her soon enough. It was time to start considering who would want to see Amber go down for murder. There had to be an old schoolmate or ex-bestie, maybe even a competitor at a rival television station with a grudge against her. Revenge, jealousy, there were all kinds of potential motives.

No matter that he'd only been employed at B&C

Investigations for a month, he'd learned a lot from the boss already. Jess had a motto: find the motive, find the killer. When looking for the source of trouble, there was no better advice. The boss didn't exactly have a lot of confidence in Sean just yet. She'd been reluctant to assign him this case—which was exactly why he had to do the best job possible. Of course, he always wanted to do a good job, but he couldn't allow even a single misstep this time. He had a feeling the first mistake and he would be out at B&C Investigations.

For damned sure he would never again allow the kind of mistake he'd made on his last security assignment. His bad judgment had cost a life.

His fingers stilled on the back door's lock mechanism. How could he blame Jess Burnett for not fully trusting him? No matter that he had years of outstanding work history under his belt, his last assignment for his former employer had gone to hell. The only reason he'd gotten the job with B&C Investigations was because Buddy Corlew and Sean's older brother, Chase, were friends. They'd played high school football together—against each other, actually. Chase had warned Sean that a year of moping around was enough. Sean had to get on with his life. During his time in Hollywood he'd built up considerable savings. Private security in the entertainment world paid extremely well. Finding a new job hadn't been necessary the first year after he returned home, but his brother was right. Sean had to get on with at least part of his life. His personal life might never recover from his mistake with Lacy, but there was no excuse for allowing his professional life to stay in the toilet.

"Is there something wrong with my door?"

Amber's question snapped him from his worrisome thoughts. He closed the door and shook his head. "I've checked front and back doors, and so far no sign of forced entry. The windows are next."

A frown dragged down the corners of her lips. She had nice lips. Full and pink. Her red hair and green eyes were a vivid contrast to her pale skin. The sprinkling of freckles across her nose she worked so hard to cover with makeup made him want to smile. She was a gorgeous lady, no doubt, but not the kind of overdone Hollywood beauty he'd disliked in California. Amber's was natural and completely unpretentious. He'd been watching her and fantasizing for months.

Fantasies and casual encounters were all he had anymore. He wasn't sure he would ever trust himself in a real relationship again, and he would never permit work to become personal. Of course, his brother warned him that a guy still six months from thirty shouldn't be throwing in the towel.

Realization dawned in the lady's pretty green eyes. "You think someone broke into my home and took my...the evidence the police found." The frown reappeared. "But how did they get my prints on the teacup?"

When he looked confused, she quickly explained about the evidence the BPD had discovered in the murder victim's home.

Sean inspected the second of three kitchen windows. "Trust me," he said in answer to her question, "there are ways to get into any place—home or business—if a person wants in badly enough."

Amber followed him into the living room. She watched silently as he confirmed the windows were locked and that all the locking mechanisms were in working order.

"You mean like overriding security codes?"

"That's one way, yes." He shrugged. "Folks who make it their business to break and enter can unlock about any kind of lock with or without a key."

Rather than continue with her hovering too close and watching his every move, he decided to run a few questions by her. Why not start with the most obvious ones she'd already answered for his boss and more than likely for the police? "Do you have any enemies, Amber?"

Her arms crossed protectively over her chest, and she dropped into the nearest chair. "Your boss and the police asked me that question along with a barrage of others. The answer is no. I've never had any sort of trouble with anyone. I've never had a stalker. Never received strange emails or Facebook messages. The fan mail from viewers is never threatening or overly negative. Someone might disagree with the way I reported an issue or event, but so far no one has taken it any further."

"Lucky you. Most celebrities get their fair share of threatening or nasty mail." Sean meant the comment as a compliment, but judging by her sigh she didn't feel so lucky. He hitched his head toward the hall that led to the bedrooms. "How about persistent fans or admirers? Any of those?"

Amber pushed to her feet and trailed after him. "The usual. I typically receive flowers at the station a couple of times a week, depending on the stories I've covered. The high-profile stories generate the most reaction from viewers. Letters, food baskets, the occasional gift." She rubbed at the back of her neck and then stretched it from side to side. "Nothing negative."

The single window in the hall bath was secure. Sean moved to the first of the three bedrooms. "Any that are unsigned or from repeat senders?"

"A few."

Both windows in bedroom one were secure. "Define 'a few.'"

Following him to the next bedroom, she shrugged and said, "Four or five fans who consistently send little gifts. The occasional unsigned letter, maybe once or twice a month."

"Have you ever met any of the four or five gift

senders?" He progressed from the first window to the second before moving on to the final bedroom—her private space.

"The station has a big community day twice a year." She crossed her arms over her chest, drawing his errant attention momentarily to her breasts. "You know, to thank the viewers. We do photos and giveaways. Have games and hot dogs. There's always a clown and a couple of cartoon characters for the kids. Sometimes the people who write to me or send me gifts or flowers come by and say hi. No drama or discomfort. Just a friendly hello and a request for an autograph."

The instant he entered her bedroom he felt completely out of place. The room smelled like her. Whatever perfume she wore was restrained but unmistakable. Light and citrusy. The delicate fragrance was barely there but so uniquely her, as if the subtle sweetness came from all that soft, satiny skin. He gave his head a mental shake. Evidently the skin-tight tee she wore had his imagination running a little wild.

The bed was big, too large for a woman to lie in alone. The bedding was pure white, lush and natural—like Amber. It didn't take much to summon the image of that long, curly red hair flowing over those white linens. His body tightened with need at the thought of climbing onto that bed and kissing his way up her naked body.

Do the job, man. “Do you keep the unsigned letters?” He walked to the nearest window and confirmed it was locked. “Some of those may be from the same person.”

She massaged her temples as if a headache had begun there. Who wouldn’t have a headache? She was a person of interest in a murder case. That was enough to give anyone a headache.

“I never looked to see if there were similarities in the handwriting. I don’t keep them all. Only the ones that touch me in some way. In fact, Gina and I did a special about how feedback from viewers added a richness to our work.” She smiled; his pulse reacted. “We each shared things about ourselves that viewers could hopefully relate to. It was one of the most watched local programs last year.”

Her bedroom windows were secure. He stepped into the en suite bath. The only window was one of the half-moon types above the shower and it didn’t open. Like the rest of her home, the bathroom was organized and well-appointed. The house was a traditional one-story brick in an upscale, older neighborhood. According to the background report Jess had given him, Amber had lived here since graduating college. She’d inherited the house from her grandmother.

He returned to the bedroom, where she waited in the middle of the room looking very much like a lost little girl. “You keep the fan mail here or at work?”

"Here." She opened the double doors leading to what he presumed would be the closet.

He hesitated in the doorway. The closet was almost as large as the bedroom with a sliding library-style ladder that provided access to the upper shelves that banded all the way around the space above the hanging clothes.

"The house used to have four bedrooms," she explained as she adjusted the ladder. "I used the fourth bedroom to expand the bathroom and for this closet."

"Looks like you made a smart move." He surveyed the rods and rods of clothes and the rows of shoes and whistled. "This could be a supermodel's closet."

"Ha-ha. Viewers notice if you wear the same outfit." She climbed up the ladder and reached for a box covered in a floral pattern resting on the first shelf.

"Let me take that." He stepped over to the ladder and reached up to take the box.

"I suppose you'd know a supermodel's closet when you saw one. My sister told me you were a bodyguard to the stars."

He accepted the box and waited for her to climb down the few rungs. "I may have seen one or two."

She pushed the ladder back into its storage position. "Don't be modest, Mr. Douglas. Barbara says you had quite the reputation in Hollywood as a top security specialist as well as a ladies' man."

Apparently she hadn't heard the whole story.

"Where do you want these?" He was damned ready to get out of her bedroom. Being surrounded by her scent and her private things in what now felt like a small space was too much.

"Kitchen table."

Rather than be a gentleman and wait for her to go first, he got the hell out of her closet and her bedroom. A few deep breaths and he still hadn't cleared her scent from his lungs. He shook off the uneasiness and placed the box on the round table that stood in the breakfast alcove of the kitchen.

The red and pink rose-patterned box wasn't a typical file storage size. Handholds were formed on each end. Judging by the weight, it was made of heavy-gauge cardboard. He'd noted several of varying sizes on the uppermost shelf of her closet. Some he recognized as photograph boxes. All were neatly arranged by size and color. His mother had similar tastes and organizing habits. From what he'd seen so far, his mother would like Amber.

He booted the concept out of his head. Maybe he needed more coffee. He was sure as hell having a hard time keeping his head on straight.

Amber joined him at the table. She pressed a hand to her flat belly and made a face.

"Look." He took her by the shoulders and turned her to face him. "I know you TV personalities don't like to eat for fear of gaining half an ounce, but you're going through some serious trauma right now. You need to eat."

Her green eyes were wide with surprise or indignation because he'd touched her or that he'd dared to give her an order or both. He released her and dropped his hands back to his sides.

"No need for strong-arm tactics, Mr. Douglas. I was just thinking that I needed to eat." She turned gracefully and marched to the refrigerator.

Strong-arm tactics? Well, at least she was smart enough to listen to good advice.

She pulled open the freezer drawer and selected a frozen dinner—the organic, calorie-conscious kind. While she removed the outer packaging, she flashed him a fake smile and said, "Take your pick. I highly recommend the pecan chicken and rice."

While she nuked her meal, he rummaged through the selection. He chose the pizza. The photo on the box looked normal enough, though he doubted one would ever be enough. The way his stomach was protesting, he could eat his weight in steak and potatoes about now.

"Water or coffee?" She grabbed a bottle of water from the fridge for herself.

"Water would be great."

Ten minutes later they were seated at the table with their little prepackaged meals—*little* being the operative word. The first bite of the pizza did two things. Burned the hell out of his mouth and confirmed that although it looked nothing like the one on the box, it tasted exactly like the box.

"Gina says you grew up in Birmingham." She twirled her fork in the noodles of her meal. She'd picked out the little chicken and broccoli chunks.

He imagined the noodles tasted somewhat similar to his pizza. "I did. When I graduated high school I went for a criminal justice degree. After that I headed out to Cali with my best friend. We both went to work for the LAPD. My friend's parents had divorced when he was a kid. His father promised him a job with the department if he wanted to move out to California after school."

"So you both became cops?"

He tore off another chunk of the tasteless pizza and nodded. "Two years later the top personal security team in the LA area offered me a position with a salary I couldn't refuse."

"You must have done something to grab their attention?" She smiled, and his pulse executed another of those crazy dips.

"I might have saved a couple of lives in a nightclub shoot-out while off duty and without a firearm." He shoved the last of the pizza into his mouth to prevent having to say more. The doped-up ex-husband who'd come after his wife in a crowded club with a cocked and loaded nine millimeter had every intention of killing anyone in the room with her. There hadn't been time to think, only to act.

Sean had thrown himself at the guy. Two shots had hissed by his head, close enough to have him wishing he'd gone to church a little more often. Clips from the club's security cameras had played on all the local networks and even a couple of national ones for days. The notoriety had bothered him. He'd done the right thing. Maybe that might have made him a hero to some.

"Had you always envisioned yourself as a bodyguard to the stars?" Amber set her fork aside and sipped her water.

"Never crossed my mind until they knocked on my door."

"What was it like? Are the big stars as difficult to work with as the gossip rags suggest?"

He really didn't want to talk about his past. Things always ventured into the territory he still couldn't revisit. The only reason he hadn't changed the subject already was because she looked relaxed for the first time since they'd met.

"Stars are like anyone else. You've got the nice ones, and you've got the jerks. They put on their pants the same way you and I do."

"According to Gina, you're the best."

He pushed back from the table and stood. "Your friend might have exaggerated just a little." He carried his plate to the sink and rinsed it before depositing it into the dishwasher. Amber did the same with her bowl and fork.

"We need a notepad or something to list the names of the people who've written to you repeatedly." He moved back to the table. The sooner they focused on the reason he was here, the quicker she would forget about all the questions she appeared to have for him. Not that he had expected anything less from the lady. Amber might not be a big-screen celebrity, but she was damned sure a big star in Birmingham. "Anyone who seems overly interested in your career or you as a person is what we're looking for."

She opened a drawer and came up with a notepad and pen.

"We should talk about your neighbors," he went on. "Friends. Ex-boyfriends. Former girlfriends. Anyone who knows your routine. Anyone who knows you well enough to have a handle on your likes and dislikes. Paradise Peach tea, for instance. Who would know about your taste in tea?"

When she'd settled back at the table, she placed the pen next to the pad and looked him straight in the eye. "My sister and my parents. My colleagues at work. None of them would do this any more than I would. Most of my neighbors are the same ones who lived here when my grandmother was still alive. They're older, and I've known them forever. I have no former girlfriends. I only have current ones."

"No fallings-out. No estrangements of any kind?"

"There are people with whom I've lost touch, but nothing like you're suggesting."

"What about ex-boyfriends? Even the one-night stands—especially the one-night stands."

"I don't do one-night stands, Mr. Douglas. This is not Hollywood."

"But it is the twenty-first century. Even people in Alabama do one-night stands, Ms. Roberts."

"Not this person." Her eyebrows shot up her forehead. "And before you jump to that conclusion, I'm not a prude, either."

"Ex-boyfriends?"

"We talked about this already."

He exhaled a big breath and reached for patience. "I need more details."

"There have been three."

Did she just say three? "Three?" he echoed.

She gave him a sharp look that answered the question. "One in high school. We started dating when we were freshmen. We broke up when we went our separate ways to college. He's married with three children and lives in Wyoming. My second boyfriend was in college. He decided he wanted to travel the world before settling down. To my knowledge he's still doing so. Last year I broke up with the man to whom I'd been engaged for two years."

"Please tell me you dated a few guys in between."

"A few. Yes. I was very busy with my education and then with building my career, Mr. Douglas."

"Sean," he countered. "The Mr. Douglas thing makes me feel old."

"I certainly wouldn't want to make you feel old, *Sean*," she acquiesced.

Like every other ridiculous reaction he'd experienced since coming into her home, the sound of his first name on those pink lips disrupted the rhythm of his pulse again. "The ex-fiancé has no reason to want to cause you trouble?"

She sent him a look. "Killing a man and leaving my panties in his bed is a little more than causing me trouble—wouldn't you say?"

He nodded. She had him there. "I'll take that as a no."

"We broke up because he confessed that he'd never stopped loving his college sweetheart. They're married with a baby on the way. They live in Mobile. I'm certain I'm the last person on his mind these days."

The guy must have been a total idiot.

Sean cleared his throat and his head. "That leaves us with strangers." More often than not, crimes of this nature were committed by an intimate, but not always. Occasionally strangers formed fantasy relationships or attachments with high-profile personalities. Once in a while those bonds led to murder.

"Okay." She stood, took the lid from the box and set it aside. "I have quite a few letters and cards here." She reached inside and lifted a mound of envelopes. She placed them on the table. She reached into the box once more and stalled. “What in the world?” Her eyes widened with horror. “Oh, my God.”

Sean moved to her side. In the box, amid the stacks of envelopes addressed to Amber Roberts, was a knife. Nothing elaborate or exotic, just a stock kitchen butcher knife, with an eight- or ten-inch blade covered in dried blood.

It was time to call his boss.

Chapter Four

Birmingham Police Department, 6:15 p.m.

Captain Vanessa Aldridge stared directly at Amber. "You want me to believe that you just happened to have a knife from the victim's kitchen in your home. A knife, I might add, that is covered in his blood."

The head of the Crimes Against Persons Division had asked Amber this same question several different ways over the past three hours. The lab had confirmed the blood on the knife was in fact Kyle Adler's. The knife apparently was part of a set from his home. Dear God, how had this happened? Why would anyone do this to her? Her home had been searched by the forensic team for any other potential evidence. It was all completely insane.

"Your prints are on the knife handle, Ms. Roberts."

Amber blinked. Her mind wouldn't stay focused on the moment.

"Of course her prints are on the handle," Teller countered. "She touched it while she was searching through a box of saved fan mail."

"Do you have some way of proving her prints weren't already there?" Aldridge argued.

"Do you have some way of proving they were?" Teller fired back. "I have no burden to prove anything, as you well know. You're the one who needs to prove your accusations. And unless you can do that, Captain Aldridge, I would suggest you stop harassing my client."

Amber felt sick. "I have never seen that knife before. I have no idea how it got in my house."

Teller put his hand on her arm to silence her. He didn't want her to make any spontaneous remarks. Only the prepared ones they had discussed before this meeting. This was wrong. All of it. And it was escalating. She was terrified at the idea of what might happen next. It felt surreal, like someone else's life was spiraling out of control.

"You have a security system. Who else knows the access code?" Aldridge demanded for the third time.

"My client is uncertain of the answer," Teller replied without hesitation.

"You don't recall who you gave something as important as your security code? An old boyfriend? An associate from work? You can't expect me to believe you have no idea who else might have access to your own home."

The captain stared directly at her, ensuring Amber understood the questions and comments were meant for her regardless of the attorney seated beside her. Amber merely stared back. She'd already answered those questions. Teller had reminded her repeatedly not to allow Aldridge to drag her into a discussion. The captain's job, according to Teller, was to trip Amber up and make her say something she didn't mean. The truth was, Amber couldn't have answered at the moment even if Teller had wanted her to. Some level of shock had descended, and she couldn't think quickly enough to piece together a proper response.

"Ms. Roberts, I'm aware your attorney is supposed to work in your best interest, but frankly I'm concerned as to why he feels compelled to answer for you—if you have nothing to hide."

Teller launched a protest.

Amber held up her hands. "Are we done here?" They had been at this for three hours. Her answers weren't going to change whether she gave the prepared ones or the ones straight from her heart—assuming she could get the right words out. "Or do you plan to arrest me?"

Aldridge laid one hand atop the other on the table and smiled. "We're done for now, but rest assured, Ms. Roberts, we will be speaking again. Soon, so don't leave town."

Amber wanted out of this room. She tried to slow her racing heart, tried to still her churning stomach. *Who would do this?* The question echoed in her brain. She could think of no one who wanted to hurt her this way.

Captain Aldridge walked to the door, glancing over her shoulder one last time before exiting. The silence that ensued left Amber feeling hollow and alone.

"Let's get you home."

Amber followed Teller's prompts and exited the interview room. Douglas—Sean waited in the corridor.

"We're going out the back," he said to Teller.

Teller nodded. "I'll go out the front and hopefully keep the media entertained long enough to allow the two of you to escape.

Escape. Amber had been one of those reporters more times than she could count. Desperate to get the story. Determined to discover what the person in the spotlight was hiding. Certain the police were holding back crucial information.

"No." Amber shook her head. "I'm not running from the press."

Teller urged her to listen to reason as they boarded the elevator. She ignored him. As the doors opened into the lobby, he launched a final plea. "I can't do my job if you don't cooperate. Every step you take makes an impression. If this case goes to trial, the jury will be made up of people who watch the news and read the paper."

Amber had had enough. She turned to him. "I'm certain you'll be able to do your job under whatever circumstances arise, Frank."

Teller held up his hands and backed off. "I've said my piece."

As she approached the main entrance, Sean pulled her close. "I'm not going to try to talk you out of something you're obviously intent on doing, but we will do it my way." Her gaze locked with his as he went on. "You will stay right beside me. You will not reach out to anyone who reaches toward you. You will stay focused on moving forward while giving whatever responses you intend to give quickly and concisely."

His eyes and the stony set of his jaw warned there would be no changing his mind. Unable to do otherwise, Amber nodded her agreement.

"Good. Let's do this." He pushed through the door, moving her along with confident strides.

Lights flashed and questions were hurled at her. As Sean had predicted, hands extended toward her. Amber felt as if she were being pulled in every direction. The few faces she recognized blurred with the many she did not.

"Amber, did you murder Kyle Adler?"

"Amber, have you been arrested?"

"Amber, were you and Kyle involved?"

She wanted to answer. Her feet stumbled, and her tongue felt tied. Her heart pushed into her throat.

"Give us your side, Amber!" a vaguely familiar voice shouted.

Behind her, Teller assured the crowd that Amber had not been arrested and was not involved with Kyle Adler. He firmly stated that she certainly had not murdered him.

Sean pushed his way through the microphones and the cameras stretching toward them. Amber moved along in his wake, able to remain upright and progress forward only because he held tightly to her arm.

They reached his car, and suddenly she was in the passenger seat. He slid behind the wheel, and they started to roll slowly through the seemingly endless crowd. The situation was completely alien to her. She felt lost and uncertain. This was what she did every day. How could she feel so completely out of place on this side of the story? Where was her professional training? Where was her courage? She should have answered those questions. She should have looked directly into the camera and told the world that she was innocent no matter what Sean or Teller told her to do.

How many times had she watched someone do exactly what she just did and doubted the veracity of his or her claims of innocence?

People watching the news would think precisely that about her. They would believe she'd killed a man. They would believe she knew all the tricks to avoid being found guilty because she was a reporter.

They would believe she was lying because her job was to spin stories into the kind of news viewers couldn't resist.

"I'm telling the truth." She turned to Sean as he accelerated, leaving the horde of reporters behind. "I *am* telling the truth."

He glanced at her. "I believe you."

Did anyone else?

"We're going to the office," he explained as he made the next turn. "My boss wants to speak with you."

Amber managed a nod. His boss was former deputy chief Jess Burnett. Gina trusted her. Amber had been working her way up the ranks when Jess first returned to Birmingham. She remembered the buzz about the FBI's top profiler helping with the Murray case. No one would ever forget how serial killer Eric Spears had followed Jess here. Amber had read the stories about her and how she could find the face of evil when no one else could.

Please let her be able to find this one.

Fourth Avenue North

"AMBER, I KNOW this is unsettling."

Amber produced a smile for Jess Burnett. "I never thought I'd say this, but yes, this is terrifying." Had she been such a coward all this time?

"Being the target of breaking news is far different

from finding the breaking news. Trust me on that one," Jess assured her.

Certainly the former profiler would know. Amber remembered well when Jess had been the target of those who thought she'd brought evil to town with her—that she was on some level partially responsible for the heinous murders committed by Eric Spears and his followers.

"I appreciate that you understand," Amber confessed. "What I really want to hear is that you can help prove I'm telling the truth. I don't think Captain Aldridge believes me."

"We'll do all we can—you have our word on that," Buddy Corlew assured her.

Buddy sat next to Jess. Amber knew a little about him, as well. He'd grown up in a rough neighborhood and he'd beaten the odds. He'd served in the military and the Birmingham Police Department. Even when his career as a detective had tanked, he'd built a thriving private investigation agency. The man was a fighter as well as the new husband of the recently named Jefferson County medical examiner.

If the people in this room couldn't help her prove her innocence, Amber felt reasonably confident she was screwed.

Next to her Sean shifted in his chair as if he'd read her mind and recognized that she had left him out of her deduction. Bearing in mind that they'd found a bloody knife in her house—which confirmed beyond all doubt that someone had been in her home without her knowledge—she was pretty damned sure she needed him, too. And her attorney, Frank Teller, was the best. Amber would need them all to get through this nightmare.

"We didn't invite Teller to this meeting," Corlew said, "since what we're about to tell you is off the record and he doesn't need to know about it. For now."

Was she thinking out loud or were they all mind readers? Amber took a breath and forced the crazy thought aside. She needed to calm down and focus. "I understand."

"Buddy and I have contacts inside the department, and they've shared details with us that Captain Aldridge might not be ready to disclose at this time," Jess explained. "However, none of what we're about to tell you is breaking the law. We're only bending it a bit."

"I'm grateful for any insights into what the captain is thinking." The woman gave every indication of being on a witch hunt. Amber had pondered the possibility that this was the captain's opportunity to get back at the press. Since taking over as head of Crimes Against Persons, she had been cast in a bad light more often than not.

"I've had the opportunity to review the findings by the evidence technicians," Jess began, "as well as the lead detective's assessment." She turned to a new page in her notepad. "The victim's home is meticulously organized and painstakingly clean. No journal or personal notes were discovered, but I've asked the detective to have another look for any items that may be connected to other ongoing or unsolved cases."

Tension coiled inside Amber. "You believe he may have been involved in some sort of illegal activity?"

Jess hesitated but only for a moment. "The china teacups found on his table were the only pieces in that pattern found in his home." She removed a photo from a folder and passed it to Amber. "I've blown up the photo provided by the lead detective on the case. Look closely at the pattern. Is it possible those teacups and saucers came from your home?"

Amber studied the image, and her breath caught. She hadn't been able to see the pattern very well in the photos Teller had shown her. "This is my grandmother's china." Her heart pounded. "He or someone he knew was in my house." *Maybe more than once*, she realized as she thought of the knife.

Jess nodded. "Now we're getting somewhere."

Amber looked from Jess to the photo and back. "What does this mean?"

"It means," Sean interjected, drawing her attention to him, "that *you* have been a victim without even knowing it."

He was right. She'd been so focused on finding something that would prove she was telling the truth that she hadn't considered herself a victim.

"Kyle Adler may have been obsessed with you,"

Jess explained. "He may have come into your home on numerous occasions. He has no criminal record, but we're operating under the assumption that he simply hadn't been caught. His need to have something of yours may have caused him to cross the line, ultimately perhaps drawing him into association with the person who murdered him."

Amber looked from Jess to Sean and back. "So it's possible his killer may have saved my life. Is that what you're suggesting?"

"In some perverted way perhaps," Jess agreed. "Envy may have driven him or her. The unknown subject—unsub—may have been Adler's lover who learned of his obsession with you and killed him in a fit of rage. When your name and face hit the news as a person of interest in the case, this person may have put the knife in your house to further implicate you as the murderer. Or if he or she was working with Adler all along, the knife may have been in your home since the day it was used as a murder weapon."

"How could he or she have known I would look in that particular box?"

"The choice was too specific to believe it's a mere coincidence," Jess agreed. "At this point my opinion would be that the unsub took his time and selected a place that wouldn't be too obvious to the police but wouldn't go unnoticed by you. Does anyone else know about the box of fan mail you keep in your closet?"

Amber started to say no, but the memory of the special she and Gina had done stopped her. "Gina and I did a special." She looked at Sean. "I told you about it earlier." To Jess she said, "We both shared a little about how our professional and personal lives intersect. I talked about the letters and..." Amber sighed. "And how I kept them in a lovely box on a shelf in my closet."

Jess nodded. "He was watching. He's using all he knows about you to frame you for murder."

"He's certainly done a top-notch job so far." Every piece of evidence in the case pointed to her as the murderer. How could her entire life be turned upside down in less than twenty-four hours?

"With your permission," Jess said, "the detective in charge of the case wants to have a couple of evidence techs go through your house a second time to see if they can pick up any overlooked prints left by the victim or any other potential unsub." Jess removed her reading glasses and placed them on her desk. "It's a long shot, but we shouldn't ignore the possibility that one or both may have been in your home many times."

Amber held up her hands. "I have no problem with them turning my house upside down if it helps find the real killer."

"There's always the possibility," Corlew warned, "they'll find more planted evidence that could hurt your case. You might want to run this by Teller before you commit."

Amber pressed her hand to her lips. She hadn't thought of that scenario. She shook her head. "I have nothing to hide. If something else has been hidden in my home, I want to know."

Jess nodded. "All right. I'll let Sergeant Wells know. She'll call Sean in the morning with a time."

"Meanwhile," Sean spoke up again, "I have a locksmith at your house changing the locks as we speak. As soon as we get back there, you should change your access code and your password for your security system."

Amber's head was spinning again. "I've never given anyone—not even my own parents—the access code or password to my security system. At least not that I can remember."

"There are other ways," Corlew assured her. "Perps can order electronic equipment on the internet that overrides or breaks access codes."

"Which is another reason," Jess cut in, "we believe the person who murdered Adler and planted the evidence in your home has done this before. He's too smooth to be a first timer."

Amber thought of the man Kyle Adler. She couldn't recall ever seeing him except for the occasional delivery. On those occasions he'd always seemed so kind and shy. His was not a face she would have associated with evil.

Sean spoke up again. “Does your station keep the original footage from your assignments or just the part that doesn’t end up on the cutting room floor—so to speak.”

“The station stores the footage that airs, but not the raw footage before it’s edited.” Hope welled in her chest. “My cameraman may keep all the raw footage. I can check with him.”

“If Adler was watching you,” Sean offered, “we might find him in the crowd wherever you were reporting breaking news. It’s worth a shot.”

Jess agreed.

Amber couldn’t believe she hadn’t thought of checking the footage. She had to clear her head and focus. Her future depended on how this turned out. She could spend the rest of her life in prison or end up on death row. Worse, a murderer could get away with his heinous act.

“Go home, Amber,” Jess said. “Try to get some rest, but don’t clean your house tonight,” she added with a smile.

“Don’t worry.” Amber stood. “I won’t touch anything I don’t have to touch.”

“Good idea,” Jess granted.

As they left the building, Sean exited ahead of her. He scanned the street and checked his car before motioning for her to cross the sidewalk and climb in. He closed her door and went around to the other side. Dusk had the street lamps flickering on against the coming darkness. She closed her eyes and leaned fully into the seat. This day couldn't be over soon enough for her.

When the car moved down the street, she opened her eyes and turned to the driver. "Do you really believe we'll be able to find all the pieces of this puzzle?"

He glanced at her. "Don't worry—we'll find him."

Amber stared out at the darkness. "I hope so."

She didn't want the next story about a person who spent years in prison before being exonerated to be about her.

Chapter Five

Hugo L. Black United States Courthouse
1729 Fifth Avenue North
Tuesday, October 18, 10:30 a.m.

Sean did not like this one bit. He'd had no sleep since Amber had paced the floors most of the night. She'd insisted that was what she did when she battled insomnia. She'd also insisted he should take one of the bedrooms and just ignore her.

Impossible.

The loose fit of the pink flannel pajamas showed nothing of her curves or all that pale, creamy skin. There wasn't one thing sexy about the overly modest sleeping apparel, and still he couldn't keep his mind off her. At one point he'd even covered his head with the pillow. The move hadn't helped an iota.

He'd opted to sleep on the sofa since the layout of the family room and kitchen gave him a view of both the front and rear doors. The house was an older one, but it had been renovated at some point, opening up the main living space. The locks had been changed and her security system had a new access code and password.

First thing this morning she had informed him that she had to get back to work. She wouldn't discuss taking a vacation. She had ongoing assignments, she'd insisted. Apparently last night's insomnia had evolved into today's determination to pretend nothing had happened.

Three cups of coffee and one caramel latte later and Amber was rushing around the station prepping for the McAllister assignment. On the way to the federal courthouse, she'd explained that Forrest McAllister had been the go-to guy for investments by the who's who of Birmingham for many years. Eight months ago he'd been charged with insider trading. Now that same who's who were doing all within their power to distance themselves from the man. His trial started today.

Sean had heard something about the big story, but he hadn't followed it. Apparently, he was going to now.

Watching Amber wasn't a hardship. The blue skirt and sweater she wore today fit her petite body perfectly. Her hair hung in soft waves, and those cute little freckles were faintly visible across the bridge of her nose.

Get your head back on the job, man. The cameraman had promised to dig through the work they'd done together. He couldn't promise he had anything Amber was looking for. Her first cameraman had retired more than a year ago. She hadn't been able to reach him yet. Sean intended to remind her to fol low up with both men later today.

Vehicles sporting the logos of television stations and newspapers from all over the southeast ringed the block. Security had the courthouse locked down. The street, however, was brimming with people—mostly newshounds. Between the horde of reporters, the occasional helicopter overhead and the blaring horns of frustrated drivers attempting to navigate Fifth Avenue, the situation was a security specialist's worst nightmare.

There was no way to cover every direction from which trouble could come. He was left with no recourse but to stay as close as possible to his client. Sweat lined his brow. He felt as if he were guiding a rocker client through the crowd for a sold-out concert. It never ceased to amaze him how many megastars felt the need to brush shoulders with thousands of fans despite the risk that one of them might be a wacko. Sean had navigated the crowds, ever watchful and barely breathing. Like now. His senses were on full alert. Adrenaline had his heart in the fight-or-flight zone. Every muscle was tense, ready to react to the first sign of trouble.

The hearing had started at nine. Since the date

and time of the hearing had been a closely guarded secret, the reporters following the case had missed McAllister's arrival. Word had traveled like wildfire as soon as the man was spotted entering the courthouse. Now they all waited for his exit and any sound bite his team of attorneys would permit to slip. Amber had managed a spot right up front, near the steps into the building. In the event of trouble, maneuvering through the crowd behind them would not be an easy task. Just his luck.

Suddenly, the towering entrance doors opened and a group of men exited. Sean recognized the main player from the shots he'd seen on the news and in the papers. The suits all around him were a combination of security and lawyers. The difference was easy to spot; the lawyers carried the briefcases while the others wore communication devices in their ears and constantly scanned the area around their client.

As if floodgates had been opened, the rush of reporters swelled into a tide of bodies, microphones and cameras. Sean wrapped his fingers around Amber's left forearm to keep her close. Intent on getting some word on how the hearing turned out, she ignored his move. Questions were hurled at the group exiting the building. Amber's was the loudest voice. For such a petite woman, she had a set of pipes and she knew how to use them.

The cameraman slipped in front of Sean, blocking his view forward. Sean held tighter to Amber and elbowed his way between her and the big guy.

Once the group reached the sidewalk, the crush of bodies was too close for comfort. Sean didn't like this. He angled his body to stay close to Amber. She stretched toward her target.

The huddle of security guards and lawyers abruptly stopped. McAllister stepped forward. A hush fell over the crowd of reporters. "Today was the first step in proving my innocence," he announced. "See you next week."

As soon as he was swallowed by his guards, the attorneys shouted, "That's all for today!"

Amber twisted to face her cameraman. "Did you get that?"

"Got it," the man fondly known as Bear assured her.

"Let's find a quiet place and do a lead-in," Amber directed.

Before Sean could suggest they get the hell off the street, she was climbing the steps to the building's entrance. She took a position and smoothed a hand over her hair.

"Hair and makeup are good," the cameraman assured her. "We are live in the studio in ten, nine..."

As he counted down, Sean scanned the crowd that had followed McAllister to the waiting limos. Behind him, Amber delivered a thirty- or forty-second overview of the case and introduced this morning's hearing results. When she signed off the air, Sean was able to breathe again.

The position they were in was far too open, not to mention they were backed against a wall—literally. No overt threats to Amber's life had been posed, but his orders were to assume the worst. If the attempts to frame her for murder failed, the perp might very well choose a different strategy.

"Can we get out of here now?" Sean asked as the cameraman packed up his equipment.

"We can." Amber moved toward him. "There's a clerk inside I want to follow up with first."

As long as they were off the street, Sean would be happy.

"See you at the station," Bear tossed over his shoulder as he hustled away.

Sean reached to open the door for her as a dozen or so of the reporters who'd only moments ago been hanging on McAllister's every move were suddenly closing in on them. He stepped in front of Amber.

"Amber, is it true the murder weapon was found in your home?" the nearest reporter shouted.

Sean turned his head and whispered to her, "Go inside. Now."

"Did they find your prints on the weapon?" another voice shouted.

"If you didn't know the victim as you claim, can you explain how this happened?"

"Were you and Kyle Adler having an affair?"

More questions speared through the crisp morning air. Rather than go inside, Amber stood stone still, staring at the people who were her colleagues—colleagues determined to get the story even if it meant turning on one of their own.

"What about those red panties they found in his bed?" a man accused as he moved to the front of the horde. "Are you going to deny they're yours?"

Sean didn't wait for Amber to react. He opened the door and dragged her inside. Two security guards immediately stopped them.

"We have a meeting," Sean announced, hoping Amber would snap out of her coma and get them past these guys.

"Paula Vicks," she said, her voice shaky. "She's expecting us."

After passing through security, Amber seemed to regain her composure. They moved to the elevators and she selected a floor. Sean kept his mouth shut as the car shuttled them upward. The elevators, like every other part of the building, would be monitored by security.

The elevator bumped to a stop, and the doors opened. She took a right down the corridor, and he eased up close beside her. "You okay?"

"Why wouldn't I be?"

He wasn't going to touch that one. "Good."

She seemed to square her shoulders as she reached for the door. He followed her inside. A woman about

Amber's age, tall and thin with blond hair and brown eyes, was waiting. She shepherded them into a small office and closed the door.

"I can't talk to you about the McAllister case, Amber. I can't talk to you about anything."

Amber appeared surprised. "What's going on, Paula?"

"Rumor is you're about to be charged with murder. I've taken too many risks giving you tidbits already. Anything or anyone related to you is about to come under intense scrutiny. I can't be a part of that. I'm sorry."

Amber nodded. "I understand. If you can just tell me the date of the next hearing on the McAllister case, we'll leave it at that."

"A week from today. Same time."

"Thanks." Amber exited Paula's office without another word.

Sean kept his mouth shut until they were back in the first-floor lobby. The tension radiating from Amber said loads. This ugly business had just trickled into her career. For a woman whose career came first, this new reality was devastating. Outside the reporters had thankfully vanished. They reached his car without incident.

Once they were inside, he asked, "Where to now?"

"My office. I need to dig up everything I can find on Kyle Adler."

"Then we need to go to Corlew's office instead."

Amber hesitated at the door he'd opened. "I thought your firm had already given me everything they had on Adler."

Sean shrugged. "You have everything obtained through the usual channels. It's time we checked out a few others."

When she didn't argue, Sean closed her door and rounded the hood. He'd call Corlew en route. If Corlew's contacts couldn't find it, it didn't exist.

The Garage Café, Tenth Terrace South, 11:15 a.m.

SEAN WAS NO stranger to the Garage, but Buddy Corlew considered the place his conference room. He held more meetings here than he did at the office. This particular meeting couldn't be held at the office anyway. Jess knew Buddy skirted the law from time to time, he'd done it for years as a PI before he and Jess formed their partnership. Jess, being the boss, had one rule: never break the law. So Buddy conducted whatever business Jess might not approve of here.

Buddy acknowledged their entrance with a nod. Sean ushered Amber to his table. She had asked a lot of questions on the way, and he'd assured her that Buddy could answer just about anything she wanted to know. Sean worried that no one was asking the right questions. To some degree the dilemma was understandable. At this point, the motive for Adler's murder was unclear. The motive for framing Amber was even foggier.

Buddy stood as Amber took the chair Sean pulled out. “I saw you on the news a little while ago.” Buddy gestured to the screens hanging around the bar. “You think McAllister is innocent?”

Amber smiled, looking relaxed for the first time this morning. “I do not, but that conclusion is based primarily on the fact that I just don’t like him.” She leaned forward. “If you tell anyone I said that, I’ll make my next exposé about you, Mr. Corlew.”

Buddy held up his hands. “No worries here. I’ve never met a woman who could tolerate a man who gave her secrets away.”

“What about Kyle Adler’s secrets?” she asked.

Sean wasn’t surprised. The lady had built a career on getting straight to the point. He’d seen her falter a bit the past twenty-four hours, but she didn’t give up.

“Mr. Adler was a strange one.” Buddy rested his forearms on the table, leaning in a little closer. “He didn’t go to college and still he was twenty-seven before he held a steady job and moved out of his parents’ basement. He rented a small home over on Eagle Ridge Drive about two years ago. He made a living delivering *things*.”

“Things besides flowers and dry cleaning?” Amber asked.

She stood by her certainty that the few times Adler had shown up at her door to make a delivery he hadn't come inside. Sean had pressed her to consider whether or not she'd ever turned her back for even a few moments. Had she gone to get a tip from her purse in the other room? Even a couple of minutes could have given him the opportunity he needed to make a move.

"Groceries, prescriptions, flowers, dry cleaning, you name it," Buddy said in answer to her question. "Your books overdue at the library? Just give him a call, and he would pick them up and drop them off for you. But he made his real money driving folks home from the clubs and bars around town."

A waitress appeared and took their orders. Buddy insisted they have lunch on him. Amber hadn't eaten that morning. After seeing what she kept in her fridge and cabinets, Sean expected her to order a salad. A woman as tiny as she was couldn't possibly eat more than a spoonful at a time anyway. She surprised him by ordering a burger, fries and a regular cola. Maybe she felt the need for carbs. He damned sure did. He'd been starving all morning.

"Did Adler ever drive you home?" Sean asked once the waitress was on her way.

Amber shook her head. "Absolutely not. I haven't spent much time on the club scene in years. Occasionally I meet friends or colleagues at a bar, but I always leave under my own steam."

Buddy pulled a folded piece of paper from his shirt pocket. "I compiled a list of the businesses he operated from the most frequently." He passed the list to Amber. "It's possible your encounters with him may have been more frequent than you realize. We shouldn't rule out anything. Start with that list and compile your own. Any deliveries, pickups, drives to the airport or to pick up your car after it was serviced, whatever you can think of that required assistance from another person."

She studied the list. "I recognize a number of these business. The dry cleaner." She pointed to another name. "The alteration shop. Still, I'm certain I've never seen him beyond a couple of flower deliveries and I think something from the dry cleaner's that once."

"We can't ignore the possibility that he disguised himself when he was delivering to you," Buddy countered. "You may not have recognized him."

"Oh." Amber frowned as she surveyed the list again. "I hadn't thought of that."

Buddy was right. If Adler was obsessed with Amber so much that he went to such extremes to be close to her, the possibilities for encounters were endless. "It's a little like looking for a needle in a haystack," Sean commented.

"It's a lot like looking for a needle in a haystack," Buddy agreed. "You just have to remember that the haystack can come apart the same way it went together, one row at a time."

"Has the BPD turned over any of the inventory

lists of things found in his home or vehicle?" Sean looked from the list of businesses to Buddy. "It would seem to me they'd find the tools of his trade. Anything he used to get into houses like Amber's. Disguises, if he used them."

"Jess received a list from Lori Wells, the lead detective on the case," Buddy said to Amber, "but there wasn't the first tool or electronic gadget one would need for breaking into a house found."

Uncertainty nudged Sean. "Then he has to have a secondary go-to place. A storage unit or somewhere he keeps his gear."

"Or a somebody," Buddy countered. "The more Jess and I learn about this guy, the less we feel he was capable of anything worse than stalking."

"If we can't find the motive or the killer, the only way his murder makes sense—" Amber met Sean's gaze before shifting her attention to Buddy and going on "—is if we were friends or lovers and I killed him."

Her words hung in the air as the waitress delivered their drinks. When she'd gone, Amber continued, "The problem is, I hardly knew him. He's a face I barely recall. A smile of appreciation for a good tip after making a delivery."

"Did Detective Wells mention whether or not Adler had a cell phone and if they'd subpoenaed the records?" Sean suspected the BPD was already working on any cell phones and social media Adler used.

"They have," Buddy confirmed. "But it'll take

a few days with all the hoops they have to jump through." He grinned. "I, on the other hand, have my own source. We'll have his phone records by morning."

"I'm impressed, Mr. Corlew," Amber said. "I guess Gina was right when she said B&C was the best."

Buddy gave her a pointed look. "First, no one calls me mister anything. It's Buddy. And second, just make sure you remember that my methods for being the best are trade secrets."

Amber smiled, the confident, relaxed expression she wore whenever she was on camera. Sean was glad to see it.

"You have my word, Buddy. I'm putting all my trust in you." She glanced at Sean when she spoke. "The two of you," she amended.

Sean would not let her down. He wondered, though, if she knew the last woman he had been assigned to protect and who had trusted him had ended up dead.

Chapter Six

Thrasher Floral, Pearson Avenue, 3:10 p.m.

Amber wasn't entirely convinced about this route, but she had nothing to lose beyond a little time by taking it.

"Stick to your story," Sean reminded her. "Don't allow your emotions to get involved."

Amber's jaw dropped. He did not just say that to her. "Excuse me?"

How many years had she been reporting breaking stories? She'd waited for hours in the rain and freezing cold. She had followed leads into the darkest back streets and alleys of the Magic City. She had endured the latest trends in health, fitness and fashion. She never lost her cool or came unglued. Never.

At least not until today…

"You're a pro at digging into a story and finding the details," he offered. "This isn't just another story—this is *your* story. It might not be as easy to do."

"I've got this." Not about to debate the subject, she grabbed her bag and reached for the door. She'd barely opened it and gotten out when he moved up beside her.

"It wasn't my intention to offend you," he said as they crossed the sidewalk.

"You didn't," she lied.

He opened the door and a bell jingled. Inside the smell of flowers overwhelmed all else. As much as she loved receiving flowers, visiting a floral shop was one of her least favorite things to do. It always reminded her of funeral homes and the day she'd had to go with her mother to select flowers for her grandmother. Amber shuddered. She hated this smell.

Sean leaned closer. "You okay?"

She flashed him a frustrated smile. "I'm fine."

Who knew how annoying having a bodyguard could be? No wonder celebrities were always coming unhinged in public. What kind of life was this? Someone watching every move a person made? Ordering that person around for her own good?

Then again, she decided as she reached the counter, there was little chance of feeling afraid…or lonely. Sean Douglas paused next to her and sent her a sideways smile. Her heart bumped into a faster rhythm. Why in the world did her bodyguard have to be so damned handsome?

"Good afternoon," the clerk announced. "How may I help you?" She looked from Amber to Sean and back. "Do you have a special occasion coming up?"

Summoning her game smile, Amber glanced at her name tag. "Kayla, I'm Amber Roberts, and this is Sean Douglas. We're here to speak to Mr. Thrasher."

Kayla made an aha face. "Sure. He's in the back working on arrangements. I'll let him know you're here."

Amber thanked her as she disappeared through the staff-only door behind the counter. She'd researched the shop on the way here. Peter Thrasher was the owner. His mother had opened the shop forty years ago, nearly a decade before he was born. An old lifestyle interview from the *Birmingham News* during Thrasher's senior year in high school quoted him as saying flowers were his life. His mother had passed away the year before last. According to the obituary, she was preceded in death by her husband and Peter was her only child. If he had ever been married, Amber had found no announcement. Kyle Adler delivered flowers for only one floral shop, and this was the one.

The door opened once more and Peter Thrasher appeared. The six-foot-two man matched the few images she'd found in her Google search. His white button-down shirt sported the shop logo over the breast pocket. His brown hair was neatly trimmed and his brown eyes appeared overly large behind the black-rimmed glasses.

"Ms. Roberts." He gave her an acknowledging nod. "Welcome to my shop. How can I help you? I've just received a beautiful shipment of fall flowers. Gerber daisies, chrysanthemums and classic roses. I'm certain I have just what you're looking for."

"Sounds lovely." She reached into her purse and removed the photo of Kyle Adler she'd printed from her Google search last night. "I was hoping you could help me with a story I'm doing on Kyle Adler." She showed him the photo. "He was murdered a few days ago."

Thrasher looked from the photo to her. "I heard about his death." He gave a shrug, the gesture uncertain. "I also saw on the news that the police were talking to you about it."

"Did you know him?" Amber forged ahead despite the turmoil of abrupt emotions his words had stirred inside her. Maybe Sean had been right to warn her. This was not the same as chasing a story about someone else.

Thrasher nodded. "Not really. Not until he started his delivery service anyway. He was a friendly guy. Easygoing, quiet. It's a real shame, what happened to him."

"It really is," Amber agreed. "I want to do all I can to ensure justice for Mr. Adler."

Thrasher glanced at Sean. "Were you and Kyle… involved? I mean, after what I saw on the news last night…" His words trailed off as his gaze settled on Amber once more.

"I didn't know him. He delivered flowers from your shop to my home a couple of times. They were lovely, by the way." She searched Thrasher's face. "Did he ever mention me?"

Thrasher's expression turned defensive. "I see. You think he was some sort of stalker or obsessed fan."

"I don't think that at all," Amber denied. "I believe whoever killed Kyle is using me to get away with murder. I'm hoping that his friends and colleagues can help me find out who killed him."

"Isn't that what the police are supposed to do?" Thrasher stared at her expectantly.

Amber couldn't get a read on the man. Was he being indifferent or accusatory? His tone gave nothing away.

"Sometimes," Sean said, his tone undeniably pointed, "the police are too busy with other leads to see the real ones they need to follow. If you counted yourself a friend of Adler's, we're hoping you can help us find the truth."

"Anything you recall," Amber cut in, "might prove helpful. Did Kyle have any close friends that we might speak to?"

Thrasher stared at her for so long without saying a word, Amber was sure he wasn't going to answer.

"Kyle was a loner. He didn't have any friends that I know of."

"How well did you know him?" Sean pressed.

Thrasher visibly withdrew. His shoulders went back and he eased a few inches from the counter. "I really didn't know him. He made deliveries for me. He was quiet and reliable. That's all I know. I have work to do, so if you'll excuse me."

He had already turned and reached for the door when Amber said, "You seemed disturbed by the idea that I might consider Kyle a stalker or an obsessed fan." Thrasher hesitated but didn't turn around. "If you didn't know him very well, why would that bother you?"

Thrasher turned back to face her. Whatever he felt or thought, he had wiped his face clean of any reaction. "I don't like the idea of anyone being made to look bad when he's not here to defend himself," he said, his tone barely above freezing. "Have a nice day."

Amber mulled over his words as she and Sean exited the shop.

"Strange guy," Sean muttered as he opened her car door.

She turned back to the shop before getting into the car. "A little."

When she was settled into the passenger seat and Sean had climbed behind the wheel, he said, "He lied about his relationship with Adler."

Amber had sensed that, as well. Thrasher's defensive reaction had been his only slip. "The question is, does he simply not want to get involved or is he protecting his friend by not revealing some not-so-flattering secret?"

"You may have missed your true calling." Sean grinned. "Maybe you're the one who should be a PI."

4:15 p.m.

"THAT'S IT." AMBER POINTED to the alterations shop. "Martha Sews."

Sean maneuvered into a parking spot. The alterations shop had a great location in one of the city's oldest neighborhoods that had gone commercial. Martha's shop was near Mountain Brook among a row of small houses converted to businesses whose front yards served as parking lots. Unlike the other shop owners, Martha had maintained the lovely flowering shrubs that lined the foundation of the house. With rocking chairs on the front porch, the place still looked like a home. Amber doubted the owner, who continued to live in the house as well as to operate her business, knew Kyle Adler any better than she did, but no stone could go unturned.

Amber sighed. She still found it incredible that the facts she needed to find were to clear her name. How had this happened? Her gaze settled on the driver as he shut off the engine. How had he handled the situation when his life was turned upside down? At some point she wanted to ask him about Lacy James. There had been endless speculation about the relationship between the star and her bodyguard in the media after her death. Sean had never acknowledged or denied they were lovers. Ultimately her death had been ruled an accidental overdose. But not before Sean had been crucified by the media. Unfortunately, being targeted by the media was only the tip of the iceberg where Amber's troubles were concerned.

"We going in or what?"

Amber blinked and turned away from the scrutiny of his blue eyes. "Yes." She grabbed her bag and reached for the door. As usual he was out of the car and waiting for her as she emerged.

He closed her door. She said, "Thank you."

As they moved toward the shop, rather than dwell on how Thrasher's slightly odd behavior had rattled her, she tried to remember all she could about Sean. She'd heard about his disappearance from Hollywood. At the time, no one seemed to know where he'd gone. She had vaguely wondered if he'd returned home, but then another local story had come along and she'd forgotten all about the disgraced bodyguard and the deceased pop star. Funny how fate had a way of bringing things and people back around. Maybe she'd have the opportunity to get the real story from him. His side should be told.

He reached for the door to Martha Sews but hesitated before he opened it. "I don't give interviews, Amber."

Clearly she was wearing her every thought on her face for all to see. It was the only explanation for how everyone seemed to read her mind lately. "I don't know what you mean."

"Part of my job is to recognize what a person is thinking before they act."

She would have disagreed with his conclusion, but he opened the door for her to go inside. It wasn't as if she could refute his statement. She had been wondering about an interview. She was curious about the man charged with her safety. His credentials should be of concern. Except he worked for Jess Burnett, and that said it all.

Annoyed now, as much with herself as with him, she struggled to pull off a smile for the lady who emerged from the back of the shop to greet them. "Martha, how are you?"

"I'm just fine, Amber. How are you this lovely afternoon?" The older lady frowned. "Were you scheduled to pick up your dress today and I forgot?"

Amber had almost forgotten the dress herself. "No. I think that's Friday." How had she let the dress slip her mind? She had a huge fund-raising event on Friday night. Assuming she wasn't in jail.

Martha nodded as she glanced at Sean. "It's always nice to see one of my favorite customers. What can I do for you and your friend today?"

"Actually..." Amber stalled. She surveyed the retail side of the shop. Martha sold all sorts of vintage items as well as one-of-a-kind scarves and handmade jewelry. If Amber recalled correctly, most of the items were on consignment. The extra income tided her over when the alternations were slow. Amber doubted that happened very often anymore. "My friend—" she wrapped her arm around Sean's "—needs a vintage bow tie for a fund-raiser we're attending."

"I see." Martha beamed. "Does your friend have a name?"

Amber put her hand to her chest, feigning embarrassment but also because her heart was suddenly and foolishly pounding after touching him. "Of course. Martha Guynes, meet Sean Douglas."

Sean extended his hand. "Nice to meet you, Ms. Guynes."

Martha blushed. "Call me Martha. Everyone does."

"Martha," he said with such charm that even Amber melted a little more.

"Let me show you what I have, Sean." Martha directed them to the far left side of the small shop, where ties and handkerchiefs stocked a vintage display case. She moved behind the case and slid open a door. "Do you see one you like?"

While Sean perused the bow ties, Amber said, "I

was telling him you'd been in business more than a quarter of a century. Everyone who's anyone brings their alternation needs to you."

Martha gave a nod. "It seems like only yesterday that I was praying for some sort of answer from the good Lord. My husband had come home from a mission in the Middle East with undiagnosed PTSD. He drank all the time and was either deeply depressed and couldn't get out of bed or was on a rampage breaking things around the house." She sighed. "It was a hard time for me and our son."

Amber reached across the counter and touched her hand. "So many husbands and fathers returned with wounds no one but the immediate family could see."

Martha drew in a deep breath. "I was worried sick about just surviving. Since his troubles were undiagnosed, there was no money coming in. I had to find a way to make ends meet. I remembered back to the days before his illness when I would have coffee and play cards with the ladies from church. It never failed that when the holidays came around and folks needed costumes or clothes altered, Ruby Jean would say, 'Don't fret, girls. Martha sews.' I suddenly realized my old friend was right, and I opened this shop in my own living room. Here we are better than twenty-five years later."

"What an inspiring story," Amber said.

Martha shrugged. "We do what we have to do."

"I'll take that one," Douglas said, selecting a classic black bow tie that required hand tying.

"One of my favorites," Martha said. "It takes a man who knows what he's doing to get the bow just right."

"My father refused to wear a tie that came with a clip," Sean said. "I learned the art of hand tying at an early age."

"A sign of character and breeding," Martha said with a smile.

While Sean paid for his tie, Amber considered all the framed photos hanging around the room. Customers, including Amber, modeling Martha's work. Everyone she knew used Martha for her alterations. The lady was a household name.

"I was sorry to hear you're having some trouble," Martha said to Amber as she passed Sean a paper bag emblazoned with her sewing machine logo. "I swear, some reporters will make up anything for headlines. Anybody with one eye and half sense would know you wouldn't hurt a fly." She shook her head. "A disgrace, that's what it is."

Amber drummed up what she hoped was a passable smile. "Thank you. I'm sure the police will get to the bottom of what really happened."

Martha came around the counter and patted Amber on the arm. "You'll be in my prayers, hon."

"I appreciate that." Amber showed Martha the

photo of Adler. "I know he made deliveries for you. Did you know him well?"

Martha considered the question before answering. "He was reliable. Pleasant. He went out of his way to be helpful." She shrugged. "I can't imagine who would want to hurt him. He was such a shy fellow."

"Did he have a girlfriend?" He may have been a very nice man, but her panties and her grandmother's teacups had wound up in his house somehow. Amber kept that part to herself.

Martha crossed her arms over her chest then and pressed a finger to her cheek as if contemplating the question. "I thought he was a bit of a loner. If he had any friends or a girlfriend, I never saw or heard about them. Why do you ask?"

The few details the police had shared with Amber had not been released to the press, which meant she couldn't share those with Martha. "Curious, I suppose. I'm hoping to find someone who knew him well."

"Are you doing a story on his murder?"

Amber shook her head. "I'm looking for the truth. And maybe a few answers about why I'm a person of interest in the case. Maybe he was an obsessed fan. I don't know. I feel like there's something the police haven't seen."

"You know," Martha said, "now that you mention it, I do remember him stopping once to watch you." She gestured to the small television that sat on one end of her counter. “He picked up the deliveries for the day, and he noticed you on the screen. He didn’t move until the channel had returned to the regular program.”

“Do you recall when this happened?”

Martha shook her head. “I’m sorry. I don’t remember. A few weeks or so ago.”

“You’re certain he never mentioned any friends or places he frequented?”

“I think he played video games,” Martha offered. “He brought my son a new game now and then.” Her smile returned. “I think they spoke the same language when it came to video games.”

“How is Delbert?” Amber felt terrible she’d forgotten to ask Martha about her son. Delbert was wheelchair bound and very reclusive. His father had died in a car crash and then poor Delbert had been paralyzed in a football injury. Keeping a roof over their heads and food on the table were only parts of the burden Martha carried. Caring for a physically challenged child was incredibly difficult to do alone. Few could handle the stress, much less the workload of operating a thriving alterations shop.

“He’s doing well—thank you for asking. These days he helps me remember where I leave things and what I’m supposed to be doing. I’d be awfully lonesome without him.”

“Does Delbert know his friend is dead?”

“We talked about it. He’ll be a little more withdrawn than usual for a while." She sighed. "I'll just have to find another way to keep him entertained. Would you like to say hello? He'd be thrilled to see you. That boy thinks you're the prettiest thing."

Amber smiled. "I'd love to say hello."

Martha ushered them through her kitchen, where the scent of something wonderful emanated from the Crock-Pot. The house had originally been a three bedroom, but Martha had turned the larger of the three into a family room since the living room and dining room were lost to the business.

Delbert sat in his wheelchair in front of the television, his focus on winning the game playing out on the screen. The cozy room had Martha's touches all over it. Crocheted throws and framed needlepoint art. Amber often wondered if sewing was Martha's way of escaping reality. Everyone needed an outlet.

"Delbert, look who stopped by to see you," Martha cooed.

Her son looked up, his attention shifting to Amber. He smiled.

Amber moved closer to him and crouched down to his eye level. "One of these days I need to learn to play that game." She couldn't remember the name of it, but it was all the rage with gamers.

Delbert glanced from her to Sean. His smile faded, and he shut off the game and stared at the floor.

After several moments of silence, Martha offered, "We'll let you get back to your game."

"I'll see you next time, Delbert," Amber promised. Back in the shop, she said, "I hope Sean's presence didn't upset him."

"He'll be fine." To Sean, Martha said. "He's just not very good with strangers."

Delbert's story was such a sad one. Not long after the paralyzing injury he'd tried to take his own life with a drug overdose. He'd survived but the close encounter with death had left him with some amount of brain damage.

"I understand. I was in his territory. By the way," Sean went on, "do you know the name of the video game store where Mr. Adler shopped?"

"That place over on Riverview Parkway, I believe."

"Game Master?" Sean asked.

Amber was glad he knew about game shops. She knew nothing about video games and had no desire to learn. Several of her friends knew the lingo and all the newest games. They warned Amber that when she had kids she would have to learn. Since she had no prospects—even if she were interested—in a relationship, she doubted there would be children. Her gaze lingered on Sean. Did he want kids?

Where in the world had that thought come from? Had to be the stress. Her mind was playing games with her.

"That's the one," Martha confirmed. "I remember the bags." She frowned. "Do you think I should call that detective who questioned me and tell her about Kyle bringing those games to Delbert?"

"It could be significant," Amber advised. At this point anything could be significant. "We should be going. We've taken up too much of your time. I hope you'll call me if you think of anything else that might help us learn more about Mr. Adler's life."

"Of course." Martha shook her head. "It's such a senseless tragedy."

Amber prayed one tragedy didn't become two. One way or another they had to find Kyle Adler's killer.

When they were back in Sean's car and he'd driven out of the parking lot, he turned to Amber. "What's the story on her son?"

Amber gave him the details Martha had given her after they became friends. "He's completely reliant on his mother."

"I guess that takes him out of the suspect pool."

No kidding. "I can't see Delbert as a suspect even if his physical and mental challenges didn't exist." These were people Amber had known for years.

"You see—" Sean glanced at her "—that's where you'd fall down in your investigation."

She shook her head. "What're you talking about? What motive could that boy possibly have?"

"First, he's not a boy. He's a man. And just because he's in a wheelchair and dependent on his mother doesn't mean he doesn't think like a man."

"Okay. How is that motive?"

"It isn't, but *you* are."

Now she was totally confused.

"He lit up like a Christmas tree when he saw you," Sean explained. "His own mother said he adores you."

Amber frowned, understanding dawning. "Then he withdrew when he saw you."

"He also shut off his game. He didn't want to share anything with me. He closed me out."

"Are you really suggesting Delbert is a suspect?" *Please.* There was no way. Even if he did think like a man where she was concerned.

Sean flashed her a lopsided grin. "I'm just pointing out how easy it is to miss clues when you're emotionally involved. Like Mrs. Guynes's comment about Adler being shy. Still waters run deep."

"Point taken." Amber tamped down her frustration. She'd thought the same thing about Adler. Just another reminder that the face of evil rarely looked the way one expected. "What we do know is that according to the police report there was no evidence of forced entry, which suggests Adler knew his killer."

"I found no signs of forced entry at your place." Sean glanced at her again. "Someone still got in and left that bloody knife in your fan mail box for you."

"Good point." Amber stared out the window. "If the police don't find the killer, how will I prove I didn't do this?"

Sean braked for a light and settled his blue gaze on her once more. "More important, how will you ever be safe if we don't find the person who did this?"

Amber's hand went to her lips. He was right. As much as she wanted to pretend this tragedy wasn't about her, somehow it was. She was part of the motive that had caused Kyle Adler's death.

"Let's go back to who might want to hurt you," Sean suggested. "And how that person could connect to Kyle Adler."

Amber wished she knew.

THE VIDEO GAME store proved a waste of time. No one who worked there recognized Adler. Defeat had set in nice and deep by the time they pulled into her driveway. Amber stared at the house where she'd felt safe as far back as she could remember. The kitchen had always smelled of fresh-baked cookies. Her grandmother had made her feel as if this house were her home away from home.

How could she ever feel that way again knowing a killer had been in her house…had touched her things?

Would there be Channel Six viewers out there—or maybe even friends—who would forever believe she'd had something to do with this man's murder?

She felt as if some part of her identity had been stolen, leaving a hole she might not be able to repair as easily as Martha mended a failing hem or split seam. No matter that she was twenty-eight years old, she suddenly wished her parents were in town. She'd insisted they not rush back. If they learned about the knife, they would be very upset. She'd have to make sure Barb didn't tell them.

"Is it your birthday or something?"

Her gaze followed Sean's, landing on the vase of flowers waiting on her porch. "No." She started around the hood of the car, but he moved in front of her.

She waited at the bottom of the steps while he inspected the large bouquet of red roses. Who would send her roses? If they weren't from her parents, she had no idea. Though she couldn't fathom her parents finding now a good time to send her flowers. The station? A fan? She went to a great deal of trouble to ensure most of her personal information, including her address, was kept private.

Sean removed the small envelope from the bouquet and opened it. He read the card and then showed it to her. "Looks like you have another admirer."

I'm watching you.

The stamp on the back of the envelope was the Thrasher flower shop. Amber checked the time on her cell. "We might be able to get back there before the shop closes."

"Let's bag the card before we do anything else."

Amber hurried into the house and returned with a sandwich bag. "We have to hurry."

"Dodging traffic is one of my finer talents," he assured her as he carefully bagged the card and tucked it away.

When they were settled in the car and he'd started the engine, he glanced at her before taking off. "You might not want to watch."

Deciding to take him at his word, Amber closed her eyes. Unfortunately, the terrifying images her mind conjured about the man who'd been murdered and the one who'd been in her house—perhaps more than once—proved utterly disturbing.

Sean was right. A connection of some sort existed between her and Kyle and maybe between her and his killer. How on earth did she find it? She'd done enough investigative reporting to know if a person didn't want to be found, they wouldn't be. A serial killer might use the same MO repeatedly and get away with it because he was too careful, too meticulous to leave even trace evidence.

Sean was right about that, too. In a case like this, the only way to find the killer was to find the motive for the murder.

Chapter Seven

Fourth Avenue North, 6:00 p.m.

The visit to the floral shop had been pointless. Sean had pushed Thrasher as far as he could without a badge and a warrant. The flowers had been ordered online, paid for with a gift card. The payment method was a dead end. It would take a warrant and considerable effort to trace the IP address of the computer used for the purchase. None of that was necessary in Sean's opinion. Whoever killed Adler had ordered the flowers the day before he was murdered with instructions they were to be delivered on this date.

The cops would see that element as proof Adler had ordered the flowers. In Sean's opinion the date the flowers were ordered didn't change the fact that Adler likely had a partner in whatever weirdness he was into. And that partner was in all probability his killer. Sean's conclusion confirmed the concept that Amber Roberts was in no way connected to the murder of Kyle Adler. She was a victim. All he had to do now was turn the card with the ominous message over to the BPD. Detective Lori Wells would follow up.

The boss called as they left the floral shop. Evidently the BPD had uncovered new evidence and wanted to meet with Amber. The drive to the office was tense. He could feel Amber growing more anxious. As soon as they arrived, he passed the card he'd bagged to Jess, told her about the flower delivery and brought her up to speed on the rest.

Ten minutes later they were still waiting in the conference room. Amber sat next to Sean. She kept fidgeting with her bag or the hem of her skirt. She was nervous, but Sean wasn't worried about her going down for Adler's murder. It didn't take a detective's shield to see she was being framed. Whatever the motive, the killer wanted Amber to suffer this roller-coaster ride or worse. It was the *worse* part that worried Sean.

Unless the detectives had found more evidence that would connect to the perp, he'd get away with murder. Why risk being caught by sending flowers to Amber? If eliminating Adler had been the goal, why continue taking risks?

"Sergeant Wells and Lieutenant Harper should be here anytime now," Jess announced, breaking the thick silence.

"You have no idea what this new evidence is?" Frank Teller asked.

Sean glanced to the other side of Amber, where Teller sat, his fingers drumming on the table.

"We'll all know soon enough what they've found," Jess assured him.

Sean liked his boss even if he wasn't so sure whether she liked him or not. He'd never met anyone quite like her. She was smart and brave. As far as he could tell, she wasn't afraid of a damned thing. She and Corlew were a strange combination. Both determined to get the job done but with different perspectives and from different avenues. Corlew didn't blink at crossing the line if that was what it took. *Oil and water*, Sean decided. Yet somehow they meshed. There was a long history between the two. One of these days Sean was going to ask Corlew about it. Maybe over a beer.

A bell jingled and the sound of Corlew's deep voice filled the lobby, followed by Lori Wells's laughter and Chet Harper's quiet response to whatever Corlew had said. The two detectives were part of the family, Jess told Sean frequently. Along with Clint Hayes, Chad Cook and Corlew's wife, Sylvia. More of those close ties, bound by history. Sean wondered if he would ever again have those beyond his immediate family. The fact that his gaze moved to Amber at the thought made him want to kick his own backside.

The truth was, he'd thought he was ready for a lifetime commitment back in LA. He'd had the woman, the friends and the job. Life had been damned good. His life-shattering mistake had sent his friends running. The great job went next. The ties fell apart.

Maybe it was better not to get tangled up in close ties. No worries about being let down if you kept your expectations low. His gaze drifted to Amber. He didn't need complications like her, either. Getting involved with a client was always a bad idea. He'd learned that lesson the hard way.

Corlew and the detectives entered the room and settled around the table. Sean nodded to Lori and Harper. Since they all knew each other there was no need for introductions.

"What is it that couldn't wait until morning, Detectives?" Teller steered the conversation to business with his usual dry style.

Lori placed a folder on the table. She removed two photographs and passed them around. "Meet Rhiana Pettie and Kimberly McCorkle."

Both women looked to be twenty-five to thirty; Pettie was a blonde, and McCorkle was a brunette. Sean passed the photos on to Jess.

"Both are deceased," Harper said. "Strangled. Ligature marks indicate they were held captive for several days before being strangled. No indication of sexual assault."

"These two victims are related to our case how?" Jess asked as she handed the photos to Teller.

"We believe both women were victims of Adler and whoever killed him," Lori said.

Next to him, Amber drew in a harsh breath. Sean resisted the urge to reach for her hand and give it a squeeze.

Lori withdrew more photos and passed them on. "We located a storage unit near Riverview Parkway rented under Adler's name. Inside were three small plastic boxes. The kind you'd purchase to store a pair of shoes." She used her hands to indicate the size. "In each box was a pair of panties. A single pubic hair as well as one from the scalp was folded into each. Analysis confirmed the respective hairs belonged to the two victims." She indicated the photos that had made their way back around to Harper. "Along with Pettie's panties was a wineglass. The lab confirmed her prints were on the glass. In the box with McCorkle's was a coffee mug bearing her prints."

"Like my teacup and…"

Amber didn't have to say "red panties." Sean had struggled to keep images of her wearing nothing but those panties out of his head more than once.

Lori nodded in answer to Amber's unfinished question.

"Where were the bodies found and how were they dumped?" Jess asked.

"Pettie was taken Valentine's Day. She left work

and never made it home. Her body was found a week later in the woods off Highway 280. McCorkle disappeared on June 20. Same scenario. She left work and wasn't heard from again until her body was discovered in a drainage ditch in Bessemer ten days later. Both were dressed in skimpy lingerie. McCorkle was still bound by the thin nylon rope used to secure her. Lengths of the rope were secured to each wrist like a bracelet. The one from Pettie's right wrist was missing."

Harper pulled yet another photo from the folder. This one showed a piece of blue nylon rope. "Considering this new evidence, we did another sweep of Adler's house. We found the rope tucked inside a family photo album."

"Did you find anything else like this?" Jess asked as she spread the photos of the items found on the table.

"We took his house apart," Lori answered. "We didn't find any other evidence anywhere on the property."

Jess removed her eyeglasses. "Ladies and gentlemen, we're looking at the work of a fledgling serial killer or killers. The MO is the same, though things were a bit sloppier with Pettie. The killer or killers had cleaned up their act a bit by the time they murdered McCorkle." She turned to Amber. "If I'm right, you were supposed to be the next victim."

Amber eyes widened. The pulse at the base of her throat fluttered. "Oh, my God."

"The third box found in his storage unit was empty," Lori explained. "The items belonging to you would have likely ended up there if Adler hadn't been murdered."

"We're assuming he was working with a partner," Harper said. "And that partner killed him and planted the evidence to point to Ms. Roberts. We just don't know why yet. We also can't say whether Adler was involved in the murders."

"Does that mean my client is no longer a person of interest in the case?" Teller demanded.

"We have every reason to believe," Lori explained, "Ms. Roberts had nothing to do with Adler's murder. But until we know more she's still a part of this case."

"But she has been cleared of suspicion—is that correct?" Teller pressed.

"She has been cleared of suspicion," Harper confirmed. "At this point, we believe she may be in danger from whoever Adler was working with."

"Crimes Against Persons is officially handing off the case to the Special Problems Unit," Lori explained. "Captain Aldridge is not happy about it since the search she ordered turned up significant evidence, but the chief called it a couple of hours ago. Chet will be in charge of the case now."

"Excuse me." Amber stood and hurried from the room.

Sean followed. She went into the restroom, and he waited in the hall. As grateful as he was certain she felt to be cleared of suspicion, the other news had been startling.

Learning you were the next victim on a serial killer's hit list wasn't exactly like being named prom queen.

At least now he knew what the *worse* part was.

AMBER LET THE faucet run until the water was as cold as it was going to get, and then she bent forward and splashed it on her face. She gripped the sink to keep herself steady.

The dead man, Kyle Adler, had come into her home and taken her things. He could have touched any or all of her possessions.

Fear twisted inside her, churning in her stomach.

He'd taken her panties into his bed and fantasized about…*her*.

He'd wanted to kill her.

He'd probably killed or been a party to the murders of those other two women.

Amber drew in a shuddering breath as she stared at her reflection. She had been next.

Another deep breath and then another. *Calm down.* She needed to get back in there and hear the rest.

Reaching for a paper towel, she braced her hip against the sink. She patted her face and dried her hands. She could do this. Adler was dead. He couldn't hurt her or anyone else now.

Except he had a partner…who'd in all probability been in her house, too.

Amber tossed the damp paper towel and opened the door.

Sean was waiting for her. "You okay?"

She pushed a smile in place. "I'm many things, but okay is not one of them at the moment."

He gestured for her to go ahead of him.

Amber squared her shoulders and returned to the conference room. She could do this. She was strong, and she had a bodyguard.

Jess offered a kind smile as Amber took her seat once more. "We were just discussing that you and the other two—" she gestured to the folder on the table in front of Lori Wells "—have nothing beyond being female in common."

Amber listened, struggling to keep her face clear of the fear pounding in her veins, as the detectives, Jess and Corlew, discussed the facts. Pettie was much taller than Amber and a little heavier. She had been on staff at one of the city's prestigious law firms. McCorkle was average height with a tiny waist and extra wide hips. She was an architectural engineer at one of the city's top firms. They shared no physical traits, as Jess said, except being female.

"The common characteristic that drew Adler may have simply been physical beauty," Jess suggested.

"Or personality. Possibly body language. Whatever the commonality, he was drawn to each victim."

Amber wanted to know more about the partner. "How does a team of serial killers work?"

"One is usually dominant," Jess said. "Adler may have been the scout. He observed the target. Perhaps even lured her into a trap. The partner may have been the one to decide when and how she died. He may have been the one to make the kill, or they may have taken that step together."

"He left no evidence?" Amber was aware there were criminals capable of operating without leaving behind even trace evidence, but she didn't want this killer to be one of them.

"None we've found," Harper confirmed. "We'll continue interviewing friends, relatives, associates—anyone who knew Adler."

Amber appreciated their efforts. She moistened her lips and asked the question ramming into her brain. "What do I do until you find him?"

"You take extra precautions," Lori said. "You watch every step you make."

"Sean will be assigned as your personal security for as long as necessary," Jess added.

The churning started in Amber's stomach again. She swallowed back the bitter taste of bile. "How long will it take to find him?" She knew they couldn't answer that question. She, of all people, understood how these things went. She closed her eyes and shook her head. "I'm sorry. That was a ridiculous question." They might never find him. She might never know the name of the man watching her…waiting for the perfect moment to act.

"We'll do all we can as quickly as we can," Harper assured her.

"We've already taken initial precautions," Sean spoke up. "New locks. New security codes."

Amber's attention drifted. How could this man—this killer—have been watching her and she hadn't realized he was so close?

Chairs scraped across the floor and fabric rustled. Amber blinked. The meeting was over. She hadn't even realized the conversation had ended. She stood. The detectives were assuring Teller they would keep in touch with any new developments. Jess was speaking quietly with Sean.

Amber pushed in her chair and picked up her purse. Corlew joined the huddle with Jess and Sean.

"Amber, don't worry." Teller moved up beside her. "Between Jess and the BPD, we'll get through this."

She tried to summon a smile, but her lips wouldn't quite make the transition. "Thank you."

Teller gave her a reassuring pat on the arm, and then he followed the path the detectives had taken. Amber took a breath and lifted her chin. She should call her sister and her parents and let them know this latest news before they heard it some other way. This was good news on one level, she argued with herself.

Sean and the others broke their huddle, all eyes turning toward her.

After more assurances from both Jess and Corlew, it was time to go home.

Sean surveyed the sidewalk and checked the car before allowing her inside. Numb, she settled in the seat. He shut the door, and she flinched. *Deep breath. They will find this guy.*

She should call the station manager and discuss the situation. Was her cameraman in danger working with her? She glanced at the man driving. He was in danger, as well. Her sister. Gina. Maybe it would be best if she took some time off work. Gina was a reasonable person. Hopefully she could convince Barb to stay away from Amber until this killer was found.

Amber stared out at the familiar landscape. The plan seemed like a good one. Reasonable.

So she was going to put her life on hold because some evil, twisted bastard had targeted her?

No way.

"I need to go to the station."

Sean glanced at her. "Did you get called in for an assignment?"

"No. The computers at the office are better for what I need to do."

He made the necessary turn for the new destination. "Would you like to let me in on what we're doing?"

She considered his profile for a moment. Strong jaw and forehead with a nice nose balanced perfectly between gorgeous blue eyes. She wondered how often he'd been asked why he wasn't on the big screen. He had the looks, the charm. He could have gone for an acting or a modeling gig. Amber dismissed the silly notion. Her mind was working overtime to distract her from the worry.

Rather than answer his question, she asked one of her own. "What did Jess and Corlew say to you after the meeting?"

He glanced at her. "Not to let you out of my sight."

"Really? I thought that was already the plan. Isn't that why you're sleeping on my sofa?"

"Guess so." His lips quirked with a need to grin.

He likely wouldn't find the situation so amusing if the shoe were on the other foot. Still, she couldn't deny that seeing his lopsided smiles and grins were almost worth the worry and frustration. Maybe that was an exaggeration. Just another indication that her mind was on overload.

"So, what's on tonight's agenda?" He shot her a look. "I'm not going to let you out of my sight, but you're still the boss."

Amber relaxed the tiniest bit and told him what he wanted to know. "We're going to find out all we can about those two women Adler and his partner killed. Those women and I shared some common trait or connection that drew Adler and his partner. We have to figure out what it was."

"We should get food," he suggested. "I work better on a full tank."

She hadn't even thought of food. She wasn't sure her stomach could handle food. Two women were dead, but Amber had survived whatever the bastards had planned for her. The least she could do was help find the other person responsible for their deaths.

Going into hiding wouldn't be fair. Rhiana Pettie and Kimberly McCorkle and their families deserved justice.

Amber had an obligation to help them find it.

Chapter Eight

Thornberry Drive, 9:05 p.m.

"You're sure you want to show up at someone's door at this hour and announce you might know who killed their daughter?"

The idea sounded much better when she said it. "I have to do something."

Was she being selfish? The McCorkles had waited four months to hear who had taken the life of their daughter; the Petties even longer. Still, Sean had a point. She couldn't just show up at their door and announce that she knew the murderer. Not to mention the detectives on the case would not be happy with her, and the last thing she needed to do was to annoy or enrage the BPD. Odds were, the lead detective in the case, Chet Harper, had already spoken to the families.

Still, Amber had to do this.

"I'll be subtler than that," she assured him.

Sean grunted in that way only males could, the sound a warning that he had his doubts. *Fine.* She didn't need his approval.

She hadn't been able to reach anyone at the Pettie home. Mrs. McCorkle had insisted she was happy to meet tonight. If Amber had a daughter who had been murdered, she wouldn't care what time of the day or night news came; she would want to hear it as soon as possible.

Sean parked at the street in front of the ranch-style home. "Just remember, Harper's going above and beyond to solve this case. Don't do anything to make them regret the extra effort to keep you in the loop."

"Is that what your boss warned you about after the briefing?"

He shifted his attention straight ahead, and Amber knew she'd hit the nail on the head.

"Something like that," he admitted.

"I would never do anything to jeopardize my relationship with the BPD or with Jess Burnett." As a journalist, she understood the value of the relationships she'd built. As her mentor, Gina had kept that golden rule in front of Amber. She was no rank amateur.

Sean flashed her one of those killer smiles as he opened his door. "Well, all righty then."

As usual he was at her door before she was out of the car. He surveyed the street and the homes on either side of the McCorkle home before ushering her up the sidewalk to the porch. Amber rang the bell and found herself holding her breath.

The door opened, and an older woman, fifty or so perhaps, with dark hair looked from Amber to Sean and back.

"Mrs. McCorkle?" Amber asked.

"You're Amber Roberts," the woman said. "I recognize you from TV."

"This is my friend Sean Douglas." Amber indicated the man beside her.

Mrs. McCorkle gave a nod. "Come in."

When the door opened wider, Amber stepped inside. Sean stayed close behind her. Maybe a little too close. The heat from his body made her tremble. *You really have lost it, Amber.*

"You're certain we're not disturbing you, Mrs. McCorkle?" The guilt was making an appearance. Damn Sean for making her second-guess this move. If she weren't so vulnerable right now, he would never have been able to accomplish that feat. Investigative reporters ferreted out information on cases all the time. It was part of the job. More often than not the police weren't particularly pleased, but it generally worked out to everyone's benefit.

The lady shook her head adamantly. "I want to do all I can to help find the monster who took my baby."

Amber understood. She glanced around the neat living room. Framed photos of Kimberly were everywhere. "Is Mr. McCorkle home?"

The older woman looked away. "He's gone to bed." She wrung her hands. "It's hard on him. Truth is, he drinks enough beer every night after work to render him unconscious by the time he goes to bed."

"We all have our own way of dealing with loss," Sean spoke up. "As long as it doesn't hurt anyone else."

Amber wondered what he had done to deal with the loss of his lover when Lacy James died. Had he struggled to sleep at night? Tried to drown his sorrows? Why was it she suddenly wanted to know all there was to know about him? Yes, he was the man tasked with her safety, but she suspected there was more to it than that.

Mrs. McCorkle nodded her agreement with Sean's understanding words. "I tell myself that every night." She sighed. "Sometimes I feel like we're muddling through some alternate reality. How can this be our lives?" She waved off the words. "Please, make yourselves at home. Would you like coffee or hot tea?"

"No, thank you," Amber said as she perched on the edge of the sofa. "Was Kimberly a hot tea drinker?"

The lady shook her head. "That would be me. Kim loved her coffee in the morning, iced tea for lunch and dinner was a cold beer. She allowed herself one or two each night, the same as her father. He always warned that overindulgence was a bad thing. But that was before..."

"I love the flavored teas," Amber said, keeping her tone light. "Paradise Peach."

"I guess I'm a purist. Earl Grey for me."

"Green tea chai for me," Sean tossed in. "Only I cheat—I buy the instant stuff."

The man drank hot tea? When he shot her another of those amused looks, Amber closed her gaping mouth. She would need to be careful around him. He kept her off balance, and he knew it.

Time to get to the point of this meeting. "Mrs. McCorkle, I believe the man or men who hurt your daughter may have been targeting me, as well."

The woman's eyes widened. "Has someone else gone missing?" Her hand went to her chest. "Mercy, I've prayed nonstop that he would be caught. I don't understand why the police can't find whoever did this. They were here this evening asking more questions, but they weren't giving me any answers."

"I'm certain they're doing all they can," Amber assured her. "I'm wondering if your daughter and I had any hobbies, shopping habits or interests in common. May we talk for a few minutes about the things she liked to do?"

Mrs. McCorkle's eyes brightened, but the perpetual sadness created by the loss of her daughter lined her face. "She always loved building things as a child. It was no surprise when she decided to become an architect. She took great pride in her work."

"What about her hobbies?" Amber reached into her purse for a notepad.

"She loved playing basketball," Mrs. McCorkle said, her eyes growing distant. "She played in high school, you know. No matter that she was a foot or more shorter than the rest of the team—she was a force to be reckoned with when she got her hands on the ball."

"Was she dating anyone in particular?" Amber asked.

Mrs. McCorkle shook her head. "She had a lot of friends and dates, but she didn't date anyone regularly. Kimberly said she was in no hurry to get serious. She was busy building her career."

Amber's instincts started to hum. "I can relate."

"Kimberly had big plans. She wanted to have her own firm one day. She was going to take care of me and her dad. She promised we'd never have to worry about anything." Mrs. McCorkle's lips trembled. "She sure saw to that. She carried a million-dollar life insurance policy. We had no idea until we saw the paperwork among her personal papers."

"Do you mind sharing the name of her insurance company?" Amber, too, carried a significant policy. The day before she'd started her job her father had insisted on a "business" talk. He'd urged her to be smart with her money from the beginning. Setting up a savings plan was at the top of his list. Insurance and investments were next. Six years later Amber was grateful for that talk.

Mrs. McCorkle told her the name of the company, but it wasn't the one Amber used. After half an hour, Amber learned that she and Kimberly had very little in common beyond their single-mindedness regarding their careers. As significant as that similarity was, their careers were so different Amber wasn't sure how that had drawn a killer's attention. The firm where Kimberly was employed was nowhere near Channel Six. Maybe they shared the same maintenance crew, or maybe Adler had made deliveries to both offices or to their homes. The architectural firm hadn't been on the list, but maybe that was only because he'd delivered there fewer times.

By ten thirty Amber realized the woman would have gladly stayed up all night talking about her daughter. She passed Mrs. McCorkle a business card. "This is my cell number. Call me anytime, day or night, if you think of anything you believe would be helpful."

Mrs. McCorkle saw them to the door. "I hope they catch him soon."

Amber squeezed her arm. "I'm certain they will."

When goodbyes were exchanged and the door closed behind them, Amber felt exhausted. The meeting had been far more emotional than she'd expected. She had conducted plenty of interviews with families who had lost loved ones, but somehow this time had been more difficult. Certainly it was more personal. Those people could have been her parents…

Sean abruptly moved in front of her. She bumped into his back. His hand went under his jacket where she'd seen the weapon stationed at his hip. She peeked around one broad shoulder and spotted the trouble. A man stepped out of the shadows.

Gerard Stevens.

Irritation seared through Amber. "What do you want?" She stepped around Sean, but he stopped her with one strong hand before she could move toward Stevens.

"So the rumors that Adler is connected to the McCorkle and Pettie murders are true," Stevens stated with a satisfied smile.

"You know this guy?" Sean asked, his fingers still biting into her arm.

"She knows me," Stevens mouthed off. "She knows me *very* well."

"Adler was stalking me," Amber said, anger building faster than she would have liked. "I'm considering an exposé on women who're murdered by obsessed men. You better watch out or you'll end up in the story."

"I'll nudge my contacts at the BPD and confirm for myself."

Sean was urging her toward the car.

"You do that," Amber tossed at the jerk before

Sean ushered her into the car. Stevens had made far too many enemies at the BPD to have any reliable contacts left. He was bluffing. How the hell had she ever been attracted to the arrogant bastard?

Sean echoed the question as he drove away from the McCorkle neighborhood. “You dated that guy?”

“Once or twice.” More like six times. She closed her eyes and shuddered at the memory of the time they’d spent together. The moment Gina had found out, she’d told Amber that Stevens liked to bed all the new female competition, and then he bragged to his male peers.

Gerard Stevens had been her one big career mistake. Cutting herself a little slack, she had been young and eager to make all the right contacts in the business. At the time Stevens had seemed like a great contact. *Live and learn.*

“I guess pretty boys like him attract lots of women.”

Amber considered the remark as they drove through the night. For such a handsome guy, Sean almost sounded envious. She wouldn’t tell him, but he was far better-looking and more charismatic than Stevens would ever be.

“Trust me—his ego is sickening. What you see is definitely not what you get. As a date he’s a massive letdown.”

“Ouch,” he teased. “Remind me never to let you down.”

During the fifteen or so minutes it took to drive to

her house, Amber weighed the few facts she knew. If Pettie had been a career-oriented woman, that could very well be the attraction the three of them shared. Still, the killer had to have come into contact with each of them somewhere. What places or people did they have in common? Mrs. McCorkle hadn't been able to provide much in the way of places her daughter frequented. She had promised to talk to some of Kimberly's friends and get back with Amber.

Now if she could just get an appointment with the Petties tomorrow.

Sean checked the street before allowing Amber out of the car. He ordered her to wait in the living room while he checked the rest of the house no matter that the security system had been armed. Honestly, she didn't see how celebrities lived like this. She would lose her mind.

"Clear," he announced as he returned to the living room.

"Great." She needed to think. A cup of tea and some quiet time would hopefully go a long way in making her feel a little more in control of her life. "I'm having tea. You want anything?"

"I'm good." He peeled off his jacket and tossed it over the arm of the sofa.

Yes, she mused, he was very good.

"I have wine," she offered as she lit the flame under the teakettle.

"No drinking while on duty." He reached up and

plowed his fingers through his hair. “I’ll just take a quick shower while you have your tea.”

She shifted her attention to preparing her tea and tried her very best to block the images of him naked beneath the hot spray of water. She was tired and confused and plenty worried. There was no other explanation for her sudden inability to think straight.

While the water boiled she went to her closet and put her shoes away. She stripped off her clothes and pulled on a pair of pajama pants and a tee. It felt good to simply relax. She washed her face and dabbed on her nightly moisturizer. Her mother had taught Amber from an early age how important the nightly rituals were. Her father had been the one to insist she set and maintain a workout routine. Her parents were health nuts, and she was glad. So many of her friends struggled with finding the time to take care of themselves in their busy lives. The routines her parents had instilled had become part of her day, so she didn’t have to make time.

The whistle of the kettle drew her back to the kitchen. She gave herself a pat on the back for only hesitating a mere second or two in front of the hall bath door. The sound of spraying water had ceased. She could imagine Sean in there toweling off that muscular body. She sighed. Maybe she just needed the relief of thinking about anything else besides her current fears. Or maybe it had been too long since she’d bothered with a personal life. So many of her colleagues had the same problem. There just wasn't enough time to establish an upwardly mobile career and to have a life, as well. A few, like her, had abandoned the idea of marriage and children for the foreseeable future. Most, however, went the other way. She had no idea how people like Jess Burnett and Lori Wells juggled such demanding careers while raising children. Maybe it was time she asked.

While her tea steeped, she prowled through the cupboards until she found a package of her favorite cheese straws. With her teacup and snack ready, she settled on the sofa with her notes. Sean wandered into the room, but she kept her attention on the notes. From the corner of her eye, she noticed he'd donned the same trousers and his shirt was only partly buttoned. She refused to look directly at him. She certainly didn't need to see any part of that body uncovered.

She sipped her tea and nibbled on the cheese straws. A short list of potential places where she and McCorkle may have run into each other was easy enough to make. A few boutique shops that catered to the professional woman. The dry cleaner. The municipal building. As an architect, McCorkle would likely be in and out checking property lines and zoning ordinances. Amber followed court cases. She spent a good deal of time at or around the city offices. Town hall meetings.

The same possibilities were true of Pettie, as well. Since she had worked for a law firm, they may have been involved with the same case at some point. Amber didn't recognize either woman beyond the reports she'd seen about their abductions and the subsequent discovery of their bodies. But then, she was usually so focused on her assignment she often had tunnel vision.

If she could get her hands on Adler's credit card records, nailing down shops and restaurants he frequented would help tremendously. Corlew was working on the phone records. Maybe he could get the man's credit card records, too.

Amber blinked. Her cup found its way to the saucer hard enough that it was a miracle it didn't crack the fine china. Her mouth felt numb. She set her notes aside and tried to stand. Her legs were rubbery. Saliva leaked from her mouth. She wiped it away. *What the hell?*

"You okay?"

Sean stood beside her. She hadn't even realized he'd moved.

"I don't know. I feel..." She tapped her lips and tried to swallow all the excess saliva. She swayed, her shoulder bumping into his.

"We're going to the ER."

She stared at him. His words were not really making sense to her. "What?"

"Are you drinking the tea from the can on the counter?"

She nodded, or she thought she did.

He sat her down in the nearest chair and disappeared. Her stomach roiled violently. "You'd better get a bag or a bucket." God, her mouth felt so damned weird. Numb and yet burning.

Sean's arms were suddenly around her, supporting her. "Let's go."

Before she could respond or catch her breath, she was in his car. How had they gotten there so fast?

He handed her a plastic trash bag, and then the car started to move.

Amber closed her eyes and fought the urge to vomit.

"Don't hold back." His words floated through the darkness. "Try to get it up."

As if his suggestion somehow triggered a response in her belly, she hurled.

"Good girl," he praised.

Funny. It didn't feel good at all.

Chapter Nine

University of Alabama–Birmingham Hospital
Wednesday, October 19, 3:15 a.m.

Sean's teeth felt ready to crack he'd clenched so long and hard. He'd only relaxed when Amber had stopped vomiting and started to get comfortable. Her mouth wasn't numb or burning anymore, and she could stand, walk and communicate normally.

"We believe whatever toxin you ingested has broken down in the digestive tract," Dr. Chaconas explained. We've taken the necessary detox precautions and given you lots of fluids. Your vitals are good. I think we're out of the woods."

"So I can go home now?" Amber asked, her voice still a little weak.

Chaconas glanced at her chart. "I don't see any reason to keep you." He made a few notes on the chart. "Come back here immediately if you experience any more symptoms, and stay hydrated. Check in with your personal physician as soon as possible."

"Thank you." Amber accepted the discharge papers.

As soon as the doctor was out the door, Harper came back in. "Looks like you're going home."

"Thank God," Amber said.

"I know you've been through a lot," Harper began, "but we're gonna need to go through your house again—top to bottom this time." He glanced at Sean. "I believe it's best if you stay somewhere else until we determine if there're any other toxins in your home. We wouldn't need more than a day or two and we should know within the next forty-eight hours what was in your tea. Is that doable?"

"My parents are out of town. I could..." Amber began. She frowned as if attempting to decide what to say next.

"She'll be staying with me."

Sean was as startled by the announcement as Amber appeared to be. Harper looked from one to the other and gave a nod. "I think that's a good idea," he agreed.

Amber drew in a big breath. "Whatever it takes."

"Good. We'll be in touch with updates."

When Harper was gone Sean offered Amber a hand as she hopped off the exam table. She swayed a bit; he steadied her.

"I, ah..." She moistened her lips. "I should probably call my sister."

Sean guided her into the corridor and toward the doors that would take them back to the lobby. "I believe I mentioned that when we first arrived."

"You're going to say I told you so? After what I just went through?"

He opened the passenger-side door. When she was settled in the seat, he passed her his cell. "You make the call—I'll get you someplace safe."

Sean rounded the hood and slid behind the wheel. He told himself he was doing the right thing. She couldn't go back home. She was his responsibility. It was his job to keep her safe. B&C Investigations didn't have a safe house as of yet. There was no need to wake up Jess or Buddy at this hour. He'd made the right decision.

Amber spoke quietly to her sister. Her sister wasn't so calm. Sean could hear the concern in her voice as she demanded answers. Amber responded steadily. He had to hand it to the lady, she was a trouper. She'd puked her guts out and was weak as a kitten, but she'd hung in there. While she had been undergoing the barrage of tests, he'd called Harper and notified him of the turn of events.

He was confident in his decision to take her home with him. Then why the hell was his gut in knots? Maybe because the last client he'd taken home with him had ended up dead.

His palms started to sweat. His heart raced. Now that they were driving away from the safety of the hospital, Amber was calmer than he was and she was the one who'd been poisoned.

Sean tightened his grip on the steering wheel. *You've got this, man. Shake it off.*

"Well." Amber passed his cell back to him. "That went over like a lead balloon."

"Yeah, big sisters like to be called during the crisis, not after." Another one of those life lessons he'd learned the hard way.

Sean braked for the traffic signal. The street lamp chased away the darkness between them. Despite the unpleasantness of the past few hours, a faint smile tilted her lips. "I see. You have an older sister?"

"Five years older and fifty times smarter." He laughed. "In her opinion, of course."

"Which is the only opinion that counts."

A smile tugged at his lips, and he relaxed a fraction. "Definitely."

The city was quiet at this hour. Back in high school he'd liked this time of the morning better than any other time of the day. The night was over, but it wasn't quite daylight…a fresh start. Anything was possible.

He had clung to that motto all the way up to the morning—about this time—when he'd made the biggest mistake of his life.

Sean checked his mirrors once more to ensure he

wasn't being tailed, then he hit the remote to raise the overhead door of his garage. Once they were inside, he shut off the engine and closed the door. He hopped out and unlocked the door that led into the kitchen.

Amber closed her door and leaned against the car. "I hope you have something I can borrow to sleep in." She pulled at her tee. "This is a little gross."

"I'm pretty sure I can come up with something."

Sean flipped on the lights as he entered the house ahead of her. He didn't have a security system like the one she had, but he had something even better.

Rebel sat in the middle of the kitchen, staring expectantly at his master. The tan-and-white boxer turned his attention to Amber. Amber stalled.

Sean patted his leg. "Come on over here, boy. He's the friendliest dog you'll ever meet."

"He's big."

"He's a teddy bear. Take a break, buddy." Sean pointed to the back door. Rebel bounded to it and scooted out the doggy door. "Follow me," he said to Amber, "and I'll get you settled."

"Why didn't he bark when he heard us coming?"

"He knows the sound of my car." He paused at the door to the spare bedroom. "Trust me—if anyone besides me had come into this house, Rebel would have taken him down."

"Who takes care of him when you're not here?" She surveyed the room as she asked the question.

His home was a classic bungalow, not nearly as

large as hers, but with a decent-size yard for Rebel. It was on a quiet street in a nice neighborhood. "My sister. She helps with rescued dogs. That's how I got Rebel. No one else wanted him since he's kind of big and he's a little past his prime."

"So you took him." Amber smiled, the genuine article despite how lousy she no doubt still felt. "I would never have guessed you have such a soft side."

"Do me a favor, don't tell anyone. It would wreck my image."

She held up a hand. "Your secret is safe with me. Besides, I'm expecting you to keep any and all descriptions of my projectile vomiting to yourself."

"No one will ever know," he promised.

"I could use a shower, the sooner the better, and something to sleep in." She tugged at her tee again and made a face.

"And bottled water," he reminded her.

She pressed a hand to her stomach. "Right."

Sean rounded up a couple of bottles of water, a toothbrush and a Crimson Tide T-shirt. Amber was already in the hall bath, frowning at her reflection.

"I look like hell."

He placed the water and toothbrush on the counter and passed her the tee. "You look damned good considering. If you need anything else, just let me know. I'm at the end of the hall."

She touched his arm, stopping him. Even through

the fabric of his shirt the contact sparked the desire already simmering in his veins.

"Thanks, Sean. I'm really glad you were there to take care of me."

He nodded and headed for his room. He needed a shower, too. A long, cold one.

8:15 a.m.

AMBER STARED AT the broth Sean had prepared for her. "I'm sorry. I just don't think I can do this." She had no appetite. She felt like hell. Her stomach still felt queasy and crampy.

"Just following the instructions on the discharge papers." Sean sipped his coffee.

Amber groaned. He was right. She needed to follow the doctor's orders. Slowly, she lifted the spoon to her lips and tasted. Her stomach clenched, but she kept going. One spoonful after the other, until she emptied the bowl. She washed it down with plenty of water. When she was finished, she pushed the bowl away and summoned a smile. "I feel better already."

Sean gave that one-sided grin that somehow made him even more handsome. "Liar."

She laughed. "Yeah. I feel..." She groaned. "Quite blah and very grateful for your quick thinking."

He gave a nod. "It's nice to be the hero from time to time."

Amber studied him a long moment. He really was

a nice guy and completely committed to the job. She didn't see him as the type to fail a client. There had to be more to the story. "You know pretty much everything about me. I'd like to know more about you."

His relaxed expression hardened the slightest bit. "You know all the important stuff."

"Wives? Kids? Significant others?"

"Nope, nope and nope."

"You've never been married or engaged?"

He shook his head.

"Long-term relationships?" She reminded herself to sip her water.

"A couple. Nothing particularly memorable." He stared into his coffee.

"What really happened in LA?" She snapped her lips together. She actually hadn't been planning to blurt out the question.

He studied her for a long moment before he answered. "I made a mistake."

"Yeah, that's what you said before, but I think there's a lot more to it than just a mistake." She smoothed a hand over her ponytail. She'd been too exhausted to dry her hair after her shower. Her only option when she'd gotten up was to restrain the wild mass of curls. "I just feel like I deserve full disclosure from the man who's seen me at my absolute worst."

His lips quirked with the need to smile in spite of that stony profile. "I guess you have a point there."

Anticipation zinged through her. "So, let's hear it."

"Lacy James was smart and talented. And beautiful," he said, awe in his voice. "No matter that I worked extra hard to stay focused on the job, I was mesmerized by her. She had this ethereal beauty and incredible depth of soul that no one ever saw onstage."

"She was incredibly talented and beautiful," Amber agreed, feeling strangely jealous of the way he described her. For the first time in ages she longed to know a man saw her that way.

"I'd been in LA for six long years. I was lonely. I'd dated plenty between assignments but nothing serious. I was almost twenty-nine and maybe I was feeling the need for something real."

Amber's stomach took a little dive, and she was reasonably sure it wasn't about the poison. She'd been feeling exactly that way—as if something was missing in her life. No matter that her career had taken off; something was still lacking. She needed more than work. More than coming home to an empty house and an equally empty bed. But how did she trust anyone with her heart? The world was so full of people who cared only for themselves. In her profession she saw so much *fake*—it felt impossible to sort the real from the make-believe. Oddly, this moment—this man—felt real.

"The next thing I knew we were…together." He fell silent for a moment. "She had a short break before the next leg of her tour started, and we never left the house. It felt exactly like what was missing in my life. It felt real and good, and I wanted it to last forever."

Amber watched the pain clutter his handsome face. The memories still hurt even though a year had passed. Was he still in love with her memory?

"When I was briefed on the assignment, her agent warned me not to trust her. She was never allowed to overindulge in alcohol, and if I spotted drugs, I was to get her out ASAP." His gaze met Amber's, and the agony there tugged at her heart. "Lacy was an addict. Had been since she was thirteen. When we met she'd been straight for two years."

"No one is responsible for what an addict chooses to do," Amber reminded him softly.

He nodded. "I know. But that doesn't change the responsibility I feel. I was with her 24/7 for weeks. I took my eyes off her for one minute at a party while she went to the bathroom and she scored. That night after I went to sleep, she overdosed on cocaine. She was sitting right there in the room watching me. I didn't even know she'd gotten out of bed." He stood and gathered her bowl and spoon. "That's what happens when you get too comfortable. Your sense of caution becomes dulled. You miss things. Lacy's dead because I didn't see how getting personally involved with me made her feel out of control. Made her wish for things she couldn't have if she wanted to keep her career on track."

"Are we all doomed to that choice?" Amber bit her lips together. She hadn't meant to say those words out loud. What was it about this man that made her feel the need to be so forthcoming? "I mean, can't a woman or a man have an astonishingly successful career and a personal life? Why do we have to choose only one?"

"There's a career," Sean said, his tone somber, "and there's a *career*. When you choose the latter, there's nothing else. It's all-encompassing. After the funeral, the one trusted friend she had told me I reminded Lacy how much she regretted the choices she'd made. She'd given up everything—her first love, the child they'd had together—to follow her dream. Falling in love again sent her hurtling back into the pain and loss."

Amber stood and pushed in her chair. "It isn't fair that she had to give up one or the other. Why couldn't she have had both?" Her heart was pounding. What she was really asking was why couldn't she have both? What made women like her—like her sister and Gina and even Jess Burnett—believe they had to give up a real life for their careers? Though the dilemma rarely affected men the same way, Sean seemed to be stuck in that same place.

"It took me nearly a year of soul-searching and no small amount of counseling to come to terms with the answer to that question, Amber. Are you sure you want to hear it?"

She blinked, taken aback. "Why wouldn't I?"

"Lacy couldn't have both because she was an addict. Staying completely focused on her career helped her keep it together—helped her stay clean. I disrupted the rhythm she'd come to depend on. I should have recognized the issue, but I was too infatuated, too caught up in my own needs. I failed to do my job, and for that I'm in part responsible for her death."

"Are you suggesting I'm addicted to my work? That I don't care about anything else?"

Sean exhaled a big breath. "I'm suggesting if you can't see yourself living a personal life in addition to your career, then you won't be able to have both. You'll have to choose one or the other, and there will always be regrets with whichever choice you make. Isn't that the true definition of addiction? Being willing to sacrifice everything else for the one thing you want most?"

The doorbell rang, and Amber jerked at the sound. "Barbara said she'd bring me some of her clothes."

"I'll get the door."

Amber took a deep breath and let it out slowly. Why in the world had they been discussing her love life and career decisions? It was her own fault. She'd started it. The conversation was meant to learn more about him and what happened in LA. It was never intended to dissect her life.

Could he possibly be right about her? Was she incapable of balance? She couldn't deny being singularly focused. She'd recognized her type A personality at the ripe old age of twelve. She'd decided then that she wanted to be the next Barbara Walters.

Barb's voice in the other room drew her from her thoughts. This wasn't the time to worry about her love life. Two women were dead—possibly murdered by the same man who had poisoned her. Finding Adler's partner and presumably his murderer had to be top priority right now. Just because Sean Douglas made her heart pound and her pulse skip was no excuse to revert to being controlled by adolescent hormones.

Amber squared her shoulders and joined her sister and Sean in the living room. Barb took one look at her and rushed to where she stood. She grabbed Amber in a bear hug. "Don't you ever do that again!"

Amber tried to breathe. Sean stood on the other side of the room, his arms loaded with clothes, shoes and a small bag hanging from his long fingers.

"Really, I'm okay," Amber assured her.

Barb drew back and surveyed her from head to toe and back. "You look like hell. You definitely need all that makeup Gina shoved into the bag the cutie-pie over there is holding."

Sean looked at the floor in an attempt to hide his grin.

"Thanks." Amber knew she was okay when her

big sister told her she needed makeup. Barbara Roberts hated makeup. How she ever fell in love with a television journalist like Gina was a mystery to Amber. "The cutie-pie," she said, using Barb's term, "is Sean Douglas."

"A pleasure." Barb gave him an approving nod and grabbed the bag he held. "Come on, little sister." She reached for one of the outfits he held, as well. "We have work to do. You'll have to excuse us, Mr. Douglas."

"Take your time," he suggested. "I'll follow up with Lieutenant Harper."

Amber flashed him a smile as her sister ushered her from the room. What was it about a near-death experience that made a woman suddenly bemoan all she'd given up for a career?

How did she capture that elusive thing called balance?

As soon as the person trying to kill her was caught, she intended to find her balance.

She glanced over her shoulder one last time. Maybe she would start with Sean.

Chapter Ten

Frontier Drive, Vestavia Hills, 11:00 a.m.

Rhiana Pettie's mother had agreed to a meeting.

Amber looked considerably better even if she still felt weak and weary. Barb had helped her pull herself together. Her head was still just a little foggy, but an extrasweet café mocha had helped immensely.

Sean parked at the curb and checked his cell. "Harper sent me a text. So far your place is coming up clean for toxins, but he'd feel better if you gave them another day just to be sure."

"I can live with that." She searched his eyes. "Can you?" After all, he was the one sharing his place.

"My job is to keep you safe, Amber. I can do that just about anywhere."

"I guess it's settled then. I'll be at your place again tonight."

His blue eyes darkened. "Technically it'll be your

first night at my place. It was already morning when I took you there today."

"I used your shower and spent time sleeping in your guest bed."

He nodded. "You did."

"I rest my case." Amber reached for the door. As usual, he somehow managed to appear at her side of the car before she emerged.

Forty-eight hours ago she'd found his persistent presence frustrating, annoying even. Now she was very grateful he was here. The reality that someone had come into her house and touched her things was bad enough. To recognize that he'd meant her physical harm made it all the worse. It was one thing to have an obsessive fan, even a stalker; it was entirely another to be targeted for death.

Amber turned her attention to the brick home nestled on the corner of Frontier and Kingswood. According to her research, the Petties had lived here for thirty-five years. Rachel and Tom, Rhiana's parents, had three grown children, but she had been their only daughter. People always pointed out statistics like those. If they'd had another daughter, would Rhiana's death have been easier? Of course not.

The door opened, and Mrs. Pettie stared at them as if she'd forgotten they were coming.

"Mrs. Pettie, I'm Amber Roberts. We spoke about an hour ago. You said my associate Sean Douglas and I could come by to speak with you about Rhiana."

She nodded and opened the door wider. “You look different than you do on television.”

Amber relaxed a little as she crossed the threshold. “Most people say I look much taller on TV.”

Pettie managed a faint smile. “I think they’re right. You do look taller on-screen.”

Rhiana’s mother went through the usual steps, offering refreshments, which they both declined, and steering them toward the sofa. Pettie was tall like Rhiana. Her blond hair was more gray now than blond, but the resemblance to her daughter was unmistakable. Amber had inherited her red hair and green eyes from her mother. Barb, on the other hand, had inherited their father’s rich brown hair and dark eyes. People who didn’t know them rarely believed they were sisters.

“The police told me they may have found the man who took her from us.”

Amber nodded. “Yes. I hope the BPD can confirm those suspicions soon. I’m certain they’ll contact you again as soon as they do.”

Pettie’s brow furrowed into a frown. “Are you reporting on the investigation?”

Amber glanced at Sean. This was where things got a little muddled and a whole lot sticky.

“Mrs. Pettie,” Sean answered for her, “the police have reason to believe Amber was the next victim on the killer’s list. As you can imagine, she’s anxious to help solve the case.”

"Is that why they thought you killed him?"

Amber hoped that debacle wasn't going to follow her forever. "I was and still am a person of interest in the case, but the police have cleared me of any suspicion related to his murder." It felt really good to be able to say those words.

"Can you tell us about the last few days before your daughter went missing?" Sean asked. "Had she met anyone new? Was she working on a new case at the firm?"

Amber flinched. He'd gone straight to the point rather than easing into the hard questions.

"The police already asked questions about those days," Pettie said, her gaze drifting to the floor. "After she first went missing and then again yesterday."

"Sometimes it helps to have new eyes and ears on a case. That's why we're here," he explained gently.

Pettie cleared her throat. "Rhiana was a hard worker," she said softly. "She put in a lot of long hours. I cleaned her apartment for her every couple of weeks." She smiled. "I didn't mind. Anytime she was home in the evenings she had dinner with her father and me. I think that's what I miss most… doing things for her. I loved hearing about her day. She would share the details she could, and it was always so exciting."

The loss she felt thickened in the room. It was moments like this when Amber wondered how on earth anyone could bear to have a child. How did a parent survive losing a child? *Keep your attention on the goal—finding this bastard.*

Amber braced for a no. “Can we see her apartment?”

Pettie hesitated, but then she stood. “I’ve left it just as it was. ’Course, the police went through her room twice, but otherwise it’s exactly the way she left it.”

“We’ll be very careful,” Sean promised.

“Follow me,” Pettie offered.

There was something immensely comforting about Sean’s hand at the small of her back as Amber followed Pettie up the exterior stairs that led to the apartment over the garage. She unlocked the door and stood back for them to enter first.

Rhiana had a large space that included a small bathroom and kitchenette. It was roomier than Amber’s first apartment out of college. She’d refused the offer to move back in with her parents. The tiny apartment had been her only option.

The pajamas Rhiana had slept in the night before she disappeared were on the unmade bed. The bowl and coffee mug she’d used that morning were in the sink. A large bouquet of dead flowers sat on the coffee table in front of the small sofa. Amber leaned down for a closer inspection. Roses…red ones, she suspected, though they had turned black, many of the petals falling to the table.

"She was excited about the flowers," Pettie said. "She thought the junior partner she'd been smitten with for a year had finally noticed her." Her face fell. "When he was questioned, he told the police he didn't send them."

"Were they delivered here or at her office?" Sean asked.

"Her office. She brought them home with her the same day she received them. She was so excited," Pettie repeated.

Amber's heart ached for her. "Was there a card?" She searched the area around the bouquet.

The older lady wrung her hands in front of her. "There was, but as far as I know the police never found it."

Rhiana had gone missing Valentine's Day, eight months ago. The chances of finding the card now were slim to none. Amber straightened. "Did some-one from the firm send home the personal items from Rhiana's office?"

Amber felt certain they would have cleared out the office reasonably soon after the body was found. The law firm where Rhiana had worked was a busy one; up-and-coming attorneys and paralegals were essential to the fast-paced operation of the firm. Of-fice space was no doubt a premium.

"One of her colleagues packed everything in boxes, and Rhiana's father brought them home." She sighed. "At the time I wasn't up to facing people. I think he put the boxes in the garage. That's usually where he puts everything." She glanced around the room. "I meant to bring them up here, but I…I never got around to it. We can go down and look for them if you'd like."

Amber and Sean followed Pettie down to the garage. Sean pulled the two boxes from the top shelf where Mr. Pettie had stored them.

"May we have a look inside?" Sean asked.

Pettie nodded. "Are you looking for the card that came with the flowers? I think the police went through her office and didn't find it."

"We know new details now," Amber offered. "Perhaps something else we find will mean more than it would have all those months ago."

Sean opened first one box, and then the other. Rather than being sealed with tape, each had been closed by folding the flaps one over the other. Careful with the items that had likely decorated Rhiana's office, Amber emptied the first box. Sean glanced at her, and she shook her head. Nothing potentially useful to the case.

Amber's hopes plummeted as the second box provided nothing relevant to the case, either. The last item in the box was a stack of business cards bound together with a rubber band. She might as well verify that the card wasn't among them. As she reached the final three, her fingers stilled. Holding one of the cards by the edges, she turned it for Sean to see. *Thrasher Floral.*

It wasn't the warning Amber had received, but it showed a connection to the same floral shop. The police couldn't have recognized the connection when Rhiana went missing.

"Mrs. Pettie, do you have a plastic bag we could put this in?" Sean asked before Amber had the presence of mind to do so.

The lady nodded and hurried into the house.

"We need to see Kimberly McCorkle's home." Anticipation seared through Amber's veins. They were on to something here. "If we can find even the smallest connection to the floral shop, we'll have something to take to Lieutenant Harper."

"We should call him first," Sean countered. "This is evidence."

Sean was a former cop. Amber understood his desire to be a team player—particularly since the cops involved were his friends. Unfortunately there wasn't time. A murderer—possibly a serial killer—was out there, and it was more than probable that he still intended to make Amber his next victim. Not to mention there were two families who desperately needed answers sooner rather than later.

Amber made up her mind. "We can call him after we see Kimberly's house."

Sean would have argued, but Mrs. Pettie returned with a sandwich baggie.

The memory of their rush to the emergency room when Amber had been poisoned surged to the front of her mind. She had to see this through. Now.

Beckham Drive, 12:45 p.m.

SEAN WAS SURPRISED when McCorkle agreed to meet them at her daughter's home without asking the first question. He parked in front of the small house near the popular Five Points district. The cottage had been a present to Kimberly from her parents when she graduated from college. Like Rhiana Pettie's apartment, the house had been closed and left just as it was the day their daughter walked out the last time—except for the official BPD investigation.

He didn't like doing this. Despite his misgivings, he climbed out and went around to the passenger side as Amber emerged. "You know Lieutenant Harper will be ticked off," he reminded her for the third time. He had no desire to step on the toes of the BPD's finest. Jess would not be happy, either. But Amber was the client. Wasn't it his job to keep the client safe *and* happy? *Damn.*

"We will call him as soon as we're done here," Amber repeated the same response she'd given him last time he'd raised the issue.

He exhaled a big breath and followed her up the walk to the front door. McCorkle was waiting just inside. She opened the door wider as they approached.

"I was surprised when you called me again so soon." The older lady looked hopefully at Amber. "Does this mean new evidence has been found?"

Amber smiled. Sean should have looked away, but he didn't. Her smile was part of what had landed her in the television business, in his opinion. When she smiled, everything else faded into insignificance. She was genuinely beautiful.

No going there, pal. He'd spent plenty of time admiring her physical attributes before they even met. If he was completely honest with himself, he'd gone way past the admiration stage. He had to put the brakes on for now. Maybe when this assignment was finished...

Had he just made a plan to pursue something beyond work?

"We're hoping to find a connection no one knew about before," Amber explained as she glanced around the cramped living room.

Her words dragged Sean back to the here and now.

Like Rhiana Pettie's house, there was no security system, Sean noted. A small sofa and cocktail table were overpowered by a massive drawing desk and light. One wall was covered with bookshelves, but rather than filled with books, the shelves were stacked with rolls of architectural drawings. The shelves were labeled alphabetically.

No flowers in the living room.

"May we see the rest of the house?" Amber asked, her anticipation showing.

"Oh, sure." McCorkle gestured to the far side of the room. "The hall leads to the two bedrooms and a bathroom. The kitchen is that way." She indicated the doorway to the right. "The police moved things around a bit, but otherwise it's all just like she left it that last morning before she went to work."

A narrow pair of swinging doors separated the living room from the tiny kitchen. In the sink sat the vase of flowers. Adrenaline fired across Sean's nerve endings. It was way past time to call the cops.

Amber leaned close and visually examined what was obviously an arrangement of dead roses. She turned to McCorkle. "Do you know when she received the flowers?"

The older woman nodded. "The day before…"

"Did she mention who they were from or if there was a card?"

McCorkle shook her head. "She didn't. She only said that she was mad that he wouldn't let go."

Another blast of adrenaline nailed Sean. "Who did she mean? An old boyfriend?"

"Yes. They had broken up the month before, but he kept calling. The police interviewed him and eventually ruled him out. They said he had an airtight alibi."

"What was the ex-boyfriend's name?" Amber asked.

"Quentin Yates. He works for another architectural firm in town."

"Do you mind if we look around for a card?" Sean didn't wait for Amber to ask. As mad as Harper would be, this could be a major break in the case.

"I'll help you," McCorkle offered.

Since the flowers were in the kitchen, that was the logical place to start. The evidence techs had taken the garbage to the lab. Sean figured if they'd found a card with a sinister note, they would have marked it as evidence. Since that wasn't in any of the reports, he was going with the theory it hadn't been found.

When they had checked every nook and cranny in the small kitchen, they moved to the living room. Amber chatted casually with McCorkle. Sean decided she could have been a cop herself. She had a way of prompting answers without directly asking the questions. McCorkle didn't hesitate even once. Sean doubted she realized she was being interrogated. By the time they moved on to the bedrooms, Amber knew all about Kimberly's social life and the long, hard path to her career.

"I'll take the bathroom," Sean offered. He had no desire to spend the next twenty minutes or so trapped in one of those little bedrooms with Amber. In the past twenty-four hours she had gotten deep under his skin. He wished he could regret it, but the necessary emotion just wouldn't come. He knew it was wrong, but he couldn't help savoring it.

As good as it felt, it could not go any further while he was responsible for her safety. He could fantasize all he wanted.

Kimberly McCorkle's bathroom was crammed with the usual female necessities. Lots of hair and skin products. Loads of fragrances. Various types of razors. Toothpaste. Bodywash in a variety of scents. Amber's bathroom looked a lot like this. The first night he'd stayed at her house he'd had a hell of a time evicting her scent from his system. The subtle citrus fragrance was fresh and clean and made him long to taste every inch of her.

"Idiot," he muttered. He moved on to the medicine cabinet. No drugs other than aspirin and a half-empty prescription of antibiotics.

"Sean!"

He closed the mirrored medicine cabinet door and hurried to the bedroom at the end of the hall.

Amber pointed to the jewelry box on the dresser. "It was under the velvet lining."

He moved to her side and took a look. Amber had removed several necklaces and a watch, as well as the lining in the bottom of the jewelry box. How had the evidence techs missed this? "Was it obviously loose?"

"No. One of the necklaces hung in the fabric and pulled it away from the bottom."

At the bottom of the box were a couple of folded notes and the card from the floral shop lying right on top. It wasn't a business card; it was the one sporting the note that accompanied the bouquet. *I'm watching you.*

"We need a plastic bag," he muttered.

"I'll get one," McCorkle said, sounding breathless.

Amber reached into the jewelry box and gingerly removed the card by its edges. "Should we look at the notes, too?"

"For sure." Sean removed the stack of notes carefully; there were four in all. Each was from the ex, Yates, who hadn't wanted to end the relationship.

"She thought the flowers were from him," Amber said. "She was keeping all this in case she needed it in the future."

But her future never came. The words echoed through Sean's head. Amber wouldn't have a future either if this bastard had anything to do with it.

McCorkle returned with a plastic sandwich bag and Sean bagged the evidence. Amber made her aware of the notes, which weren't particularly threatening, simply obsessive. Sean's mind wouldn't quit replaying those haunting words.

Did Amber have any idea how lucky she was to be alive? His throat tightened.

By the time they were at the front door, McCorkle's composure had frayed.

"We'll get this evidence to the police," Sean assured her. "They'll get this guy."

When they were in the car and headed downtown, Amber turned to him. "Before we go to the police, I want to go back to the floral shop."

Sean moved his head firmly side to side. "No way."

"It can't be a coincidence that all three flower arrangements came from the same florist and that at least two had the same warning."

Sean wouldn't deny the point. "It's still circumstantial and—" he shot her a pointed look "—we're playing fast and loose with evidence that may prove necessary to solving a double homicide."

She twisted in the seat and pled her case from a different perspective. "We have no idea what this guy does to stay ahead of the police. We do know he got past my security code. He could be listening to a police radio. I don't want him tipped off."

Sean shook his head. He had to be nuts, and yet she had a point. "What do you expect to say to Thrasher?"

She sighed. "I don't know. All I know for sure is that I don't want him to get away."

Sean braked for a light, and she touched his arm. He turned to her, and the stark fear on her face startled him. "How will I ever feel safe again if he gets away?"

Before he could stop the words, he made a promise he hoped like hell he could keep. "I won't let that happen."

Chapter Eleven

Thrasher Floral, Pearson Avenue, 3:00 p.m.

"Can we go in now?" Amber asked again.

Sean didn't like the idea of going in before they called Harper, but he'd put off the inevitable for a full fifteen minutes. If he didn't agree to going in soon, Amber would likely ignore him and go in anyway. Keeping her reasonably cooperative was essential.

"As soon as that customer comes out," he promised, "we're going in."

Amber acquiesced to his latest delay tactic with nothing more than a roll of her eyes.

The shop was in a small building on Pearson Avenue. Thrasher was thirty-one, the same age as Kyle Adler. Birmingham and its surrounding suburbs made for a fairly large population, so the two might not have grown up in the same neighborhood or have gone to school together, but they knew each other. Adler made deliveries for the floral shop—two of those deliveries had carried cards with warnings. Sean was damned certain a third one had, as well; he just couldn't prove it.

Since Adler was dead, who had delivered Amber's flowers? Thrasher? He'd denied making the delivery and claimed the employee who filled the order was out sick when Harper questioned him. If Harper had located the employee and questioned her, Sean hadn't heard about it. There was a lot happening in a short period of time. So much so that keeping everyone in the loop was difficult. Not that he and Amber had been keeping anyone informed. That had to change soon. They were way over the line already. Jess wouldn't be happy. The boss considered B&C's relationship with the BPD sacred. Maybe he'd still have a job when this case was finished.

At this point, he didn't have much to lose by putting off calling Harper for a few more minutes. If they were going to do this, they might as well do it right. It was time to ask Thrasher different questions.

The entrance opened, and the brunette they'd been watching at the counter exited with a small arrangement.

"That's our cue." He climbed from behind the wheel and moved around to meet Amber on the sidewalk. "Careful what you say," he warned. "We need him cooperative, not defensive."

She made a face. "Trust me—I've done this once or twice, Mr. Douglas."

"So I'm Mr. Douglas now?"

She eyed him skeptically. "For the moment."

Shaking his head, he opened the door. The bell jingled as they entered. The lady behind the counter looked up. "Good afternoon. Welcome to Thrasher's. How can I help you?"

"Is Mr. Thrasher in?" Amber asked, taking the lead.

Sean suppressed a grin. She might be petite, but there was nothing small about her personality. She was pretty damned fearless. Like most people who met her in person for the first time, he'd thought she would be taller, too. He decided then and there the reason was her personality. Amber Roberts was larger than life.

The clerk shook her head. "He called me this morning and said he was sick. I rushed over and opened the shop."

"Thank you—" Sean noted the name on her badge "—Louanne. We'll try to catch him again later."

Amber glared at him as he guided her out the same door they had just entered.

"What're you doing? I want to have a look around in that shop."

He ushered her to the car and opened her door. "Get in and I'll explain."

With a reluctant huff, she dropped into the seat. Sean hurried around to the driver's side and joined her.

"Let's go to his house." She dug through her purse. "I can locate his address in about thirty seconds."

"We have to call Harper. Now. No more putting it off." He pulled his cell from his pocket, ignoring her irritated glare. "We want whatever evidence we find to be admissible in court, Amber. We can't just go rummaging through the man's shop looking for clues."

"You didn't mention having issues with the idea when we were going through Rhiana's and Kimberly's homes."

"We had permission," he reminded her. "Their mothers were right there with us. We've gone as far as we can with this. It's time to let the cops do their job."

She stared at the street for a long moment. "Fine. Make the call."

Sean entered Harper's number and brought him up to speed. With the order to back off ringing in his ears, he ended the call and gave Amber the bad news.

"Detective Harper says it will take some time to get a warrant. He *suggested* we go home and wait for his call. The techs are finished at your place. He thinks it's safe if you want to go home."

"I knew this would happen." She folded her arms across her chest. "We should have nosed around when we had the chance."

He didn't bother pointing out once more that rendering evidence unusable was not their goal. "We skipped lunch. After what you went through last night, we need to rectify that oversight."

"I'm not hungry. I..."

When she remained silent, he glanced her way. She stared forward, her lips slightly parted. He licked his own and shifted his attention back to the street. The woman had amazing lips. He'd spent a lot of time watching those lips, and even when she'd been sick as a dog in the wee hours of the morning they were still tempting.

"We've been so focused on finding the evidence," she said, more to herself than to him. "We've ignored what it means." She turned to him. Her eyes round with something like disbelief. "They were watching us, and I don't mean from afar. I'm talking about up close."

Sean braked for a four-way stop. "Adler and Thrasher?"

She nodded, her gaze seeking his. "The flowers were delivered the day before each victim went missing. Mine had been ordered several days before they were delivered. They were watching." She pressed a hand to her lips. "One or the other or maybe both came into my house—into their houses—and took souvenirs, but that's not all they did while they were there."

A horn blared behind them, forcing Sean to take his eyes off her and to move forward. He got where she was headed. "You're thinking they planted cameras so they could watch."

"Oh, my God." Both hands went to her face then. "There's no other explanation."

Harper hadn't mentioned finding any surveillance devices. Sean reached over and took her hand in his. "You're okay. Adler is dead, and we're on to Thrasher. Whatever one or both did, it won't happen again."

She scrubbed at her eyes. "We have to search my house. Now. I need to know if they were watching me… I need to be sure."

"Since no other toxins have been found, I think it's safe to have a look. But I'm not letting you stay there again until this is over." Sean gave her hand a squeeze before letting go.

She held his gaze a beat longer. "Okay."

His entire being aching to lean across the seat and kiss her. He shifted his attention straight ahead. What he really wanted to do was pull over and make her feel this raging desire building inside him. She needed kissing. She needed to feel safe and cared for. For the first time in a very long time, he hoped he got the opportunity to make her feel that way.

Forest Brook Drive, Homewood

AMBER STARED AT her home for a long moment after the car stopped moving. Sean was getting out and would be at her door any second, but she suddenly couldn't move. Growing up, she had spent endless hours in this house. Louisa Roberts had been the perfect grandmother. She always baked cookies for Amber's arrival. If it was summer, there would be fresh-squeezed lemonade. If it was winter, there would be homemade hot chocolate. They read together and played games. Grandma Louisa owned every good board game made between 1950 and 1980, she'd boasted.

In this house Amber had felt completely safe and loved her entire life.

Until now.

Her door opened, and Sean waited for her to climb out. She stared up at him, conscious of her need to throw herself into his arms. She suddenly felt so isolated and completely alone. He was the one person that made her feel remotely safe right now. She wanted to know the shelter of his arms…she wanted to know him.

Shaking off the overwhelming reactions, she emerged from the car and steadied herself. When this was over, she intended to take a serious vacation. She hadn't taken a real vacation since the summer she graduated college. The job at the station was already hers, so she'd taken two weeks on the West Coast to relax and shop for a fashionable wardrobe. She'd returned well rested and seriously broke. Her grandmother had laughed and given her a high five. That winter Louisa Roberts had passed away.

Amber pushed aside the tender memories and waited while Sean unlocked her front door. The silence inside made her belly clench. Normally her security system would be screaming for attention, but she had left it disarmed for the police. Actually, they hadn't armed it when they'd raced out of here headed for the ER. How had this place that had once felt so safe suddenly become so filled with potential danger?

Her heart was pounding by the time she crossed the threshold. As terrifying as the reality that someone had broken in and touched her things was, it was still good to be home on a level no one could touch.

The evidence technicians hadn't left the mess she had expected. Everything looked just as she'd left it when they'd hurried off to the ER last night. The teacup she'd used as well as the can of tea were missing. Both were evidence now. In a day or two the lab would be able to tell her what sort of poison had been added to her tea. She'd done some Google searches before she'd fallen asleep this morning, but the symptoms for most toxins were so similar it was impossible to narrow down the possibilities. She was, however, relatively certain the culprit was some sort of plant.

"Where should we begin?" she asked, shifting to what they'd come here to do.

"The cameras might be really small. Basically they could be planted anywhere, but—" he met her gaze "—we should check the bedroom and bathroom first."

The idea made Amber sick to her stomach. "How do you want to do this?"

"Do you have a stepladder?"

She nodded. "In the garage."

Rather than go to her bedroom, Amber waited in the living room for Sean to return. She hoped the feeling of uncertainty in her own home would pass quickly. When this was over and she was on that nice, long vacation, she intended to have the house cleaned and painted. All the food products were going in the trash. Every dish and spoon and utensil would be sanitized in the dishwasher. Every single item she owned was going to be washed or dry-cleaned.

It was the only way she would ever feel comfortable in her home again.

While Sean checked the overhead light fixtures and tops of the windows, Amber started the challenging task of going through the bookshelves and clutter on the chest of drawers and dresser.

"Here we go."

She turned from the bookshelf to see him take a small object from the narrow shelf made by the plantation shutters on the window. Her heart lurched.

"We need a box," he said. "A shoe box, hatbox, whatever you have handy."

Amber rushed into her closet and grabbed the first shoe box she could get her hands on. She dumped the contents and hurried back to where he waited. He placed the small gadget in the box. She positioned the lid over it. If the thing was still live, she didn't want whoever might be watching to see anything else.

Before moving on to the next room, they covered every square foot of her bedroom and discovered one more camera, this one on top of a family portrait that her grandmother had commissioned when Amber's father was five. Even if the evidence techs had moved the painting, they wouldn't have noticed it unless they were looking specifically for something so tiny.

A third camera was found in the bathroom on the cabinet above the toilet, angled to ensure she was captured taking a bath or shower. The fear she had felt earlier was gone. Fury had taken its place. This was her home! The living room and the kitchen were bugged with one camera each. She stood in the middle of her kitchen now and allowed the rage to course through her. It was either that or throw up, and she'd done enough of that last night.

"We should take all this to Harper," Sean suggested.

Amber didn't argue.

When they left she armed the security system for all the good it would do.

Sean called Lieutenant Harper, who suggested they meet at Thrasher's home since he was en route there with a warrant.

"Did they find him?" Amber wanted to know. Sean hadn't mentioned the floral shop owner.

He shook his head. "One of the neighbors said he left this morning at the same time he always does to open the shop and he hasn't returned."

"He's gone." Amber didn't need confirmation. The man knew the police were getting close to figuring out his connection to Adler and the murdered women and he'd run. *Damn it!*

"I'm sure the BPD issued a BOLO. Thrasher won't get far."

Amber hoped he was right.

Killough Circle, 6:15 p.m.

A BPD CRUISER sat on the street in front of the house belonging to Peter Thrasher. The sedan Lieutenant Chet Harper and Detective Chad Cook had arrived in was parked in the driveway alongside the evidence techs' van. Yellow tape marked the area as a crime scene. The two uniforms guarding the perimeter had informed Amber and Sean they had to wait on the street until further notice. Two other cruisers had blocked both ends of the block. No reporters were getting in.

Amber had been pacing the sidewalk for a good forty-five minutes. She was dying to know what was going on inside the house. Had they found evidence tying Thrasher to Adler? She rubbed at her forehead. Had they found photos or videos of her or the other women?

She hugged her arms around herself and paced in the other direction. Had the two sold the intimate look at her life to some adult site? Her stomach churned. If they had uploaded the videos they made to the internet…

"You're going to wear out that sidewalk," Sean commented.

Amber stalled and glared at him. Leaning against his car, his arms folded across his chest, ankles crossed, he appeared completely unperturbed. How could he look so calm? Two women had been murdered. She would have been number three if someone hadn't killed Adler. She might still end up murdered if Thrasher wasn't found. Reality washed over her like a dash of icy water. She would be looking over her shoulder for the rest of her life if he got away.

She couldn't fall apart now. *Deep breath.* "We've been waiting almost an hour." She looked back at the house. "Do you think they've found evidence to connect him to the cameras we found in my house?" She had stood outside the yellow tape at plenty of scenes where a crime had been committed. In her experience the longer the investigators were inside, the more likely the findings were significant.

"Chances are if they'd found nothing, we'd know it by now."

Of course they had found evidence. She really was out of sorts here. How long had she been reporting the news? Going on seven years. Granted, she rarely landed the major crime stories like serial killer Eric Spears—that was Gina Coleman's domain. Frankly, it didn't matter how many times she had worked a crime scene like this; this was different. This was personal. She was on the other side of the event this time. The reporters following this case were talking about her, which was in part why her boss had insisted she take a few vacation days. She'd been thinking about calling to do exactly that. He'd beat her to it.

Sean abruptly straightened away from his car. Amber's gaze followed his to the detective exiting the front door of Thrasher's home. Her pulse fluttered.

Detective Cook was only a couple of years younger than Amber. She'd seen him at Gina and Barb's engagement party. Cook had just popped the question to Dr. Sylvia Baron's daughter. Amber remembered feeling vaguely jealous of the couple. They had looked so in love.

Her gaze drifted to Sean. She blinked and looked away. God help her.

Cook gave Sean one of those male nods of acknowledgment, then he turned to Amber. "Ma'am, Lieutenant Harper will be out shortly. He'll brief you on what we found."

"Thank you." It was about time.

"We've got Ricky Vernon headed over here to take a look at the computers," Cook said to Sean. "Harper doesn't want to risk triggering any safety features that might shut down or wipe the systems."

"Are you saying there's more than one computer?" Amber's stomach sank.

Cook shifted his attention back to her. She held her breath as he seemed to decide how much he could tell her. "Yes, ma'am, four desktop computers and one laptop. It looks like he was watching a fourth woman. The lieutenant has sent a couple of uniforms over to check on her."

"Is she okay?"

Cook hesitated again. "We're not seeing her on any of the cameras. We've made a couple of calls already, and she wasn't at work today."

"Thrasher may have taken her." A chill bored into Amber's bones. And he was out there somewhere. She turned all the way around, scanning the neighborhood. He could be anywhere.

Chapter Twelve

Magic City Beer & Burger, 8:00 p.m.

Amber needed to relax. She sat on her side of the booth, her back ramrod straight. Sean had hoped that coming to an out-of-the-way place—one he doubted she'd ever set foot inside—would help make that happen. No such luck. She jumped every time the bell over the door jingled with a new customer.

"You should stop worrying about who walks in and just eat." He nodded to the house special on her plate. "You know the sauce is a closely guarded secret."

"I'm sure it's great." She forced a smile into place. "I'm really not hungry."

"The fries are the best in town." For emphasis he stuffed one into his mouth. Bad move. Rather than follow his example, she watched him chew. Out in LA he'd dated plenty of celebrity types. Every single one had been unique, but the one thing they all had in common was the inability to hide certain basic feelings. The flare of desire he spotted in Amber's green eyes startled him almost as much as he felt certain it did her. They'd had a couple of moments the past few days, but this was the first time she'd shown true hunger, and he was relatively certain it wasn't about the food.

"Eat," he encouraged. "You'll thank me later. Besides, you don't want to offend the chef."

She glanced over at the counter as the owner and cook shouted, "Order up," and placed a meatloaf special on the counter of the pass through window. With a sigh, she picked up her burger and took a bird-size bite. The surprise that captured her expression made him smile.

"I told you." He tore off another bite of his own sandwich.

For a few minutes they ate in silence. Amber stopped sizing up every customer who entered, and she ate not only the burger but every single fry. Apparently the lady hadn't realized how much she liked burgers. She'd polished off a good-size one at the Garage Café, too. All this time he'd been watching her on the news he'd had her figured for a vegan.

She patted her lips with her napkin. "Wow. I can't believe I ate so much."

"Good." He tossed his own crumpled napkin into his now-empty serving dish. "Would you like dessert? They make the best deep-fried Oreo cookie on the planet."

Amber held up her hands. "No, thanks. I couldn't eat another bite."

"Coffee then," he suggested.

She nodded. "Coffee would be great."

Sean waved over the waitress and ordered coffee. When she was on her way, he watched as Amber drifted back into her own troubling thoughts. "They'll find him."

She blinked as if resurfacing from a faraway place. "I hope so."

"Harper and Cook are the best."

She nodded. "They were part of the team Jess had when she was still with the department."

Sean's boss was pretty much a celebrity herself. "Lori Wells and Clint Hayes were on the team, too." Clint was the senior investigator at B&C now. One of the things Sean liked most about the older man was his straightforwardness. He didn't tolerate the games some people liked to play. Amber appeared to share that feeling. So far Sean had found her to be honest and direct. He liked that about her.

"Gina is always telling stories about Jess's FBI days and how her profiles were responsible for bringing down the worst of the worst."

"Eric Spears." Sean was still living in Hollywood when the infamous serial killer followed Jess to Birmingham, but he'd heard plenty about it from his family.

"Eric Spears was at the top of the evil scale," Amber said. "Gina did an exposé on the way Jess profiled using a scale she called the faces of evil." She laughed. "I'm sure you've heard a great deal about how amazing your boss is."

"She is amazing and tough." Sean had experienced the latter firsthand.

Amber pushed her empty plate aside and braced her crossed arms on the table. She leaned forward and looked directly into his eyes. "How many other women have been hurt or murdered by Thrasher and Adler? What if Pettie and McCorkle weren't their first victims?"

"Jess doesn't think there were other victims, but we may never know for sure," Sean allowed. The waitress arrived with two steaming cups of coffee. Sean gifted her with a smile and thanked her. He sipped his coffee, hoping Amber would do the same rather than dwell on the what-ifs.

When she followed his lead and tasted the coffee, she made an approving sound. "This place is full of surprises."

The place looked a little rough on the surface, especially with the old truck front end hanging on the wall behind the bar. Rustic but homey in Sean's opinion. The staff was extra friendly, and the craft beers were second to none. "My folks used to bring us here here as kids. It was a ritual after church on Sundays."

Amber smiled, that genuine one that made his heart beat a little faster. "You went to church?"

"Didn't you?" he teased. "You grew up in Birmingham—you must have."

"I did. I still do occasionally. Work sometimes gets in the way." She sipped her coffee and turned thoughtful for a moment. "Even when we traveled, we found a house of worship. Whether it was a Jewish temple or a Buddhist one. My parents embrace all people and their cultures."

"More people should raise their children that way." Sean damned sure intended to—if he ever had any. Now there was a thought that came out of left field. Just because he would turn thirty this year didn't mean time was running out. As far as he know guys didn't have so-called biological clocks. He drowned the crazy idea with more coffee.

"Why does Jess believe there aren't other murder victims?" Amber's smile had disappeared. The worry was back in her eyes.

"She read the case files on Pettie and McCorkle. She concluded that the first murder, Pettie, was likely a surprise to both men. The work was sloppier. They were more careful and organized with the second victim, McCorkle. Even the way the cameras were placed in the homes, Pettie's versus yours, was progressively more precise."

"So they may have started out as Peeping Toms hiding in the girls' bathroom at school or watching their sisters or mothers?"

"Exactly. The BPD confirmed the two attended the same schools. Jess believes they probably teamed up as school chums and things grew from there."

Amber shivered visibly. Sean reached across the table and placed his hand on hers. "Even if Thrasher is stupid enough to try, he'll have to go through me to get to you."

A faint smile trembled across her lips. "I'm really grateful you're here."

The warmth that had spread up his arm and across his chest from nothing more than touching her hand had him wondering how grateful she would be if she knew how much he wanted to touch all of her.

She straightened away from the table, breaking the contact. "I think maybe I'll have one of those deep-fried Oreos after all."

Rather than summon the waitress, Sean went to the counter and placed the order. He needed the distance. Allowing personal involvement with a client was a mistake he did not intend to repeat. Too bad the only part of him sticking by that motto was his brain—everything else was pulsing with need. He returned to the booth only a few minutes later with their desserts, and they both dug in.

Whether the sugar rush had her thinking again or just gave her the courage to do so, she waded into sensitive territory. “Do you think they shared the videos on the internet? Will the FBI have to be involved?”

“The guy from the BPD’s lab is the top in his field. He’ll be able to determine how far the sharing went, if at all,” Sean explained. “If Adler and Thrasher were sharing their peep shows with friends via the Net, the FBI will more than likely be involved.”

She shuddered. “I feel so exposed.”

He understood. It was one thing for her to report the news on camera, but another one entirely for her private moments bathing and dressing to be videoed without her knowledge or consent. He knew a little something about feeling exposed.

“We’ll know more about what we’re looking at tomorrow,” he promised.

“I hope they find the other woman alive.” She nibbled at another bite of her dessert. “The timing would be right, you know, for another kidnapping. Pettie was in February, McCorkle in June. October makes four months. Isn’t that the way serial killers work?”

“Most have a pattern.” He nodded. “If Thrasher stuck to the pattern he and Adler followed and abducted a fourth victim, he did so in the past twenty-four hours. Since the other vics were held for several days before they were murdered, it makes sense that she would still be alive. Assuming, of course, the death of his partner hasn't sent him off in a different direction."

Amber sat her coffee down and stared into the cup for a moment as if searching for the right words. "Why do you suppose I was skipped? It was obvious they'd been watching me longer."

"If Thrasher murdered Adler, we have to assume the two had a falling-out. I imagine the event put Thrasher into a tailspin. Before he could regain his bearings the body was discovered and you were brought in for questioning. I've been with you since. My guess is he moved on to the next name on the list."

Amber leaned her head in her hand and rubbed her temple with her fingers. "I guess I'm the lucky one."

Sean had learned enough from Jess to know luck had nothing to do with it. Something went down between Thrasher and Adler that disrupted the timeline of the two killers. In Sean's opinion it was somehow related to Amber.

He wished the feeling that it was far from over would stop gnawing at him.

Oxmoor Glen Drive, 9:15 p.m.

SEAN TOSSED THE tennis ball across the room, and the big dog bounced after it. When he tried to take the ball back a tug-of-war ensued. Amber moistened her lips and bit back a grin. She found it far too endearing that her bodyguard played with his dog as if it were a child. He obviously loved the animal. She'd never had time for pets. Come to think of it, she rarely found time for anything other than work. Why was it the idea suddenly felt so wrong?

When Rebel had tired of playing, he curled up on the fluffy round bed in the corner. Sean gestured to the sofa. "Feel free to turn on the television. I should make sure the guest room is presentable."

"I slept in it for a couple of hours this morning," she reminded him. "I didn't have any complaints. Besides, why would I turn on the television and listen to all the speculation and theories connecting me to Adler's murder?"

"Good point." He backed into the hallway and then disappeared.

Amber released a long, weary breath and surveyed Sean's place. She hadn't really taken in many of the details in the wee hours of this morning. The kitchen, dining and living space were one fairly large room. The place was nice with most modern amenities. A gas fireplace in the living room, stainless steel appliances in the kitchen and nice high ceilings. The decor was American bachelor simple: big, comfy sofa, huge television hanging over the fireplace and a coffee table littered with sports magazines and remotes.

On the bar that separated the kitchen from the rest

of the space where he'd tossed his keys, there was a framed photograph of a young Sean, his siblings and their parents. His hair was considerably longer. She estimated the shot had been taken before he left for the West Coast. A built-in bookcase next to the fireplace held several books by one of her favorite mystery authors. She reached for last year's release and smiled. So they had something besides the lack of a personal life in common after all.

"Have you picked up his latest?"

Amber closed the book and tucked it back onto the shelf. "I haven't, but I plan to. You?"

"It's on my bedside table. You're welcome to it."

Was he inviting her to his bed or to borrow his book? Her nerves jangled foolishly. She was nervous. The realization startled her. Hoping to keep that embarrassing revelation to herself, she pointed at him and gave a knowing nod. "You saw the stack on my bedside table, didn't you?"

He shrugged. "I might have noticed." He glanced at the clock in the cable box. "Would you like a beer?" Another of those completely male shrugs lifted his shoulders. "Sorry. I've been meaning to pick up a good bottle of wine for company. I'm pretty sure I have popcorn and a stash of peanuts."

Was it her imagination or was he feeling as nervous as she was? "Nothing for me, thank you."

For several seconds they stood there staring at each other.

She should say something. "I think I might shower and go to bed early." She propped her lips into a broad smile. "Do a little reading maybe—if you don't mind me borrowing that book."

"Sure thing." He hitched a thumb over his shoulder. "I'll get it for you."

Scrubbing her unexpectedly sweaty palms against her hips, she followed him down the short hall. Butterflies had taken flight in her belly. She stopped at the door rather than follow him into his bedroom. Like the main living space, the decorating was minimal. A big bed, bedside table and a chest of drawers. She was surprised not to see another massive television. What she did see was a stack of books that rivaled her own.

He grabbed a pair of boxers and a lone shoe from the floor. "You need anything else to sleep in?"

She thought of the faded crimson tee that sported the Roll Tide logo she'd slept in that morning. "The T-shirt works."

"There're clean towels in the bathroom closet." He winced. "Did your sister bring bodywash? You might not like my soap. I know you used it this morning, but that was kind of an emergency."

"It's fine." It smelled like him, but she'd been too sick to care.

He tossed the shoe and boxers into his closet and then grabbed the hardcover from the bedside table. He crossed the room, coming toward her, and her heart beat considerably faster. She tried to swallow, but her throat felt closed.

He passed the book to her. "If you get past the sixth chapter, don't tell me if he gets the girl."

Her fingers brushed his and need ignited deep inside her. "Doesn't he always get the girl?"

Sean was so close now the scent of his skin filled her senses. She wanted to reach out and run her hands over those broad shoulders. She wanted to trace every ridge and valley of the lean torso beneath that khaki shirt. She wanted to lose herself in the sensations and pretend her world wasn't a total mess.

He leaned his face toward hers. "I would really like to kiss you right now, but that's a bad idea."

She lifted her face, leaving no more than a couple of inches between their lips. "I was thinking the same thing."

He moistened his lips, and her breath caught.

"What do you want to do about it?"

Amber reached up slowly and fisted her fingers in his shirt. "I say we get it over with so we can move past it." She wet her lips. "My grandmother always said to go for whatever you wanted, otherwise you'd just go on wanting it."

"Smart lady."

His lips lowered to hers. The first contact had pure pleasure erupting inside her. His mouth was hot, his lips firm, but his kiss was slow and restrained. His fingers landed on her cheeks, tracing the lines of her face as his lips tasted and teased hers. She pulled at his shirt, drawing that amazing body nearer.

By the time he drew his lips from hers, her thighs were trembling and every part of her was on fire. He pressed his forehead to hers and whispered, "That was good."

"Uh-huh." She licked her lips, shivering at the taste of him.

"Should we do it again just to make sure we get it out of our systems?"

Amber closed her eyes and inhaled a slow, deep breath. She wanted to say yes so badly. "I think we should maybe wait until tomorrow and revisit the idea then." Otherwise she was going to drag him into that big, unmade bed.

"Agreed."

He drew away first and stuffed his hands into the pockets of his jeans as if he didn't trust himself.

Amber's entire being protested the loss of contact. "Well, good night."

He managed a stiff nod. "'Night."

Amber didn't breathe again until she was in the guest room with the door closed. She tossed the book onto the bed and dragged in a couple more deep breaths to calm her galloping pulse. When she felt in control again, she grabbed the tee and some clean underwear. She opened the door and peeked into the hall. Clear. She moved to the bathroom. He'd gone back to the living room and turned on the television.

Once inside the bathroom, she closed the door and locked it. A glance in the mirror made her wince. She looked frightful. Her skin was even paler than usual. Dark circles had formed under her eyes.

With a groan, she turned on the water in the shower and undressed. How in the world had she allowed that to happen? What had she been thinking? Shaking her head, she stepped into the shower, and the hot water instantly banished all other thought.

For a while she stood there and allowed the water to work its magic on her tight muscles. It felt so good. She'd been so tense all day. Slowly, she reached for the soap and lathered it up. The clean, fresh scent of Sean filled the tiled space. She shivered despite the hot water.

A glutton for punishment, she closed her eyes and rubbed the soap over her skin. When she moved it over her breasts, her breath caught and she let the memory of his kiss consume her. By the time she'd lathered her skin, her body felt weak with want. In her mind his hands replaced hers, sliding the soap over her skin, his fingers tempting her nipples and trailing down her ribs. She trembled.

The soap slipped from her fingers and hit the floor. Amber jerked out of the fantasy. This was a perfect example of how badly the past few days had shaken her. She was fantasizing about a stranger. Sure they had spent the last forty-eight or so hours together, but they still didn't know each other.

Hurrying through the rest of her shower, she rinsed her body with cool water. Even after she'd toweled off, she was still burning up. She dragged on the tee and her underwear and reached for the door. Maybe she should give herself a few more minutes before chancing an encounter with Sean.

After taking a deep breath, she prowled for a hair dryer and set to the task. She massaged her scalp with one hand while directing the hot air with the other. Her fingers slowed as she studied her reflection. What did Sean Douglas see when he looked at her? She was attractive enough, she supposed. Braces had taken care of her teeth back in middle school. She hadn't suffered with acne like a lot of her friends, but she'd been teased endlessly about her freckles.

She didn't mind the freckles really. The makeup when she was on the air basically covered them up, but she didn't bother trying to hide them when she wasn't on the job. She hung her towel over the shower door while the dryer cooled off, and then she searched the cabinet under the sink for a spare toothbrush. She'd left hers in the guest room.

A knock at the door made her jump. She bumped her head on the counter.

"I noticed your toothbrush on the bedside table," Sean announced, his deep voice filtering through the door and wrapping around her. "You want it?"

Man alive did she want it, only it wasn't the toothbrush. Amber rubbed at her head. She cracked the door open the tiniest bit and reached out. "Thanks."

He placed the toothbrush in her waiting hand. "Welcome."

When he walked away she closed the door and leaned against it for a long moment. *Get a grip, Amber. Adrenaline is messing with your head.*

Five minutes later, teeth brushed, dryer put away and her clothes folded in her arms, she exited the bathroom and headed straight for the guest room. "See you in the morning," she called without a backward glance.

His deep voice followed her into the room. "Count on it."

Chapter Thirteen

Fourth Avenue North,
Thursday, October 20, 10:20 a.m.

The story was out.

For six years Amber had chased the story. She had gone to great lengths to uncover details and insights no one else could find.

Now *she* was the story.

She and Sean had been summoned to the B&C office right after breakfast. On some level she was glad for the escape. All night the memory of that kiss had haunted her. Meeting his gaze this morning had been difficult. Primarily because she'd wanted to resume right where they'd left off. *So, so not smart.*

On the way here, she'd focused on the case, hoping the summons meant there was good news, but judging by the look on Jess Burnett's face that was not the case. Buddy Corlew had called first thing this morning to let them know the phone records had been a bust. There were plenty of calls between Adler and his customers, but none between him and Thrasher except those to the floral shop.

Amber braced for more bad news.

Jess closed the folder on her desk and looked first at Amber, then at Sean. "Thrasher is still at large. His car was found abandoned near the Nineteenth Street bus station. It's possible he fled the city, but there's always the chance he could be in hiding close by."

It wasn't necessary to be an FBI profiler to understand why Thrasher would choose not to run. "He may want to finish what he and Adler started," Amber proposed.

Jess nodded. "Lieutenant Harper and I believe it would be best if you continued to keep a low profile for a few more days. We want to be sure you stay safe."

"Wow." Amber slumped in her chair. "This keeps growing more complicated." So many times she had interviewed victims and expressed her sympathy. Now she understood the look in their eyes after she offered the usual words of commiseration. A person couldn't possibly understand how *this* felt…unless he or she was the target. "So *you* believe I'm still in danger."

"I do. I've had time to review all the available information on Thrasher and Adler," Jess began. "Thrasher has spent his adult life dealing in flowers. He never married. No long-term relationships. His father died when he was ten and his mother passed away two years ago, so there's no family. No record of mental illness or counseling of any sort. No health issues on record. According to the interviews conducted by the lieutenant's team, his employees like him."

"Is that typical in a killer?" Sean asked.

The sound of his voice wrapped around Amber and made breathing difficult. She wasn't at all sure she could handle another night in the same house with him. She'd gone to sleep and awakened dreaming of making love with him. His voice, the way he moved, it all got under her skin somehow.

"Many killers are loners," Jess explained. "Most psychopaths are quite charming. Not all are murderers. In fact, I'm not convinced Thrasher is a killer. Adler may have been the dominant one, but I haven't found evidence suggesting as much. According to the interviews conducted by the BPD, Adler's parents are very religious. They raised their son in a strict environment. Those who knew him called him a loner, shy, quiet. Nothing was found in either man's home that tells us the rest of what we need to know." Jess clasped her hands atop the folder. "I'm not willing to take the risk there's another layer to one or both that I'm not seeing yet. Until we know more, we need to make sure you stay safe."

Sean glanced at Amber. "I guess that means you're stuck with me for a little while longer."

She produced a smile. “I guess so.”

“If Thrasher and Adler were obsessed with you,” Jess said, “he won’t be able to stay away. He’ll need to see you. To be close.”

Her words sent goose bumps spilling over Amber’s skin. “I understand. The station isn’t expecting me back to work for a few days.” She swallowed, wishing her mouth hadn’t gone so dry. “I should stay home and not answer the door?”

A rap on the door drew Jess’s attention there. Amber glanced over her shoulder to see the receptionist poke her head into the office.

“There are at least a dozen reporters lining the street out front. When Ms. Roberts is ready to leave I would suggest the alley exit.”

Any hope of getting through this without mounting attention in the media curled up and died in the pit of Amber’s stomach.

“Thank you, Rebecca.” Jess shifted her attention to Amber. “The more your face is in the news, the more Thrasher will be incited to make a move—if he’s watching, as I suspect he is. If he’s obsessed with you, he can’t help himself.”

“How difficult do you believe it’ll be for the police to find him?” Amber pressed.

“His resources are limited, which helps, but there’s no guarantee he’ll be found.”

She could be looking over her shoulder for the rest of her life. This time the inability to draw in a deep breath had nothing to do with the man next to her. Something Jess had said suddenly elbowed its way to the front of her worries. “You said you’re not convinced Thrasher is a killer and that there’s no absolute evidence Adler is. If they aren’t killers, then who murdered those women?”

“Therein lies the rub,” Jess admitted. “Consider Adler’s murder. He was seated at the dining table having tea, presumably with his killer. If that killer was Thrasher, who is a far larger man than Adler, why get up from the table and go to the kitchen for a knife when you can easily overtake the victim?”

“You think there’s a third killer involved.” It wasn’t a question. Amber could see the conviction in Jess’s eyes.

“Lieutenant Harper has expanded the parameters of his investigation to include a potential third killer,” Jess explained. “In my opinion, it’s a necessary step.”

Amber felt completely unnerved. Totally unsettled. “Wow.”

“I would advise you to go someplace not a part of your routine,” Jess offered. “Someplace the killer or killers won’t know to look. Just for a few days. Let the BPD and us do what we need to do without having to worry about adding names to the victim list.”

“What about the other woman who was being watched?” Amber worried Jess hadn’t provided an update on the woman because it was more bad news. “Has she been found?”

"She has," Jess said. "Her name is Emma Norton. The employee the BPD spoke to had just returned from vacation and didn't realize Emma had taken her vacation this week. The lieutenant has spoken to her. She's visiting her father in Seattle. I received the call just before you arrived."

"I'm glad to hear it." Amber felt immensely relieved. It was bad enough two women were dead.

"Take a day or two someplace quiet while we sort this out," Jess repeated. "Sean will see that you stay safe."

He stood. "I'll make sure the alley is still clear."

Amber pushed to her feet. "I appreciate all you're doing, Jess. I can't imagine doing this alone."

With effort Jess stood and rested a hand on her rounded belly. "I'm glad we can help. You are our top priority."

Sean returned and ushered Amber to the rear entrance. Since the slots in front of the B&C office had been full when they arrived, he'd parked two blocks away. To avoid being spotted by her colleagues from the various stations around the city, they detoured another couple of blocks.

He opened her door, and Amber settled in the passenger seat. What if Thrasher wasn't found by Monday? How long was she supposed to keep her life on hold? She should call Barb and let her know what was going on. Was her sister in danger? Jess hadn't mentioned any concerns about Barb's safety.

Calling her boss was unavoidable. He would insist she take as much time as she needed.

She didn't want to take more time. She wanted her life back. She wanted to avoid getting tangled up with her protector. She wanted to stay alive.

Amber looked around to get her bearings. She couldn't say how long Sean had been driving before she snapped out of her pity party. "Where are we going?"

"My parents have a place on the river. I thought we'd go there."

She hoped it was larger than his house. "What about clothes?" And other stuff, like a toothbrush and deodorant?

"We can drive past your house, but I'm guessing there are more reporters waiting there. We can stop for what we need once we're out of the city."

Amber resigned herself to her fate. It was either risk a confrontation with an obsessed killer or killers or spend time in a remote location alone with the man who had kissed her like she'd never before been kissed.

She stole a glance at him. She was in trouble either way.

River Road, 3:30 p.m.

JUST OVER A year ago Sean had escaped the hurt and anger by coming here. For six months after Lacy's death the press hounded him. The official investigation had cleared him of any criminal wrongdoing related to her death, but he hadn't been able to forgive himself. If he had paid closer attention...if he hadn't allowed things to become personal, she might still be alive.

Intellectually he understood that the choices she had made in her life were not his responsibility, but in his heart he carried the burden. He had trusted her...trusted the love they shared.

What an arrogant fool he'd been.

"So this is where your family spends Christmas?"

Sean shook off the painful memories and focused on the woman standing in the middle of the family room. "This is the place."

During the forty-five-minute drive from the city she'd initially remained silent. He imagined she grappled for some way to come to terms with the situation. As if she'd reached some understanding with herself, she had kept the conversation going from that point on, asking him question after question about the family cabin. His great-great-grandfather had built the room they were now standing in nearly a hundred years ago. Each generation had added additional square footage and renovated to include multiple bedrooms and bathrooms. His grandmother had been the one to insist on the huge eat-in kitchen.

"Take any bedroom you'd like." The sooner they were settled, the sooner he could walk the grounds to clear his head. In the past twenty-four hours the lady had managed to breach his defenses entirely. That kiss had blown him away. Even a month ago he wouldn't have believed he could feel that way again. He wanted to touch her and to kiss her...and a whole lot more.

She's an assignment, blockhead. Work. You can't go there.

"Which one do you usually take?"

Her question dragged him from the disturbing thoughts just in time to watch her turn all the way around again, taking in the enormity of the place. There were no frills, no chef's kitchen or jetted tubs, just homey spaces with decent plumbing and incredible views of nature.

"Top of the stairs, first door on the left." He hitched a thumb toward the door. "I'll batten down the hatches and bring in the supplies."

Since no one had stayed here since spring, there were a few things to be done before dark, like turning on the water and checking the generator in case there was a power outage. Then he had to bring in the food supplies and get the refrigerated goods stored. As long as he stayed busy, he would be good to go.

Maybe.

Sean did a quick walk-through of the house before heading outside. When he'd been a kid he'd dreamed of living here full-time. Of course puberty and girls had changed his mind. The occasional weekend here had felt like a world away from his school friends and whoever he'd been sweet on at the time. If only he had known how complicated life could be.

The sky was darker than usual. The rain would be here soon, along with a potential thunderstorm or two. All the more reason to check the generator. His father had taught him to ensure all the mechanics were in working order before getting comfortable. It wasn't like you could call for a service man who would show up in an hour or so.

With the water on and the generator checked, he took a walk around the house and confirmed all was as it should be. Down at the road a passing car drew his attention. He should probably call his parents and let them know he was here. Neighbors were few and far between out here, but they kept an eye on each other's property. His folks would no doubt get a call when the house lights were spotted tonight. Having his parents show up to investigate would not be a good thing. His mother had been complaining for years that she wanted grandchildren. Since his older siblings hadn't stepped up to the plate, his mother was now eyeing him to fill that void.

The image of little redheaded girls frolicking around the pond made his heart stumble. Shaking his head at the crazy fantasy, he carried the first load of grocery bags into the house. When he returned with the rest, Amber was putting away the refrigerated goods.

"You didn't tell me there was a basement with a wine cellar." She put the quart of milk in the fridge. "This is no run-of-the-mill cabin, sir."

"When my grandmother insisted on the kitchen expansion, my grandfather demanded the wine cellar with a smoking room."

A smile spread across her lips as she set the sandwich bread on the counter. Man, he loved the way she smiled. "Sounds like your grandfather knew how to drive a hard bargain."

"He did." Sean placed the bag of mixed greens in the fridge. "He died three years ago, barely three weeks after my grandmother."

"I'm so sorry."

He met her sympathetic gaze. "They were like that. Did everything together, and wherever one went, the other followed."

Sean had decided years ago his grandparents had the kind of love that couldn't be found anymore. People had stopped learning how to love that way. For the most part his parents' relationship wasn't far off the mark. He couldn't hope to ever share that kind of devotion with anyone.

"My grandparents were like that." Amber scooted onto a stool at the kitchen's center island. "My parents, too. I never really noticed until they retired and started traveling so much. It's like they've fallen in love with each other all over again. My sister says she and Gina have that deep bond. I'm not so sure people our age know how to love like that. Maybe we can't give so deeply."

"Is that what you're looking for?" He could have bitten off his tongue. Why the hell had he asked that damned question? Because he was this close—he mentally imagined his thumb and forefinger a fraction of an inch apart—to being a fool twice in one lifetime. At least he hadn't announced that he'd just been thinking the same thing. He'd already noticed far too many commonalities between them.

Her brow furrowed as she contemplated the question. He busied himself with stuffing the plastic grocery bags into the recycle bin.

"I absolutely want it, just not now. My career is top priority." She drew in a big breath. "Before I'm forty I'd like to be married and focused on making a family."

He allowed his gaze to rest on hers once more. The seriousness in her green eyes made his gut tighten. "Sounds like a plan."

He could see himself taking a similar path when he was older. Just another example of how alike they thought. Sean stopped himself. He was intensely attracted to Amber and they had a great deal in common, but that didn't mean they belonged together. *Get your head out of your—*

"Would you mind taking a walk with me?"

Sean blinked. "Sorry. What?"

"I've felt like a prisoner for two days. I need to get outside, breathe some fresh air and just walk off some of the stress. I hate to ask, but apparently I'm not supposed to go anywhere alone."

"Sure." He reached for the key. Usually he wouldn't bother locking up for a stroll around the property, but this was different. Until Thrasher and whoever else might be involved were found, Amber had to be protected.

The sky had darkened a little more but there was still plenty of daylight for a short walk. Over the years several paths had been formed along interesting views on the property. A long circle around the pond and then a meandering trail through the woods to the river. The air was crisp but not actually cold.

Maybe a walk had been a good idea.

"Do you come here every Christmas?"

The soft, lyrical sound of her voice meshed perfectly with the natural beauty around them. Funny how he noticed all those little things when he didn't want to. He should never have kissed her. That sweet taste would never be enough. "I do."

"I'll bet you cut your Christmas tree from these very woods."

Sean laughed. "We do actually. My grandfather insisted that two be planted for each one we cut. Every year on Christmas Eve, my parents drag two small evergreens up here to plant."

"Your grandfather was a smart man."

Sean wished he were a lot smarter and maybe he wouldn't be standing here dying to kiss her again. Then again, maybe what he really needed was courage.

Chapter Fourteen

7:30 p.m.

The scent of marinara sauce filled the kitchen, and Amber's stomach grumbled. She placed the salad she'd prepared on the dining table. The long farmer's table seated ten. She could imagine the big family gatherings around the holidays. The large fireplace on the other side of the room would be roaring at Christmastime. The freshly cut tree would stand tall before the front window. She closed her eyes and imagined the smell of freshly baked cookies. Though her family holidays were usually celebrated in the city at her parents' Mountain Brook home, she'd gotten a taste of a true country Christmas as a child. Her grandparents on her mother's side had lived on a small farm in Blount County. She'd spent a few Christmases there.

She remembered the towering, freshly cut trees. Her grandparents always waited until Christmas Eve to place the final decoration on their tree. The star that topped its peak was saved for Amber's mother to set in place. Her grandmother insisted that her only child, Amber's mother, had placed that star atop the tree since she was old enough to hold it, and she wasn't letting go of that tradition as long as she was breathing.

By the time her grandmother reached thirty, she'd already been married with a daughter running around the home where she and her husband had started many wonderful traditions. Amber straightened the linen napkins next to the two plates. Her only traditions were spending holidays with her family—if work didn't get in the way. Those traditions were actually her parents', not hers. She didn't have any holiday traditions, or any other kind for that matter. She had work.

"Hot stuff headed your way," Sean announced as he moved around her to place the bowl of sauce and the mound of plated pasta on the table.

Amber bit her lips together to prevent mentioning that the food wasn't the only hot stuff in the room. Then and there she admitted defeat. The man got to her. He made her want to explore feelings she'd spent the past year telling herself she no longer cared about. After the breakup with her fiancé, she had decided she would wait a few years or ten before getting involved in another serious personal relationship. How had this man—in a mere seventy, give or take a few, hours—changed her mind so completely?

A hand waved in front of her face. "You still with me?"

Her gaze settled on his, and she melted a little more even as the sound of his deep voice made her shiver.

"Are you cold?" He rubbed his hands up and down her arms.

Her pulse skittered, and she mentally scrambled to find her voice. "No, no. I'm not cold at all." In fact, she was burning up.

"Sit." He pulled out a chair. "I'll run down to the cellar and get a bottle of wine."

Amber prepared her plate. A small serving of salad and pasta. The smell of the sauce had her mouth watering and her appetite resurrecting. Maybe eating was what she needed to take her mind off sex and Sean. Really, her inability to ignore her attraction to him surely had to do with twelve months of celibacy. Had she chosen to abstain from sex since the breakup? Not really. She simply hadn't taken the time to socialize.

The truth was she hadn't been on a date in six or seven months.

Sean returned with a bottle of wine and a bottle of water. He placed the bottle of water next to his glass and deftly opened the bottle of wine. He reached for her glass. "Say when."

Amber moistened her lips as he poured the red wine. "When," she remembered to say as the stemmed glass grew half full.

He set the bottle aside and claimed his chair. Rather than pour himself a glass of wine, he added water to his glass, and then reached for the pasta.

"You're not having wine?" She downed a hefty swallow to calm her nerves.

"Can't." He grinned as he smothered the angel-hair pasta with sauce.

The heat that had kindled inside her at just being in the same room with him extinguished. "Right. Of course. You're on duty." It was his job to be here with her.

She really, really was losing her grip. None of this was real. The silky texture of the full-bodied wine soured on her tongue. What was wrong with her? A man was dead, two innocent women—his victims—had been murdered. Being trapped on the radar of this former killing partnership had turned her life upside down. Had left her vulnerable to her own fundamental desires. The fear of death made her want to celebrate life. She downed another swallow of wine.

Since he'd already dug in, she forced herself to eat. Her appetite had vanished again, but she had the foresight to understand the wine would go straight to her head if she didn't eat. They had forgotten to pick up rolls. Saved her a few carbs.

"Is everything okay?"

She realized then that he'd already cleaned his plate and was going for seconds. "It's great." Another mouthful of wine covered the bitter taste of the lie.

He talked endlessly about his family and how much he'd missed the traditions when he'd lived in LA. To a large degree he felt the loving traditions of his family had helped him move past the tragedy. Amber hung on his every word—hard as she tried not to.

When he tossed his napkin aside, she realized he had stopped talking and was staring at her.

"Now I'm really worried."

She reached for her glass, but it was empty. She blinked and cleared her throat. "Worrying won't find the bad guy." She laughed. "We can do nothing but wait it out." The truth in her words made her shudder. There really was nothing she could do. For the first time in her adult life she felt helpless.

He reached out and entwined his fingers with hers. "This is hard—I know. We'll get to the bottom of what's going on soon. The BPD is moving quickly. Jess and Buddy are doing all they can." He squeezed her fingers. "I'm right here, and I'm not going anywhere until you're safe."

And then he would be gone.

Amber stood. "Thank you for a great meal. I'll be back to help clean up."

She hurried up the stairs to the room she'd chosen. She slammed the door shut and tried to calm her breathing. Squeezing her eyes shut, she cursed herself for jumping back into the pity pool. Her mood swings were about nothing more. She was a grown woman—an educated woman with a great career. There was no excuse for feeling sorry for herself. Yes, a bad man or men had put her life in danger, and, yes, her emotional neediness had prompted her to get all sentimental and filled with what-ifs, but this would be over eventually and she would be okay.

The least she could do was act like a grown-up about it instead of falling apart just because the man who had kissed her like she'd never been kissed before wasn't the knight in shining armor with whom she was destined to ride off into the sunset.

And then she laughed. When the laughter started, she couldn't stop it. Two women were dead, and she was upset because her bodyguard wasn't as enamored with her as she was with him.

A knock at the door had her wiping the tears from her eyes.

"You okay in there?"

Was she okay? *Absolutely not.* Would she be okay? *Probably.*

Squaring her shoulders and wiping her cheeks, she crossed to the door and opened it. "I'm perfectly fine."

He searched her face with those incredible blue eyes, and she realized that he really was worried about her state of mind.

Amber laughed. Startled at her reaction, she pressed her fingers to her lips and muttered, "Sorry. I think I'm hysterical."

Concern lined his face. "Maybe I should get you another glass of wine."

Barely suppressing a second outburst of side-splitting laughter, she held up her hands stop-sign fashion. "No, no. Really, I'm fine. I just…I just…" She burst into tears. "Oh, God. I don't know what's wrong with me."

Could she do any more to embarrass herself? She simply could not get it together.

Sean pulled her into his strong arms and hugged her close. "Everything's going to be all right," he promised softly. "I'll keep you safe."

She drew away and shook her head. "I know the police will find Thrasher and whoever else is involved, and this will all be over eventually. That's not the reason I'm upset."

He squeezed her arm and smiled. "You're scared."

A burst of anger flared inside her, instantly drying the ridiculous tears. "I am not scared." She wasn't. She really wasn't. Not at the moment anyway. She had him…for protection.

He held up his hands in surrender. "Sorry. I'm only trying to help."

Calm down, Amber. It isn't his fault you're having trouble holding it together.

She smoothed a hand over her blouse and reclaimed her composure. "I apologize. I don't know why I fell apart there for a moment. I'm fine—I assure you. I should probably call it a night a little early."

Under no circumstances did she trust herself alone in the same room with him just now. She was on some sort of emotional roller coaster, and she had no idea where the tracks ran out. Ending up in bed with him was not where she wanted to crash-land tonight.

His face changed as if an epiphany had occurred to him. "Is this about that kiss last night?"

Her jaw dropped. The very idea that he would call it *that kiss* made her inexplicably angry. "What about the kiss? It happened in a moment of…a moment of neediness. It wasn't a big deal."

He frowned. "Ouch. I thought it was a huge deal." His gaze dropped to her lips. "I really hoped we might go for an encore." His gaze slid up to hers. "If you're as interested as it felt like you were."

A multitude of new sensations cascaded over her, shaking her newly regained composure. "I told you I don't do one-night stands." Even as she said the words she couldn't stop looking at his lips.

Before she could dodge the move, he had closed the short distance between them and forked his fingers into her hair. "Good, because I have no interest in a one-night stand with you." He pulled her mouth to his but hesitated before kissing her. "I want a whole lot more, starting with this."

He kissed her, his lips applying just the right amount of pressure. No matter that her mind was set to protest, her body melted against his. Her hands slid up his sculpted chest and curled around his neck. He cupped her bottom and lifted her into him, showing her the intensity of his desire.

"Say the word," he murmured against her lips, "and I'll stop."

"Don't stop." She kissed him hard, tangled her fingers in his hair and held his mouth firmly against hers.

He lifted her against him and carried her to the bed. They fell onto the plaid quilt together. He took his time undressing her and helping her nervous fingers undress him. It had been so long and she was so excited she couldn't seem to make her fingers work.

When they lay skin to skin, he slowed things down even more. He kissed her gently, tracing her face with his fingertips. She did the same, loving the ridges and planes of his handsome face. The high cheekbones and square jaw, the straight nose and strong brow. The silky feel of his blond hair and the amazing blue of his eyes.

He whispered sweet words to her as he kissed his way down her throat. *You're so beautiful. Your skin is so soft. Your hair drives me crazy.* He traced every inch of her with his lips and fingers, and she repeated each move with hers. By the time he moved on top of her, spreading her legs wide, she was gasping for air, her entire body pulsing with need.

They made love twice before moving to the shower and making love a third time. Afterward he dried her hair and teased her body to the point of insanity all over again. He brought her to climax again with those magic fingers and those equally skilled lips, and then he held her tight until she drifted off to sleep.

Friday, October 21, 6:30 a.m.

SEAN WOKE TO the sweet scent of Amber. He smiled and resisted the urge to wake her. He wanted to make love to her again, but he had to be sure she wanted to go there. Last night had been an emotional one for her. He didn't want her to look back and see one minute of their time together as a mistake.

He was serious when he'd told her he wanted more than just one night together. If he was lucky, she would want the same. The idea of a serious relationship had been the furthest thought from his mind. Since Lacy, he hadn't wanted to feel this way again. Amber Roberts had shattered his defenses and stolen his ability to resist without even trying. He was pretty sure she had been as surprised by the development as he was.

Her eyes opened, and she stared at him in surprise. Holding his breath, he hoped regret wouldn't be the next emotion he saw in those beautiful green eyes. A smile widened across her kiss-swollen lips, and happiness was what he saw in her gaze.

"Good morning," she whispered.

He grinned. "It's a damned good morning." He brushed her lips with his own. "I was thinking we'd make pancakes. You like pancakes?"

She nibbled at his lips with her teeth. "I haven't indulged in pancakes in forever, but I'm not really ready to get out of bed yet." One delicate hand slid along his hip until those cool fingers found his arousal. "It feels like you're ready for something besides breakfast."

He teased a rosy nipple with his tongue. "Always."

They made love slowly. Her soft whimpers made him want to go faster, made him want to plunge hard and deep into her over and over, but he refused to hurry. He wanted to show her how important she was to him. How much he adored every part of her. How much he wanted to know her innermost thoughts and secrets.

His body arched with the building need as she cried out his name. He could hold back no longer. Still, he set an easy rhythm and pace, determined to make this last.

AFTER A SHOWER and a long morning walk, they were both ready for breakfast. She made the pancakes from a box of mix he found in the pantry. He brewed the coffee and rounded up the syrup.

"I don't know what your family does for the holidays," he ventured.

She licked her finger, making him smile. "Barb and Gina insist on hosting the family for Thanksgiving this year. We're eating lunch at one, so Barb and Gina can have the evening meal with the Colemans."

"That works out perfectly," he said, grabbing his courage with both hands. "Maybe you can come to dinner here with me and my family."

The smile started at one corner of her mouth and spread across her face, and the whole room lit up. "I could do that, if you're sure your family won't mind."

He downed a bite of pancake. "My family would be ecstatic. I warn you, though, they'll jump to conclusions. If you're not careful, my mother will start suggesting wedding venues."

Amber's tinkling laughter filled the air and made his heart glad. "I'm an expert at changing the subject."

He bit his tongue to prevent asking her if she had given up on the idea of weddings. He damned sure had—or he'd thought so. Funny, the notion of marriage didn't feel so difficult to imagine anymore. The realization should terrify him. Strangely it didn't.

Silence enveloped them for a minute or two. Sean recognized reality had intruded. They weren't kids punch-drunk after a night of incredible sex.

She set her fork aside. "What're we really doing, Sean?"

All of a sudden he didn't know how to answer that question. This—whatever it was—had happened so damned fast.

She nodded. "I can't answer the question, either." She exhaled a big breath. "I really like you. You make me feel things I haven't felt before, not even when I was wearing an engagement ring. I just don't know what it means."

"I'm in the same place." He shrugged. "I swore I'd never make this mistake again."

"Is that what *this* is? A mistake?"

The hurt in her eyes tightened his chest to the point where he couldn't draw in a decent breath. "I hope not." All that bravado he'd felt earlier abruptly deserted him. "I honestly don't know."

Obviously his answer wasn't the one she'd wanted to hear. "Wow. Okay." She stood and carried her plate to the sink.

Damn it. He grabbed his plate and joined her there. "I just meant—"

She backed away. "Let's not do this right now, okay?"

He piled his plate on top of hers and set his hands on his hips. "Is this your way of protecting your feelings? You just blow it off and walk away?" That was exactly what she was doing. Maybe instead of arguing he should take the easy way out and forget the whole damned thing.

"You're the one who called it a mistake."

Before he could respond, his cell in his pocket vibrated. He dug it out and glared at the screen. *The boss.* He dragged in a calming breath and answered. "Hey, boss. You have news?"

Sean listened to the update and tried to feel relief. Didn't happen. "Thanks. I'll let her know."

He ended the call and tucked his phone away. He had a bad feeling that what he was about to tell Amber would be the end of whatever *this* was. "The BPD found Thrasher. He's dead. He left a note apologizing for all he'd done."

Chapter Fifteen

Birmingham Police Department, 11:00 a.m.

"Peter Thrasher appears to have committed suicide. We can't officially call it a suicide until we have the autopsy report, but based on the ME's examination at the scene and the note he left, the preliminary call is suicide."

Lieutenant Chet Harper opened the folder in front of him and passed an eight-by-ten photo to Jess. Next to Sean, Amber tensed. He'd tried a dozen times on the way here to apologize for not being able to explain himself, but she refused to talk. She had been vulnerable, needy. He should have protected her without allowing personal feelings to get in the way. How could he make her see what he meant if she wouldn't hear him out?

He was supposed to be a professional. He was supposed to keep her safe. He'd fallen down on both counts and he'd taken advantage of her need to grab on to life with both hands. He had to find a way to explain to her that the mistake he'd meant hadn't been what she thought.

Jess passed the photo to Sean, yanking him back to the present. The preliminary report indicated Thrasher appeared to have taken an overdose of over-the-counter sleep aids. The empty bottle had been found in his pocket. Apparently when he'd abandoned his car, he'd hitched a ride to the greenhouses where he grew flowers. One of his employees, a worker who spoke little or no English, had given him a ride. The employee had no idea Thrasher was embroiled in a murder investigation. He claimed Thrasher acted like he always did. When they had arrived at the greenhouses, Thrasher had told everyone to take the rest of the week off with pay.

"Forensics found evidence from both victims, McCorkle and Pettie, on Thrasher's computer. He and Adler were sharing the videos via a cloud service."

Jess studied the forensic report before passing it to Sean. "Is there any possibility the evidence was planted?"

Sean had been about to ask the same question. As badly as he'd screwed up with Amber, he hadn't forgotten the case entirely.

"Are you suggesting that someone may have set up Thrasher?" Amber asked. "The potential third killer you mentioned before?"

"That's exactly what I'm suggesting," Jess confirmed. "Thrasher knew the BPD was looking for him and he goes to a greenhouse and puts himself to permanent sleep? Why not just disappear? Did he call anyone on his cell? This is not typical behavior for a serial killer, and I'm always suspicious of an alleged suicide note that ties everything up in a nice, neat little bow."

Chet Harper shook his head. "We haven't located his cell. We're hoping to have his cell phone records later today." Harper directed his attention to Amber. "The case will remain open until we've tied up the last of the loose ends, but we're confident Adler and Thrasher murdered McCorkle and Pettie. It's difficult to say who actually did the killing or if it was a joint effort. As for the potential third perpetrator, we'll either rule out the scenario or we'll find him." When he turned back to Jess, he flared his hands. "Any additional input you have is always extremely valuable to the team."

"I agree with your conclusions to a degree." Jess surveyed the photos and reports now spread across the table. "But we're missing something."

"One other thing." Harper reached into another folder and removed a report. He passed it to Amber. "The toxin that made you sick was azalea leaves. Someone chopped up the leaves and added them to your tea. Do you have a regular tea routine?"

Amber looked from the report to Harper. "I have a cup every evening when I get home from work."

"Adler and Thrasher would have known that routine," Harper said. "Since Thrasher worked with flowers and small shrubs, we checked the greenhouses. He was growing a variety of azaleas. The lab is attempting to determine if the leaves in your tea came from a plant in his greenhouse. The azalea leaves may have been added to your tea to disable you. One or both men were likely watching, prepared to act when the time was right for abducting you."

Sean gritted his teeth. The son of a bitch's carelessness with Amber's life made him want to beat the hell out of something...or someone.

"Did you find evidence that similar methods were used with McCorkle and Pettie?" Jess wanted to know.

"We've got the ME's office taking a second look," Harper confirmed. "Dr. Baron believes the screening tests wouldn't have picked up all potential plant toxins. She wants to run additional tests."

"I understand that the case is ongoing," Amber spoke up. "But are you saying Emma Norton and I are no longer in danger?"

Sean turned to Amber. She kept her gaze away from his. He'd made a mess of this morning and now she couldn't wait to get away from him. *Damn it.*

Harper and Jess exchanged a look. Harper said, "As

far as the department is concerned, any threat these men posed no longer exists, but we are still investigating the possibility of a third person's involvement."

"I'm not completely comfortable with the facts in front of us," Jess said with obvious caution, "but to our knowledge the source of the threat is gone. If there is a third killer involved, he may believe he's tied up all the loose ends and will escape any consequences."

"But we can't be sure." The words were out of Sean's mouth before he'd taken the time to think through the statement.

All eyes were on him now. He might as well say the rest. "We can't say that Amber is no longer in danger until we rule out the third killer scenario."

A beat of silence echoed in the room.

"No doubt," Jess said, backing him up. "Amber." She turned her attention to the woman beside Sean. "The choice is yours. If you'd like to continue our security services a few days longer, we're more than happy to do so. Lieutenant Harper, I'm certain, will have more answers soon."

"I won't stop," Harper assured her, "until we know for certain. You have my word on that, Ms. Roberts."

Sean braced for Amber's decision.

"The cameras have been removed from my home," she said. "Adler and Thrasher are no longer a threat." She took a breath. "At this point, I feel secure on my own. I'll, of course, be watchful." She met the gaze of everyone at the table except Sean. "I appreciate all you and the BPD have done to bring a swift conclusion to this nightmare."

"Amber," Sean protested, "you should—"

"Get back to work." She stood. "I've had way more time off than I'm comfortable taking." She flashed a smile at Jess and Harper but still refused to even glance at Sean. "Thank you again."

"If you change your mind," Jess offered, "call. Day or night. We'll be there."

Amber gave her a nod and started for the door.

Sean pushed back from the conference table and followed her. He would owe his boss an explanation, but right now he couldn't let Amber leave this way.

"Amber, wait." He caught up with her at the elevator.

She jabbed the call button and reluctantly met his gaze. "We both have careers that need our attention, Sean. We don't need any distractions or personal entanglements. Spending more time together would complicate things. I'm not ready for complications. Clearly you aren't, either."

He touched her, wrapped his fingers around her forearm. Even that innocent contact made his pulse rush. "We should talk about us first."

For one instant he thought she was going to agree, but then her green eyes shuttered. "There is no us,

Sean." She pulled free of his touch. "I have a very important event to attend tonight. Everybody who's anybody in Birmingham will be there—including your boss. I barely have time to pick up my dress from Martha's and get ready. Goodbye, Sean."

The elevator doors slid open, and she stepped inside. Sean watched her go. There was plenty he wanted to say, but none of it would come to him just now.

Eagle Ridge Drive, 2:00 p.m.

SEAN CLIMBED OUT of his car. Maybe he was way off base, but like his boss he wasn't convinced this case was as cut-and-dried as it seemed. It didn't feel right. He fully understood that part of what he felt was prompted by his feelings for Amber.

God almighty, he couldn't pretend those feelings didn't exist.

Problem was, he had his work cut out for him. Convincing Amber to give *them* a chance wasn't going to be easy. He had to find the right words to rebuild the trust he'd crushed with this morning's hurtful ones. Before he could worry about their relationship, he had to do whatever necessary to ensure she was safe.

He moved around to the back of Adler's house. What he was about to do was breaking and entering. At least the house was no longer a crime scene. His boss wouldn't be happy when she found out, but if he found a connection to a third killer, she would likely let his methods slide. He removed the lock pick from his pocket, glanced around and set to the task. He'd learned how to pick a lock from Buddy Corlew, but he wasn't supposed to tell Jess.

The door opened easily. Inside the place still smelled like blood. He wasn't exactly clear on what he expected to find. Mostly he intended to look until he was satisfied there was nothing to find. He pulled on a pair of latex gloves and started with the living room.

He scanned the framed photos, the books, unopened mail. As he moved through the house he checked drawers, shelves, cabinets and closets. Nothing.

Before closing the door to Adler's bedroom closet, he hesitated. Might as well check the guy's pockets and shoes. One by one, Sean went through his jackets, his shirts and his trousers. Nothing in the pockets.

"Damn it."

There was only one thing to do. Check out Thrasher's place.

Unfortunately, it was still a crime scene.

Killough Circle, 3:30 p.m.

SEAN WAS INSIDE Thrasher's house without a glitch. As he did at Adler's place, he moved from room to room, checking every available space.

He'd almost called it a bust, when he backed up to check a framed photo next to the television. A younger Thrasher with a couple of buddies. It wasn't the sort of thing the cops would consider relevant; still it was worth a look.

"Well, hell." Sean picked up the photo and scrutinized at it. There were three guys. Thrasher was in the middle, Adler on the left. Sean studied the dark-haired guy on the right. The kid, seventeen or eighteen, looked vaguely familiar. He flipped the frame over and removed the back. As he'd hoped, the names were written on the back of the photo. Thrasher, Adler and Guynes. Where had he heard that name? The three looked high school age. The clothes were definitely last decade's.

Sean went back to the spare bedroom and opened the closet door. School yearbooks were piled on the top shelf. He grabbed the stack and went through the autographed pages. The threesome had been friends for years. Maybe they'd lost touch, but then why keep the framed photo displayed? People, especially men, didn't do that unless the people in the photograph were more than a little important to their lives.

The senior yearbook gave him the answer he was looking for. Delbert Guynes had been injured in a football game his senior year. Making the winning touchdown, he'd suffered a spinal cord injury, which had left him paralyzed from the waist down. Sean skimmed the dedication page. Guynes was touted as a hero, as was his mother who always tailored the cheerleader uniforms.

Martha Guynes… Martha Sews.

She had spoken as if she hardly knew Adler. She certainly hadn't mentioned that her son and Adler were best friends all through high school.

Amber was picking up a dress there today.

Sean shook his head. The theory didn't make sense. Delbert Guynes was paralyzed and sentenced to using a wheelchair for the rest of his life. He was a big video game player. Did that mean he was also a computer buff? What did a guy whose life consisted of being stuck in a wheelchair and under his mother's thumb do for fun…or for pleasure? *The videos.* Maybe the cameras had been for Delbert.

Still, how could Delbert be involved with Adler and Thrasher's criminal activities without his mother knowing?

Memories from his and Amber's visit to the shop the other day flashed one after the other through Sean's mind.

Were those shrubs lining the front of her shop azaleas?

Martha Sews, 4:30 p.m.

AMBER PEERED OVER her shoulder at the mirror. The back of the dress looked great. She smiled. "It's perfect, Martha." She turned back to the lady who had single-handedly kept Amber's wardrobe fitting right for years now. Being what the fashion world considered petite was a real pain. Not even the most expensive labels managed to make clothes that fit her body. "I don't know what I'd do without you."

Martha beamed. "I love taking care of you, Amber. You're my favorite customer."

Amber gave her another big smile before stepping back into the dressing room. "I'll change and pay so you can call it a day." It had to be five already. Thankfully that still left her enough time to get ready.

"Take your time. I'm locking up," Martha called. "Would you like some tea before you fight the rush hour traffic?"

Arching her back, Amber reached for the zipper. "Oh, that would be wonderful."

"Paradise Peach still your favorite?"

Amber almost stumbled stepping out of the dress. "Yes." She cleared her throat. "But whatever you have will be fine." Her stomach roiled. The ugly few hours she'd endured the other night had made her wonder if she would ever drink another cup of her favorite tea. Her response to Martha had been automatic. Amber's grandmother had taught her to love hot tea. Louisa Roberts would be immensely offended that someone would use tea as a weapon.

"I have tea cakes if you'd like one," Martha called. "You should treat yourself more often, Amber. You deserve it."

Amber paused again as she wiggled into the unwashed jeans she'd bought yesterday. She tugged the sweater on next. The memory of rushing through the discount store grabbing clothes with Sean made her heart hurt. How had he stolen a place in her heart in a mere four days? She hadn't meant to let that happen, but control had been taken from her so quickly her head was still spinning. Walking out of that meeting on her own today had been her way of taking back control. Adler and Thrasher were dead. She would be okay.

"You'll love the cakes," Martha said loud enough for Amber to hear. "They're my grandmother's recipe."

Evicting thoughts of Sean, Amber considered that she really wouldn't have time to eat before heading to the fund-raiser. A quick snack would be nice. "I would love a tea cake."

She stepped out of the dressing room, and Martha was waiting for her. Amber jumped.

"I'm sorry. I didn't mean to startle you, dear." She took the dress from Amber's hand. "Come along before your tea gets cold."

"You don't want me to pay you first?" Amber followed her to the kitchen.

"That won't be necessary." Martha draped the dress across the back of a chair. "Sit down and I'll serve."

Amber exhaled, feeling a burst of uncertainty. What was wrong with her? This was Martha. She'd known her for years. There was time before she had to get dressed. She needed to relax. If she were honest with herself, she would admit that it was Sean. Making love with him had touched her in a place no one had reached before. It was ridiculous. She barely knew the man and somehow it felt as if they'd always known each other. He felt like the perfect fit… her other half.

Ridiculous. Tomorrow Sean would wake up and realize the circumstances had triggered an out-of-control moment, and he'd never think of her again.

"Amber?"

She snapped to attention. "I'm sorry—what did you say?"

"I was asking about your friend Mr. Douglas."

"Oh." Amber accepted the cup of tea. "His assignment concluded."

"So you were working together." Martha gestured to a chair. She then placed a tea cake on a delicate china plate and set it in front of Amber.

"We were." *Close enough*, she supposed as she sipped the warm refreshment.

"He seemed like a nice young man." Martha settled into a chair across the table from Amber. "Quite handsome. I thought he was smitten with you—the way he looked at you, I mean."

"I…don't think so." Amber sipped her tea to avoid saying more.

"You certainly appeared quite taken with him."

Before Amber could protest, a howl reverberated through the house.

Martha jumped up from her seat. "Delbert?" She rushed from the room.

Amber sat there for a moment, wondering if she should check to see if everything was all right. The silence that followed felt entirely wrong. She should see if Martha and her son were okay.

Amber stood and the room tilted.

Good grief. What was wrong with her?

She stared at the porcelain cup. *The tea.*

Where was her phone? Her purse?

Turning around, Amber grabbed at that table to maintain her balance.

"Now, now, take care there."

Amber tried to steady herself. Martha was suddenly at her side, guiding her forward. At least it felt as if they were moving.

"Martha…" Amber's tongue wouldn't work right. She felt horribly ill. Vomiting felt imminent.

"Don't you worry, dear. I'm going to take extra good care of you."

Amber leaned heavily on Martha. She couldn't

hold herself up anymore. She tried to plead with her…but the words wouldn't come out.

"Here she is, Delbert."

Amber felt her body plop into a chair. The room was shifting again. In front of her a man in a wheelchair stared at her. Delbert. Martha's son. Behind him the computer screen that usually sported a video game was focused on a small room. Was that the dressing room she'd just been using to try on the dress? Amber groaned. She couldn't be sure. Her vision kept fading in and out. She just didn't know. She felt horribly sick.

"We thought we'd lost you," Martha was saying.

What was she talking about?

"You're the one he wanted," Martha cooed. "Of all the ones we offered, it was you he wanted."

Amber didn't understand. She tried to move. Couldn't.

"Rhiana turned out to be nothing but a whore." Martha heaved a big sign as she knelt in front of Amber and tied her feet together.

Amber told herself to pull away from her. To get up and run, but her legs wouldn't work.

"And Kimberly was a closet alcoholic. He just didn't like either of the two the boys and I picked out for him. It was you. It had always been you. He'd been watching you for years. He said you were perfect. You were the one. I even tried to discourage him. How could someone as famous as you be bothered, but then I understood what I had to do. I had to make you available."

Amber tried again to cry out. She tried to get up. Her body wouldn't work.

"And those stupid so-called friends of his almost ruined everything. You just can't depend on anyone anymore. They were only supposed to install the cameras on the candidates. But I knew when Kimberly went missing that they were up to something. The bastards were messing with those girls, and they killed them. But don't worry—I took care of those idiots. As soon as I found out what they were up to, I made them pay. All I had to do after that was find a way to get you here. I'm sorry about the tea the other night. That wasn't supposed to happen until I was ready. You'll be fine, though. I was careful about the dosage."

She tied Amber's wrists together. "Now. We're ready. I'm going to be taking you and Delbert to a special place where no one will ever bother us. You are to love him and take care of him from now on. He's ready for a life of his own, and he has chosen you to share it with him. I'll make sure you have whatever you need."

Another of those eerie howls echoed in the room.

"Hush now, Delbert. She's all yours." Martha got to her feet. "You can play with her all you want, every day from now on, and she'll take good care of you."

Amber closed her eyes in an effort to stop the spinning. She had to do something.

Martha screamed, and Amber's eyes snapped open.

Sean.

Her heart leaped. He was here.

He and Martha struggled. Amber tried to keep her eyes open, but she couldn't.

The darkness consumed her...and then the silence.

UAB Hospital

AMBER OPENED HER EYES. She felt weak. Her brain seemed swaddled with cotton. She remembered throwing up in the ambulance. She remembered... *Sean.* He'd been right beside her through it all.

"There you are." His blue eyes twinkled as he smiled at her.

Her heart squeezed. She really liked his smile. She like his eyes and everything else about him. "Martha...oh, my God." Her mouth felt cotton dry. "She's done my alterations for years. How did you know?"

"Thrasher kept a framed photo of him and his best buds from high school—Kyle Adler and Delbert Guynes. I couldn't get the idea out of my head that there was a third player in all this. When I saw that photo, I knew I was right."

Amber reached for the water on the bedside table.

"Let me do that." Sean poured water in the cup and added a bendable straw; then he held it to her lips. "This should help."

The water cooled her raw throat. She drew back and he set the cup aside. "I don't see how Martha thought she could get away with this." Amber shook her head. "They were helping her find a caregiver for Delbert. Why in the world would she do something so insane? She always seemed so normal." The whole idea was ludicrous.

"Jess called a little while ago and gave me an update." Sean's expression turned somber. "Martha is dying. It's cancer. The doctors have given her maybe six months to live. She doesn't want her son in some institution. When she found out Thrasher and Adler were using her shop to video women changing and then sharing that video with her son, she threatened to call the police."

"Wait." Amber's brain was still a little fuzzy from the poisoned tea. "Why did she threaten to call the police?"

"To make them cooperate with her. At some point after that she found out they were using the women for sex slaves. She killed Adler when she found out he was obsessed with you. She was after Thrasher next, so he killed himself. He knew his life was over anyway, so he ended it himself. Martha found him and left the note."

"The whole thing is just horrible." Amber fiddled with the edge of the stiff sheet. "What happens to Delbert now?"

Sean took her hands in his. "He'll be placed in a facility and receive the care he needs. It isn't what his mother wanted, but there's no other family. The important thing is that you're safe now and the Pettie and McCorkle families don't have to wonder if their daughters' killers will get away with murder."

"You were right." Amber squeezed his hand, tears burning in her eyes. "Still waters do run deep."

"Sometimes being right is not so much fun." He leaned forward and kissed her forehead.

"I was thinking," she ventured. "I feel like maybe it's time we learned how to have a real personal life. Together, I mean. Unless, of course, you really believe what happened was a mistake."

"You're behind the curve, Roberts." He grinned and shot her a wink. "I've already started. For the record, I never thought what happened between us was a mistake. I worried that the circumstances were the wrong time and place." He kissed her hands. "I don't care what brought me to you, all that matters is that I found you. I want to explore what we have more than I want to see the sun come up tomorrow."

That was the best news she'd heard all week. "I'm sure we can arrange for both to happen."

"Good." He kissed her lips this time.

Amber closed her eyes and savored the sound of his deep voice as he promised her the world. As soon as she was out of this hospital she intended to hold him to every single one of those promises.

Chapter Sixteen

3309 Dell Road, Mountain Brook, 9:00 p.m.

"She's growing too fast." Jess smoothed the hair back from her sweet baby girl's face.

Dan tucked the pink blanket around Bea. He turned to Jess, took her by the hands and drew her away from their daughter's crib. "She'll always be our little girl no matter how big she gets."

Jess leaned into his chest and closed her eyes as his arms went around her. "Is she going to be jealous of her little brother?" Jess peered up at him. "I don't think I could bear it if they hate each other when they become teenagers. Lil and I went through that stage, you know."

"You need some hot cocoa." Dan kissed her forehead and ushered her from Bea's room.

He looked back one last time before turning out the light. The princess night-light kept the room from being completely dark. Jess had always been afraid of the dark. She hoped her children weren't, but just in case she intended to make sure they felt safe.

"We have to finish decorating your son's room soon. He'll be here before we know it." She was feeling a little overwhelmed lately. The agency was off to a great start and even Sean had turned out to be a top-notch member of the team. Still, there was just so much to do, and she felt tired all the time.

Dan guided her to her favorite chair in their family room. Toys were scattered all over the floor. Jess groaned. She had sworn she would never be one of those people—the ones who spoil their children with far too many toys. And look at their home. Toys were lying about in every room.

"You sit tight, and I'll make the hot chocolate." He backed toward the door and stumbled when the stuffed animal he stepped on made a high-pitched sound. He swore under his breath and snatched up the pink bear to ensure it still worked. It did not.

"You killed it," Jess warned. "You better get rid of it before she notices."

Dan nodded. "Good idea."

He hurried away, damaged pink bear in hand.

Jess huffed out a big breath. This was her mother-in-law's fault. Katherine spoiled Bea endlessly. "Like you don't," she muttered.

With much effort and no shortage of groaning, Jess hefted herself out of the big plush chair and followed the path Dan had taken to the kitchen. He'd just put the milk in the microwave. She slid onto a stool at the island and watched as he readied the instant cocoa mix. It might be instant, but it tasted like the real thing. With a toddler in the house, they had both learned to appreciate plenty of *instant* fixes.

"What's on your mind?" Her handsome husband leaned on the island and studied her. "I can always tell when you're unsettled."

It was true. They had been in love since they were teenagers and could read each other like a book.

"This case reminded me of the one that brought me back home." The similarities were disturbing.

Dan nodded. "Me, too. I was terrified Andrea would end up dead, like the two women in this case."

Jess placed her hand on his arm and smiled. "But she didn't. She's in her senior year of college and doing great." Andrea was Dan's stepdaughter from a previous marriage. Though the marriage had been over for years, Dan still loved Andrea. Jess did, as well. She was a wonderful young woman.

"She didn't because you found her when no one else could." He touched Jess's cheek. "I am so thankful you came back to me."

"This is where I was always supposed to be."

The microwave dinged and he straightened away from the island. "First you had to go catch all those serial killers for the FBI."

She rubbed her belly as Dan prepared her cocoa. One of those bad guys had followed her back to Birmingham and no matter that two years had passed since she ended his reign of terror, he still haunted her sometimes.

The steaming cocoa appeared in front of her, marshmallows floating on top. “Drink up before it gets cold.”

She arranged her lips into a smile. “Thank you. Where’s yours?”

“I—” he reached into the fridge “—am having a beer.”

She made a face. “Don’t brag.”

He twisted the top off the glass bottle. “The case brought up memories of Spears and Holmes.” He traced his fingers over her forehead. “Whenever you’re worried about a case you frown. And since the big case B&C was investigating is closed, it has to be about those two bastards.”

He knew her too well. “Spears is dead. I don’t worry about him. It’s all his sick followers that keep me awake sometimes.” Ted Holmes had tried his best to reenact Spears’s obsession with her. He’d gotten far too close to her child. “I’ve had my moments since leaving the department,” she confessed, “when I thought I’d made a mistake. That maybe I couldn’t do as much to stop the evil out there.”

Dan held his tongue and allowed her to continue in her own time.

“This case showed me I made the right decision.” She held up her mug. “To the future.”

Dan tapped her mug with his bottle of beer. “Hear, hear.”

One more face of evil down. Jess sipped her hot cocoa and relished the victory.

* * * * *

FALCO: THE DARK GUARDIAN

SANDRA MARTON

CHAPTER ONE

THERE were those who said that Falco Orsini was too rich, too good-looking, too arrogant for his own good.

Falco would have agreed that he was rich, that he was probably arrogant, and if you judged his looks by the seemingly endless stream of beautiful women who moved in and out of his bed, well, he'd have had to admit that perhaps he had something going for him that women liked.

There were also those who called him heartless. He would not have agreed with that.

He was not heartless. He was honest. Why let a competitor buy an elite investment bank if he could scoop it up instead? Why let a competitor get the edge in a business deal if he could get it first? Why go on pretending interest in a woman when he no longer felt any?

It wasn't as if he was a man who ever made promises he had no intention of keeping.

Honest, not heartless. And in the prime of life.

Falco was, like his three brothers, tall. Six foot three. Hard of face, hard of body. Buff, women said. That was true but it had nothing to do with vanity. He was fit the way a man must be when he knows keeping himself that way could mean the difference between life and death.

Not that he lived that kind of existence anymore.

Not often, at any rate.

Not that he talked about.

At thirty-two, Falco had already led what many would consider an interesting life.

At eighteen, he'd grabbed his backpack and thumbed his way around the world. At nineteen, he'd joined the army. At twenty, he became a Special Forces warrior. Someplace along the way, he picked up a bunch of disparate university credits, a skill at high-stakes gambling and, eventually, a passion for high-stakes investing.

He lived by his own rules. He always had. The opinions of others didn't concern him. He believed in honor, duty and integrity. Men who'd served with him, men who dealt with him, didn't always like him—he was too removed, some said—but they respected him almost as much as women coveted him.

Or hated him.

It didn't matter.

Family was everything.

He loved his brothers the same way they loved him, with a ferocity that made the four of them as formidable in everything as they were in business. He would have given his life for his sisters, who would happily have returned the favor. He adored his mother, who worshipped all her sons as perhaps only Italian mothers can.

His father…

Who gave a damn about him?

Falco, like his brothers, had written off Cesare Orsini years ago. As far as his wife and daughters were concerned, Cesare owned a carting company, a construction firm and some of New York City's priciest real estate.

His sons knew the truth.

Their father was the head of something he referred to only as La Famigilia.

He was, in other words, the same as the thugs who had originated in Sicily in the last half of the nineteenth century. Nothing could change that, not the Brioni suits, not the enormous mansion in what had once been Manhattan's Little Italy and was now Greenwich Village. But, for their mother's sake, there were times Falco and his brothers put that aside and pretended the Orsinis were just another big, happy Sicilian-American family.

Today, for instance. On this bright, late autumn afternoon, Dante had taken a wife.

Falco still had trouble getting his head around that.

First Rafe. Now Dante. Two brothers with wives. And, Dante, it turned out, wasn't just a husband, he was also a father.

Nicolo and Falco had spent the day smiling, kissing their new sisters-in-law and grinning at Dante and Rafe. They'd done their best not to feel like jerks cooing at their infant nephew—not that it was difficult because the kid was clearly the world's cutest, most intelligent baby. They'd danced with their sisters and shut their ears to Anna's and Isabella's not-so-subtle hints that they had friends who'd make them perfect wives.

By late afternoon, they were more than ready to slip away and toast their bachelorhood with a few well-earned cold beers at a place the four brothers owned. Not their investment firm. This place was called, simply enough, The Bar.

Cesare headed them off before they could get to the door. He wanted to talk to them, he said.

Not again, Falco had thought wearily. One look at Nick's face and he knew his brother was thinking the same thing. For months now, the Don had been giving his "after I'm dead" speech. The combination to his safe. The names of his attorney and his accountant. The location of important papers. Stuff none of the brothers cared about; none of them wanted a penny of their father's money.

Falco's initial instinct was to ignore Cesare and keep walking.

Instead, he and Nick looked at each other. Maybe the long day had put them in a mellow mood. Maybe it was the champagne. What the hell, Nick's expression said, and Falco replied with a sigh that clearly said, Yeah, why not.

Their father had insisted on talking to them separately. Felipe, Cesare's capo, jerked his head, indicating Falco should go first.

Falco gave a moment's thought to grabbing the capo by his skinny neck, hoisting him to his toes and telling him what a slimy bastard he was to have spent his life as the Don's guard dog, but the family celebration was still going strong in the conservatory at the rear of the house.

So he smiled instead, the kind of smile a man like the capo would surely understand, moved past him and entered Cesare's study. Felipe shut the door behind him….

And Falco found himself in an endurance contest.

His father, seated at his desk, the heavy drapes behind him drawn so that the big room with its oversized furniture seemed even more gloomy than usual, looked up, nodded, waved a manicured hand toward a chair—a gesture Falco ignored—and went back to leafing through the contents of a manila folder.

According to the antique mahogany clock that hung on a wall, all but lost among photos of politicians, old-country ancestors and age-yellowed religious paintings, four minutes ticked away.

Falco stood perfectly still, feet slightly apart, arms folded, dark eyes locked on the clock. The minute hand ticked to yet another marker, the hour hand made its barely perceptible jump. Falco unfolded his arms, turned his back on his father and went to the door.

"Where are you going?"

Falco didn't bother turning around. "*Ciao,* Father. As always, it's been a pleasure."

The chair creaked. Falco knew the Don was pushing back from his desk.

"We have not yet had our talk."

"Our talk? You were the one who requested this meeting." Falco swung toward his father. "If you have something to say, say it—but I assure you, I recall your touching words the last time I saw you. Perhaps you don't remember my response so let me remind you of it. I don't give a damn about your safe, your documents, your business interests—"

"Then you are a fool," the Don said mildly. "Those things are worth a fortune."

A cool smile lifted the corners of Falco's mouth. "So am I, in case you hadn't noticed." His smile vanished. "Even if I weren't, I wouldn't touch anything of yours. You should know that by now."

"Such drama, my son."

"*Questa verità*, Father. Such truth, you mean."

Cesare sighed. "All right. You've made your speech."

"And you've made yours. Goodbye, Father. I'll tell Nicolo to—"

"What were you doing in Athens last month?"

Falco stood absolutely still. "What?"

"It's a simple question. You were in Athens. Why?"

The look Falco gave the older man would have made anyone else take a hurried step back.

"What in hell kind of question is that?"

Cesare shrugged. "A simple one. I asked you—"

"I know what you asked." Falco's eyes narrowed. "Did you have me followed?"

"Nothing so devious." Cesare moved his chair forward

and reached for an elaborately carved wooden box. "Pure Havanas," he said, opening the box to reveal a dozen fat cigars. "They cost the earth. Have one."

"Explain yourself," Falco said sharply, without a glance at the box. "How do you know where I was?"

Another shrug. "I have friends everywhere. Surely you know that by now."

"Then you also know that I was in Athens on business for Orsini Brothers Investments." Falco smiled again, even more coldly. "Perhaps you've heard of us, Father. A privately held company started without any help from you."

Cesare bit the tip off the cigar he'd chosen, turned his head and spat the piece into a wastebasket.

"Even in these bad economic times, we've made our investors wealthy. And we've done it honestly, a concept you couldn't possibly understand."

"You added a private bank to your stable when you were in Athens," Cesare said. "Nicely done."

"Your compliments mean nothing to me."

"But banking was not all you did there," the Don said softly. He looked up; his eyes met Falco's. "My sources tell me that during that same few days, a child—a boy of twelve—held for ransom by insurgents in the northern mountains of Turkey, was somehow miraculously returned to his fam—"

Falco was around the desk in a heartbeat. His hand closed on his father's shirt; he yanked him roughly to his feet.

"What is this?" he snarled.

"Take your hands off me!"

"Not until I get answers. No one followed me. No one. I don't know where you got all this crap but—"

"I was not foolish enough to think anyone could follow you and live to talk about it. Let go of my shirt and perhaps I'll give you an answer."

Falco could feel his heart racing. He knew damned well no one had followed him; he was far too good to let that happen. And, yes, though he would never admit it, there had been more to his trip to Greece than the acquisition of a bank. There were times his old skills came in handy but he kept that part of his life private.

Falco glared at his father. And silently cursed himself for being a fool.

He had not let Cesare get to him in years. Fifteen years, to be exact, on a night one of his father's henchmen had caught him sneaking back into the heavily guarded house at two in the morning.

The Don had been furious, not at where his seventeen-year-old-son might have been, not at how he'd defeated the alarm system, but at how he'd gotten by the silent men who kept watch from the shadows outside the front door and deep within the walled garden.

Falco had refused to explain. He'd done more than that. He'd smirked as only a badass teenage boy could.

Cesare had backhanded him, hard, across the face.

It was the first time his father had hit him, which was, when he'd had time to think about it, a surprise. Not the blow; the surprise was that it had not happened before. There'd always been a hint of violence in the air between father and son; it had grown stronger when Falco reached adolescence.

That night, it had finally erupted.

Falco had stood still under the first blow. The second rocked him back on his heels. The third bloodied his mouth, and when Cesare raised his hand again, Falco grabbed his wrist and twisted the Don's arm high behind his back. Cesare was strong, but at seventeen, Falco was already stronger.

He was also fueled by years of hatred.

"Touch me again," he'd said in a whisper, "and I swear, I'll kill you."

His father's expression had undergone a subtle change. Not fear. Not anger. Something else. Something swift and furtive that should not have been in the eyes of a powerful man who'd just lost a battle, physically as well as figuratively.

Falco's face was badly bruised the next day. His mother questioned it, as did his sisters. He said he'd fallen in the shower. The lie worked but Nicolo, Raffaele and Dante had not been so easy to fool.

"Must have been a pretty awkward tumble," Rafe had said, "to blacken your eye as well as give you a swollen lip."

Yeah, Falco had said calmly, it was.

He never told anyone the truth. Had the beating been too humiliating to talk about? Was it his shock at the intensity of the quicksilver flash of rage that had almost overcome him?

Eventually, he understood.

Power had changed hands that night. It had gone from Cesare to him…and then back to Cesare. What he'd seen in his father's eyes had been the knowledge that despite Falco's vicious threat, he, Cesare, had actually won the battle because Falco had let emotion overtake him. He had lost control of his emotions and somehow, he had no idea how or why, that loss of control gave the other person power.

And now, here he was, fifteen long years later, losing control all over again.

Carefully, he unfisted his hand, let go of Cesare's starched white shirt. Cesare fell back into his chair, his jowly face red with anger.

"If you were not my son…"

"I'm not your son in any way that matters. It takes more than sperm to make a man a father."

A muscle knotted in the Don's jaw. "Are you now a philosopher? Trust me, Falco, in many ways, you are more my son than your brothers."

"What's that supposed to mean?"

"It means that what you so self-righteously claim to hate in me is what is also inside you. The lure of absolute power. The need to control." Cesare's eyes narrowed. "The willingness to shed blood when you know it must be shed."

"Damn you, old man!" Falco leaned over the desk and brought his angry face within inches of the older man's. "I am nothing like you, do you hear? Nothing! If I were, God, if I were…"

He shuddered, drew back, stood straight. What was he doing, letting his father draw him deeper into this quagmire?

"Is this what you wanted to talk about? To tell me you've come up with absolution for yourself by pretending your genes are my destiny? Well, it won't work. I am not you. And this so-called discussion is at an—"

Cesare took something from the folder on his desk and pushed it toward Falco. It appeared to be a glossy page, an advertisement, torn from a magazine.

"Do you know this woman?"

Falco barely spared the picture a glance.

"I know a lot of women," he said coldly. "Surely your spies have told you that."

"Indulge me. Look at her."

What the hell did it matter? Falco picked up the photo. It was an ad for something expensive. Perfume, jewelry, clothing—it was hard to tell.

The focus of the page, though, was clear enough.

It was the woman.

She was seated crossways in an armchair, one long leg on the floor, the other draped over the chair's arm, a shoe with the kind of heel that should have been declared lethal dangling from her toes. She wore lace. Scarlet lace. A teddy. A chemise. He had no idea which it was, only that it showed almost as much cleavage as leg.

A spectacular body. An equally spectacular face. Oval. Delicate. The essence of femininity. High cheekbones, eyes as amber as a cat's, lashes long and thick, the same ebony color as her long, straight hair.

She was smiling at the camera. At the viewer.

At him.

It was, he understood, a deliberate illusion. A damned effective one. Her smile, the tilt of her head, even her posture, dared a man to want her. To be foolish enough to think he could have her. It was a smile that offered as much sexual pleasure as a man could want in a lifetime.

Something hot and dangerous rolled through Falco's belly.

"Well? Do you recognize her?"

He looked up. Cesare's eyes locked on his. Falco tossed the photo on the desk.

"I told you I didn't. Okay? Are we done here?"

"Her name is Elle. Elle Bissette. She was a model. Now she is an actress."

"Good for her."

Cesare took something else from the folder. Another ad? He held it toward Falco, but Falco didn't move.

"What is this? You expect me to spend the next hour playing Name the Celebrity?"

"*Per favore*, Falco. I ask you, please. Look at the photo."

Falco's eyebrows rose. Please? In Italian and in English. He had never heard his father use those words or anything close to them. What the hell, he thought, and reached for the photo.

Bile rose in his throat.

It was the same ad but someone had used a red pen to *X* out her eyes. To trace a crude line of stitches across her lips.

To draw a heavy line across her throat and dab red dots from her throat to her breasts. To circle her breasts in the same bright, vicious crimson.

"Miss Bissette received it in the mail."

"What did the cops say?"

"Nothing. She refuses to contact them."

"She's a fool," Falco said bluntly, "if she won't go to the authorities."

"The parents of the Turkish boy went to you, not the authorities. They feared seeking official help."

"This is America."

"Fear is fear, Falco, no matter where one lives. She is afraid or perhaps she does not trust the police. Whatever the reason, she refuses to contact them." Cesare paused. "Miss Bissette is making a film in Hollywood. The producer is, shall we say, an old friend."

"Ah. I get it now. Your pal's worried about his investment."

"It concerns him, yes. And he needs my help."

"Send him some of your blood money."

"Not my financial help. He needs my help to safeguard Miss Bissette."

"I'm sure your goons will love L.A."

Cesare chuckled. "Can you see my men in Beverly Hills?"

Falco almost laughed. He had to admit, the idea was amusing—and, suddenly, it all came together. The talk of what had happened in Turkey, this conversation about Elle Bissette…

"Okay."

"Okay?"

Falco nodded. "I know some guys who do bodyguard work for celebrities. I'll call around, put you in touch—"

"I am already in touch," Cesare said gently. "With you."

"Me?" This time, Falco did laugh. "I'm an investor, Father, not a bodyguard."

"You did not say that to the people you helped in Turkey."

"That was different. They turned to me and I did what I had to do."

"As I am turning to you, *mio figlio*, and asking that you do what must be done."

Falco's face hardened. "You want some names and phone numbers, fine. Otherwise, I'm out of here."

Cesare didn't answer. Falco snorted, turned on his heel, headed for the door again, changed his mind and decided to exit through the French doors hidden by the heavy drapes. The mood he was in, the last thing he wanted was to risk running in to his mother or his sisters.

"Wait." His father hurried after him. "Take the folder. Everything you need is in it."

Falco grabbed the folder. It was easier than arguing.

By the time he'd taxied to his mid-sixties town house, he'd come up with the names of four men who could do this job and do it well. Once home, he poured a brandy, took the folder and his cell phone and headed outside to his walled garden. It was close to sunset; the air was chill but he liked it out here, with the noise of Manhattan shut away.

There was nothing of much use in the folder. Stuff about the movie; a letter from the producer to Cesare.

And the pictures. The one with her in lace. The marked-up duplicate. And another that his father had not shown him, a photo of Bissette standing on a beach, looking over her shoulder at the camera. No lace. No stiletto heels. She was dressed in a T-shirt and shorts.

Falco put the three pictures on the top of a glass table and looked from one to the other.

The one of her sexy and mysterious was a turn-on if you liked that kind of thing. He didn't. Yeah, he liked crimson and lace and stiletto heels well enough; was there a man who didn't? But the pose was blatantly phony. The smile was false. The woman looking at the camera had no substance. She might have been looking at a million guys instead of him.

The mutilated picture made his gut knot. It was an outright threat, crude but effective.

The third photo was the one that caught him. It was unselfconscious. Unposed. A simple shot of a beautiful woman walking on a beach, needing no artifice to make her look beautiful.

But there was more to it than that.

She'd sensed someone was watching her. He'd been the watcher often enough in what he thought of as his former life to know how subjects looked when they suspected the unwelcome presence of an observer. He could see it in her eyes. In the angle of her jaw. In the way she held her hair back from her face. Wariness. Fear. Distress.

And more.

Determination. Defiance. An attitude that, despite everything, said, *Hey, pal, don't screw with me.*

"Goddammit," Falco growled.

Then he grabbed his cell phone and arranged for a chartered plane to fly him to the West Coast first thing in the morning.

CHAPTER TWO

ELLE HAD spent most of the morning in bed with a stranger.

The stranger was tall and good-looking and maybe he was a good kisser. She didn't really know.

The thing was, she didn't like kissing. She knew less about it than, she figured, 98 percent of the female population of the United States over the age of sixteen, but that didn't mean she didn't know how to make kissing seem fantastic, especially with a guy who looked like this.

Kissing, the same as walking and talking, laughing and crying and all the other things an actress did, was part of the job. She had to remember that. This was a movie. Kissing the man in whose arms she lay was, yes, part of the job.

No question that women everywhere would change places with her in a heartbeat. Fans, other actresses… Chad Scott was world-famous. He was box office gold. And, for this scene, at least, he was all hers.

Elle knew how lucky she was. She hated herself for not being able to get into character this morning. Love scenes were always tough but today…

Today, things were not going well at all.

It wasn't her co-star's fault. She'd worried he might be all walking, talking ego, but Chad had turned out to be a nice guy.

He'd shaken her hand when they were introduced days ago, apologized for arriving after everyone else. She knew he hadn't had to do that. They'd spent five minutes in small talk. Then they'd run their lines. Finally, they'd shot their first scene, which was actually a middle scene in the film. Movie scenes were rarely shot sequentially.

Today, they were shooting their first love scene. It was, she knew, pivotal to the story.

The set was simple, just a seemingly haphazard sprawl of blankets spread over the sand near a big Joshua cactus. She was wearing a strapless slip; the camera would only catch her head, her arms and her bare shoulders, suggesting that she was naked. Chad was shirtless and wearing jeans. They were surrounded by a mile of electrical cable, reflectors and boom mikes, and the million and one people it took to film even the simplest scene. Antonio Farinelli, as hot a director as existed, had told the two of them he hoped to do the scene in one take.

So far, there'd been four.

A sudden gust of wind had ruined the first shot but the three others… Her fault, every one. She'd twice blown her lines; the third time she'd looked over Chad's shoulder instead of into his eyes.

Farinelli sounded angrier each time he yelled, "Cut."

Elle sat up, waiting while the director spoke with the lighting guy. Her co-star sat up, too, and stretched. Chad had been really good about all the delays. He'd obviously sensed she was having a problem and he'd made little jokes at his own expense. She knew they were meant to put her at ease. *Heck*, he said, *I'm pretty sure I shaved this morning. And don't feel bad, kid, my wife once told me the ceiling needed paint at a moment just like this.*

Everyone who heard him laughed because he was not just a hot property, he was a hot guy. Elle laughed, too. At least, she did her best to fake it. She was an actress. Illusion was everything.

In real life, she could never have lain in a man's arms and gazed into his eyes as he brought his mouth to hers, but then, reality was a bitch.

And reality was the phone call that had awakened her at three o'clock that morning.

"Darling girl," the low male voice had whispered, "did you get the picture? Did you get my note?" A low, terrible laugh. "You're waiting for me, aren't you, sugar?"

Her heart had slammed into her throat. She'd thrown the telephone on the floor as if it were a scorpion that had crept in under the motel room door. Then she'd run to the bathroom and vomited.

Now, all she could hear was that voice in her head. All she could see was that mutilated ad from the magazine, the note nobody knew about. Bad enough Farinelli knew about the ad. If only he hadn't walked into her on-set trailer just as she'd opened the innocent-looking white envelope she'd found propped against the mirror of her makeup table.

"Elle," Farinelli had said briskly, "about tomorrow's schedule…"

But she wasn't listening. The blood had drained from her head. She'd been as close to fainting as she'd ever been in her life.

"Elle?" Farinelli had said, and he'd plucked the envelope and what she'd taken out of it from her hand.

"Madre di Dio," he'd said, his words harsh with fury. "Where did this come from?"

She had no idea. Once she got her breath back, she told him that. A crazy person must have sent it. She'd had nasty little notes before, especially after the Bon Soir lingerie ads, but this marked-up photo…

Still, anything was possible. Her face was out there. In those two-year-old ads and now in stuff the publicity people for *Dangerous Games* had started planting. It was nothing, she and Farinelli finally agreed, but if she received any more things like this, she was to tell him and they'd go to the police.

Elle had agreed. She'd told herself the photo was a one-shot. Whoever had sent it would surely not contact her again.

Wrong. A few days later, a note arrived in her mail. Its message was horrible. Filthy. Graphic. And it was signed. The signature stunned her but it had to be a hoax. She told herself she would not let it upset her. She was an actress, she could pull it off.

Evidently, she was not as good an actress as she thought.

Farinelli had taken to asking her if she was okay and though she always said yes, certainly, she was fine, she knew he didn't believe it. He'd proved it two days ago when he stopped by her trailer during a break. Was she ill? No, she assured him. Was she upset about her part? No, no, she loved her part. Farinelli had nodded. Then he could only assume that the photo he had seen was still upsetting her because she was most assuredly not herself.

Elle had tried telling him he was wrong. He silenced her with an imperious wave of one chubby hand. He had given the situation much thought. The photo had been *of* her but it had been meant for him. She had been in, what, two, three films? She was almost unknown. He, however, was famous. He was taking a big chance, starring her in *Dangerous Games*. Obviously, someone understood that and wished to ruin his film.

But, by God, he would not permit it. He had millions of his own money tied up in this project and he was not going to let someone destroy him. He was going to contact the police and let them deal with the problem.

Elle couldn't let that happen. The police would poke and pry, ask endless questions, snoop into her past and find that the story of her life that she'd invented had nothing to do with reality.

So she'd resorted to high drama. She pleaded. She wept. She became a *diva*. A risky gambit but she had not come as far as she had by playing things safe. No guts, no glory. Trite and clichéd, maybe, but true. Besides, really, what did she have to lose? A police investigation would destroy the burgeoning career she had worked so hard for. She was twenty-seven, a little long in the tooth to go back to modeling….

More to the point, she could not face her ugly, ugly past all over again.

In the end, Farinelli had thrown up his hands. *"Basta,"* he'd said. "Enough! No police."

A disaster avoided. She'd forced herself to forget the ad, the note, to keep focused on the movie. And then that phone call at three this morning…

"Okay, people" Farinelli said. "Let's try it again."

Elle lay back. Chad leaned over her, waiting for the camera to roll. She felt his breath on her face….

"Hey," her co-star said softly. "You okay?"

"I'm fine," she said, with no conviction at all.

Chad sat up and looked at Farinelli. "Tony? How 'bout we break for lunch?"

The director sighed. "Why not? Okay, people. Lunch. Half an hour."

Chad stood up, held out his hand and helped Elle to her feet. One of Farinelli's gofers rushed over and held out an oversized white terrycloth robe. Elle snugged into it and Chad squeezed her shoulder.

"Sun's a killer, kid," he said softly. "Some shade, some water and you'll be fine."

Her smile was real this time. He truly was a nice man, a rare species as far as she was concerned.

"Thank you," she said, and she knotted the belt of the robe, slid into the rubber thongs the gofer dropped at her feet and made her way quickly to the half-dozen Airstream trailers clustered like Conestoga wagons awaiting an Indian attack a couple of hundred yards away.

Chad Scott was right, she thought as she went up the two steps to the door of her trailer. Cool air, cool water, some time alone and she'd be fine.

"Absolutely fine," she said as the door swung shut…

A man was standing against the wall just beyond the closed door. Tall. Dark-haired. Wraparound sunglasses. Her brain took quick inventory…and then her heart leaped like a startled cat and she opened her mouth to scream.

But the man was fast. He was on her, turning the locking bolt, one hand over her mouth before the scream erupted. He gripped her by the shoulder with his free hand, spun her around and hauled her back against him.

She could feel every hard inch of his leanly muscled body.

"Screaming isn't going to help," he said sharply.

A waste of time.

Falco could damned near feel the scream struggling to burst from her lips.

To say this wasn't exactly the reception he'd expected was an understatement. He'd spoken with the director, Farinelli, on his cell from the plane. He'd told him when he'd be arriving, more or less, and the director had said that was fine, it gave him lots of time to brief the Bissette woman and that it would be best if he, Falco, met with her in private because she'd probably want his presence on the set kept quiet, so—

"Hey!"

She had kicked him. Useless, as kicks went, because she

was kicking backward and wearing ugly rubber beach thongs, but it told him what he needed to know about whether or not she'd calmed down.

Okay. He'd try again.

"Ms. Bissette. I'm sorry if I startled you but—"

She grunted. Struggled. Her backside dug into his groin. It was a small, rounded backside and under different circumstances, he'd have enjoyed the feel of it—but not when the backside might as well have belonged to a wildcat.

"Dammit," Falco said. He swung her toward him, one hand still clasping her shoulder, the other still clamped over her mouth. "Pay attention, okay? I. Am. Not. Going. To. Hurt. You."

Mistake.

She slugged him. Two quick blows, one to the chest, one to the jaw. He was damned if he knew what to do with her now. He had only two hands and she was already keeping both of them occupied.

"Okay," he said grimly. "You want to play rough? That's fine."

He shoved her, hard. She stumbled back against the door and he went with her, pinned her there with his body. Her hands were trapped against his chest; her legs blocked by his. She was tall but he was a lot taller; her head was tilted back so that she was staring up at him with eyes even more tawny than they'd seemed in the defaced magazine ad.

Eyes filled with terror. And with what he'd seen in the candid photo that had brought him out here.

Defiance.

Okay. Instead of saying to hell with this and walking out the door, he'd try and get through to her one last time.

"Ms. Bissette. My name is Falco Orsini."

Nothing. Still the hot blend of fear and defiance shining in those eyes.

"I'm here to help you."

Fear, defiance and now disbelief.

"Trust me, lady. This isn't my idea of a good time, either. I'm here as a favor. And if you don't calm down and talk to me, I'm gonna walk straight out that door and leave you to handle this thing on your own."

She blinked and he saw confusion sweep across her face. Yeah, but she couldn't be any more confused than he was, unless—unless—

Oh, hell.

"Didn't Farinelli tell you I was coming?"

Another blink. A delicate vertical furrow appeared between her dark eyebrows.

"He said he would. He said you'd want to keep this private and that I should wait for you here, in your trailer."

Her eyes widened. "What?"

It sounded more like "wmf" because his hand was over her lips but there was no mistaking her surprise. Everything was starting to come together. She, a woman who'd been sent a picture defaced by a madman, walks into her trailer and finds a stranger waiting for her.

Merda! That fool, Antonio Farinelli, had never told her he was coming.

"Okay," Falco said, "here's the deal. Somebody sent you a picture." She began to struggle again. He shook his head. "Just listen. You got a picture. A bad one. Your boss wanted to call the cops. You refused. Am I right?"

He could see he was. So far, so good.

"So your boss contacted someone I—someone I know, and that someone contacted me. I agreed to talk to you, check things out, see if there were a way to deal with this so it all goes away quietly. No muss, no fuss. Yes?"

She exhaled sharply. He felt the warmth of her breath flow

over his hand, just as he could feel a fraction of the tension ease from her body. Her eyes were still locked to his, bright and distrustful, but now, at least, curious.

"My name," Falco said, "is Falco Orsini. I, ah, I sometimes do what you might call security consulting. That's why I'm here. I know about the picture, I know that you're worried about it, I know you don't want the authorities involved. I'm here to discuss the situation and offer some advice. That's the only reason I'm here—and the only reason I scared you is because your boss was too stupid to tell you about me." He tried for what he hoped was a reassuring smile. "I'm going to take my hand off your mouth. And maybe we can have that talk. Does that work for you?"

She blinked. Nodded. Now she was wary—but she was ready to listen.

He took his hand from her mouth.

She didn't scream.

Instead, the tip of her tongue came out and slid lightly over her bottom lip. Falco watched its progress. His gaze fell lower, to the rise of her breasts in the vee of her bulky terrycloth robe. He knew what she had under it; he'd watched the scene Farinelli had been filming at a safe distance before he'd slipped into the trailer. What she had on was a slip. Plain. Unadorned. Not like what she'd worn in that ad.

This slip was plain. Sexless.

Not that she was.

She was gorgeous. That hair. Those eyes. That mouth. Still, even with theatrical makeup on, there was another quality to her that he had not seen in the ad. A kind of innocence.

Which was, of course, ridiculous.

She was an actress. She played to the camera. To men. She could be whatever a particular part called for. Maybe she'd decided this part called for wide-eyed and innocent. Not that he gave a damn. He was only interested in her problem, and every problem had a solution.

"Antonio shouldn't have hired you," she said.

"He didn't."

"But you said—"

"I'm doing someone a favor."

"Whatever you're doing, I don't want you here."

Her voice was husky. Shaken.

"Listen," Falco said, "if you want to sit down—"

"I can handle this myself."

"The hell you can," he said bluntly.

Her chin rose. "You don't know what I can and can't do."

"I saw that picture. You can't handle that. No woman can. And there'll be more."

Her gaze sharpened. "What's that supposed to mean?"

Her answer, her body language, gave her away. Falco took off his sunglasses.

"There's been more already," he said grimly. "Hasn't there?"

"No," she said, but far too quickly.

She turned her head away; he reached out, cupped her chin, gave her no choice but to meet his eyes.

"What was it? Another picture? A letter? A phone call?"

No answer, which was answer enough. Her mouth trembled; Falco fought back the illogical desire to take her in his arms and comfort her. It was an uncharacteristic reaction for him in this kind of situation and he didn't like it.

"Have you ever seen a cat play with a mouse?" he said. "He'll keep things going until he tires of the game."

Elle shuddered. "You mean, until he does the things he drew on the picture."

"Yes," he said bluntly.

She nodded. And said, in a low voice, "And you think you can stop him?"

Falco's lips curved in what nobody would ever call a smile. "I know I can."

She stared up at him. "You can keep him from—from doing anything to me?"

"Yes."

"A man of few words," she said, with a little laugh. "How can you be so sure?"

"It's what I do. What I used to do," he said evenly. "I can find him and keep him from hurting you."

Elle stared at this stranger with eyes so dark they resembled obsidian. Why should she believe him? The answer was agonizingly simple.

Because, otherwise, she might not have a life.

Perhaps this man, this Falco Orsini, really could help her.

"If I agreed to let you get involved," she said slowly, "you won't—you won't contact the police?"

"No."

"Because, uh, because the publicity," she said, scrambling for a reason he'd accept, "because the publicity—"

"I told you. I'll handle this alone. No cops."

"What would you do, if I hired you?"

"You can't hire me. Remember what I said? I'm here as a favor. As for what I'll do… Leave that to me."

"The thing is…I wouldn't want anyone to know I had a-a bodyguard. There'd be talk. And questions. And questions are the last thing I want."

"I already figured that."

"So, how would we do this, then? I mean, how could you watch over me, go after whoever this is, do whatever you need to do without people knowing?"

Falco had considered that dilemma during the six-hour

flight from New York. There were lots of ways to move into someone's life to provide protection and search out information without raising questions. The idea was to assume a role other people would accept. He could pass himself off as her driver. Her assistant. Her personal trainer.

Personal trainer was pretty much what he'd decided on. Hollywood was filled with actors and actresses who worked on their bodies 24/7. He was fit; he'd look the part. And it would give him access to her no matter where she went.

Okay. Personal trainer it would be…

"Mr. Orsini?"

"Falco," he said, looking down into her eyes. He saw the rise and fall of her breasts, remembered the soft, lush feel of her against him, and he knew he wasn't going to pretend to be her trainer after all.

"Simple," he said calmly. "We'll make people think I'm your lover."

She stared at him. Then she gave a little laugh.

"That's crazy," she said. "No one will believe—"

"Yeah," he said, his voice low and rough, "yeah, they will.

Falco reached out, gathered Elle in his arms and kissed her.

CHAPTER THREE

THE FEEL of her mouth under his was incredible.

Warm. Silken. And soft. Wonderfully soft.

Not that he cared about that.

He was kissing her only to wipe that smug little smile from her face. To show her, in no uncertain terms, that they sure as hell could play the part of lovers, fool anybody who saw them.

Did she think she was the only one who could stick to a script?

Or did she think a bodyguard was too far out of her class to seem a convincing lover for a woman like her?

She was fighting him. Trying to twist free of his arms, to drag her lips from his. To hell with that. That who-do-you-think-you-are attitude of hers deserved a blunt response. She was wrong and he wasn't going to let her go until she knew it.

"No," she gasped against his mouth, but she might as well have saved her breath. Falco speared his fingers into her hair, tilted her face to his and kept on kissing her.

So what if she tasted of honey and cream? If she felt warm and soft against him? Those things were meaningless. This was about nothing else than teaching her that she couldn't laugh at Falco Orsini and get away with it.

He nipped lightly at her bottom lip. Touched the tip of his tongue to the seam of her mouth. With heart-stopping suddenness, she stopped fighting, stopped struggling.

She leaned into him, sighed and parted her lips. His tongue plunged deep.

The taste of her made his mind blur.

And his body react.

In an instant, he came fully erect, not just aroused but hard as stone, so hard it was painful. Desire pulsed hot and urgent in his blood. He slid his hands to her shoulders, cupped them, lifted her to her toes, drew her so close he could feel the race of her heart against his.

This was what he had wanted since he'd seen her in that first, unaltered ad. The eyes and mouth that promised passion, the made-for-sex body

The knife that pressed against his belly caught him fully unaware.

Falco went absolutely still.

Where she'd gotten the knife was irrelevant. The feel of it wasn't. With instincts and sharp reflexes honed by his time in Special Forces, he locked one hand around her forearm and grabbed her wrist with the other, bending it back until the knife clattered to the floor. He kicked it into a corner, saw that it wasn't a knife at all but the slim plastic handle of a hairbrush. Not that it mattered.

It was the intent that counted.

"Let go of me!"

Her hands clawed for his face. He grunted, shoved her back against the unyielding door, used his weight to keep her in place. The only way she could hurt him was if she managed to throw him off and that was about as likely as the trailer sprouting wings. He had at least seven inches in height on her and probably eighty, ninety pounds of muscle.

"Stop it," he snarled.

That only made her fight harder. Falco tightened his grasp on her wrists, brought her hands to her sides and pinned them to the door.

"I said, stop it! You want me to hurt you, I will."

She made a choked sound but it wasn't of rage, it was of terror. Her face, bright with color a moment ago, blanched. Those enormous topaz eyes turned glassy.

He'd flown out here to protect this woman. Instead, he was scaring her half to death. Kissing her had been a straight and simple matter of ego and he wasn't into BS like that. He was who he was; he didn't need anybody's applause to do whatever job he set out to do, certainly not a client's. He'd let his pride, whatever you wanted to call it, get in the way.

And he didn't like it, not one bit.

"Listen to me."

She wouldn't. She was lost in her own world, fearing the worst.

"Ms. Bissette," he said sharply. "Elle. Pay attention. I'm not going to hurt you."

Her eyes met his.

Hell. He'd seen a dog look at him like this once, years back when he was just a kid. He'd found the animal wandering an alley not far from the Orsini mansion in Greenwich Village. Its ribs had showed; there were marks he hadn't wanted to identify on its back. *Come on, boy*, he'd said, holding out his hand, but the creature had looked at him through eyes that said it damned well knew his soft voice didn't mean a thing.

He'd won the dog's trust by squatting down, holding out his arms, showing his hands were empty. What was the human equivalent of that kind of message?

Falco cleared his throat.

"Okay. Here's what happens next. I'll let go of you and step back. You stay where you are. No hands, no fists, no weapons. And we'll talk. That's it. We'll just talk."

He gave it a couple of seconds. Then he did what he'd told her he'd do. Another couple of seconds went by. She didn't move. Neither did he. That was some kind of success, wasn't it? A little color had returned to her face. Another plus. Finally, she took a deep breath.

"I want you to leave."

Her voice was low but steady. Her eyes had lost that terrified glitter. Good. Maybe now they really could talk.

"Look, Ms. Bissette—"

"I said—"

"I heard you. But we need to discuss this."

"We have nothing to discuss."

She was back. He could see it in the way she held herself, in the lift of her chin, the steadiness of her gaze.

"Actually, we do. I'm sorry if I frightened you but—"

"Frightened me?" Her eyes narrowed. "You disgusted me!"

"Excuse me?"

"Putting your hands on me. Your mouth on me." Her chin went up another notch. "Men like you are…you're despicable!"

Falco felt a muscle jump in his cheek. He'd been called similar names, a long time back, though they'd been names that were far more basic. It happened when you were a kid and your old man was Cesare Orsini.

He'd learned to respond to such remarks with his fists.

Not this time, obviously. This time, he flashed a cold smile.

"Trust me, Ms. Bissette. The feeling is mutual. I'm not into women who look into a camera as if they want to screw the guy behind it. I was simply making a point."

"You made it. You're contemptible."

Falco gave an exaggerated sigh. "Disgusting, despicable, contemptible. Yeah, yeah, yeah. I've heard it all before."

Elle Bissette folded her arms. "I'll bet you have."

"You said we couldn't fool anybody if we pretended we were lovers. I figured I could save us ten minutes of talk by showing you that you were wrong."

"Well, you didn't. And I wasn't. I'm an actress but playing at being your lover would take more talent that even I possess."

Her insults almost made him laugh. From poor little victim to haughty aristocrat in the blink of an eye. Damned right, she was an actress.

But he was willing to bet that her terror a little while ago had not been an act.

"Look," he said in as conciliatory a tone as he could manage, "why don't we start over? We'll go somewhere, have a cup of coffee, you'll fill me in on why you need a bodyguard—"

"I do not need a bodyguard. Are you deaf? I want you out of here, right now."

She pointed an elegant hand at the door and tossed her head. Her hair, a mane of jet black, flew around her face. He'd bet she'd practiced the gesture in front of a mirror until it looked just right.

"Get out or I'll scream so loud it'll bring half the world running."

Enough, Falco thought grimly. He took a step forward and clasped her elbows.

"That's fine," he said coldly. "Go right ahead. Scream your head off."

"You think I won't? I will! And five minutes after that, you'll be in jail."

"You left out a step. The part where the cops show up." He tightened his hold on her and hauled her to her toes, his head lowered so their faces were inches apart. "They'll want to have a nice, long chat with you, baby. Are you up for that?"

She stared at him. The color drained from her face and she became still.

"What's the matter, Ms. Bissette? Don't you like that idea?" She didn't answer and he flashed a smile as cold as a New York winter. "Maybe, if we're really lucky, the paparazzi will come by along with the cops. Then you can talk to the whole world."

Whatever fight was left in her was gone. She went limp under his hands, her head drooped forward and all at once he thought, to hell with this! He had not flown 3,000 miles to play games. She found him disgusting? Her prerogative. She had a reason to keep the cops away? Her prerogative again. She was not his problem, none of this was. How he'd let himself be drawn into the mess was beyond him but no way was he going to get drawn in any deeper.

The lady had said "no," and "no" it was.

"Relax," he said, his tone flat as he let go of her and stepped back. "You don't need to scream to get rid of me. Just move away from the door and I'm out of here."

She didn't move. He rolled his eyes, shouldered past her and reached for the knob.

"Wait a minute."

Falco looked over his shoulder. Elle Bissette swallowed; he saw the muscles move in her throat. Which color were here eyes? Amber or topaz? The thought was so completely inappropriate, it made him angry.

"What now?" he growled.

"Mr. Orsini." She hesitated. "This is your—your line of work? You're a bodyguard?"

He smiled thinly. "I am any number of things, Ms. Bissette, but it's a little late to ask for my CV."

"The thing is…I didn't ask for a bodyguard."

"Here's a news flash, baby. I didn't ask for the job."

"But you said someone sent you."

"I said someone I know told me you had a problem and asked me to check it out." His mouth twisted. "And here I am."

"Look, it's not my fault you agreed to do a favor for a friend and—"

"He isn't a friend and I don't do favors for anybody." Falco heaved out a breath. Why get into any of that? How he'd come to be here didn't matter, especially since he was about to leave. "It's a long story and it doesn't change the facts. I came here because I was under the impression you needed help." Another thin smile. "I was wrong."

"You *were* wrong," she said quickly. "You can see for yourself, I'm just fine."

He thought of the terror that had shone in her eyes a little while ago. Well, maybe it was true. Maybe she was fine. Maybe all that fear had been strictly of him.

"Really, I'm fine. I'm just wondering why you…why someone would have thought otherwise."

Falco dug his hands into the pockets of his flannel trousers. "You posed for a magazine ad," he said. "A provocative one."

Her chin rose again. He'd seen pro boxers with the same habit. It wasn't a good one, not if you didn't want to end up in trouble.

"It was a lingerie ad, Mr. Orsini, not an ad for—for Hershey's chocolate."

He grinned. "No argument there, Ms. Bissette." His grin faded. "Fifty thousand lovesick idiots went out and bought their girlfriends whatever it is you were wearing in that ad, then wondered why it didn't look on them the way it looked on you."

She stiffened. He could almost see the gears working. She

was trying to figure out if what he'd said was a compliment or an insult.

"For your information," she said coldly, "statistics show that women are the target audience for lingerie ads."

"Great. So fifty thousand broads went out and bought that outfit, put it on, looked in the mirror and wondered what the hell had gone wrong."

For a fraction of a second, she looked as if she wanted to laugh. Then that chin rose again.

"Is there a point to this, Mr. Orsini?"

"Damned right. All those people looked at an ad and saw an ad." His voice became chill. "One sicko saw something else and decided to—what's today's favorite psychobabble term? He decided to 'share' what he saw with you."

A flush rose in her cheeks. "You've seen what that—that person sent me."

Falco nodded. "Yes."

He expected a rant. Indignation, that Farinelli had sent the thing to someone. Instead, she shuddered.

"It was—it was horrible," she whispered.

A fraction of his anger dissipated. She looked tired and vulnerable; she was frightened even though she was determined to claim she wasn't, but she wasn't going to do anything to protect herself. It made no sense.

"It was worse than horrible." He waited a beat. "Why won't you go to the cops?"

"You said it yourself. It was just the work of some—some crazy."

"Crazies can be dangerous," Falco said. "He should be found."

She stared at him, her eyes suddenly filled with that same despair he'd seen in the photo of her on the beach.

"That would mean publicity."

"Publicity's better than turning up dead."

His blunt statement was deliberate. He'd hoped to shock her into telling him the real reason she didn't want to go to the police—he'd have bet a thousand bucks there wasn't an actor or actress on the planet who didn't want publicity, good or bad—but he could see that wasn't going to happen.

"It's just a prank," she said, very calmly. "Stuff like that happens. I mean, this is Hollywood."

"Has he contacted you again?"

"You already asked me that. I told you, he hasn't."

She'd lied again. So what? So what if there was more to this than she was letting on? Fifteen minutes from now, he'd be on a plane heading back to New York.

"Just that one thing?" he heard himself ask. "Nothing else?"

"Isn't that what I just said?" A smile as false as the one she wore in that lingerie ad curved her lips. "Look, I'm not worried. Really. There's security on the set. I have an alarm system in my house." Another smile. A toss of the head. Forget despair. What he saw in those topaz eyes now was dismissal. "At any rate, thank you for coming to see me."

Falco shrugged. "No problem."

She held out her hand. It was a queen's gesture. She was discharging him, her subject.

Something flickered inside him.

Had that softening of her mouth under his, that barely perceptible sigh, really all been an act? Had she been diverting him so he wouldn't expect that phony knife at his belly? Or had it been real? That sudden, sexy little sound she'd made. The way she'd parted her lips beneath his.

One step forward. One tug on those slender fingers extended toward him. Then she'd be in his arms, her breasts soft against his hard chest, her thighs against his, her lips his for the taking. And he would take them, he'd kiss her again and again, taking each kiss deeper than the last until she moaned and rose to him, whispered her need and her hunger against his mouth…

Dammit, was he insane?

She didn't go for men like him. Hey, that was fine. He didn't go for women like her. And he sure as hell wasn't turned on by women who flaunted their sexuality, who all but invited a faceless sea of men to get off on thinking what it would be like to take her to bed.

Falco ignored her outstretched hand.

"Goodbye, Ms. Bissette," he said, and he opened the door of the trailer and stepped briskly into the heat of the desert.

The afternoon's shoot began badly and went downhill from there.

It made the morning's attempts look good.

Everybody was unhappy.

The heat was awful; they'd been breaking early because of it but Farinelli announced that they were going to get this scene filmed or, *per Dio*, nobody was leaving!

Elle just could not get the scene right. Not her fault, she kept telling herself. The encounter with Falco Orsini had shaken her. She'd done her best to be polite to him at the end but it hadn't been easy. Finding him in her trailer, a stranger so tall, so powerful that he'd seemed to fill the space…

And the way he'd kissed her, as if he could make her want to kiss him back.

Some women might; even she knew that. Not her, though. She hated the whole sex thing. It was like a bad joke, a woman hired for her sex appeal in an ad, but it wasn't a joke, it was the terrible truth. A man's wet mouth, his rough hands…

Falco Orsini's mouth had not been wet. It had been warm

and hard and possessive but not wet. And his hands…hard, yes. Strong. But he hadn't touched her roughly….

Elle gave herself a mental shake.

So what? The point was, he'd had no right to kiss her even though he'd done it in response to her telling him she and he could never pretend they were lovers. Besides, it didn't matter. He would not be her bodyguard. Nobody would. Nobody would poke and pry and ask questions she had no intention of answering….

"…listening to me, Elle?"

She blinked. Antonio was standing close to her while everyone waited. "This is a love scene. A very important one. You must convey passion. Desire. Hunger. And you must do it with your eyes, your hands, your face. There is no kissing in this scene, *sì*? There is only teasing. Of your character, of Chad's character, of the audience." He took her arm, looked up at her, his expression determined. "You can do this. Relax. Forget the cameras, the crew. Forget everything but whatever brought that look to your face in the advertisement you did for Bon Soir."

Elle almost laughed. She'd had small movie roles before but that ad had gotten her this big part. What if people knew that "that look" had been the lucky result of an unlucky sinus infection? A heady combination of aspirin, decongestant and nasal-and-throat spray had miraculously translated to glittering eyes, slumberous lids and parted lips.

Better not to mention that, of course.

"One last try," Farinelli said softly. "I want you to imagine yourself in the arms of a man whose passion overcomes your most basic inhibitions, a man who stirs you as no other ever could. Imagine a flesh-and-blood lover, *bella*, one you have known and never forgotten. Put Chad out of your mind."

Chad rolled his eyes. "Damn, Antonio. You really know how to hurt a guy."

The joke was deliberate. A tension reliever, and it worked. Everybody laughed. Elle managed a smile. Farinelli patted her hand, stepped away, then raised his hand like the Pope about to give a benediction.

"And, action!"

Elle lay back in her co-star's arms. Her heart was racing with nerves. What had she been thinking, letting her agent convince her to take this part? What Antonio wanted of her was impossible. She couldn't do it, couldn't look into a man's eyes and want him not even when it was make-believe.

Having a man's hands on her. His wet mouth on her mouth. God, oh, God…

"Look at me," Chad's character said. It was a line of dialogue he'd repeated endless times today. Elle looked up, just as *she* had done endless times today….

And saw not his movie-star handsome face, but the beautiful, proud, masculine face of Falco Orsini.

Obsidian eyes. Thin, aristocratic nose. Chiseled jaw and a hard, firm mouth—a mouth that she could still remember for its warmth, its hunger, its possessiveness.

An ache swept through her body, heat burned from her breasts to low in her belly…

"And, cut!"

Elle blinked. She stared at the man looking down at her Chad, her co-star, who flashed a toothy grin.

"Elle, *mia bella*!" Antonio Farinelli hurried toward her. She heard a smattering of applause, a couple of whistles as he held out his hands and helped her to her feet. "*Brava*, Elle. That was *perfetto*!" He brought his fingers to his lips and kissed them. "The screen will sizzle!"

Chad rose beside her and winked. "I don't know who you were thinkin' about, honey, but he is sure one lucky guy."

* * *

A quarter of a mile away, half-concealed by a Joshua tree, Falco Orsini slammed a pair of high-powered binoculars into a leather case and tossed it into the front seat of his rented SUV.

What a hell of a performance! Elle Bissette and a cameraman. Elle Bissette and an actor. And when this movie hit the theaters, Elle Bissette and a couple of million faceless men.

She was hot for every guy in the world.

Except him.

No that he gave a damn.

What got to him was that he'd flown 3,000 miles and she'd sent him packing. Her choice, but he couldn't stop thinking about that look in her eyes in the beach photo and again in the trailer, a look that spelled FEAR in capital letters.

Something was happening and no way was he leaving until he knew what it was. Falco got into the SUV and settled in to wait.

CHAPTER FOUR

AN HOUR passed before he saw her. She was heading for the cars parked near the set. He'd figured her for something bright and expensive. He was right about the bright part, but expensive? He smiled. The lady drove a red Beetle.

He'd been wrong about her destination, too. He'd figured her for a rented house in Palm Springs or maybe a glitzy hotel but she headed northwest. To L.A.? It was a fairly long drive but this was Friday. She was probably heading home for the weekend.

Following her wasn't a problem. There was plenty of traffic, plus she turned out to be a conservative driver, staying in the right-hand lane and doing a steady 65 miles per hour.

He settled in a few of cars behind her.

After a while, her right turn signal light blinked on. She took an exit ramp that led to the kind of interchange he was pretty sure existed only in California, a swirl of interlocking roads that looked as if somebody had dumped a pot of pasta and called the resultant mess a highway system.

Freeway. That was what they called them here. He remembered that when the Bissette woman took a freeway headed north.

Still no problem but where was she going?

Another thirty minutes went by before her turn signal

came on again. This time, the exit led into a town so small he'd have missed it had he blinked. Following her wasn't so simple now, especially after she hung a couple of lefts and ended up on a two-lane country blacktop.

Traffic was sparse. A couple of cars, a truck carrying a load of vegetables, that was about all.

Dusk had fallen. There was no other traffic now. Bissette's taillights came on. Falco kept his lights off and hung farther back.

They'd been on the road a long time and the passing minutes had only made his suspicions sharpen. Why was she so determined to handle the mess she was in all by herself?

Why was she so smugly certain nobody would buy into him as her lover?

Did she want him to believe she could convince a million horny guys looking at her in an ad or in a movie that they turned her on, but that she couldn't play the same act one on one with him?

His hands tightened on the steering wheel.

Was that the real reason he was tailing her? To confront her again, show her what could happen if he wanted it to happen, if he kissed her not to make a point but to make her damned well admit she wanted to respond to him, that it wouldn't take any acting at all for her to come alive in his arms?

"Merda!"

Falco slowed the SUV to a crawl. Was he going nuts?

It was years, hell, it was more than a decade since he'd cared about proving himself to anybody. And it had never, ever involved a woman. "The Orsini Stud," his brothers had laughingly called him when they had been in their teens. They'd all done just fine in that department but yeah, some of the local girls had burned extra hot for the neighborhood bad boy.

It had been like that as he got older, too; it still was.

Women, beautiful women, were easy to come by. Women even more beautiful than Elle Bissette. Women who didn't play games. So, what was he doing following her into the middle of nowhere?

It wasn't logical, and it wasn't like him.

Okay. It had been a long day. He needed to kick back, have a drink, a meal…

Yes, but what was Bissette doing in the middle of nowhere? Maybe that was the real question. This all but empty road, curving now like a snake as it climbed into the mountains, tall trees on either side. It wasn't a good place to be if some crazy was after you. Crowds. Bright lights. People. There was safety in numbers. A cliché but also a fact.

Falco frowned.

Maybe the whole thing was a lie.

Maybe it was her idea of publicity. Or the director's. He didn't think so, after talking with Farinelli, after seeing that mutilated ad, but anything was possible.

Or maybe she was all the way out here to meet some guy. A lover. A woman like this, lush and sensual, sure as hell would have a man around. A weekend of sex, of lying in her lover's arms, of giving him what she had made clear she would never give Falco, her body naked under his, her hands on him, her mouth…

His body reacted so quickly, so completely, that it was embarrassing.

Forget needing a drink. What he needed was a run, a long one. Or a workout. Better still, he needed both. He'd been in L.A. before, he knew a couple of gyms where he could sweat whatever this was out of his system and—

Falco blinked. Bissette's taillights, two dots of crimson bleeding far into the distance, flashed brightly, then disappeared.

Had she made him?

He picked up speed. Slowed when he reached the approximate location where she'd seemingly vanished. Without headlights, it was difficult to see much of anything, but, yeah, he spotted something, a pair of old wooden posts to the left of the road and between them, a rutted track barely wide enough for a car. The VW had taken it; he could see its taillights and, in the sweep of its headlights, the murky outline of a house in a small clearing.

The lady had reached her destination.

A muscle flickered in Falco's jaw.

A strange place for an actress to rendezvous with her lover. A dangerous place, if she wasn't meeting anyone and would be here alone, but hey, not his problem…

"Dammit," Falco said. He pulled to a cleared space fifty feet ahead, parked and got out of the SUV.

Elle sighed with relief as her headlights picked up the shape of the cabin.

She parked her VW under a soaring pine, stepped out and shut the door after her. The clearing was dark; there were stars overhead but the moon had not yet risen.

No matter. She knew every foot of the clearing and the cabin by heart.

And loved all of it.

She'd rented it for a while and she'd been heartbroken when the owner decided to sell it or tear it down. She couldn't blame him. The cabin was small, it needed lots of work, and the ski resort that had once been planned a few miles away had never materialized.

Nobody wanted the run-down cabin but her. It was her sanctuary but she couldn't afford to buy it.

And then, a miracle. She'd signed with Bon Soir. Her contract called for more money than she'd ever imagined she might earn and she'd taken the entire check and plunked it down on the cabin.

Now, it was hers.

She was still fixing it up. It needed a new porch, a new roof, but what did that matter? It belonged to her. Nobody else. No one knew about it, either. It was the one place where she could relax, be herself…

Be safe.

She'd always felt safe here, despite the isolation. The cabin, the surrounding woods, took her back to her childhood. Part of her childhood, she thought quickly, the only part she ever wanted to remember, when her mother was still alive and there'd been just the two of them living in a cabin like this in a woods like this…

An owl called from the trees.

Elle jumped. Silly. The woods were home to lots of creatures, none of them frightening. It was the day that had left her feeling unsettled, she thought as she climbed the porch steps. The scene that just wouldn't end, the movie role she should never have taken…

The man.

Falco Orsini.

Elle took her keys from her pocket and unlocked the door.

How dare he show up the way he had? Without warning, without permission.

She stepped inside the cabin, shut the door behind her.

Part of it was Farinelli's fault. The director had no right going behind her back; he should have told her he was going to hire a bodyguard and she'd have told him to do no such thing. But that man. Orsini. Entering her trailer. Waiting for her there. Acting as if he owned her. Kissing her. Forcing her into his arms, forcing her to endure the feel of his hands, his body, his mouth.

A tremor went through her.

Awful, all of it…

It *had* been awful… Hadn't it?

She could still feel his embrace. The strength of his arms. The hardness of his body. The warmth of his mouth. And—and the sudden, incredible quickening of her blood.

No. That was impossible. What she'd felt had been disgust. What else would a woman feel when a man touched her? She knew all she needed to know about men and their needs, their appetites, their hunger. Some women endured it all, some pretended to like those things. Not her. She knew. She had always known, and what did that matter?

Falco Orsini had burst into her life and now he was gone.

All that talk about protecting her… Elle tossed her purse aside. Baloney, her mama would have said. He had his own agenda; hadn't he proved it by trying to kiss her? Men always had their own agendas. Her co-star acted like Mr. Nice Guy, but, really, it was only because he wanted to get this movie over with. Her director wanted the same thing and had proved he'd do anything to have it happen, including hiring a bodyguard that he had to know she would not want.

Especially a bodyguard like Falco Orsini.

The hard, handsome face. The powerful body. The low, husky voice. The veneer of good manners laid over the persona of a street tough.

Elle shook her head, reminded herself she'd come all the way up here so she could spend the weekend ridding herself of all those thoughts and reached for the nearest light switch.

Nothing.

Click. Click. Click.

Dammit, the light wasn't coming on. Moving carefully, feeling her way, trying to ignore the sudden unease tiptoeing up her spine, she made her way to a table and reached for the lamp centered on it.

Click. Click. Click.

The hair rose on the nape of her neck. Two bulbs dying at the same time? Coincidence? Yes. It had to be. Hadn't she just thought about the fact that nobody even knew the cabin existed? She'd kept it as her secret hideaway from the start. She had an apartment in Studio City, but this was where she came to restore her soul. Mama would have said that, too. The woods were like a cathedral where you went to find peace.

Coincidence, absolutely.

Briskly, she moved forward, hand outstretched, feeling for the little round table beside the sofa. Yes. There it was. Her fingers found the slender column of the lamp centered on it, skated up its cool surface, closed around the switch.

The light came on.

Elle breathed a sigh of relief…

And saw what had been hung on the planked pine wall beside the fireplace.

A scream rose in her throat but she couldn't get it out. It seemed to take forever before it burst, full-blown, into the dark silence of the night.

Falco was standing on the edge of the woods that surrounded the cabin, asking himself—for the third time—just what, exactly, he was doing here.

He'd come out of curiosity or maybe out of anger and a slightly dented ego, and none of that justified following her here. Elle Bissette didn't want his help. She didn't want any part of him. Fine. End of story. By now, he should have been on a plane, halfway to New York.

His mouth thinned. Hell, he thought, and he turned and started jogging toward the road.

He'd already made a fool of himself, trying to protect this woman. Why would he do it again? She wanted to spend the night in a place that looked like a leftover from a *Friday the 13th* movie? Her business, not—

Her scream tore apart the night.

Falco turned and ran to the house. He charged up the porch steps. This was not the textbook response to trouble. He had no weapon, no knowledge of what awaited him, but that scream…

The door opened and Elle flew through it, straight into his outstretched arms.

"No," she shrieked, "no, no, no…"

"Ms. Bissette. Elle. It's me. Falco Orsini."

He knew she couldn't hear him, not in the state she was in, eyes wide with terror, face white with it. Panting, sobbing, she beat at him with her fists but he had no time to worry about that. Instead, he shoved her behind him, braced himself to take on whoever was in there…

Nobody.

The cabin, brightly illuminated by a lamp at the far end, was empty.

Falco turned to Elle, huddled in the corner of the porch. Her breath was coming in desperate little gasps. Her teeth were chattering. She was cold and shaking and he cursed, reached for her and gathered her into his arms.

"Elle. You're safe. You're with me."

Slowly, she raised her head and focused on his face. "Mister—Mister Orsini?"

"Yes. That's right. Tell me what happened. Was someone waiting for you here?"

She shook her head. "N-no."

"But something scared you. What was it?"

"I saw—I saw…" Her expression changed, her voice was still weak but not it was tinged with suspicion. "What—what are you doing here?"

"I followed you."

"You followed…?" Her hands flattened against his chest. She pushed back a couple of inches. "Why?"

Why, indeed? "We can talk about that later. Right now you need to tell me what frightened you."

Her eyes clouded; she dragged them from his and looked down. "It's—it's nothing. A—a spider."

Falco's mouth twisted. "That's bull and you know it." He cupped her face, forced her to meet his steady gaze. "Here's the bottom line, lady. You won't call the cops? I will."

"No. You have no right—"

"You need help. If not from me, then from the police."

"All right!" She took a breath. "Someone—someone left something here. Something for me."

He felt his belly knot. "Another picture?"

She shook her head. Her hair whispered across his hands like ebony silk. "Not a picture. An an animal. A dead animal."

Falco nodded. "Okay. Here's what you're going to do. My SUV is parked on the road about fifty feet up. Here are the keys. Go to it, get inside, lock the doors and—"

"No!" Her fingers curled into his jacket. "I don't want to be alone."

Falco put his arms around her again. She stiffened but she let him hold her. He could feel her heart racing. She felt fragile and female and hell, any man would show a woman compassion at a moment like this.

"All right. Forget the SUV. You stay here while I check things out."

"Okay."

Her voice was low and shaky. He'd have liked it better if she'd given him a hard time. She was tough, he already knew that, and this show of obedience told him, even more than her pallor and her trembling, that she was far too close to shock.

"Good girl." Her eyes had not left his. Instinct took over. He bent his head and brushed his lips gently over hers, told himself it was simply another way of offering her the reassurance she needed. Her mouth trembled at the touch of his; the warmth of her breath was a shocking contrast to the icy feel of her skin. "I'll be right back."

She nodded. He stroked a strand of hair back from her cheek. Then he took a deep breath and stepped inside the cabin.

It wasn't much. Anybody expecting the palatial digs of a movie star would have been disappointed. One room, simply furnished. A couple of small tables. A couple of chairs. A door to his left stood open and led into a no-nonsense bathroom. Sink, shower, toilet. An alcove to the right held an apartment-sized stove, refrigerator and sink.

The lamp at the far end of the cabin burned as brightly as the sun.

There was a light switch by the door. A lamp on a table a couple of feet away. Why would Elle have ignored both, made her way through a dark cabin to reach the most distant light source in the room?

He tried the wall switch. The table lamp. Got useless clicks both times. Coincidence? He doubted it. A quick look confirmed it. There was no bulb in the wall fixture, none in the lamp.

Someone had set things up so Elle would be drawn farther into the room.

To the wall beside the fireplace.

To something he could see hanging on that wall.

Falco moved forward slowly. The thing on the wall became easier to identify. His belly knotted. Yes, it was an animal. A possum? A squirrel?

A cat. Yes, but not a real—

"Falco?"

He spun around. Elle stood in the doorway, hands clasped at her waist, face a pale oval against the darkness behind her. Her gaze was fixed on the wall.

"Is it—is it dead?"

"It's okay," he said, but she shook her head. Falco moved toward her. "Honestly, baby, it's okay. It isn't a real animal, it's a toy. A toy cat."

Elle made a little sound. She began to sway. Falco cursed and got to her just before she went down in a boneless heap.

CHAPTER FIVE

IT COULD have been an act.

Bissette was an actress, wasn't she? Maybe she thought she could play him for sympathy if she did an old-time swoon.

But the light-as-air feel of her limp body in his arms, the way her head lolled back against his shoulder, was all too real. She was out like the proverbial light.

Falco cursed under his breath and carried her to the futon. "Elle," he said urgently. "Elle, can you hear me?"

Nothing. Her face was devoid of color. For all he knew, she was going into shock.

The cabin was cold. And damp. There was wood and kindling on the fireplace hearth but no way was he going to let her remain here long enough for a blazing fire to matter. The time for her to make her own decisions was over.

When he left this place, so would she.

A patchwork quilt, almost translucent with age, was neatly folded across a ladder-back maple chair. He shook open the quilt, drew it over her then lay his fingers against her throat.

Good.

Her pulse, though rapid, was strong and steady. She'd stopped shaking and now tinges of color were starting to stain her cheeks.

His throat tightened.

God, she was beautiful. Even now, with no makeup, her hair wild, she was the most beautiful woman he'd ever seen.

And what did that matter at a time like this?

He had to get Elle Bissette up and moving and out of this dreary, isolated place. She might not want a bodyguard but she was in no condition to make that determination. She was his responsibility. For the moment, anyway.

A man didn't turn his back on his duty.

Falco went quickly to the alcove that passed for a kitchen, pulled a dish towel from a rack, checked the minuscule fridge, found a bottle of water. Halfway to the futon he made a quick detour, ripped the toy cat from the wall and put it aside.

Elle gave a soft moan.

He squatted next to her, opened the bottle of water, poured some onto the towel and patted it over her forehead and cheeks.

"Elle," he said firmly. "Open your eyes."

A sigh. A murmur. A flutter of lashes so long they seemed to curve against her cheekbones. Her eyes opened. Confusion glittered in their amber depths. Then she gave a hoarse cry, jerked upright and went for his face.

"Dammit," he said, and caught her wrists. "Elle. Take it easy. You're all right. It's me. Falco."

She stilled. Her eyes cleared. "Falco?" she whispered.

He let out a breath he didn't know he'd been holding.

"Yeah," he said gruffly. "It's me."

She fell back against the futon. "What—what happened?"

"You fainted."

"That's impossible. I've never fainted in my life."

Her voice was thready but the determination was there just the same. He would have laughed if he hadn't figured that would only send her into attack mode again and there wasn't time for that.

"Yeah," he said, "well, there's a first time for everything." He leaned forward, wrapped a strong arm around her shoulders, drew her toward him and held out the water bottle. "Drink."

"What is that?"

Falco rolled his eyes. "Gin and tonic with a slice of lime. It's water, babe. H_2O."

"But I'm not—"

"Thirsty. Do you ever do anything without an argument?"

She gave him the glare he figured the Medusa had used to turn men to stone. That was good, considering she'd been out cold only a few minutes ago. Then she snatched the bottle from his hand, put her head back and took a long drink. He watched the play of muscle in her throat, watched a trickle of water make its way over her bottom lip.

All he had to do was lean in, put the tip of his tongue to that tiny bit of moisture…

Falco shot to his feet. "Okay," he said brusquely. "Are you ready to tell me what just happened?"

"What do you mean, what just happened? I passed out."

"Somebody that knows about this place broke in to it and left something for you."

"Oh, God." Her voice turned thready. "The cat."

Idiot, he said to himself, and squatted beside her again.

"It was a toy, Elle. It wasn't real."

"I know. You said so."

He nodded. "But you fainted anyway."

Her gaze met his, then skittered away. "From relief."

"Or because that toy has some meaning to you."

"No," she said quickly. Much too quickly.

"I saw you, Elle. You thought the cat was real… That was bad." A muscle knotted in his jaw. "But finding out it was a toy was even worse." His eyes drilled into hers. "Why?"

Elle gave him another of those cold glares. He could see

the defiance, the tough independence coming back, but he knew enough this time to recognize it for what it was.

A shield.

She knew something. And she wasn't about to let him in on it.

Still, he couldn't demand answers now. He wanted her out of here. He didn't like the cabin's seclusion, the impenetrable wall of tall trees that surrounded it, the fact that he had no idea what, or who, might be hiding within those trees.

Most of all, he didn't like the fact that whoever had wanted to scare the bejeezus out of her had damned near done it. If she'd been alone when she saw that thing on the wall…

"Okay," he said, as he stood up, "the questions can wait."

"I'm not answering any questions, Mr. Orsini—but I have one for you. Exactly what are you doing here?"

"I see we're back to formalities."

"We're back to the fact that I didn't hire you as a bodyguard."

"Nobody hired me. I told you that. Consider me a volunteer."

"This is not a charity," she said coldly. "I don't accept volunteers."

Despite everything, he laughed. She didn't. She just fixed him with that look again. He figured it had surely sent other men running. Too bad she was wasting it on him.

"You followed me." Her tone was as sharp as a well-honed blade. "Why?"

He thought of taking her in his arms and giving her a graphic answer to the question, kissing her until she responded to him—and he could make that happen, he was certain—but it was a crazy idea. Besides, everything had to take a backseat to getting her the hell out of this place. They'd already been here too long.

Whoever had tacked that stuffed animal to the wall could still be outside. Okay, it was doubtful, but why take chances?

"Answer me, Mr. Orsini. Why did you follow me?"

"Maybe I like red VWs."

Elle rose to her feet. "Maybe I don't like smart answers."

"Look, baby—"

"Do not call me that!"

"Look, Ms. Bissette, you want conversation, fine. But not here."

"I am not the least bit interested in conversation. What I want are answers."

"So do I, but not here."

"On second thought, forget the answers. All I want is you out of here."

Falco narrowed his eyes. "Is it me, or do you just like giving men a tough time?"

"I don't give men anything," she snapped. "Why would I?"

Why, indeed. Was she into women? No way. That kiss in the desert assured him of that. Was she a woman who used men to suit her purposes, then discarded them when it was time for a change? Did she change lovers as often as some women changed hair color?

Not that it mattered. He had nothing to do with her life. Somebody was out to get this woman. The obscenity of it was not just wrong, it was vicious.

"Look," he said, trying hard to sound reasonable, "you can't stay here."

She laughed. It made his fists clench.

"Did I say something amusing?" he said.

"I don't know how to break this to you, Mr. Orsini, but I can do whatever I want."

"Somebody broke into your cabin. Left you a—a message."

"Oh, please! Break-ins happen in wild country like this. It was vandalism. Kids, plain and simple."

Falco smiled thinly. "Did kids nail that toy to the wall and send you that marked-up advertisement, too?"

It was a low blow. He knew it, wanted to feel guilty about it but if it forced her to see reality, it was worth it. He waited for her to retaliate. To his surprise, she didn't. Instead, she swung away from him, wrapped her arms around herself, and that did it. Falco clasped her shoulders and turned her toward him.

"Don't you see, Elle? These two things must be related."

She shook her head. "No," she whispered, "they aren't."

"And the sun won't set in the west."

She swallowed hard. "That's different."

"Yeah, it is. The sun isn't interested in hurting you."

For a few seconds, nothing happened. Then her eyes filled with darkness. "Oh, God," she whispered, "God…"

Falco muttered an obscenity, reached for her and gathered her close against him. A sob broke from her throat and he cupped her face, lifted it to his.

"I'll protect you," he said softly. "I swear it."

"I don't need anyone to protect me," she said, her voice breaking, and instead of arguing and telling her she was wrong, he drew her to him again and held her.

She felt warm and soft against him; the fragrance of her skin and hair was delicate and clean. He wanted to kiss her. Undress her. Take her to bed. Make love to her until she forget fear, forgot sorrow, until he was all that mattered.

Carefully, he cupped her shoulders, took a step back, waited until her eyes met his. Her nose was red and running. It made him want to hold her close again. Instead, he reached into his pocket, took out a pristine white handkerchief and handed it to her.

"Thank you," she said, and mopped her eyes, blew her nose.

He nodded.

"So. I'm assuming you don't live here full-time."

"I don't, no."

"Is this a rental?"

"It's mine." Her voice was low; he had to strain to hear it. "I bought it with my first big paycheck."

"From that lingerie company?"

Damn, he hadn't meant to sound accusatory. What did he care if she smiled and pouted for the eyes of every man on the planet? But she simply nodded and said yes, that was right.

"I'd always wanted a place like this. Quiet. Tucked away."

The cabin was definitely both. Still, someone had found it. A lover she'd brought here one weekend? The very possibility made him furious. That a man would violate a woman with such calculated cruelty. That a man would violate this particular woman—

Falco frowned. He was wasting precious time.

"Okay," he said briskly, "here's the plan. Get together anything you think you'll want. We'll leave your car. I'll arrange to have—"

"No." Elle shook off his hands. No more tears. No shaky voice. She was the portrait of composure.

"No, what? Your car will be fine. I'll arrange to have somebody pick it up and—"

"I'm not leaving."

"Dammit, woman, be reasonable."

"I'm being totally reasonable. If anybody—if anybody had wanted to—to do anything to me, they'd have been here, waiting."

"That's one way to look at it."

"It's the only way to look at it."

It wasn't, but telling her about similar situations that had ended in blood and disaster wasn't on the agenda right now. She thought she was being reasonable? Okay. He'd appeal to that.

"Look, there's nothing complicated about this, okay? Pick a friend. I'll drive you there and you can spend the night."

"I don't have friends."

His eyebrows rose. She made the announcement without drama, the way another woman might say she didn't have a potted geranium.

"It doesn't have to be a bosom buddy. Just somebody who'll put you up until tomorrow while I check things out."

Her expression went from composed to icy.

"Have I asked you to, as you so brilliantly put it, 'check things out' for me, Mr. Orsini?"

"Dammit, woman—"

"No. I have not. That's because I am perfectly capable of making my own plans."

"Then make some." Falco narrowed his eyes. "Otherwise I'll make them for you."

"You are an arrogant man, Mr. Orsini. That may impress some of your clients but it doesn't do a thing for me."

"I don't have 'clients,'" Falco said, each word dipped in ice. "And if there's anybody here who's arrogant, baby, it's not me."

"My name is not 'baby.' And I am not going to explain myself to you."

Forget arrogant, forget determined. Her tone, her posture, the look on that gorgeous face was downright hostile.

"I have a car. If I want to go somewhere, I'll drive myself."

"Fine. You take the VW. I'll follow you."

"Are you hard of hearing, Mr. Orsini? I'm staying right here."

The hell she was, Falco thought grimly. She was not staying here—and neither was he. It was too late, too dark to check the woods. Somebody was stalking her; why she refused to acknowledge that was a question that needed answering but he'd screwed around here much, much longer than was prudent.

And he wasn't about to waste more time arguing with a woman who gave new meaning to the word *mulish*.

"Don't you get it, Mr. Orsini? You are dismissed."

That did it. Falco scooped Elle Bissette off her feet and dumped her over his shoulder. She was an egotistical, irritating, obstinate witch, but no way would he leave her in a place like this.

She punched, kicked, shrieked. None of it mattered. He walked straight through the cabin, along the dirt track to the road, right to where he'd left the SUV, its ebony surface lit by a newly risen ivory moon.

"Son of a bitch," Elle huffed. "You no-good, no-account—"

"Do us both a favor," Falco said, "and shut up." He shifted her weight, yanked open the passenger door and dumped her in the black leather seat. She responded by trying to scramble out, but he'd expected that and he put one big hand in the center of her chest and unceremoniously shoved her back. "Stay put," he warned, "or so help me, I'll tie you up and stuff you in the cargo compartment."

She looked up at him, starlit eyes hot with fury.

"You bastard! For all I know you—you pinned that—that thing to the wall in there."

Okay. She knew he hadn't but the look on his handsome, arrogant face was worth the stupid taunt.

"Right." His voice dripped with sarcasm. "I figured out where you were heading, got here before you, hung kitty up, drove away, hid out and waited until you arrived." His mouth twisted. "Man, I am one clever dude!"

"You have no right to—to kidnap me."

He laughed. Laughed, damn him, as if she and the entire situation were amusing.

"Is that what you're going to tell the cops? You are one lucky lady. I mean, two chances to call the cops in one day?" His laughter died; his voice turned cold and he leaned down until their eyes were almost level. "Go on, baby. Use your mobile. Call the cops, tell them how you found that message in your cabin—"

"What message?" she said and, once again, her words tumbled out too fast.

"Oh, it was a message, all right. We both know that. The difference is, I don't understand it—but I have a feeling you sure as hell do."

Her chin lifted. "That's ridiculous."

"Good. So call them. Tell them what you found, tell them how I dragged you out of the freaking middle of freaking nowhere to save your pretty ass. Tell them that's what you call a kidnap, and I'll stick around for the laughs."

Pay dirt. He could see it, see the fight drain out of her.

"Bastard," she hissed.

"If only," Falco said with a quick, dangerous smile.

"I hate you!"

"And that breaks my heart."

"It couldn't. You have no heart, Orsini."

"I've been told that before."

"Oh, yes, I'll just bet you have."

Her mouth was trembling, that soft-looking mouth. He remembered the taste of it, the hint of sweetness she had not given him time to savor and then he thought, what the hell, she might as well hate him for cause and he leaned in, captured that sweet mouth with his, kissed her, swept his hands into her hair when she tried to turn away…

And heard the soft catch of her breath, the whisper of acquiescence that told him all he needed to know.

The need burning hot inside him burned inside her, too.

"Elle," he said, and her lips softened. Parted. Clung to his.

He said her name again and she moaned, curled her hands around his wrists as he took the kiss deeper and deeper.

The world fell away.

He could have her.

Everything in him knew it, knew as well that having her would be like nothing he'd ever known before. There had been women all his life but there'd never been a woman like this.

All he had to do was lift her from the SUV, carry her back into the cabin, undress her, bare her to his hands, his eyes, his mouth, take her again and again until he stripped her of that cold arrogance…

An owl hooted from the forest.

Falco pulled back.

Elle's eyes opened.

They were pools of deepest, darkest amber, shining with bewilderment. He could hardly blame her. Kissing her, wanting her, made no sense.

Neither did leaning in and kissing her again, his lips featherlight on hers.

"I'm in charge," he said in a low voice. "I'll take care of you. Nothing will happen to you, Elle, I swear it."

Then he slammed the door shut, went around to the driver's side, got behind the wheel and took the SUV away from the cabin fast enough to make dust rise into the moonlight.

CHAPTER SIX

THE NIGHT was magnificent, the ebony sky shot with silver starfire, the cool air fragrant with the tang of pine and fir.

The isolation, the beauty of the coastal mountains and the ever-present sound of the Pacific, beating against a rocky beach, were what had drawn Elle here in the first place.

In some ways, it reminded her of home and her earliest, happiest memories. No ocean, of course. She had grown up in a secluded valley hundreds and hundreds of miles from anything, least of all the sea. It had been a wonderful place, a wonderful life….

And then it had ended.

Elle frowned.

Why think of that now? She hadn't, for years. Until a few weeks ago. Until the ad torn from the fashion magazine…

"Are you cold?"

Startled, she turned to Falco Orsini.

"What?"

"You were shivering. If you're cold—"

"No. No, I'm fine. I just…" She bit her lip. "I'm fine," she said again, and looked down at her hands, tightly knotted in her lap.

Why had she let him carry her off? He'd given her little

choice, but the truth was, she could have stopped him. Could have made the attempt to stop him, anyway. But she hadn't. She'd let this stranger stuff her into the SUV and drive away with her.

And she'd let him kiss her.

Elle closed her eyes against the unwanted memory. She'd let him kiss her, force a response from her…

Liar!

He hadn't "forced" anything. He'd put his lips on hers and something had happened deep inside her, something she had never believed could possibly happen if a man kissed her.

But it had.

She'd kissed him back, kissed him and wanted to go on kissing him.

Which only proved what bad shape she was in.

She did not respond to—to that kind of thing. Why would she? She knew women did but she'd never been able to understand it. And what impression had she made with that one moment of irrational behavior? Did the man beside her think she would repay him for coming to her rescue by having sex with him?

Not that he'd come to her rescue.

He'd turned up, unwanted, uninvited. Not once. Twice. In the trailer. At the cabin. Yes, she'd flown into his arms when he'd burst through the door but she'd have been fine if he hadn't been there. She'd have gotten over her fear.

She would have.

Absolutely, she would have.

"Elle. If you're cold, just say so."

"I told you, I'm—"

He reached out, touched a button. The windows went up; a whisper of warm air drifted through the vehicle. He looked at her.

"Is that better?"

It was, actually. She hadn't realized it until now but he was right, she felt chilly.

"Yes. Thank you."

He nodded. Looked back at the windshield.

More silence.

They'd been driving for the better part of an hour, virtually alone on the narrow road. She'd never been on it this far past her cabin, hadn't even been curious where it led. Falco had turned onto it going fast, no signal light, checking and rechecking the mirrors. After a while, he'd settled into a steady, what, sixty, seventy miles an hour? They'd seen only two other vehicles, both heading toward them and then, a little while ago, headlights had come up behind them.

Falco had known it well before she did. She knew because she'd been watching him from the corner of her eye. That hard, handsome profile. The long fingers of one hand splayed over the steering wheel, the others lying loose on the gearshift lever.

Both hands had suddenly tightened.

A long minute later, the pinprick of headlights had illuminated the interior.

Logic told her his eyesight was better than hers. Instinct told her it had nothing to do with eyesight. He had sensed the presence of the other vehicle. He was like a predator, sleek and alert to every nuance of what might be prey, or what might prey on him.

Such a breathless analogy from a woman not given to breathless analogies, but she suspected it was accurate. Falco Orsini was different. At this point, nothing about him could surprise her.

Well, yes, she thought. Something could. Or, rather, something had. The way he'd kissed her.

The way she'd responded.

Back to that.

Elle turned her face to the window and stared blindly into the night. She responded to music. To art. That didn't come close to describing how she had reacted to that kiss. The quick, reflexive sense of disgust. Of revulsion. The shock at the feel of a man's mouth on hers…

And then, oh, God, and then the incredible explosion of heat that had swept through her thighs, her belly, her breasts…

"Take the ramp, on right, in four-point-eight miles."

Startled, Elle swung toward him. "What was that?"

"My navigator."

"Your what?"

"My navigator," he repeated. "She says we turn off just ahead."

Was she losing her mind? "Who says?"

Falco flashed a quick grin. It was so unexpected that she was half-afraid her mouth had dropped open.

"The GPS," he said, jerking his chin toward the dashboard. "The Voice of the Robot Queen. She has all the charm of a machine but she's generally right on the money."

The global positioning system. Of course. Elle looked at the lighted panel. Was she so far gone that she hadn't noticed it glowing like a TV monitor?

"I turned it on only a few minutes ago," Falco said, as if he'd read her thoughts. "I don't know this area and I don't want to just keep driving without doing some reconnoitering."

"Reconnoitering?" she said blankly.

"Checking things out. Making some plans."

"What plans? As soon as we get to Los Angeles—"

"Is that where you live?"

"In Studio City. Yes. The street is—"

"We're not going there."

Elle cocked her head. "What do you mean, we're not going there?"

Falco shifted his weight. "I told you before. I want you someplace safe."

"And I told you—"

"Turn right in point-three miles."

"I know what you told me." Lights glowed faintly in the distance ahead; a sign flashed by. The name of a town she'd never heard of, logos for food, for gas, for motels. "Remember? I asked if you had a friend who'd take you in for the night and you told me that you didn't."

He was right. He'd asked and she, idiot that she was, had stupidly said she had no friends. It was true enough but she hadn't meant he could take her wherever it was he was taking her.

"Look, Mr Orsini—"

"I'd think, after all this, we could give up the 'Mister' thing, don't you?"

She looked at him, felt the rush of color climb her face until she realized he hadn't meant the remark the way she'd taken it. His tone was level, his concentration still on the road. He'd been referring to what had happened in the cabin, not to the kiss.

The kiss hadn't meant anything to him. Why would it? He'd probably kissed more women than he could remember. She wasn't a fool, she knew that most women would be eager to be kissed by a man like him.

She also knew the reason he'd kissed her. To show control. He'd even told her that. Not that it had been necessary. She knew all about that kind of thing.

The SUV slowed, took a right.

"Pick one."

Bewildered, she swung toward him. "One what?"

"A motel. Your choice." He slowed the SUV and now

she saw the line of motels fronting what had become a four-lane road.

Her belly knotted.

What she'd feared was happening. He had taken that kiss as permission to take her. A bitter taste filled her mouth. Despite everything she knew about men, a tiny part of her had hoped he was different.

She should have known better.

None of them were different, she thought coldly, and sat up straight in the leather seat.

"Forget it," she snapped.

"Yeah, I know. They're not up to your usual standards but it's the best we're going to do."

"You've miscalculated, Mr. Orsini."

Her voice was cold enough to turn water to ice. What now? Falco thought wearily. He was bone tired; the last thing he wanted was another battle.

"Look," he said, "it's late. I told you, I don't know this area. I punched in a request for a place to stay the night, the GPS came up with this as the closest loc—"

"I am not sleeping with you."

Her tone was quick and sharp. Another time, another place, he might have seen her reaction as having some logic to it. She was a movie star; she was paid to turn men on. Maybe that was a crude way to put it, but, basically, it was what women like her did. He was a stranger, a man who had shown up, uninvited, in her life and now he'd told her they were going to spend the night at a cheap motel.

So, yes, maybe her attitude bore some semblance of logic.

Unfortunately, he wasn't in the mood to see it.

For starters, he didn't like Elle Bissette. She was a gorgeous package on the outside, but on the inside, she was the worst kind of snob. She'd taken one look at him and decided he wasn't in her league. He despised that kind of thinking; he'd never be interested in a woman who made judgments like that, not even for a night's worth of sex with a woman most men would crawl over each other to reach.

Besides, sex was the last thing on his mind.

He was tired and hungry and what he wanted was a shower, a hot meal, enough strong coffee to keep him awake while she told him what in hell was going on because, come hell or high water, she was going to tell him.

Then he wanted to fall into bed and sleep.

And all Elle Bissette could think of was that he was going to jump her bones?

Anger rose inside him, quick and hot. At her, at himself. He slammed on the brakes and pulled into the parking lot of the nearest motel, stopping the engine and swinging toward her even as he did.

"Has anybody ever told you that you have one incredibly overblown idea of where you stand on the desirability scale?"

Elle undid her seat belt and reached for the door handle. "Good night, Mr. Orsini. It's been—"

Falco's hand wrapped around her elbow. He spun her toward him.

"You really think that's what this is all about? That I took one look at the famous Elle Bissette and began plotting a way I could get my hands on her?"

Color shot into her face. "You're disgusting!"

"Or maybe you think that's the way I get women into my bed. Wander around, find one who looks as if she needs a little help, then tell her she owes me."

"Let go of my arm!"

"Well, let me set the record straight. I'm not interested. Have you got that, or you want it spelled out?"

"Damn you! I said—"

"I heard what you said." Falco, eyes glinting, mouth hard, leaned forward. "You are nothing I would ever want."

"And nothing you could ever have!"

"You don't get it. A man would have to be crazy to put up with an egotistical psycho like you."

"Thank you for the personality analysis," she said coldly. "Be sure and add the cost to your bodyguarding bill."

"Trust me, honey." Falco's lips twisted. "My services cost nothing. The whole thing is free of charge."

"Fine, because that's exactly what your services are worth."

"I'd sooner go to bed with a block of ice than with you."

She flashed an ice-queen smile. "Whatever turns you on, Orsini."

"Not you, babe, that's for sure."

Elle recoiled. His words were like a slap in the face and that was ridiculous. She had no wish to turn anybody on, certainly not a man like him, all that overbearing arrogance, that swaggering masculinity…

All that strength, the courage, the sudden hints at tenderness…

Qualities he didn't have, she thought grimly. Qualities she'd assigned him because she had the imagination that went with being an actress.

Elle raised her chin. "Are you done?"

"I'm done, all right." Falco lifted his hand from her arm. "You want out?"

"Damned right I do."

"Fine." He dug in his pocket, hauled out his wallet. "You'll need cash."

"I won't need anything from you."

"Yeah, you will. Or did you remember to grab your purse before I hauled you out of that cabin?"

That stopped her. Her eyes narrowed.

"Hauled me out, is right. Carrying me out of there as if— as if I were a recalcitrant child."

Dammit, how could she do this? How could she accuse him of being the worst kind of bastard? And how could she be so beautiful?

Her eyes blazed. Her mouth was set in a sulky pout. She was full of passion and life and no matter what he thought of her, the fact that some crazy wanted to hurt her made his belly knot.

"Exactly as if I were a recalcitrant child, if you even know what the word means!"

"That's enough." His voice was low, rough, filled with warning.

"You think you can—you can pretend you want to protect me when all the while, all the while you just want to—to overpower me—"

"Elle." He grasped her wrists. "You know better than that."

"Oh, I know better, all right. I know all about men like you…"

Her voice broke. Falco was looking at her as if she were crazy and perhaps she was. Everything he'd said was true. He'd done nothing but offer her kindness and she—and she—

Tears rose in her eyes and spilled down her cheeks. Falco cursed and reached for her. She gave a little mew of protest, but when he pulled her into his arms, she burrowed against him.

"I didn't mean—"

"I know." And he did know; she was terrified and doing one hell of a job of not showing it. Beautiful as well as brave, he thought, and drew her closer.

"I just— Everything seems so out of control—"

"It isn't," he said with more conviction than he felt. "You're safe and I'm going to keep you that way."

She gave a wet sniffle. "I know you didn't bring me here to—to seduce me."

"No," he said, trying for a light touch as he held her, rocked her gently in his arms. "I'm more a hot sheet motel man myself."

She gave a hiccupping laugh. It was a start. He went on rocking her, his lips pressed lightly to her hair. It smelled of the night and, incongruously, of roses. After a few seconds, she lifted her head from his shoulder. "Falco?"

"Yeah?"

"I know—I know you didn't bring me here looking for—for payment."

"Damned right, I didn't," he said gruffly.

"But—but you have the right to know that—that it isn't you. I mean, I'm just not— I'm just not—"

"That's okay," he said, and wondered why the words sounded hollow. A few seconds went by. Then he cleared his throat. "Is it that make-believe cowboy actor?"

"Chad?" Elle gave a low laugh. "He's got a wife he's crazy about and six kids. No. It's not him. It's just—it's just that I don't do that."

"Sleep around." Why did that admission make him feel so damned good? "I'm glad."

"No. I mean—I mean, I don't—I don't do the—the sex thing."

She felt a stillness suddenly settle over him. What in the world had made her make such an admission? Sex was not something she thought about, much less talked about, not in any way, not with anyone.

"The sex thing," he said, as if he'd never heard those words before.

Elle winced. What he'd never heard were those three words infused with such special meaning. How could she have shown such little discretion? Irritation at herself made her tone turn cool.

"Is that a problem?"

Yes, Falco thought, it damned well was. That a woman should not like sex, because that had to be what not "doing" the sex thing meant, that a woman, especially one who looked like this, who felt warm and soft in a man's arms, whose mouth tasted of honey, should feel that way about sex was, well, unfortunate.

But was it a problem for him?

No.

He was, okay, attracted to her. Never mind all that stuff he'd told himself a little while ago. She was incredibly easy on the eyes and she needed help.

His help.

Whatever mess she was in had *Danger* written all over it. That kind of thing upped the ante. A maiden in distress. A knight on a white charger, and never mind how tarnished his armor might be. Add it all together and you had a hot thing going.

Hell, he'd been there enough times to know.

But there were other women. There would always be other women. That was the cold, honest, down-and-dirty truth. Women liked to think the world was full of kindred souls searching for each other.

Men knew better.

He did, anyway.

At seventeen, he'd made out with Cathy Callahan in the backseat of her father's Buick. A month later, Cathy was history and he'd repeated the performance with Angie Baroni under the creaky stands of a high school on Staten Island where he'd won an "away" football game with a last-minute touchdown and she'd waved her pom-poms and cheered.

Of course, he'd polished his style over the ensuing years but even his brothers, no one man/one woman forever enthusiasts themselves—though that seemed to have changed recently for Dante and Rafe—had laughed and said it would be a day at the beach in Antarctica when Falco Orsini decided he needed one woman to the exclusion of all others.

"Mr. Orsini?"

Falco frowned, focused on the lovely and suddenly composed face inches from his.

"Just in case you see this as a challenge to your masculinity…"

Her voice had become cool. It irritated him, the sudden change from tender to tough, but, hell, he admired it, too.

For a couple of seconds, he wondered how she'd react if he said yes, that was exactly how he saw it, that she'd melted in his arms a little while ago and was he really expected to believe she wasn't in to, as she put it, "the sex thing"?

But none of this was about sex. It was about keeping her safe.

That was all that mattered.

Time to lighten the mood again, he decided. He put a serious look on his face and drew back. She sat up straight, her eyes wary as they met his.

"Here's my best offer," he said politely. "You stop calling me 'Mr. Orsini,' I'll try and survive the blow to my ego. How's that sound?" He almost laughed at the expression on her face. Clearly, his answer was not what she'd expected. "Deal?" he said, holding out his hand.

He watched her think it over. Then she gave a quick smile and put her hand in his. "Deal."

And just the brush of her palm against his, the touch of her fingers, made every muscle in his body leap to attention.

Something told him celibacy wasn't going to be as easy as he'd made it sound.

He left her in the SUV while he got them a room.

The clerk must have been asleep. He showed up at the desk

looking bleary-eyed. Falco signed the register as E. Presley, 10 Blue Suede Lane, Memphis, Tennessee, and ignored the line where you were supposed to enter your license plate number. He didn't mention there was anyone else with him, paid cash, took the room key card—he suspected it would turn out to be the most up-to-date feature in the place—and asked if there was somewhere nearby to get a meal.

"Diner's one block that direction," the clerk said, smothering a yawn.

Falco nodded, thanked the guy and strolled out to the parking lot. Elle was still there. She was sound asleep, her head resting on the seat back.

He got behind the wheel and watched her for a couple of minutes. She looked exhausted, incredibly young…and there it was again, that sweet vulnerability that had brought him to Hollywood in the first place.

A muscle knotted in his jaw.

He drove to the rear of the two-story building. He'd requested a corner room on the first floor and the parking space directly in front of it was empty. Most of the spaces were; it didn't take much effort to figure out that the world had long-ago bypassed this little town.

He got out of the SUV, went around to the passenger door, opened it.

"Elle."

Nothing. Not even a flutter of her lashes.

"Elle," he said more loudly, "come on, wake up. We'll get washed, then go get something to eat and have a long talk." He sighed. "Okay, we can talk tomorrow. Showers, food, and then you can climb into a real bed."

Still nothing. Falco leaned into the car, touched her shoulder.

"Elle, come on. Open your eyes."

She murmured something and turned her face toward him. Her hair brushed over his fingers. Her breath caressed his cheek. The muscle in his jaw knotted again. Okay. Let her sleep. He'd carry her into the motel room, give her a few minutes, then wake her.

Lifting her was simple. One arm under her, the other around her. He stepped away from the car, kicked the door shut. It was easy enough to shift her weight, carry her to the room and maneuver the key card into the lock. The door opened to a dark room that smelled of disinfectant and disuse. He used his elbow to feel around for a wall switch, found one and hit it.

A dull light came on.

The room was small, shabby but clean. The furnishings were utilitarian. One window. One chair.

One double bed.

Her carried her to it, stood her on her feet while he kept one arm clamped tightly around her. She slumped against him like a rag doll as he drew back the patterned bedspread, pulled down the thin top sheet and equally thin blanket.

"Come on, baby," he said softly. Slowly, gently, he eased her down on the mattress.

She gave a deep sigh. So deep, he thought, so weary. It was a sigh of exhaustion.

He took off her shoes. Thought about taking off her clothes and getting her down to her underwear and just as quickly decided against it. Instead, he pulled up the covers, tucked them around her shoulders, all his movements brisk and businesslike…

Yeah, but brisk and businesslike didn't keep him from thinking of how much he wanted to bend down and brush her lips with his. Just that. A light kiss. A way to repeat his pledge to keep her safe.

"Hell," he muttered.

He checked the window lock, pulled the curtain. Double-locked the door. Located the heating unit and turned it to high.

Okay. To the john next. He used the facilities, washed his hands, his face, tore open the plastic pack that held a plastic cup, filled it with a tepid mix of water and chlorine from the tap and rinsed his mouth. It wasn't the best hygiene in the world but it would have to do.

In the bedroom again, he turned out the light, waited a few seconds until his eyes adjusted to the dark. The single chair looked as if it might support a dwarf but not a man who stood six-three. And the last time he'd weighed himself at the gym near the Orsini Brothers Investments building in Manhattan, he'd been at 220.

There was always the floor, but he needed a night's rest.

"Okay," he said, as if there were someone there to hear him.

Falco toed off his mocs and lay down on the bed as far from Elle as he could. The mattress sagged, the heater was making noise though it wasn't producing much heat, but he'd slept in places that made this look like a palace.

Elle Bissette, Hollywood actress, surely had not. That cabin she owned wasn't luxurious by any means but she'd made it clear it had sentimental value to her as her first big purchase.

Her day-to-day home, in L.A., was certain to be movie-star impressive.

Shabby motel room or not, she had not awakened. But she'd started dreaming, making little noises, arms and legs twitching. Not a good dream, whatever it was.

"Elle," he said softly. "You're okay."

She whimpered. Her lovely face contorted.

The hell with it.

Falco moved closer and gathered her in his arms, whispering reassurances. He felt the tension ease from her body. After a minute or two she sighed, turned toward him and lay her head on his shoulder, her hand over his heart. Her breathing went from choppy to relaxed.

He told himself he could let go of her now.

He could…

But he didn't. Instead, he drew her closer. Shut his eyes as he inhaled the clean, sweet fragrance of her skin.

And followed her into sleep.

CHAPTER SEVEN

ELLE CAME awake slowly, rising from the depths of a deep, dreamless sleep.

It was the first time in longer than she could remember that she hadn't spent the night trapped within fragmented dream landscapes…

Unless she was dreaming right now.

She felt the sudden leap of her heart.

Yes. This had to be a dream. How else to explain coming awake in a strange bed in a strange room, the half light of dawn visible behind the curtain?

How else to explain coming awake in the warm, strong arms of a man?

"Morning," a husky male voice murmured into her hair, and Elle knew it wasn't a dream at all.

Frantic, she tried to pull free of Falco's embrace. That didn't work. His arms only tightened around her.

"Don't panic," he said softly. "It's me. Falco."

If that was supposed to calm her, it didn't. Elle's struggles increased.

"Elle," he said quietly, "we shared the bed, that's all. Nothing happened. Absolutely nothing."

They'd shared the bed. Shared a night's rest. Elle stopped struggling, took a long breath.

"We're both still fully dressed." His words took on a touch of light humor. "If we'd done anything except sleep, trust me, honey, we wouldn't be."

He was right. She was wearing all her clothes. So was he. But his arms were around her… His arms were around her, and she was safe.

Elle let out a breath and went still in his embrace.

"Okay?"

She nodded and slowly, carefully, looked up at him. Her heart gave another leap but it had nothing to do with fear. What a beautiful man he was! Instinct told her he'd laugh at hearing himself described that way but it was true. His face had the elegant bone structure of Michelangelo's *David*: the strong nose, chiseled lips, firm jaw. His eyes were very dark, all obsidian pupils in the dusky early morning light; his lashes were long and enviably thick.

Beautiful, indeed.

The night had brought the shadow of morning stubble to his cheeks. Male models often cultivated that look to give them a macho aura but it never quite worked.

It did on Falco Orsini.

He looked masculine and beautiful and dangerous.

And sexy. Incredibly sexy. It was just a reasonable conclusion. A woman didn't have to like sex to admit a man looked sexy.

"What are you thinking?"

Falco had a little smile on his lips. It was intimate and knowing, as if he'd read her thoughts, and it brought a rush of color to her cheeks.

"Nothing," she said quickly. "I mean—I mean, I was trying to remember what happened last night. The last thing I can recall, we were sitting in the car."

"Yeah." He caught a strand of her hair in his hand, let it

trail through his fingers. Her hair felt like silk. How could a woman look so beautiful after what she'd gone through last night, and without a drop of makeup? For years, he'd joked about what he called the 5:00 a.m. face, the one he swore women put on while a man was still sleeping rather than let him see her as she really was. This, what he saw now, was Elle's true five-in-the-morning face and it was spectacular. Skin as creamy as satin. Eyes bright with intelligence. Cheekbones washed with light color. And that mouth. That lovely mouth, so pink, so soft, so perfect…

Falco forced himself to breathe normally, dragged his thoughts away from entering what could only be dangerous territory.

"I left you in the SUV, booked this room…" He smiled. "When I got back, you were sound asleep. So I carried you inside." He smiled again. "You missed your chance to get a first look at our deluxe, six-star accommodations. Does that do it?" He could see that it didn't. "No, huh? You're wondering what you're doing here, in bed with me."

She felt her face fill with heat. Falco nodded.

"Well, it never occurred to me to ask the character in the front office what the sleeping arrangements were. Turned out we have only the one bed. I put you on it. Then I looked around and saw that I had a couple of options. I could sack out on the Aubusson on the floor—"

Okay. That had helped. Elle's lips curved in a smile. It was faint, but yes, it was a smile.

"Definitely an Aubusson," she said.

"My other option was that very comfortable Eames chair."

She peeped over his shoulder. Eames, indeed. The battered chair reminded her of one in a shelter where she and her mother had once stayed. Something of the memory must have shown on her face because Falco put his hand under her chin and tilted her face to his.

"Hey," he said softly, "are you okay?"

"Yes, of course." She forced a smile. "Lucky man, to have had two such great choices."

He grinned. "I thought so, too. That's why I went for option numero three. Share the bed by taking the far side of it." His smile faded; his eyes turned dark again. "But you started dreaming. It didn't take much to see it wasn't a good dream so I got you out of it and you sort of turned toward me and I figured if I pushed you away you'd fall back into that dream so I stayed where I was and you—you settled in."

She wanted to tell him she didn't believe him, that she'd never, as he'd called it, "settled in" a man's arms and never would. But his tone was calm, his gaze steady. And the way they were lying, she in his arms, her hand on his heart, was proof that he was telling the truth.

How could she feel safe with this man? With any man, but especially one this big, this strong, this sure of himself?

He was watching her with an intensity that would have sent her running just twenty-four hours ago, but now—

Now, she found herself wondering what the stubble on his jaw would feel like under the brush of her fingers. Would it be bristly or soft? She could find out in a second. All she had to do was lift her hand, touch his face and then—then, maybe that tingle in her breasts, her belly would go away.

"Elle."

His voice was low. Rough. The sound of it thrilled her.

"Baby. You keep looking at me like that and—"

She knew what she had to do. Stop looking at him. Move away. Get up from the bed.

"And what?" she said in a voice she hardly recognized as her own.

Falco groaned, bent his head and kissed her. It was the lightest of kisses, just the soft brush of his lips over hers.

And it wasn't enough.

She heard the sharp intake of her own breath and then her hands were lifting, lifting, moving up his chest, over his shoulders, capturing his face and yes, oh, yes, that stubble on his cheeks felt incredible. Soft, like his mouth. Rough, like his voice when he'd said her name.

He said it again now, whispered it against her mouth, and then he groaned and rolled her onto her back, came down over her, cupped her face as she was cupping his and his lips moved against hers, his kiss changed, hungry now, hot and wild and she yielded to it, more than yielded, wanted it, wanted his kiss, wanted him.

She moaned and flung her leg over his. He made a rough sound, slid his hand under her shirt, cupped her breast. A cry broke from her throat. She put her hand over his, felt her nipple swelling, beading, felt a liquid heat forming low in her belly…

Felt a wave of sheer terror sweep through her.

"No!"

Her cry of fear was fierce. She tore her mouth from Falco's and at first she thought he wasn't going to let go of her but then his big, hard body went still and he rolled away from her and got to his feet.

Silence filled the dingy room. She wanted to say something, anything. But he spoke first.

"It's getting late," he said brusquely. "I want to be out of here ASAP."

Elle scrambled up against the creaking headboard. Falco's mouth was a flat line, his eyes were cold. She knew she owed him an explanation but how could she offer one when she couldn't even explain what had happened to herself?

"Falco, I'm sorry. I didn't mean to—to lead you on."

He looked straight at her. What she saw in his face made her breath catch.

"It was my mistake."

"No, it was me. I don't even understand why—"

"No," he said coldly, "neither do I. I'm responsible for your safety. I lost sight of that but it won't happen again." He swung away from her. "I'm going to take a shower. When I'm done, you can do the same."

"Falco…"

"Five minutes," he said curtly. "Then we're out of here."

He was impossible.

Caring one minute, unfeeling the next.

She knew she'd hurt him. Not him. His pride. She'd had a couple of minutes to think and she was pretty sure she knew what had happened. She was frightened, she'd reacted in the most primitive way to a primitive man.

No. Falco was a lot of things but "primitive" wasn't one of them despite the long, muscular body, the quick reflexes, the ability to think and react like a predator.

And he wasn't a man who'd take advantage of a woman's emotions.

He wouldn't have to.

Elle took her turn in the bathroom. She stood under the lukewarm spray—that was as hot as the water would get—and wondered what twist of fate had sent him into her life. The better question was, how would she get him out of it?

That arrogant declaration. *I'm responsible for your safety.* The hell he was! Nobody was responsible for anything about her except her.

Was that true? What about what she'd found waiting at the cabin last night? What if Falco hadn't been there to take her in his arms and ease her terror?

She shut her eyes, lifted her face to the tepid spray.

The toy cat had frightened her more than the marked-up Bon Soir ad, more than the note, more than anything she could have anticipated. The toy cat, her toy or one that was its absolute image, pinned to the wall of a cabin nobody knew existed except her…

Ever since this started, she'd told herself she didn't know the reason for it or who could do this to her. A lie. She knew. At least, she had a very good idea. And she could no longer avoid admitting it to herself, but, dear heaven, not to anyone else.

A fist banged on the bathroom door. "One minute, Bissette. After that, we'll pass on breakfast."

Elle's eyes narrowed. Forget caring. Falco Orsini was a bullying dictator. She didn't want him poking his nose into her life. She couldn't afford to let him poke his nose into her life!

Once they returned to the real world from wherever this place was, she'd get rid of him. *Here's a check for your time, a handshake, and goodbye, Mr. Bodyguard.*

As for that ridiculous threat about passing on breakfast… Did he really think he could scare her with such nonsense?

Her stomach growled.

Elle rolled her eyes, shut off the water and reached for a towel.

Falco worried that someone might recognize her. Her face was famous. The last thing he wanted was to have word go out that Elle Bissette was in whatever in hell you called this town.

Once they were in the rented SUV, he grabbed the pair of sunglasses he'd left on the dash and handed them to her.

"Put them on," he said curtly.

She looked at them as if she'd never seen dark glasses before.

"I don't need them," she said, "but thank you for the offer."

He almost grinned. The thank-you was as close to being a four-letter word as anyone could have managed. The lady had balls, he had to give her credit for that.

"Put them on anyway."

"I just said—"

"You want a meal? Or you want some truck driver spotting the famous Elle Bissette and calling the local news station?"

She glared at him, obviously hating that he'd out thought her. Then she snatched the glasses from his hand and plopped them on her nose.

Better, but not perfect.

Falco made a quick left and pulled in to a gas station. He pumped the tank full, went into the minuscule office to pay and came out with a red ball cap emblazoned with the oil company's logo.

"Put your hair up and wear this."

She looked at the cap, gave a little shudder—a shudder that would have been lots more dramatic had she seen the guy who'd been wearing the thing before Falco bought it for twenty bucks. But she twisted her hair into something like a ponytail, held it at the crown of her head, then pulled on the cap and yanked it low over her eyes.

Definitely better. You could still see her nose, her mouth and her chin, all delicate, all beautiful, all pure Elle Bissette, but he knew damned well that the only man who'd realize that was the one who'd held her in his arms through the night, who'd awakened long before she had and imagined what might happen if he woke the sleeping princess with a kiss.

He was a damned fool.

He stepped hard on the gas even though the diner was only a couple of hundred feet ahead and lurched into a parking slot.

"I know it's not what you're accustomed to," he said coldly, "but we all have to make sacrifices."

She shot him a look. "You have no idea what I'm accustomed to," she said, and before he could respond, tell her he damned well did and that third-rate motels, greasy-spoon diners and stuck-up females were not what he was accustomed to, either, she was out of the car and striding toward the door.

What had happened this morning was what had to happen when a man woke up tenting the sheets. Elle had been handy, that was all. He hadn't liked her from the start and the more time he spent with her, the more that assessment was validated.

As for that heart-wrenching little story about not "doing the sex thing"… Bull. What she did understand was how easy it was to use men. A little teasing, then pull back. It probably kept guys on the edge of sanity until she got things her own way.

She was almost at the front door. Falco went after her, grabbed her wrist, jerked her against his side.

"I can walk without your help, Orsini," she snapped.

"Not while you're with me," he snapped back, and the way she looked up at him said, as clearly as words, that being with him was a situation that wasn't going to go on much longer.

And that was just fine with him.

She didn't open the menu.

"I'm not hungry," she said and when the waitress showed up, she ordered coffee. Black.

"The house special," Falco said. "Do the eggs over easy, make sure the bacon's crisp. Hotcakes, not French toast, extra syrup on the side." He looked up at the girl and smiled. "Please."

Please was all it took, Elle thought coldly. The waitress's answering smile made it clear she'd have walked on burning coals to provide whatever this particular customer wanted.

"Toast?"

"Rye. And do the whole thing twice."

Elle waited until the girl hurried away. "I hope you didn't order the extra meal for me. I told you, I'm not—"

"Hungry. I'm not deaf. Just let the food sit there if you don't want it."

They waited in silence until the waitress brought their breakfasts, one gigantic platter for him, one for Elle. He spread a napkin in his lap, picked up his fork and dug in. He could feel Elle's eyes on him. After a couple of seconds, she put her napkin in her lap, too, and reached for her fork.

He raised an eyebrow. She flashed him a murderous look, but when she spoke, her voice was surprisingly young, almost childlike.

"It's a sin to let food go to waste."

Then she dug in.

She ate everything.

He wondered about that. Was it because she believed leaving it would have been wrong? Or was she starved for a solid meal? Despite what she obviously thought about him, Falco had dated a lot of models, a couple of actresses and a well-known Broadway star. All of them had moaned about having to watch their weight; they'd order endless courses, then poke at them.

Not Elle.

She ate as if it mattered. Then she slugged down two mugs of black coffee, made a quick trip to the ladies room and they were on their way again.

"Where are we going?"

"To your cabin."

"Good. I'll get my car—"

"I want to see if anyone's been there since we left. Assuming they didn't, you can pick up your handbag and anything else you can't do without. Then you're going to tell me where you live and we'll go there."

"That's ridiculous. I am perfectly capable—"

"That's how we're going to do it," he said in a take-no-prisoners tone. "You don't agree, we'll bypass the cabin and head straight for your place."

He felt her eyes on him. "I really dislike you intensely, Mr. Orsini."

Back to square one. "That breaks my heart."

"Such a childish attitude. Just because I didn't—I didn't succumb to your pathetic attempt at seduction…"

Elle gasped as Falco turned the wheel hard, brought the SUV to the shoulder of the road and shifted into Park.

"Is that what you think this is all about?"

"I know that's what this is all about."

"You seem to know everything you need to about me," he said coldly. "Well, here's a flash. I wasn't the one who started things this morning."

"Not true," she said, even as a small voice inside her said *He's right, it was all your doing.*

His smile made her wedge herself as far into the corner as her seat belt would permit. "You're good, I'll give you that. The dramatic little scene about not doing 'the sex thing'—and then, the next second, you're looking up at me with big, innocent eyes and asking me to make love to you—"

"I didn't do anything of the sort! I never asked you to—"

His fingers flew, undoing his seat belt, then hers, and he hauled her into his arms.

"Do you think that's the way to keep a guy like me in line?"

"What are you talking about?"

"Play that kind of game again, baby, I can promise you how it will end."

"No. It wasn't a—"

He kissed her, his lips taking hers, parting hers, possessing hers. She formed a hand into a fist, pounded it against his shoulder but he was ruthless, determined—and suddenly she felt fire ignite in her blood, felt it rush from her breasts to her belly.

Falco lifted his head.

"No more games," he said gruffly. "Not unless you're prepared to play straight to the end."

Calmly, as if nothing had happened, he closed the latch of her seat belt, then his, turned on the engine and pulled back onto the road.

The cabin stood silent, the door open as he'd left it and stirring idly in the soft breeze.

He could tell no one had been there since they'd left but he wasn't about to take chances. He took a long look before he opened the car door.

"Stay," he commanded.

Elle smiled sweetly. "Woof woof."

He couldn't help it. He laughed.

"Good girl," he said, and laughed again when she bared her teeth.

He checked the cabin. Nobody. Elle's purse and car keys were where she'd left them. He grabbed them, did another walk-through, then went back to the SUV.

"Has anyone…"

Her laughter was gone. Her eyes were big and filled with anxiety.

"No," he said. "The place is untouched."

She let out her breath. "That's good. That's very good. And since that's the case, Mr. Orsini—"

Falco raised his eyebrows.

"Since that's the case, Falco, you can surely leave me here."

"Forget that."

"I'm not going to stay." She shuddered. "I'm never going to stay here again. I'll just get into my car and drive myself home."

"To find what? Something similar to what you found here?"

"Oh, for God's sake," she said, no more dulcet tones wrapping the words in sugar, "I'll be absolutely fine!"

"That's the way it's going to be, Elle. I'll drive you to your place. Check it out. If everything's okay, I'll leave."

Her eyes searched his. "Promise?"

"Promise," he said, but why spoil things by adding that he'd first telephone a guy he knew out here who did excellent bodyguard work because he wasn't about to leave Elle on her own and he sure as hell wasn't about to go on guarding her. He had a life to go back to. Anyone could do this job; it didn't have to be him. He didn't have to like his clients or whatever you wanted to call them, but he had to at least get along with them.

He and Elle were not getting along, that was for sure—especially in those moments when he crossed the line he always kept between himself and those who needed his help. He'd never done that, until now. And he didn't like it…

"Promise," he said again, and crossed his heart, but with his fingers crossed the way he and his brothers used to when they were kids lying to each other. "So, if there's anything you want inside…"

She hesitated. Then she nodded, her face expressionless. She stepped from the SUV and headed for the cabin. He started after her but she held up her hand.

"It's just one thing. I can handle it by myself."

He waited, leaning against the SUV, arms folded while she went up the porch steps and into the cabin. The "one thing" was probably a sack full of cosmetics. Or jewelry. Or clothes. Just because she wasn't wearing makeup or jewelry, just because she was dressed like a couple of million other American women her age didn't mean—

How wrong could a man be?

She came out of the cabin a minute later, a small silver-framed photo in her hand.

"That's it?" he said in disbelief.

"That's it," she said.

He had questions. A thousand questions. But the expression on her face—sorrow, distress, despair so profound it made him forget his anger—kept him from voicing them.

"Okay," he said, and because it was too late to think, he leaned down when she reached him and kissed her. It was a soft kiss. Tender. And, for just long enough to make his heart kick against his ribs, she fitted her lips to his and kissed him back.

Then she got into the SUV, put the picture in her purse, told him her address in L.A. as if nothing had just happened and they made the two-hour trip in silence.

She lived, as she'd already told him, in Studio City.

A condo. The area was pleasant, the building was well-maintained, but Falco knew something about property costs out here and though prices in this part of Los Angeles might be astronomical by the standards of the American heartland, it didn't have the feel of super-priced real estate.

He went in alone, left Elle in the car.

"Stay put," he warned, but this time, he didn't get a sarcastic "woof" in response. She seemed remote. Was it because of that kiss? Or was she hoping everything would be okay here?

Part of him wanted to think it was because he'd told her he'd be leaving and that she was anticipating that and wishing it wouldn't happen, which was ridiculous. They were like oil and water; besides, he had work waiting back East, a tough meeting Monday with a banker from Indonesia, lunch Tuesday with a contingent of money men from Zurich.

As soon as he'd finished checking the condo, he'd put in a call to a guy he'd served with. Rick lived out here, he was top-notch at what he did.

Elle would be well-protected.

Her place was small, just a living room, small dining room, kitchen and lavatory on the lower level, all of it spotless and undisturbed. The rooms were nicely furnished but walking into it was pretty much like walking into a high-end hotel suite.

Falco climbed the steps to the upper level. A bathroom. Fine. A small room that seemed to be a home office. Also fine. The last door had to open on Elle's bedroom…

"Merda!"

Someone had taken the place apart. Drawers had been flung open, the contents dumped on the pale birch floor. Clothes had been yanked from the hangers. Words, ugly words describing women, had been scrawled on the pristine walls in what he at first thought was blood, but when he touched it, was red paint.

Worst of all was Elle's bed. Someone had gone at it with something sharp. A knife. A big knife. Nothing else could have left such devastation behind…

"Omigod!"

Falco whirled around. Elle stood in the doorway, her face white.

"My God," she said, "my God, my God, my God—"

He went to her, scooped her into his arms, carried her down the stairs to the SUV, got inside with her on his lap, his lips against her hair, his hands sliding up and down her spine, whispering words of reassurance.

Her arms were tight around his neck. She was shaking, sobbing, repeating "Why? Why? Why?" like a litany.

"Shhh, baby," he said, his arms tightening around her, holding her, rocking her, wanting to turn back the clock so she would not see what someone had done as much as he wished he'd been here when it happened so he could have killed the bastard who had done it with his bare hands.

At last, her trembling stopped. She took a couple of deep, shaky breaths. He felt her heartbeat slow. "Elle," he said softly, framing her face with his hands, drawing back so he could look into her eyes. "Elle. Who did this, honey? Who wants to hurt you?"

Her lips parted. She started to speak. Then she made a sad little sound and buried her face against his throat.

"I can't stay here," she whispered.

Falco nodded. "No," he said calmly, "you can't."

"There's a—a hotel on—"

"You can't stay there, either."

He was not only calm, but he also was possessed by a deadly quiet. His brothers, anyone who'd ever had anything to do with him, would have recognized it.

"I told you, there's no one I can impose on."

"It wouldn't matter. I don't want you in L.A." His mouth thinned. "Hell, I don't want you in California."

"Falco. That sounds good but—"

"Hawaii," he said. "Hawaii's perfect."

Elle sat back, Falco's arms enclosing her. She gave what might have been a laugh.

"Hawaii is six hours away. I've never been there. I don't know anything about it. I don't know anyone who lives there. I don't have a plane ticket. And then there's the movie. My contract. Antonio will expect me on the set Monday morning."

He smiled. "Details," he said softly, and when she parted her lips to tell him that going to Hawaii was impossible, he drew her close and kissed her until she sighed, leaned into his protective embrace and kissed him back.

CHAPTER EIGHT

DETAILS, Falco had said.

That turned out to be an interesting way to describe things.

As soon as they were in the SUV and heading for the freeway, he flipped open his mobile phone and hit a speed dial number. Elle fought back the desire to tell him using a phone while driving was illegal. She had the feeling the man beside her never cared too much about legalities.

The thought should have been worrying.

It was, instead, reassuring. While she was trying to figure out how that could be, she heard him say, "Farinelli? Falco Orsini here."

He was talking with Antonio. Her director. He would not be thrilled to hear Falco didn't want her on the set Monday. An understatement. He would not permit it; she was certain of it. They were on the freeway now and the roar of traffic drowned out Falco's side of the conversation, only the end of it when he said, "Yes, that's correct, I'll be in touch."

Surprised, she looked at him. "Antonio said it would be all right?"

Falco shrugged. "He'll shoot around you."

"Yes, but—"

He reached for her hand and brought it to his mouth.

His lips brushed her fingers. His breath whispered over her skin.

"Stop worrying, okay? I told you, I'll handle everything."

He put her hand back in her lap, flipped his phone open again. She could still feel the electric tingle of his lips on her flesh.

Her heart raced.

She was turning control of her life over to this man. How had that happened? She certainly hadn't given him permission to take charge—but then, she couldn't imagine him ever asking for permission to do anything.

Being with him, putting herself in his hands, was like riding a roller coaster. The nervous anticipation of the long climb to the top, the sharp bite of fear that began at the moment of descent and then the rush, the breathless realization that you'd let go of everything solid and real in favor of the transcendent excitement of just being.

Elle swallowed hard. She didn't like roller coasters. Then, why go on this particular ride? She swung toward Falco, ready to tell him she wouldn't go along with his plans.

"Falco—"

He raised the index finger of the hand that held the phone in acknowledgement.

"Right," he said. "On the ocean. Very private. Limited access. Top-notch security system. Yes, Maui would be perfect. And I'll need a car waiting at the airport. No, I don't care about the make. Just something with lots of horses. And black. Yes, fine. That will do."

Do for whom? No one had made decisions for her in years, especially not a man. Why was she letting such a thing happen now?

"Falco," she said sharply. "We need to discuss this. I've been thinking it over and I'm not at all sure I want to go to Haw—"

But he was already deep in call number three.

"Yes," he said, "that's correct. Immediately. To Hawaii. Just two people."

"Two people?" she blurted.

Falco shut the phone and glanced at her.

"You and me," he said. "Or did you think I'd let you go alone?"

She stared at him. The truth was, she didn't know what to think.

Not anymore.

He drove to LAX, parked at a section new to her and walked her quickly through doors marked ReadyServe Charter Flights.

"We're renting a plane?"

"How long do you think it would take for the world to know Elle Bissette is going to Hawaii if we took a commercial flight?"

"They'll know anyway, once they see my credit card."

"We're using mine."

"But a chartered flight will cost…" She bit her lip. She didn't want to insult him but surely he had to realize that this would run to thousands of dollars. "I mean, my card has no—"

"No dollar limit. But neither does mine."

Did her reaction show on her face? It must have, because he squeezed her hand.

"Trust me," he said quietly. "Can you do that, do you think?"

A better question was, did she have a choice?

There was a counter ahead of them, staffed by a young woman. Falco tugged the ball cap lower on Elle's forehead.

"Keep to the side," he said in a low voice. "Let me do all the talking." Then he let go of her hand, strolled to the counter and flashed a sexy, dazzling smile.

"Hi," he said. "I'm Falco Orsini. I phoned a little while ago."

"Oh, Mr. Orsini. Of course, sir. I have your paperwork all ready."

Elle was all but invisible. The girl hardly glanced in her direction, but then, why would she when Falco was flirting with her?

Not that it mattered.

He was her bodyguard. Their relationship was strictly business. When had she ever wanted any other kind of relationship with a man?

"Never," Elle said under her breath as Falco caught her elbow and began hustling her toward the double doors at the rear of the office.

"Never what?" he said mildly. "Or don't I want to know?" She would have jerked away but his fingers clasped her elbow more tightly. "Just keep moving."

"Don't you want to say goodbye to your little friend?"

Falco chuckled. "Why, honey, I do believe you're jealous."

"You wish."

A sleek silver jet was waiting on the tarmac. Falco walked her toward it.

"When we get to the plane, go up the steps, straight into the cabin."

"Why? Do you expect your fan club to follow you onto the field to say goodbye?"

Falco chuckled. "Nicely done, don't you think?"

"You mean, how you turned her head? Very nicely done, indeed."

"The idea was to keep her eyes from you."

"Yes, well you managed that." Dammit, why did she sound so irritated?

"And without a card from Actor's Equity, either."

She shot him a cold look. His face was expressionless

but amusement danced in his dark eyes. That annoyed her even more.

"Or maybe you'd have preferred it if she'd asked you for your autograph."

Elle narrowed her eyes. "Don't be an ass!"

"An ass." He arched one eyebrow. "Very nice."

"You know what I mean. Of course I didn't want that."

"So, what's the problem?"

The man was infuriating! "There is no problem."

"Yeah, there is." They'd reached the plane. Elle went up the steps, Falco close behind her, and they entered a handsomely appointed cabin. "You're ticked off because I kept that kid from noticing you."

"She wasn't a kid. And there were other ways you could have kept her from noticing me instead of—instead of flirting with her!"

A grin angled across his chiseled mouth. "Ah."

"Ah, what?" Elle folded her arms. "It was wrong, that's all. For all she knew, you and I were—we were—"

"Together," Falco said, a sudden roughness in his voice.

"Yes. No. I only meant—"

He caught her face between his hands and kissed her. Hard. Deep. Kissed her until she moaned into his mouth and wound her arms around his neck. Then, only then, he put her from him.

"I know exactly what you meant," he said, his voice still rough, his eyes hot, his hands slipping to her shoulders. Then he took a long breath and let go of her. "Sit anywhere," he said, as calmly as if nothing had happened. "I'm going to talk to the pilot."

She stared after him, watching that very male walk, that arrogant and, yes, incredibly sexy I-own-the-world swagger. Her heart was beating so hard she could hear it.

What was she doing, going to Hawaii with this man? What

did she know about him, really, beyond the fact that he could talk Antonio Farinelli into changing a shooting schedule, that he was as at ease checking into a cheap motel as he was chartering a flight that had to cost twenty thousand bucks or more?

Was she going from one kind of danger to another?

Logic told her to get off the plane. There was still time.

Falco strolled back into the cabin. "All set," he said. He took a seat and reached for a magazine.

Elle hesitated. Then she sat down as far from him as she could get.

Moments later, they were in the air.

She slept most of the flight, awakening once as Falco draped a light blanket over her.

"Mmm," she whispered, and she must have dreamed that he smiled, leaned down and pressed a kiss to her temple because she surely would not have permitted that to really happen.

She woke to the impersonal touch of his hand on her shoulder.

"We'll be on the ground in twenty minutes," he said briskly. "If you need to use the facilities, now's the time."

Great. Now he was taking charge of her bathroom habits. Elle unsnapped her seat belt, used the lavatory, shuddered at her reflection over the sink. Her hair was lank, her face was pale, she hadn't changed her clothes in, what, almost two days.

As soon as they touched down, she was going to find the nearest mall.

That turned out to be a foolish hope.

The plane landed, taxied to a stop at the terminal. Falco clasped her elbow as if he expected her to bolt and led her to a low, gorgeous shiny black Ferrari. You didn't have to drive one to recognize one, not when you lived in LaLa Land where driving anything that cost less than the national budget of a small nation was evidently against the law.

Falco gave the car a glance, held out his hand so the teenaged kid who'd delivered it could give him the necessary papers to sign. He handed the papers back along with a bill that made the kid's grin spread from ear to ear.

"In," he said brusquely to Elle.

The kid looked at her. Hidden safely behind the ball cap and dark glasses, wanting to stay that way, she had little choice but to obey the command. Still, she couldn't resist clicking her heels and saluting.

"Yessir!"

The kid started to laugh, saw Falco's face and thought better of it.

"All the house stuff—the keys, the gate opener, the paperwork—is in an envelope on the seat."

But Falco had already found the envelope, handed it to Elle and put the car in gear.

Forty minutes later, they pulled up at a massive iron entrance gate.

They had passed no one since leaving the main road. Now, a seemingly endless tangle of grasses and palm trees stretched ahead. If there was really a house here, it was well-hidden.

Elle peered through the windshield. "Are you sure this is it?"

"The GPS says it is." Falco aimed the control device at the gate and depressed the button. There was an audible click and then it swung open.

"Here we go," he said.

The narrow road beyond, bordered by tall native plants, twisted in a series of lefts and right. Whatever lay ahead of them was obscured by the foliage. Then, gradually, the heavy growth cleared, revealing a long shell drive lined with stately palms.

And a house.

Elle caught her breath.

It was an amazing house, all angles and planes standing on a low promontory overlooking a sea so blue it could have been a stage set, except for the white froth of waves breaking against the sand of an equally white beach.

She had spent the flight telling herself whatever Falco had arranged for them here would not matter.

A lie.

This house, this beach, this magic mattered. How could it not? The place was magnificent and secluded and like nothing she had ever seen or imagined.

She must have made some little sound because Falco looked at her as he stopped the Ferrari a few yards from the house.

"Not bad," he said.

Elle swung toward him. "Not bad? It's—"

She saw his face. The big grin. She grinned, too.

"It's not bad," she said, and he laughed, got out of the car and came around to her side, but she was already out of her seat, out of the car and staring at the house. "How did you find it?"

He shrugged and reached for her hand. "I didn't. I called a realtor we've used in the past."

"We?" Elle said carefully.

Falco looked at her. "I'm not involved with anyone."

Her cheeks blazed scarlet. "I didn't mean—"

"Yes," he said, "you did."

He waited for her to deny it. She didn't. She just stared at him, those incredible eyes filled with a variety of emotions. Anger. Embarrassment. And something more, something that made him want to take her in his arms and kiss her.

He closed the distance between them. Said her name. Reached out toward her…

And, as if Fate were the director and this was a movie set, a fat drop of rain hit his head, another hit her nose. In seconds, they'd be caught in a tropical deluge.

They ran for the house.

Just as well, Falco told himself, absolutely just as well. The last thing he needed was to get into this any deeper than he already was.

They went through the house together.

Falco wanted to see how it was set up.

The alarm system was at the top of his list. It was good, maybe very good but he could see ways, low-tech ways, to tweak it. As the realtor had promised, there were absolutely no other houses nearby.

Everything else was fine, too.

The house was built around an atrium. Glass-enclosed. An infinity pool, complete with waterfall. All the rooms opened onto it, and the rooms seemed endless.

Four bedrooms. Six bathrooms. Two half baths. A dining room, a kitchen, a wine storage room, a den, a media room. A living room the size of a basketball court with one entire wall that could be completely opened at the press of a button. A teak terrace wrapped around the part of the house that faced an empty stretch of private, white sand beach. Two miles of beach, according to a cheerful note the realtor had left stuck to the Sub-Zero fridge with a hula dancer magnet.

And, of course, there was the incredibly blue Pacific stretching to the distant horizon.

Elle stood on the terrace and threw her arms wide, as if to encompass all 10,000 or so square feet of the house.

"My God," she said, "it's huge!"

Falco, lounging, arms folded, in the door to the den,

watched her. For a movie star, the lady was surprisingly easy to please.

"Well, yes," he said, "but you never know when you're gonna need some extra space."

She laughed. It was, he thought, a lovely thing to hear.

"When I was growing up, in Beaufort Creek…"

She bit her lip, flashed him a look that could only mean she'd said more than she'd intended.

Falco said, very softly, "Beaufort Creek?"

"Just a place," she said brightly. "Where did you grow up?"

A neat change of subject, but he went with it. "New York. Greenwich Village. Or Little Italy."

She raised her eyebrows. "Which was it?"

"Well, it was Little Italy when my old man bought the first house, maybe even when he bought the second. By the time he'd bought the third, real estate mavens were calling the neighborhood part of the Village."

"I don't understand. You grew up in three different houses?"

Falco grinned. "Three houses, side by side, that he converted into one big house. Believe me, there were times so much construction was going on, we didn't understand it, either."

"We?"

"My brothers and my sisters," he said, and frowned.

How had she managed that? Getting him to talk about himself, especially about his family? He never discussed his family with anyone. Besides, he was the one who was supposed to be getting information from her.

It was just that she was easy to talk to…

"It must be nice," Elle said in a soft voice. "Having brothers and sisters."

"Didn't you?" he said, seeing a way to way to change directions and going for it. "Grow up with brothers and sisters, back in Beaufort Creek?"

She looked at him. "I'm not going to discuss my life with you," she said calmly.

Yes, he thought as she walked back into the house, oh, yes, she would. She was hiding something and she had to tell him what it was. She had to talk to him, and soon.

She had to, if he was going to keep her safe.

The kitchen was clearly a woman's dream.

It was only that he hadn't figured this particular woman was into things like that. But she was, he thought, suppressing a smile as she poked into cabinets and oohed and aahed over the appliances, the dishes, even the flatware.

"Don't tell me you can cook," he said.

She tossed her head. "If you don't want me to tell you I can, then don't ask."

He laughed as he poked into cabinets, too, though his interests were not in dishes but in food. All he came up with was the realtor's idea of a gift basket. A tiny box of crackers. A wedge of cheese. A split of champagne. Two small bottles of Fiji water and a note that said Welcome to Maui.

"Welcome to a tea party for dolls," Falco said glumly. "Okay, we'll head for town. Get some supplies." He made a face. "And clothes. I don't know about you, Bissette, but I'm starting to want to stand upwind of myself."

Elle gave up ogling the Viking range long enough to look at him. "I saw a Walmart on the way here."

He grinned. "You, in a Walmart?"

"There's nothing wrong with Walmart."

"No," he said quickly. Good God, was she actually bristling? She was. There were glints of fire in her eyes. "Absolutely not. Walmarts are, uh, they're great."

"I worked in one."

"Ah. The famous 'what I had to do before I got my first acting break,' huh?"

"I worked in one long before that. And I bought my clothes there, too."

Amazing. A town called Beaufort Creek, and now this. She'd told him more about herself in the past half hour than she had since they'd met…and from what he could remember, there hadn't been a word about Walmart or Beaufort Creek in the studio-scripted story of her life he'd found tucked within the folder his old man had given him.

"Well," he said, with a little smile, "here's your chance to buy some again. How's that sound?"

"Perfect," she said.

Wrong, Falco thought.

The only perfect thing he knew was her.

They drove to town, made a stop at a gas station.

"Pit stop," Falco said, with a quick smile.

There was no need to tell her he'd made a call on the plane while she slept, to a guy who'd served with him and lived here, in the fiftieth state.

"I need a weapon," Falco had said. "Something powerful, not big, easily carried."

The gun was waiting for him there, in bottom of a full wastebasket in the men's room. Falco retrieved it, got behind the wheel of the Ferrari and headed for Walmart.

"It's safer," he said. "It'll probably be more crowded than a regular store and—"

Elle touched a fingertip to his lips. It scalded him. He fought back the desire to suck that sweet finger into his mouth, told himself it was enough that she had touched him without him first touching her, added it to the list of amazing things that had already happened since they'd gotten to Maui.

"Honestly," she said, "I really am fine with Walmart. I can get everything I want here."

She did. Shorts. Tees. Sandals. Jeans. A zippered hoodie for cool evenings. Underwear—white, plain, utilitarian but that didn't keep him from imagining her wearing it and nothing else. Toothpaste, toothbrush, toiletries. Falco dumped similar things into the cart.

They loaded a second cart with groceries. Falco picked up wine, steaks and chops, eggs and bacon, butter and cream and coffee. Elle added vegetables, fruit, whole grain bread and yogurt. She read the labels with the attentiveness of a doctoral student in a chemistry lab.

Amazing, he thought. She didn't just seem comfortable doing this mundane stuff, she seemed to be enjoying it. He knew part of it was probably that they had, at least for the moment, left whomever was stalking her behind. Then again, maybe it was more than that. Maybe it was that she enjoyed being with him…

"All done," Elle said. She smiled at him and that was all it took. He looked into that lovely face, all but hidden by the brim of her cap and the oversized sunglasses, and right there, surrounded by cookies and snacks, he took Elle in his arms and kissed her.

What made it even better was that she sighed and kissed him back.

She was quiet on the drive back to the house.

So was Falco.

Why had he kissed her? He wasn't given to impulsive acts, not in public, especially when they involved women. There'd just been something about the easy way she had of making the best of things, the motel and now the shopping trip. He couldn't imagine any of the women he'd been involved with pushing a cart up and down the aisles of a big box store, picking out plain clothes without complaint.

Ahead, the light turned red. He eased the Ferrari to a stop, glanced idly at the mall across the way. It was small but clearly upscale. That figured, considering the price of real estate once you got along the coast. A Starbucks. A jewelry store. A hair salon.

A place called La Boutique.

There was only one thing in the window. A long gown. Slender straps, supple, softly clinging silk in a color that could only be called topaz.

Or maybe amber. The color of Elle's eyes.

A horn beeped behind them. Falco blinked, put the car in gear, made a sharp turn into the mall and pulled to a stop.

"Forgot to buy coffee," he said briskly.

"But we bought coffee," she said, but he pretended not to hear her and headed for the Starbucks.

He went in. Bought coffee. Mocha Java Bliss, Heavenly Espresso, Capriccio Cappuccino. It didn't matter. He paid for it, then went out the door, gave the Ferrari a quick glance. Elle's face was turned to the road.

Quickly, he slipped inside the boutique.

Five minutes later, he returned to the car and tossed the Starbucks bag into the rear seat. Did Elle notice its bulk? Probably not, because she was silent the rest of the way.

And, once again, so was he.

CHAPTER NINE

OKAY. Maybe he was losing his grip on reality.

First he'd kissed her in a crowded store. An impulsive act he'd quickly regretted. So, how had he made up for it?

Falco's jaw tightened.

By doing something not just impulsive but insane. Why had he bought that gown? Shoes, too. Hey, how could a woman wear a fall of silk the color of autumn leaves with flat leather sandals?

He was out of his mind.

He thought about turning around, going back to the little shop where he'd felt as out of place as snow on a Hawaiian beach, but what would he say to the sales clerk? Sorry but I shouldn't have bought this stuff? The way she'd looked at him, he figured she'd thought he was weird to start with, a man who looked as if he'd slept in his clothes because he had, a two-day stubble on his face…or was it three?

"I want that gown," he'd said, "size six or eight. And shoes to go with it."

The woman hadn't moved until he pulled out his wallet and his black Amex card. That won him a big smile.

"Of course, sir," she'd chirped.

No. Falco blew out a long breath. No, he wasn't going back

there. He'd just hustle the gown and the shoes into the trash and nobody would be the wiser.

Certainly not Elle.

He glanced over at her. The folded arms, the taut profile, eyes straight ahead, chin raised. Thinking about it, it was clear she'd enjoyed the shopping excursion because she'd seen it as a game.

He was, without question, out of his mind.

She wanted this situation to be over with ASAP. And so, absolutely, did he.

What was Falco thinking?

Elle could feel his eyes on her every few minutes but she kept her own focused straight ahead, as if the road that led out of town, then down toward the ocean, required her complete concentration.

Falco knew the way and he was a competent driver. Competent? An understatement. The car was like a growling jungle cat; he handled it with easy self-assurance, one hand on the wheel, one resting lightly on the shift lever.

How could the sight of a man driving a car be sexy?

Elle rolled her eyes.

It wasn't. He wasn't. Not to her, anyway. The word, the very concept, was foreign to her unless she was wearing a designer's creation on a runway or inside character on a film set. Even then, she was pretty much a disaster.

Something was happening. Something was changing. Inside her. Between them. Whatever it was, she didn't understand it, didn't like it, didn't want it…but it was happening just the same.

That kiss. In, of all places, a crowded aisle in a crowded store. Falco's lips moving lightly against hers; hers clinging to his. She'd done nothing to stop it. She hadn't wanted to stop it. He hadn't touched her. No hands. No embrace. Just that hot, sweet, electric fusion of lips until a grumpy female voice said, "Excuse me!" and they'd sprung apart, each of them grabbing a shopping cart, and made for the registers as if their lives depended on it.

It there hadn't been all those people around…

Her throat constricted.

Stress. That's what it was. That, or incipient insanity. There was no other explanation, no reason for that kiss or for her to wonder how it would feel if the house ahead of them—this beautiful, isolated, romantic house Falco had rented—had nothing to do with safety and expediency and had, instead, everything to do with his wanting to be alone with her….

Elle folded her arms.

What on earth was she thinking? She didn't want him wanting that. He was her bodyguard. She was his client. His not altogether willing client, when you came down to it, and that was it.

Why would she ever be stupid enough to want more?

They'd reached the house. She reached for the door handle before he'd brought the car to a complete stop.

"Hey!" He grabbed her arm and jerked her back into her seat. "Didn't anybody ever tell you it's a good idea to wait until a car stops before you get out?"

His tone was curt. It would be. Mr. Orsini didn't like anyone doing something he hadn't given them permission to do. Too bad. She wasn't in the mood to take orders.

Maybe that was the problem.

He'd stormed into her life, uninvited, and taken over. He made decisions without a word or a question, and when had she said he could do that? Never, and that was the point. He had taken over and now she was paying the price for letting him do it. That "woof" she'd barked when he'd told her to stay put today or yesterday or whenever in hell it had been, was no longer a joke. She was behaving like a well-trained dog. Compliant. Obedient. Malleable. And, she was tired of the act.

"Thank you for that helpful information," she said coldly. "I'm sure I'd never have figured it out for myself."

"You have a problem accepting advice?" he said, just as coldly.

"When I need your advice, I'll let you know."

"Do us both a favor, baby, and—"

"That's another thing. I've asked you not to call me that."

His eyes narrowed. From that soft, sweet kiss to this? Never mind that he regretted the kiss. Obviously, so did she. But why? Why should she? That had to be what this was all about, that she'd kissed him in the middle of a store, and whose fault was that? She'd wanted him to kiss her. She'd melted straight into him.

It was time to take a step back. Reassess things. He already knew he'd violated his own rules. What had become of his commitment to keeping things professional? Well, he was returning to that, right now. And she needed to know it.

"Okay," he said briskly, "here's the way things are going to be from now—"

"We need a change in plans."

His eyebrows rose. "Meaning?"

"Meaning, starting now, you're to consult me on decisions."

A cold knot was forming in his gut. "Consult you," he said calmly.

"Yes. You made all these plans—the plane, the house, Hawaii—as if I weren't involved. I don't want that to happen again."

"And I'm to do this because…?"

"Because this is my life!"

"That last I checked, you were standing in a bedroom that had been turned inside-out, wringing your hands and trying to figure out what in hell to do with that life."

She looked as if she wanted to slug him.

"I did not wring my hands. And you didn't give me the chance to figure out anything!"

Falco's lips drew back in a dangerous smile.

"This is all about that kiss."

Elle started to answer. Then she thought better of it and reached again for the door. Falco's hand closed around her wrist.

"You kissed me," he growled. "Now you're behaving as if it was a crime. Would you like to explain that?"

"I kissed you?" She laughed. "Funny, but I don't remember it that way."

"We kissed, okay? So what?"

Pointedly, she looked from him to her wrist.

"Let go of me, Orsini."

"I want an explanation, Bissette. What's this all about?"

What, indeed? She was so angry that she was shaking. He knew damned well what this was all about. He had kissed her. For some reason, she had let it happen. And, yes, she'd let it happen several times and she didn't understand it but she didn't have to.

All that mattered was that it would not happen again.

She knew how these things went.

A man came along, he offered his help, he made you feel safe and then—and then—

Falco's hand tightened on hers. "Answer me, dammit. What's going on?"

Elle raised her chin and looked into his anger-filled eyes.

"What's going on is that you are here solely to protect me."

"You have complaints about how I've been doing that?"

"Yes, I have. You seem to have forgotten your place."

God, where had those horrible words come from? She saw Falco's eyes cloud with rage. She wanted to call back what she'd said, not because she feared him but because it was a lie. She never, ever thought that way about people and she wasn't going to start now, especially with someone like Falco, an honorable, decent man whose only crime was –

Whose only crime was that he had somehow turned her world upside down.

"I've forgotten my place," he said, repeating her words in a low, dangerous voice.

"No," she said quickly, "that isn't what I meant!"

It was too late. He flung her hand from him, opened the door and got out of the car. She scrambled out, too.

"Falco! Please. I didn't mean—"

"Yeah. You did." He swung toward her. She stumbled back. "And you're right. I did forget my place."

"No. I swear, I didn't –"

"Get in the house."

"Falco—"

"I'm going to take a look around."

"What for? We already—"

"It's part of what I have to do to protect you." He reached inside the car, rifled through the bags until he found the one from Starbucks. "You're one hundred percent correct, Ms. Bissette. That's why I'm here."

Elle shook her head. "Listen to me. Please."

"Don't worry about getting the rest of the stuff inside. It's probably within my job description to haul in the groceries, but I'll get your things inside, too, even though some might call that fetching and carrying. But I'll oblige and do it—if you approve, of course. I mean, consider this a consultation."

"You're twisting everything I said!"

"Yes or no? You want me to deal with this stuff or not?"

Shaking with anger, she glared at him over the roof of the Ferrari. "A decent man would accept an apology."

His smile was quick and cold. "But I'm not a decent man. Isn't that pretty much what you just told me?"

"You can go straight to hell!"

"Sounds like a plan," he said, and he turned his back and walked away.

It took her three trips to get the all the things they'd bought into the house, including the groceries, but leaving them for Falco was not an option.

She didn't need anything from him, didn't want anything from him, not even his services as a bodyguard. She'd been doing just fine, handling things on her own.

And she'd handle things on her own, again.

Letting the all-knowing Mr. Orsini into her life had been a mistake, one she'd remedy right away. First thing in the morning, she'd call the airport, call for a taxi, get out of here so fast it would make his head spin. She'd have done it now but she wasn't even sure what time it was.

All she knew was that she needed a bath and a meal and a solid night's rest.

Choosing a bedroom was easy. She took the first one she came to, dumped the bags that held the things she'd purchased on the bed and locked the door behind her.

Falco Orsini was an infuriating, heartless bully. Her temper outburst was his fault. Kissing her, then trying to blame the incident on her…

Elle stalked into the attached marble bathroom, flicked on the light and turned on the hot water tap in the deep soaking tub.

Wait. She'd forgotten something. She hurried into the

bedroom, emptied the contents of her purse on the bed. There it was. The silver frame that held the picture of her and Mama. Tears burned behind her eyes as put her index finger to her lips, then to the picture. She gazed at it for a while. Then she took a deep breath, found the toothbrush and toothpaste she'd bought and returned to the bathroom.

She sniffed at little packets and bottles of oils and bath salts, chose an oil called Tranquility and a matching bar of elegantly wrapped soap. Elle brushed her teeth, stripped off her clothes, made a face and stuffed the clothes into a wicker basket.

The bath was steaming and fragrant. She climbed into the tub, moaned with pleasure and lay back.

Falco Orsini was impossible. He was not a knight in shining armor; he was a man like all other men. That she'd let that slip her mind, even briefly, proved how exhausted she was. The mutilated picture, the note, the mess at the cabin and the condo… All of that had worked against her, had made her vulnerable to letting a man make decisions for her.

And what would you have done if he hadn't made the decisions? If he hadn't followed you to the cabin, or hadn't refused to let you return to your place that night?

Elle gave herself a mental shake. She'd have done what had to be done, that's what. She didn't need the high-and-mighty Mr. Orsini, the police or anyone else. And she'd make that clear tomorrow. Not that Mr. Orsini needed or deserved an explanation. She was taking her life back in her own hands and that was her choice, not his.

She sank lower in the tub. The bath was wonderful. Absolutely wonderful, she thought, closing her eyes as the water lapped against her breasts. Its touch was gentle. Soothing. How would Falco's hands feel against them, instead? His palms cupping their weight. His thumbs moving over her nipples. Lightly. Gently. Then harder as he bent his head to her, pressed his lips to her throat.

Her breasts tingled. A heaviness made its slow way from them to a place low in her belly.

His hands would make their way there, too.

Elle's thighs fell open. The scented water brushed against her flesh. She could feel a pulse beating deep inside her. Beating. Throbbing. Her hand drifted over her belly. Falco's hand would follow that same path and then his mouth. He would stroke her. Part her. Touch her…

She shot upright in the water, heart racing, mind whirling, bile rising in her throat as she shoved the ugly images away. Not just ugly. Horrible. Painful. She knew that, she'd known it forever.

Quickly, she pulled the drain plug and traded the tub for the shower stall, where she scrubbed her skin until it was reddened, washed her hair and made quick work of it.

To hell with the shampoo and conditioner she'd bought. All she wanted now was to get dressed.

The clothes she'd bought lay on the bed. The clothes Falco had bought. He'd used his credit card as if the shopping trip was his to control.

Control was what he was all about. What men were all about. Whatever security company he worked for would, she knew, pick up the tab, but to hell with that. Before she left tomorrow, she'd write him a check for the chartered flight, the house, the shopping trip…

How could an hour in a faceless store have been so much fun?

"What kind of cereal do you like?" she'd said, and he'd answered by plucking a box of sugar-sweetened junk from the shelf. "Yuck," she'd said, grabbing it and putting it back, laughing at the way he'd groaned when she added a box of unsweetened granola to the cart instead, laughing just before he'd kissed her, before he'd made her heart almost stop with that sweet, sweet kiss....

"Stop it," Elle said firmly.

Hell. She'd forgotten to buy pj's. No matter. She dressed quickly: underwear, T-shirt, white jeans, everything clean and fresh against her skin. She'd caught Falco biting back a smile at her choice of underthings. It had made her blush. Would he smile if he saw her wearing them? Not that he ever would but...

Her breath caught. "Stop it," she said again, her voice sharp and a little raw.

Her thoughts were wandering across a wild landscape that had nothing to do with reality. She was tired, was the problem.

And hungry.

Her belly gave a monumental growl.

Breakfast seemed a lifetime ago. There was lots of food in the kitchen. They'd bought cheese and ham, and peanut butter and jelly because Falco had said—with a straight face—that PB and J on white bread was a staple of life.

Elle eased the door open.

The house was silent. Falco's plans had probably mirrored hers. A hot shower, then a nap. She could picture him now, that long, leanly muscled body sprawled naked across the bed.

A frisson of heat shimmered through her body.

Enough. She needed a meal and then some sleep. No. Not a meal. A sandwich would be quicker. She could be out of the kitchen before Falco so much as stirred.

She moved down the hall quickly, silent on bare feet. The kitchen was just a couple of feet away....

Damn, damn, damn!

Falco had beaten her to it. Shirtless, barefoot, wearing only jeans, his dark hair damp and glittering with drops of water, he stood with his back to her at a long granite counter. The loaf of white bread was beside him, the opened jars of peanut butter and jelly next to it. From his motions, she figured he was making a sandwich.

She watched, transfixed, as the muscles in his shoulders and triceps flexed. Her eyes swept downward. He had a powerful-looking back, a narrow waist. His jeans were low on his hips. Was the top button undone? Was that why they hung that way?

And what did it matter?

Why this sudden dryness in her mouth? The equally sudden leap of her heart? Elle took a quick step back.

"Want one?" he said casually.

Falco had sensed her presence and asked the question without turning around. A peace offering? Well, why not. They had hours to get through before she could leave, Elle reminded herself, and she moistened her lips with the tip of her tongue.

"I, ah, I… Yes, thanks. I'd love a sandwich."

He motioned toward one of the counter stools to his left. She shook her head, even though she knew he couldn't see her.

"There must be something I can do to help."

"You can pour us some milk. I'm not usually a milk kind of guy but when it comes to PB and J…"

"The drink of choice. I know."

Elle searched for tall glasses, found them, poured the milk. She put the glasses on the counter, added napkins and silverware and plates.

There was nothing left to do except sit down and watch him put the finishing touches on the sandwiches.

"Kind of like being at one of those sushi restaurants," he said. "You know, where you sit at the counter and get to watch guys wielding knives like homicidal jugglers."

She laughed. "I'm always surprised they end their shifts with five fingers still on each hand."

Falco turned toward her, reaching for the plates. The breath caught in her throat. She'd guessed right. Yes, button at the waistband of his jeans was undone. And, yes, the faded denim hung precariously low on his hips. And yes, oh, yes, he was a magnificent sight, all those sculpted muscles in his shoulders and arms, the cut abs, the dark whorl of hair on his chest that arrowed down and disappeared under the waistband of the jeans…

"What I think," he said, "is that I owe you an apology."

Elle's gaze flew to his. "It was my fault," she said quickly. "I don't know what made me say such an awful thing."

He nodded, his eyes on hers.

"We were both quick on the trigger. And some of what you said was right. I have made a lot of decisions without checking with you first. I shouldn't have done that."

"You made necessary decisions. I know that. It's just that—"

"You're accustomed to making your own decisions."

"Yes."

"Sure. I understand." He hesitated. "And about that kiss…"

She felt her face heat. "Really, there's no need to—"

"I was the one who initiated it. I've initiated every move I've made on you, baby, but they weren't 'moves,' not the way you think. I…hell, I never get involved with the people I'm helping, never step over the boundaries." He snorted and ran a hand through his hair. "There I go again. Calling you 'baby' when you've specifically asked me—"

"Don't stop."

His eyes met hers. "What?"

"I said—I said, don't stop calling me 'baby.'" By now, she knew her face was blazing. "I—I like it. The way you say it. As if—as if it means something to you."

His eyes turned black. "You mean something to me," he said in a low voice.

"You don't have to say—"

He came toward her, put a finger gently over her still-parted lips. His skin was warm; all she had to do was ease the very tip of her tongue between her lips and she could taste him.

"That's one of my flaws," he said. "I tend to say the things I mean. And I mean that, Elle. You—you've become important to me."

She sighed. Her breath was warm against his finger. A shudder went through him as he slid his hand into her hair.

"I want to kiss you," he said roughly. "Hell, I'm going to kiss you. And if that isn't what you want—"

Elle made a little sound, leaned forward and brought her mouth to Falco's. He didn't move, not for a long minute. Then he groaned, wrapped his arms around her and lifted her from the stool. Her arms went around his neck; her legs closed around his hips and he kissed her again, the kiss deepening and deepening until she was moaning into his mouth.

"Elle." He leaned his forehead against hers. "Honey, I want to make love with you."

"I know."

He gave a gruff laugh. Of course, she knew. His erection was enormous and her pelvis was pressed hard against it.

"Tell me it's what you want, too."

He could feel her heart, racing like a tiny bird's against his. She was trembling, breathing fast. He drew her even closer.

"Baby. What is it? Are you afraid of me?"

"No," she said quickly. "Never of you."

"What, then? The—" He hesitated. "The 'sex thing'? Have you had a bad experience? Because if you have—"

"It's—it's something like that."

Who had done this to her? How? What had some bastard done to this beautiful, intelligent, amazing woman? His arms tightened around her.

"I've never—I've never wanted to be with a man before. I can hardly believe it's what I want now. At least—at least, I think it's what I want. But if it's not… I wouldn't want to disappoint you."

"You could never disappoint me," he said fiercely. "If it's not what you want, we'll stop." And I'll die, he thought, but he'd do that rather than do anything to hurt this woman.

She gave a watery laugh. "Men don't stop."

Falco fought to control his fury.

"I am me, honey. Falco Orsini. I am not 'men.' I'd never do anything to hurt you, Elle. I swear it, with all my heart."

She drew back a little and looked at him.

"Just what a guy wants, I'm sure," she said, with a sad attempt at a smile. "To talk a moment like this straight into the ground."

"What this guy wants is to hold you. To kiss you. To sleep with you in my arms. And maybe that's all we should even consider tonight." He gave a little laugh. "Assuming it is night," he said. "I seem to have lost track of time."

Elle stared at him. "Do you think you could really do that?"

What he thought was that by morning he might be dead from the aching need to make love to her, but if being held in his arms was all she wanted, that was all that would happen.

"Remember what you said," she told him solemnly, "about only saying what you really mean."

Falco sighed. "I want to make love to you, baby. To change whatever it is you think you know about sex. If that's not what you want, I'll just hold you while we sleep." He paused. "Or you can trust what I said. About making love and stopping if you want to stop." He smiled. "Your decision to make, Ms. Bissette."

A day ago, an hour ago, she might have said no man could manage sleeping with a woman without sex, but if Falco said he could do it, she believed him. If he said he could stop—stop doing the things men did if she asked him to stop doing them—she believed that, too.

So—so maybe she could let him kiss her. Caress her. And he'd stop when she told him to stop. Because she would tell him to stop. Absolutely, she would.

"Elle?" He cleared his throat. "There's a third option, honey. I'll let go of you, we go to our separate rooms—"

Elle leaned forward and stopped his words with a kiss.

"Take me to bed, Falco," she whispered. "Please. Take me to bed and make love to me."

CHAPTER TEN

ELLE'S WHISPERED words raced through Falco's blood like a fast-moving drug.

If someone had asked, he'd have said he knew all the sexy things a woman could whisper to a man.

Wrong.

Elle's simple words were the most erotic he'd ever heard.

His answer was in his kiss as he carried her through the silent house, not to the bedroom he'd chosen only because it had been the nearest at hand, but past it, to the master suite. Its walls were almost entirely glass, open on one side to the sea and on the other to the cascade of water that tumbled into the atrium pool.

The bed, a four-poster, hung in sheer white lace, dominated the room.

He imagined taking her to it, laying her on it, baring her to his eyes, his hands, his mouth.

But he didn't.

Elle's lips trembled beneath his. Her heart raced against his palm. She wanted him but she was frightened.

Falco was determined to replace that fear with joy even if it took every bit of self-control he possessed.

He kissed her again. Then, slowly, he put her on her feet.

She made a little sound when her breasts brushed his bare chest, caught her breath when the heavy thrust of his erection pressed against her belly. When she would have stepped back, he gathered her in his arms, kept her close.

"That's just my body telling yours how much I want you." His voice was low and rough but the hand he put under her chin was gentle. "Don't be afraid, baby. I won't hurt you. I promise."

He kissed her, soft kisses that belied the hunger inside him until finally he felt her lips soften and cling to his. He took the kiss deeper little by little, touching the tip of his tongue to the tender inside flesh of her bottom lip. He knew he had to go slowly, that everything that came next hinged on it.

And he could do it.

He was a man who had built his life on self-discipline.

Surely, he could carry that ability into this. Into holding back. Into being content just to taste her. Into keeping from cupping her face, parting her lips with his, plunging deep, deep into the honeyed sweetness of her mouth…

Falco groaned.

Elle tensed. "What?" A quick, uneasy breath; she put her hands on his chest. "Am I doing this wrong?"

His throat constricted. He wanted to groan again. Or maybe curse, not at the woman in his arms but at whatever—whomever—had left her feeling this way. Instead, he forced a quick smile.

"No, honey. No, you're doing it just right. It's just that you taste so good…." The hell with it. He could cup her face, lift it to his, kiss her gently. Like that. Exactly like that. Again and again and suddenly she was on her toes, her hands locked around his neck, her lips open to his.

"Yes," he whispered, "yes, that's the way."

"Falco," she said, just that, and he gathered her against him, kissed her mouth, her throat, and she was trembling again but he knew it wasn't with fear, it was with what was happening, what she felt, what he was making her feel, and then he stopped thinking, stopped planning, and his kisses deepened, his hands moved over her, stroking, cupping, caressing until she was making soft little cries and clinging to him as if he was all that could keep her from falling.

He slid his hand under her T-shirt. Up her back, along the sweet, silken warmth of her skin. His palm spread over the side of her breast. She caught her breath and he waited, waited…

His thumb brushed over her nipple.

She sighed against his mouth.

He stroked her again. Felt the nub of flesh harden, felt it press against his thumb. Another sigh. A moan. Falco moved his hand, cupped her breast, bit back a groan at the delicate weight of it in his hand.

She moved.

Moved against him.

Her hips. Her thighs.

A shudder went through him.

He drew back. Put an inch of space between them but it wasn't enough, how could it be when it felt as if an entire room wouldn't be enough to keep his erection from pressing into her belly? He was harder than he'd ever been in his life, so hard that he hurt…and she wasn't leaving space between them anyway, she was moving closer, clasping his shoulders, raising herself to him.

On a low growl, Falco caught Elle's elbows and put her from him. She swayed, blinked her eyes open and stared up at him.

"Falco?"

He dragged air into his lungs.

"I can't," he said. "Honey, I'm sorry. I thought I could do this. I really thought…" Another harsh breath. "But I can't."

Tears rose in her eyes. "Yes. I mean—I mean, no. Why should you?" Elle stepped back, wrapped her arms around herself. "Of course, you can't. I shouldn't have asked—"

"Dammit!" He grabbed hold of her shoulders, lifted her to her toes. "What I'm trying to tell you is that I can't go slow and easy. I want too much. Do you understand?"

Elle swallowed hard. "You want to—to go to bed. Straight to bed. I should have—"

"Hell, no. I don't want to drag you into bed. I want to touch you first. See you. And you're not ready for that."

"See me, how?" Her eyes flew to his. "You mean, undressed?"

Her voice was low. In any other set of circumstances, her answer, the look she gave him, might have made him laugh, but laughter was the last thing in his mind at that moment. Instead, her expression, the response…both filled him with an awful combination of anger and sorrow.

"Undressed," he said gruffly. "Yes."

She nodded. He could almost see her processing his words. Then she crossed her arms, grasped the hem of her T-shirt. Falco caught her wrists, brought her hands to his lips and kissed them.

"No. I don't want you to do anything just for me, baby. That's not what making love is all about."

"I want you to see me," she whispered.

"Are you sure?" She nodded. "Then," he said, "then, let me do that."

Her hands fell to her sides. Falco reached for the hem of her T-shirt, drew it over her head and tossed it aside. God, she was beautiful. Honeyed skin. Demure white cotton bra. He'd watched her buy it, watched her bypass lace and satin for this. It had made him smile.

Now, it made his body tighten with hunger.

He waited, mentally counted to ten before he spoke again.

"I'm going to take your jeans off, too." His voice was rough as sandpaper. He cleared his throat. "Is that okay, Elle?"

"Yes," she whispered, her face bright with color.

His hands felt huge and clumsy as he reached for the button, then the zipper of her jeans. The hiss of the metal teeth parting seemed inordinately loud, but then, maybe not.

Maybe it wasn't half as loud as the hammering beat of his heart.

Slowly, he slid the jeans down her hips. Her legs. He wanted to squat down, lift her foot, ease the jeans all the way off, but he didn't trust himself, he knew the temptation to put his face against her belly might be more than he could handle. He let the jeans slither to the bamboo floor, took her hands, held them to steady her as she stepped free of them.

Then he looked at her.

Long, dark hair, falling over her shoulders. A face free of makeup. The plainest possible bra and panties. And a beauty so pure it stole his breath away.

Falco's heart kicked against his ribs as he drew her into his arms and kissed her. Lightly. Gently. Told himself to keep it that way but she moved closer to him, framed his face with her hands. Opened her mouth to his and he slid his hands behind her. He hadn't had trouble opening a bra since high school, but now his fingers felt huge and clumsy and, it seemed forever but, thank you, God, at last, the bra opened.

Elle's reaction was to clasp it to her.

Falco's hands closed over hers.

"I want to see you, baby," he said thickly.

A heartbeat's hesitation. Then she let go of the white cotton and it drifted to the floor. His eyes held hers. Then, slowly, he let them fall to her breasts. Ah, they were perfect. Small. Round. Nipples a pale, seashell pink. He raised his eyes to her face, watched her as he traced the outline of one perfect nipple with the tip of his index finger.

"Do you like that?" he whispered.

She moaned. It was all the answer he needed. His hands went to the waistband of the innocent white cotton panties; slowly, he eased them down her long legs. He bent, steadied her as she stepped free of them, fought back the desire to kiss his way up those long legs and bury his face in the soft, dark curls between her thighs and, instead, stood up straight and reached for her again.

Elle shook her head.

"I want…" Her tongue swiped across her bottom lip. "I want…" The rest was an inaudible whisper.

"Honey. I don't know what you said. I couldn't hear—"

"I said—I said, I want to see you, too."

He swallowed. "What?"

"I want to see you naked. That's all. Just to see you."

Sweat beaded on his forehead. He was never going to survive this. Why had he thought he could?

"Falco? Could I—could I see you? Please?"

His hands fumbled at the zipper of his jeans. He took a breath, got it open, pushed the jeans down. He had not put on underwear after he'd showered and now his swollen penis sprang free. His sense of relief was profound.

Profound, but short-lived because—

Because, she was looking at his aroused flesh. Just looking, not touching, and if this kept up, he was going to disgrace himself.

Where was his self-control? That control he prided himself on, that control that always, always kept him in charge of what happened, in bed and out.

"Dammit," he growled, and when she looked up at him he thought, the hell with this and he gathered her into his arms and kissed her, kissed her hard, one hand in her hair, the other holding her tightly against him. He'd do this, kiss her, feel her, let her feel him and then he'd tell her he'd been crazy to think he could pull this off, that he was too old to play doctor.

But how could he do any of those things when Elle was rising on her toes, winding her arms around his neck, meeting his kisses with kisses of her own?

"Please," she sobbed against his lips, "Falco, please, please, please…"

His heart thundered.

Whispering her name, he scooped her up, carried her to the bed. Tumbled onto it with her. Kissed her mouth, her throat, her breasts, exulting in her cries, her sobs.

And tried, one final time, to hang on to sanity.

"Elle…"

There was warning in his voice. She heard it but instead of frightening her, it filled her with ecstasy. She wanted this, wanted him, wanted everything he was, everything he had to give.

"Falco," she said softly, and she touched him. Danced her fingers the length of his rigid flesh, closed as much of her hand around him as she could, felt the throb of life within that part of him that was all male.

"Elle!" The breath hissed from his lips. He took her hand, brought it to her side. "Elle…I'm not a saint…"

She reached up. Kissed his mouth. Kissed him long and deep and sweetly until he groaned and parted her thighs.

She sobbed as he entered her. Slowly. God, so slowly.

Her head fell back against the pillows. She was coming apart. Coming undone. She was flying, blazing across the sky like a shooting star.

"Falco," she sobbed and he said her name, threw back his head and flew into the heavens with her.

* * *

She awoke hours later.

At least, it felt like hours later. Time had lost all meaning.

Perhaps they'd slept the day away. Or the night. Whichever it was, Elle came awake draped over Falco like a blanket, her face buried against his throat, his arms holding her close.

It should have been uncomfortable. He was hard, muscled, lean. And his embrace made it almost difficult to breathe.

But it wasn't uncomfortable. It was wonderful. Her lips curved in a smile. She had never felt this happy, this safe. It was as if she belonged here, with this man, as if she'd been created for this.

Her smile faded.

What was she thinking? This, being here, being with Falco…it was all a fantasy. It was worse than that. Falco had only come into her life because the past was finally catching up to her.

If he knew that past, if anyone knew it…

"Hey."

He was awake. She shut her eyes, opened them again, lifted her head and forced a smile.

"Hey, yourself," she said, and her heart turned over. He was so beautiful! She knew he'd groan if she told him that but it was true, he was beautiful. His dark hair was mussed, he had even more of that five o'clock shadow she'd always thought made a man look grungy but made him look almost unbearably sexy. There were laugh lines at the edges of his eyes and a tiny little white line she'd never noticed until now….

"It's a scar," he said softly.

"Was I staring?" She blushed. "Sorry. I didn't mean to—"

"No, it's cool." He smiled. "I like it when you stare at me." His hand slid into her hair; he brought her face to his and kissed her. "Are you all right, baby?"

"Yes." She could feel her color deepening. "I mean—"

"I know what you mean. And I'm happy to hear it."

His words were spoken in a tender whisper. "Tender" was something she couldn't afford. She couldn't let him get too close. For her sake—

And, she thought with a shudder, for his. How come that hadn't occurred to her before?

She took a breath, drew back as far as his encircling arms permitted and flashed a bright smile.

"Yes," she said, "and thank you for that."

His eyes narrowed. "For what?"

"For, you know, for helping me, ah, for helping me get past my, ah, my problem."

She squealed as he rolled her onto her back. He lay above her, his body pinning hers to the mattress, his hands wrapped around her wrists, cold fire in his eyes.

"Thank you?" he said in an ominous whisper.

"Yes. You know. For—"

"Maybe you're going to recommend me to your friends."

"No!" Her breath caught. "I didn't mean that as an insult, I only meant—"

His mouth swooped down and captured hers, his kiss hard and merciless until, despite her best intentions, she moaned his name in a way that made him let go of her hands. His arms went around her; she wrapped hers around him and the kiss changed, became soft and yes, tender, so tender that she wanted to weep.

"I'm sorry," she whispered. "Falco, I'm so sorry. What happened just now—"

"You and me," he said gruffly, "making love."

"Yes. It was—it was—"

"Yeah." A cheeky grin tweaked the corners of his mouth. "It damned well was."

Elle snorted. "Did anyone ever tell you that you have an oversized ego?"

He moved against her. "I'm just an oversized guy."

She didn't want to laugh but she couldn't help it. He was impossible. She told him so.

"You are impossible," she said, trying for stern and not even coming close.

Falco smiled. He kissed her. Kissed her again. Soft, teasing kisses that lengthened and deepened until her bones had absolutely melted.

"So is this," he whispered, "impossibly wonderful." And then he was inside her again, moving inside her, taking her up and up and up and within seconds, nothing else mattered but him.

She wouldn't shower with him.

She wouldn't even leave the bed as long as he was still in the room.

She knew it was foolish, that he knew her body with shocking intimacy, but that didn't mean—it didn't mean she could walk around in front of him without clothes on.

He didn't argue, not once he saw that she meant it. Instead, he kissed the tip of her nose, rose from the bed and strolled toward the adjoining marble bathroom. She tried to avert her eyes. Yes, they'd been intimate, but seeing him, seeing him naked, that part of him naked…

"I would never hurt you, Elle," he said softly.

She looked up. He was standing in the bathroom doorway, not just unashamedly naked but unashamedly beautiful.

Tears rose in her eyes.

She blinked them back, took a deep breath, tossed back the duvet and went to him. He gathered her against him.

"What happened to you?" her knight in shining armor said, so ferociously that it almost broke her heart.

She shook her head, burrowed closer. After a very long time, he brushed his lips lightly over hers.

"Okay," he said, as if nothing had happened, "shower time."

The peanut butter and jelly sandwiches he'd made hours ago were still on the counter.

Elle touched one with a fingertip and winced. "Hard as stone." She looked up and smiled. "I don't think the *P* in PB and J is supposed to stand for 'petrified.' They must have sat here for hours...."

She realized what she'd said and blushed. Lord, he loved the way she blushed, Falco thought as he drew her into his arms.

"Hours," he said softly. "But not half long enough."

He kissed her. Sweet kisses that grew deeper. Quick kisses that grew longer. Kisses that made their breathing quicken until he groaned and leaned his forehead against hers.

"If we don't eat something soon," he said huskily, "the realtor's going to come by one morning and find us as petrified as those sandwiches."

Elle laughed and gave him a gentle push. "I'll cook something. What would you like?"

"Hey, you think I've waited for peanut butter and jelly all this time only to give up on them now? Let's go, woman. Same as before. You pour the milk, I'll make the sandwiches."

They worked side by side and wolfed down their meal while sitting on stools at the granite kitchen counter. Four for Falco, two for her.

"The wardrobe mistress will kill me," Elle said mournfully.

He grinned. "That's how I got this scar," he said, touching his finger to the little white line she'd noticed earlier. "Defending myself against a PB and J attack."

Elle raised her eyebrows.

"My brother, Nick. We were maybe four and five, something like that. He made himself a sandwich. I stole half of it and he came after me. We'd been playing *Star Wars*, you know, the lightsaber thing? Anyway, Nick swung, got lucky and got me. I retaliated, of course—"

"Of course," Elle said. She didn't really accept the story. She suspected the truth was something much darker, but she smiled, picturing him as a little boy.

"And we both went down in a heap. Well, Rafe had left a Tonka Payloader on the floor and—"

"You have two brothers?"

"Three. Nicolo. Raffaele. And Dante." Falco ate the last bite of his sandwich. "And two sisters. Anna and Isabella."

"Oh, that's nice. To have such a big family, I mean."

Falco laughed. "It's nice most of the time. Sometimes, it's a pain in the, ah, in the butt. How about you?"

Elle's smile faded. "How about me, what?"

"Do you have sisters? Brothers?"

"No."

"No, what?"

"No," she said, "there's just me."

Her tone had become cool. Falco cocked his head. "And?"

"And, what?" Elle slid off the stool and put her plate in the sink.

"And, why is talking about family such a big deal?"

"It isn't," she said, even more coolly.

"Trust me, honey. It isn't always my favorite topic, either. I mean, Izzy and Anna, Nick and Rafe and Dante… They're great. So is my mom. But anybody mentions my old man—"

"Don't tell me," Elle said, her voice not cool but frigid. "You and your father have—what's the current term? You have 'issues.' What, he didn't let you borrow the family car when you were seventeen?"

Falco narrowed his eyes. "My father's a thug," he said carefully. "His name is Cesare Orsini. Maybe you haven't heard of him, but, trust me, the cops sure have."

"Oh." Elle reached out her hand. "Falco. I didn't mean—"

"I know you didn't, baby. So, whatever it is about your family that upsets you—"

She laughed. At least, he thought it was a laugh. But it wasn't. She was weeping.

"Ah, honey, I'm an idiot. Come here. Let me hold you."

She shook her head and pushed past him. He thought about stopping her but he didn't. Instead, he watched her go through the atrium doors and on into the starlit night, watched as she padded barefoot through the sand, to the beach. Then he went after her. They were as safe here as he'd been able to make it: the gates, the alarm system, the little touches he'd added of his own, but no way would he let her out of his sight until he got the son of a bitch who was stalking her.

A chill danced down Falco's spine.

He knew a lot of people who had what Elle had called "issues" with their families. It was, more or less, a sign of the times. Hell, he had his own thing about his father. So did his brothers.

But Elle's reaction just now…

His steps quickened.

He had held off asking her what she knew about her stalker though he suspected she knew something. He hadn't pushed her on why she didn't want the cops involved, either; she was a celebrity and maybe she just didn't want that kind of press. He hadn't pressured her because she'd been through a lot in the past few days. He'd figured on giving her a little time before asking more questions.

Some seventh sense, some instinct told him that the time for asking them was now.

He caught up to her at the surf line, fell in beside her as she walked. She shot him a poisonous look but he ignored it.

"What's going on?"

"I don't know what you're talking about."

"Elle," he said firmly. He caught her elbow, turned her toward him. "You have to tell me. You know you do."

"Go back to the mainland, Falco. Just—just leave me alone."

"The hell I will! I can't protect you without knowing what you know about this maniac."

Her eyes flashed. "Is that what you call taking me to bed? Was that about protecting me?"

She was deliberately trying to make him angry. He knew it, but that didn't make it any easier.

"Answer the question. Tell me what you know."

"What I know is that that we had sex."

He wanted to shake her. Or kiss her. Instead, he grabbed her by the shoulders and hauled her to her toes.

"Dammit, woman! We made love."

"It was sex," she said bitterly. "And I should have known you'd think that grants you some kind of ownership—"

Falco cursed, pulled her against him and captured her lips with his. She struggled, tried to twist free—and then she sobbed his name, wound her arms around him and kissed him back with all the hunger in her heart. He swept her into his arms, carried her to the house and to bed. They made love again and again, until she wept with joy. One last kiss and then she fell asleep in his arms.

Falco remained awake, eyes fixed on the ceiling.

He had violated the principles by which he lived, giving in to his emotions, letting them take him deep into uncharted waters—but he didn't care. If he had to, he would give his life for the woman beside him.

He had only known her a few short days but she had come to mean more to him than he'd ever imagined possible….

And more than he wanted to define.

CHAPTER ELEVEN

HE ASKED no more questions.

His time with Special Forces had taught him the importance of knowing as much about the enemy as he could. Later, doing clandestine work for private clients, he'd adhered to that rule. The Turkish couple he'd recently helped had accused him of indifference because he'd demanded they bare their souls to him, but what he'd ultimately learned had been instrumental in helping him find, and save, their son.

The bottom line was that the one stipulation he always required was full access to information. A client either gave it up freely or Falco would go after it.

This was different. There wasn't a way in hell he'd do that to Elle.

It made his job more difficult but he cared too much about her to force her to divulge whatever dark secrets she possessed. And he cared more and more about her as the days, and the nights, slipped by.

Time had become as fluid as the ocean. There was no beginning, no end. There were only long, sweet days and long, hot nights. The hours blurred into each other, every one of them filled with pleasure.

Not that they did anything special.

Long walks on the beach, with Elle plucking what Falco would have sworn was every shell they saw from the sand. Lazy hours by the pool. They played poker after Falco taught her the game, betting with the shells she'd collected, then with play money filched from a Monopoly set they found on a shelf in the den.

He let her win most of the hands and then, to make it interesting, he said, he suggested betting with the clothes they were wearing.

Surprisingly enough, he began winning.

"You lost all those other times on purpose," she said with mock indignation when she'd been reduced to only an oversized white T-shirt and her panties.

"Hey," he said, eyes filled with innocence, "are you calling me a liar?"

"I'm calling you a cheat, Orsini," she said, squealing as he tossed his cards aside and grabbed her.

They laughed and tussled, and gradually the laughter became sighs and the tussles became touches, and they forgot all about poker and made love until Falco thought his heart would burst with happiness.

Because, God, he was happy. Not that he hadn't been happy before but never like this, doing such mundane things. He was not a man who enjoyed mundane things, at least, he never had before. He lived for risk, for danger, for walking on the edge. And there was nothing risky about those long walks or lying in the sun or driving to the little farm stand they'd discovered, buying fresh mahi mahi and grouper, dew-covered fruits and vegetables.

He'd found condoms there, too, and he bought an amount he figured would have made Elle blush if she knew, but the simple truth was, he wanted to make love with her all the time and to his joy, she wanted the same thing.

And then, one night as he grilled their meal in the atrium and Elle emerged from the house with the salad he looked at her and he thought maybe there was something a little dangerous about this, about what he felt when he looked at her….

Something must have shown on his face.

"What?" Elle said.

"I, ah, I was just thinking that, uh, that my brothers would be proud if they could see me now."

Smiling, she poured two glasses of chilled Prosecco and handed him one.

"Because?"

"Because I've turned into a world-class chef." He grinned at the look on her face, cut off a tiny bit of the grilled fish with a fork and held it out. "Taste this and tell me it isn't the best grilled mahi mahi you've ever eaten."

She leaned forward. Parted her lips. Falco moved fast, pulled back the fork and put his mouth against hers.

Elle sighed. "Delicious," she said softly.

He kissed her again, then popped the bite of fish into her mouth.

"Mmm. That's delicious, too."

"What did I tell you? Falco Orsini, master chef. Don't laugh. Compared to the last fish-type dish I cooked, this is fancy stuff."

"'Fish-type dish,' huh?" Elle smiled as she propped her hip against the table. "I'm almost afraid to ask."

"Oh, ye of little faith." Falco slid a spatula under the fish and flipped it onto a platter. "Tuna."

"Ahi tuna?"

His lips twitched. "Bumble Bee. Chicken of the Sea. I'm not particular about the brand."

"You mean, canned tuna?"

"Toss in some penne pasta, cream of mushroom soup…"

"Yuck."

"Okay, then." He drew out a chair for her. She sat down, and he sat opposite. "The tuna, parmesan cheese, frozen peas—"

"Double yuck." She paused. "You want a gourmet meal, it's macaroni and cheese."

He laughed.

"Go on, Orsini, laugh. But until you've cooked up a box of mac and cheese, maybe add some diced ham if you want to be fancy…" She laughed, too. "No, huh?"

Falco spread his napkin in his lap. "My mother already figures I have the eating habits of a barbarian."

"Is she a good cook?"

"Is she a…" He rolled his eyes. "She's Sicilian. Of course, she's a good cook. Well, she is just as long as you don't balk at what she thinks you like to eat."

"Thinks you like to eat?"

"Yeah. She's got these ideas. For instance, my sister, Izzy, went on this vegan kick one time and Mama said no problem, she'd cook vegan."

"But?"

"But, she thought 'vegan' meant adding vegetables to things. There was no convincing her that chicken and pork and steak, vegetables tossed in or not, wasn't 'vegan.'"

Elle forked up some salad. "Uh-oh."

"Uh-oh, is right. It was interesting."

"I'll bet."

"And then there's Dante, who can't stand the sight of pesto. Somehow, Mama got the idea he loves it." He chuckled. "You cannot imagine all the ways she's come up with to serve my poor brother what she's sure is his favorite dish."

Elle's smile was soft and wistful. "It must be nice, having a big family."

They'd had this conversation before. It hadn't gone well.

Falco figured it was worth another try. He knew, in his gut, whatever Elle wasn't willing to talk about was somehow connected to the topic of family.

"So," he said casually, "you didn't, huh?"

She shook her head. "No."

"Just, what, you and your mom and dad?"

"My dad died when I was little."

"Ah. Just you and your mom, then."

There was a slight pause. Then Elle shrugged. "Yes."

"She never remarried?"

Another pause. "She did, after a while."

Her voice was suddenly tight. Falco felt a tingling on the nape of his neck.

"Nice. That she met somebody, I mean, and fell in love."

"Very nice," Elle said in a flat voice.

"It wasn't?"

"He said he'd take care of us. See, we were dirt poor."

That surprised him. "But your bio—"

She looked up. "You've read that nonsense?"

"On the plane flying out to L.A. It said—"

"I know what it said. That I grew up in San Francisco. That I had private tutors."

"Not true, huh?"

She shook her head, kept her eyes on her plate as if it were the most interesting thing she'd ever seen. "I grew up poor."

"In a place called Beaufort Creek."

She looked up. "Yes. That's where I was born. But I lived in different places after that before I finally moved to New York."

"Moved to New York, and started modeling."

"And started modeling," she said, her tone flat again. "You have a problem with…" She sighed. "Sorry."

"No," he said quickly, reached for her hand and held it

tightly in his. "I'm the one who's sorry. I guess I seemed a little, you know, a little hinky about the lingerie stuff."

The breath sighed from her lungs. "I didn't want to sign that contract. But I knew it was a big chance, that it could lead to bigger and better work—"

"Elle." Falco put down his fork. "Honey, you don't owe me or anybody else an explanation."

"If I'd never posed for that last damned picture, he might never have found—"

She fell silent. Falco's hand tightened on hers.

"Who?" he said softly. "Who is he?"

"I only meant—you know, I meant 'he' as in—as in the man stalking me."

She was lying. Her eyes were dark with despair. Her mouth was trembling. Now, when she was so vulnerable, was the time to pursue the topic. She'd break in five minutes….

Instead, Falco shot from his seat, went to her and wrapped her in his arms.

"I can't," she whispered. "Please, please, don't ask me to talk about it…."

"Hush," he said, and he tilted her face to his, kissed her until the darkness in her eyes faded and despair died in the flame of passion.

They went for a drive a couple of days later. On the way home, Falco pulled in to the big mall where they'd bought food and clothes, and stopped outside a FedEx store.

"FedEx?" Elle said, puzzled.

"Man does not live by mahi mahi alone."

She laughed. "Seriously, Orsini…"

"Seriously, Bissette," he said, dropping a light kiss on her mouth. "Just stay put. I'll be right back."

He returned with a package, dropped it in the rear seat

and pretended he didn't hear her questions. After a while she gave up.

"Nap time," he said, once they'd returned to the house.

That made her smile. Nap time had become an important part of their day, not that it actually involved napping. This time, however, after they made love—long, sweet, incredibly tender love—she fell asleep, curled against her lover's side.

And awoke, alone, in the bed.

She sat up, yawning. What time was it? It felt late. A glance at the clock proved that it was almost seven. Where was Falco? She loved waking with him in their bed. Not that this was actually "their" bed. It was so easy to fall into the fantasy, to let herself think that this would go on forever, that what he seemed to feel for her was…that it was real.

It wasn't, of course.

He was attracted to her. And concerned about her. But then, that was his job. Falco was her bodyguard. Her guardian. Yes, he'd developed some feeling for her, but it was sexual and that was okay because her feeling for him was the same and that was enough, that she'd gone from terror at the thought of a man touching her to wanting to be touched.

By Falco. Only by him. Always by him…

"Hello, sweetheart."

Elle looked up—and blinked at the apparition in the doorway.

"Falco?"

He grinned. "Nobody else."

Nobody else, indeed. Her bodyguard wore a black tux with black silk lapels, black trousers that emphasized his narrow hips and long legs, a white shirt, a black bow tie…

He was beautiful.

"Am I dreaming?" she said, as he came toward her.

He laughed softly. "Close that gorgeous mouth, baby," he said, putting a finger lightly under her chin. "On second thought…" He bent down and kissed her, ran the tip of his tongue lightly over the sweet surface of her bottom lip. Then he straightened up and struck a pose. "Well? What do you think?"

Elle sat up against the pillows, the duvet drawn to her chin. If this was a dream, it was lovely.

"I think," she said, "that neither Walmart nor FedEx sells custom-made tuxes."

"Good conclusion."

"But?"

"But, FedEx is a wonderful thing, especially when a guy can call at least one brother with a key to his town house."

"You called your brother and had him send you a tux?" Elle laughed. "Because…?"

"Because, of course, we're going out to dinner."

"Out? You and me? But you said I had to keep a low profile."

"We're going to a very private place, baby."

"But—"

"Trust me."

Trust him? With all that she was, all she would ever be…

"Come on, Bissette. Get yourself all dressed up and meet me in the atrium."

Get dressed up. In what? Shorts? A T-shirt? Rubber thongs? He was more handsome than any actor in Hollywood, any male model in New York, and she was going to look like—

"Oh. One last thing." He smiled. "You might want to check the closet."

"For what?"

He cupped the back of her head, bent to her again and gave her a long, lingering kiss.

"What did I say, baby? Just trust me."

The instant the door shut after him, Elle scrambled from the bed and flung open the closet door….

"Oh," she whispered, "oh, Falco…"

A gown of amber silk hung before her. It was beautiful, the kind of thing she'd have picked for herself to wear for an evening with him. There were shoes, too, as delicate as if they'd been spun from gold. The only possible word for them was sexy. Narrow straps. Slender, spiked heels…

Tears rose in her eyes. Silly, to weep over something so sweet, so generous, so thoughtful…

Even more silly, to weep at the realization that she had fallen deeply, deeply in love with her bodyguard.

She showered.

Washed her hair.

Dried it, brushed it until it shone, then let it flow down her back. She put on mascara and lip gloss, which was twice the makeup she'd worn all week. Then she went back into the bedroom.

The gown lay across the bed. She didn't know how Falco had bought it; maybe his brothers had sent it. It was exquisite but there was a problem. She had no undergarments to go with it. The white cotton bras had straps that would show; the panties would be outlined under the softly clinging silk.

Elle shut her eyes.

She could wear it without underwear.

No. No, she couldn't. No underwear? Just the kiss of cool silk against her skin? The knowledge, all evening, that she was naked beneath it?

Her breath hitched.

She let the bath towel fall to the floor, picked up the gown and slipped it over her head. The silk slid down her body. It did, indeed, feel cool.

And she felt sexy. Wicked. Wonderfully, gloriously wicked. Wicked in a way that had nothing to do with Madison Avenue photo shoots or the artful fakery of Hollywood movie sets. She felt wicked the way a woman would surely want to feel for her lover.

She stepped into the sexy shoes and adjusted the straps. Ran her hands through her hair. Took a quick look at herself in the mirror and then, knowing she was a breath away from losing her courage, opened the door that led to the atrium and stepped outside.

Stepped into a world of glittering, shimmering candlelight.

There were dozens and dozens of candles. All shapes, all sizes, all glowing as brightly as stars.

A round table, draped in ivory linen and set with delicate china and gleaming sterling flatware, stood near the pool. There were candles on the table, too, elegant pink tapers on either side of a crystal vase overflowing with pink and white orchids. A serving cart laden with silver chafing dishes stood nearby; a bottle of champagne stood chilling in a silver wine cooler. Music played softly from hidden speakers, something soft and romantic and perfect….

But most perfect of all was Falco.

He stood beside the waterfall, watching her, and when she saw the look on his face, her heart soared.

"Elle," he said softly, "my beautiful, beautiful Elle."

His Elle. Yes. That was what she wanted to be. Smiling, she turned in a graceful circle.

"It's the gown. The shoes. How did you—"

"Magic," he said.

She laughed. "Magic, indeed."

He came slowly toward her, arms outstretched. "May I have this dance, Ms. Bissette?"

"Most assuredly, Mr. Orsini. My card is reserved for no one but you."

He gathered her to him. She looped her arms around his

neck. He made a sound deep in his throat. Had he realized she had nothing on beneath the gown? Surely he must have: her nipples were beaded against his chest, his hand lay at the very base of her spine. But he said nothing, simply held her as they began moving to the music.

"I was afraid the gown wouldn't do you justice," he said softly.

She leaned back in the circle of his arms and looked up at him. "The gown couldn't be more beautiful."

"Neither could you."

He meant it. She was, without question, the most beautiful woman he'd ever known. If only he'd bought her something else, something more to bring out the topaz fire of her eyes….

"Diamonds," he said. "Canary-yellow diamonds."

She laughed. "What?"

"It's what you need. One perfect heart-cut stone that would lie right here." He bent his head and kissed the hollow of her throat. He could feel her trembling against him, could feel her heart beating as fast as the wings of a hummingbird.

His heart lurched. He said her name, drew her closer and they began moving again, lost in the music and in each other.

"Falco." His name was the softest whisper on the still night air. "Falco," she said again, "Falco…"

He kissed her.

He wanted to take her inside, strip away the gown, bury himself deep inside her, but had planned this night for her. Nick, who had sent the tux, had started to ask questions but he'd cut them off with a terse, *I'll explain when I see you…*

Except, how could he explain what he didn't understand himself? When had this gone from being a mission to something else, something even more dangerous than the violence he knew he would eventually face? When had Elle become everything that mattered in his life?

What did all of that mean?

Falco cleared his throat, laced his fingers through hers and led her to the table. He seated her, took the chair across from hers and took the bottle of champagne from the silver bucket. The cork made a soft pop when he eased it free. He filled two flutes, gave Elle one.

"To this night," he said, touching his glass to hers.

"This perfect night," Elle said, smiling at him.

Her lover had thought of everything. Vichyssoise. Lobster. Asparagus. Chocolate mousse. Kona coffee with heavy cream, all as perfect as the night. At least, Elle assumed it was perfect. She couldn't taste anything. Her senses were all centered on him.

He poured the last of the champagne. Then he took her hand and brought it to his lips. "I wish we could have really gone out to dinner." He smiled. "Someplace where every man in the room would have cheerfully killed to change places with me."

She laughed. "What a wish!"

Falco flashed that gorgeous, macho grin. "What can I tell you, baby? Under all the smooth veneer, a cave is a guy's natural habitat."

"Well, for a caveman, you clean up pretty good." Elle looked around them, at the candles, the serving cart, and shook her head. "How did you manage all this?"

"I told you. Magic."

He was the magic. She came within a heartbeat of telling him that.

"Nobody ever…nobody in my entire life ever did anything like this for me."

He pushed the flowers aside, leaned forward and kissed her. "Part of me wishes someone had," he said softly. A smile of blatant male satisfaction angled over his mouth. "But the part that's living in that cave is glad I was the first."

She touched her hand to his face.

"You were the first for so many things," she whispered. "Especially about—about making love. I never…until you, I thought…I always thought—"

Her admission filled him with pleasure as well as pain. He hated knowing she'd feared sex…and yet, he exulted in the knowledge that he was the man who'd freed her of that fear.

"Hush," he said gruffly. "You don't have to explain."

"I didn't mean to embarrass you."

He turned his head and pressed a kiss to her palm.

"You could never embarrass me," he said roughly, "especially if you talk about what I make you feel."

Elle took a deep breath. "And me?" she murmured. "How do I make you feel?"

She waited for his answer, asking herself what had ever made her foolish enough to ask him such a question….

"As if you and I are alone on this planet," he said huskily. "As if nothing matters but us." He rose to his feet, drew her to hers, his eyes hot as fire. "As if the only thing under that gown is you."

Her heart leaped as he reached behind her for the zipper. He had undressed her many, many times over the past days and nights, but never like this. A week ago, this would have terrified her. Now, it sent waves of hot excitement through her blood.

The zipper opened. The thin straps of the gown fell from her shoulders and the slender column of amber silk drifted sensuously over her naked skin and became a discarded chrysalis at her feet.

Falco groaned. "Elle," he said, "God almighty, Elle…"

She trembled as his eyes swept over her. The look on his face… Her body's response was swift. She felt her breasts lift, her nipples bud. Heat pooled between her thighs.

"Falco," she whispered.

"Yes," he said, and he kissed her eyes, her mouth her throat.

Then he dropped to his knees and did what he had longed to do since the first time he'd made love to her, put his face against the soft curls that guarded her femininity.

Elle gasped. "No! You can't—"

His hands closed on her wrists as she reached out to stop him.

"I can," he said. "I have to."

Gently, he gently nuzzled her thighs apart. And kissed her.

Her cry tore through the night and he kissed her again, licked her, tasted her. Her orgasm raced through her, shattering her, turning her bones to liquid. He rose to his feet, scooped her into his arms, carried her to a *chaise longue* beside the pool and tore off his clothes. He entered her on one hard, deep thrust and she screamed as she came again. And again.

"Elle," he said, watching her face as he rode her, knowing that what he had told her the night they'd quarreled was the truth.

This wasn't sex.

It was far more than that.

It was—it was—

"Falco," she sobbed, and he flung back his head and let go.

They fell asleep wrapped around each other.

The night grew cool. A breeze swept in; the candles sputtered and went out. He woke with a start.

Elle was gone.

Falco shot to his feet…and saw her, at the far end of the atrium, wrapped in an oversized pool towel and staring blindly at the thin white line of surf beating against the sea.

He pulled on his trousers and went to her, slid his arms

around her and tried to pull her back against him but she stood stiff and unresponsive within his embrace.

"What's wrong, honey? Are you cold?"

"Falco. I have—I have to tell you—"

The words were heavy with meaning. A coldness that had nothing to do with the night went through him.

"You were right when you said I knew who's stalking me. I do know. I've known, all along." She swallowed, the sound audible in the silence of the atrium. "I just—I just don't know how to tell you...."

Falco held her closer. "Just tell me," he said softly. "Whatever it is, we'll deal with it together."

"His name is Willy Joe Johnson. He is...he was my stepfather." Elle drew a shuddering breath. "I told you that my real father died, remember? He was a coal miner. We lived in a little town in West Virginia and—and one day, there was an accident in the mine. My daddy and ten other miners didn't make it out."

Her voice had undergone a subtle change. It had taken on an accent, the softness of vowels he associated with small town girls from places where men risked their lives in the bowels of the earth.

"Go on," he said softly.

"My mama wasn't well. She hadn't been for a long time. With Papa gone, it was worse. We had no money. We got a little money from the union, but—but mostly, we lived on charity."

Falco shut his eyes, trying to block out the vision of a little girl with dark hair and topaz eyes, living on the kindness of strangers.

"Mama had a sister in Ohio. We moved there. But her sister had her own troubles. So we moved again, to Kentucky. Mama got a little better and she took a job but then she got sick again. We started going to this storefront church where there was a soup kitchen." She paused. "And a preacher."

Falco's gut knotted. Whatever came next would be dark and ugly. He wanted to turn Elle toward him, tell her she didn't have to say any more, but she did. What came next was at the heart of what had been happening to her.

"Willy Joe liked Mama. He seemed nice. And he said—he said he'd always wanted a little girl of his own. So, when I was thirteen, Mama married him. She did it for me. So I'd have food to eat and a roof over my head and—and—"

Falco turned her to him and set aside everything he knew about maintaining distance between himself and a client.

"You don't have to do this tonight, honey. It can wait until morning."

"No. It can't. It's waited too long as it is. You need to know. You have the right to know." Her voice broke. "I—I want you to know, do you see?"

So he let her talk.

She told him that she knew, almost right away, something was not right. Her stepfather barked at her mother, shouted at her. Even the house was unpleasant. It was dark and dirty. It had a bad feel to it.

And the walls were thin.

"They were very thin. I could hear what was happening in the next room, his and Mama's room, at night. Mama crying, Willy Joe grunting, but when I asked Mama, she said everything was fine. I knew it wasn't but I couldn't do anything to help her."

Falco cursed, swept Elle into his arms and carried her into the house. He sat down in an overstuffed living room chair and held her close.

"Mama got sick again. Real sick. And that was when—it was when Willy Joe started looking at me. Watching me. He'd brush against me as if it was an accident, come into the bathroom—the lock didn't work—and say he hadn't known I was in there. And then, one night, he came into my bedroom."

Falco said something ugly. Elle kept talking.

"He—he came every night after that. And he—he did things. But I wasn't there. Not really. I had this little stuffed animal my daddy had given me—"

"A toy cat," Falco said, because by now he knew, he knew.

Elle nodded. "I'd hold on to that cat and hold on to it, no matter what happened. I didn't scream, I didn't cry, I didn't tell anybody anything because Willy Joe told me what he'd do to Mama if I did."

And then, one morning, she said, her mother didn't wake up. The day of the funeral, her stepfather put his meaty hand on Elle's shoulder. He said that now, she really belonged to him.

He moved her into his room. Into the bed he'd shared with her mother. And that night—that night…

Elle began to sob. Falco went on holding her, rocking her, but his heart had become as cold as ice.

"I went to school the next morning," she said raggedly. "It was safer than staying home. But something must have showed because Miss Toner, my English teacher, asked if I was okay." She dragged in a breath. "'You can tell me, Ellie,' she said, and it was like a light coming on because she was right, I didn't have to protect Mama anymore. So I told her everything."

The rest of the story was straightforward. The teacher took her to the principal; the principal called the sheriff. Her stepfather was arrested. Elle, sixteen by then, was scheduled to testify at his trial but she didn't have to. Willy Joe pleaded guilty. He said only his God had the right to judge him.

"They sentenced him to fifty years and my teacher said he could never hurt me again…."

"But she was wrong," Falco said tonelessly. "When did he get out?"

"Six months ago. He found out where I lived. Sent me that—that horrible picture. He wrote to me. He told me I was going to pay for defying him and God. And then—and then, right before you showed up, he telephoned me…."

"Ah, baby. My sweet baby. Why didn't you go to the police?"

"Don't you see? Nobody knows what happened to me, Falco. Nobody but you. To have the whole world know—and it would be the whole world, this time—to have them stare and whisper, to have to live through the nightmare again…" She shuddered. "I was Ellie Janovic until Willy Joe was sentenced. The next day, I took a bus to New York. I became Elle Bissette. And I'm never going to be that other person again."

"Yes," he said, "yes, baby, I see."

And he did. Elle's scars went deep. She had survived a horrendous ordeal but if the media got hold of the story, she'd be victimized all over again.

He held her for hours, stroking her, comforting her, telling her that he would never let anything hurt her. Gradually, she stopped weeping and fell asleep, safe in his arms.

He wanted to hold her forever, but he couldn't. The monster had to be dealt with. To do that, he had to contain his anger. Hell, his rage. He had to formulate a plan.

Discipline. Self-control. Logic. Those had always been the bastions of his life.

Until he caught the bastard who'd done this to his Elle, he needed them more than ever.

CHAPTER TWELVE

A MAGICAL evening.

But everything changed, the next day. Everything including Falco.

He became…removed.

Elle couldn't think of another way to describe his behavior. He was there but he wasn't, not in the ways that mattered. There were no more long walks on the beach, no easy laughter, no drives along the back roads.

Something was wrong. The question was, what?

The change had been painfully abrupt. He'd been so wonderful that night. So tender, holding her in his arms until she slept, soothing her with whispers and caresses. At dawn, she'd felt him slip from the bed. She'd assumed he was going to use the bathroom but then she heard the rustle of cloth and she'd looked from under her lashes to see him putting on a T-shirt and a pair of denim cutoffs.

Come back to me, she'd almost said, but there'd been such caution in the way he moved that she'd remained silent. Silly, because he probably only wanted to make sure he didn't wake her, but when he left the room without at least dropping a light kiss on her lips, the first tendrils of doubt crept in. Had the things she told him changed the way he saw her?

No. That was crazy. He wasn't that kind of man, Elle told herself as she dressed and went looking for him. He wasn't in the kitchen or the atrium, he wasn't anywhere in the house. He was on the beach, making one call after another on his cell phone. When he was done, he stripped off his T-shirt and began exercising. One hundred push-ups. One hundred squats. And then what appeared to be a wild combination of kickboxing and kung fu and tae kwon do.

After a while, sweat glistened on his body. A beautiful body she'd come to know with heart-stopping intimacy and yet—and yet, even his body seemed different. Beautiful, of course, but now she saw it could be a tool of violence.

She went back into the house and waited for him.

"Hey," she'd said as lightly as she could manage when he finally came in, "what's going on?"

"I've let things go," he'd answered. "Now I'm making up for it."

No kiss. No smile. Just those cool words as he headed for the shower.

By now, four days had gone by. Falco's morning workout routine became more intense. He seemed to be always on his phone. He spoke to her in short, clipped phrases. The most difficult thing to accept was that they didn't go to bed at the same time. They always had, since becoming lovers. Not anymore.

"You go ahead," Falco would say when it grew late. "I'll be a little while."

She fell asleep alone. Or didn't fall asleep, but it didn't matter. When he finally came to bed, he didn't touch her. Didn't hold her. And yet, during the darkest hours of the night, she'd awaken to his hard body against hers, to the drugging heat of his mouth, the skill of his hands moving over her and then the almost savage power of his possession.

No words. No whispers. Just that stunning, exciting joining of flesh to flesh.

In the morning, no matter how early she awoke, he was already gone.

At first, she wept. Not where he could see. Never that. Her heart ached; she longed for the man she'd come to know as Falco Orsini. Then tears gave way to anger. What was the point to self-pity? If she'd given in to that kind of defeatist behavior years ago, Elle Bissette would not exist.

What had created Elle Bissette was determination, guts and, yes, anger. Anger at her stepfather and then anger at herself for not getting on with her life. Anger was a strong, safe emotion. And by day four, it consumed her.

If Falco had a problem accepting the truth about her, why in hell had he insisted on hearing it? Why had he been so caring after she'd told him everything? Given time to think things over, had he regretted making love with a woman who, face it, Elle, was damaged goods?

Did he think he could have sex with her under cover of darkness and reject her when daylight came? If so, he had another think coming.

Elle glared out the window. She could see him down by the water, doing those ridiculous martial arts moves.

"Enough," she said through her teeth, "is enough."

She went out the door and strode toward him. If he heard her coming, he didn't show it. He went on grunting and straining, whirling around on one foot, kicking and jabbing. She snorted. He looked ridiculous….

Except, he didn't.

He looked graceful and almost dauntingly masculine, and for one desperate moment she almost flung herself into his arms to tell him that she wasn't angry or ticked off, she was in pain because he was breaking her heart…

"What do you want?"

She blinked. Falco stood glaring at her, his hands on his hips.

"Elle. If you have something to say, spit it out. I'm busy here."

Elle narrowed her eyes and slapped her hands on her hips, mimicking his posture without realizing it.

"I want to know what's going on."

"I'm working out. That's what's going on."

"You know what I mean. Where have you been all week?"

He stared at her. She thought she saw awareness in his eyes, but then he grabbed a towel and rubbed it over his face. When he looked at her again, his eyes were blank.

"I've been doing what I should have been doing from the start. A bodyguard's not much use if he's not in shape."

"And this occurred to you because…?"

Falco struggled to remain unmoved. She was angry. Her color was high. Her voice was sharp. She'd obviously tumbled out of bed and put herself together in a rush because her hair was tangled and she hadn't bothered with a bra; he could see the pout of her nipples against the thin cotton of her tank top.

She was, in other words, mouth-wateringly delicious. She always was.

Going to bed without enfolding her in his arms each night was agony. Leaving her each morning was just as tough. He didn't think about it so much during the day because he was busy from morning until night, getting back in shape, talking with the guy who'd gotten him the gun here in Maui and another guy he knew and trusted back in L.A., planning every move a dozen times over because if he made a mistake, his Elle was the one who would pay.

Even so, there'd been times the last few days she'd walked by him and he'd wanted to grab her. Haul her into his arms.

Tell her he was doing this for her, that this was the only way he knew to pull off something so dangerous, that it was the most important thing he'd ever undertaken because of what he felt for her.

He didn't, of course.

Control. Containment. Discipline. Making plans and reviewing them until they were part of him. It had to be handled like this.

That he lost all that control and containment and discipline in the dark hours of the night, that he was too damned weak to keep from turning to her, taking her in his arms, seeking comfort in her warmth, her silkiness, her almost pagan response to him…

That he permitted that to happen was wrong.

How could he prepare for what came next unless he kept his mind and body separate? And that was the problem. He couldn't seem to keep them separate anymore. Something inside him had changed; he didn't just want to touch Elle, he wanted to think about her. All the time. To make her part of him. To tell her—to tell her that he—that he—

His cell phone beeped. Falco almost groaned with relief as he snatched it from his pocket and shot a look at it. It was the guy from L.A.

"Yes?"

"Bingo," the guy said. "My contact at the *L.A. Times* came through. The article reads…" There was the rustle of paper. "It reads, 'Everybody can stop wondering why Elle Bissette walked off the set. She's been spotted canoodling with her latest at a private estate off Paradise Road on the beach at Maui.' Plus, his wife works for *Entertainment Tonight*. She got the same item online and on TV yesterday."

"Perfect. And the rest?"

"Well, you already know I located your man three days back, and that I've been on him ever since."

Falco looked at Elle, then swung away from her. "And?"

"And, he's getting ready to make his move. In fact, I'm standing a few feet away from him right now. He bought a ticket to Maui at the American Airlines counter. His flight's due to land at midnight, your time."

Falco nodded. "Good work," he said softly. "And Rick? Thanks."

"*De nada*, dude. Feels like old times, right?"

"Right." Falco disconnected, hit a speed dial button. Jack, the guy in Maui, picked up on the first ring.

"Yeah?"

"Time to rock and roll, Jack."

"I'm ready, man. I'll be there in an hour."

Falco closed his phone and turned to Elle. This would be the hardest part of all.

"Who," she said coldly, "was that?"

"A couple of friends." He paused. "I need their help so I can take care of your problem."

Elle saw something cold and primitive flicker in his eyes. All her anger drained away.

"Oh, God," she whispered, "Falco—"

"Your stalker is on his way here. You and I both know what he intends to do." A muscle tightened in his jaw. "Except, things won't go exactly the way he figures."

"Falco." Elle took a step toward him. "What are you saying?"

He tucked his phone in his pocket, draped the towel around his neck, grabbed his shirt and started for the house. Elle had to run to keep up.

"Answer me," she said. "What are you going to do?"

"Whatever needs doing."

"No!" She caught his arm, swung in front of him. "He'll kill you!"

Falco laughed. Elle shook her head.

"Falco. Please. Call the police."

"You gave me good reasons why the police shouldn't get involved in this," he said, shaking her off and continuing towards the house.

"I've changed my mind. If you get hurt—"

"I won't."

"Dammit, nobody's immortal!"

He stopped and swung toward her again. "I told you. I'm not going to get hurt."

"But—but if—if you should…" Her eyes searched his. "I'd be—I'd be—"

"What?" he said in a low voice.

"I'd be—" She stared at him. Heartbroken, she thought. Devastated. Lost for the rest of my life because I love you, love you—

Did the words spill from her lips? All she knew was that Falco cursed, grabbed her by the shoulders, hauled her to him and took her mouth in a bruising kiss. Elle sobbed his name, all but jumped into his arms, wrapped her arms and legs around him and kissed him back. His hands snaked under her tank top; he said something she couldn't understand as he tore it from her. Her shorts and panties followed.

Naked, she moaned his name as he backed her against the house, fumbled at his fly and then he thrust into her, hard, deep, all of him hot and rigid within her wet, welcoming heat. She screamed with pleasure, screamed again and again until he had emptied himself into her. He held her for a long moment, her face against his throat, his arms tight around her. Then, slowly, he lowered her to her feet.

"I'm not going to let you do this," she said in a shaky whisper. "You don't know what he's like. He'll—"

"I know precisely what he's like." Falco scooped up her clothing and handed it to her. He didn't want to see her naked like this. It made him want to take her in his arms and hold her to his heart and there wasn't a way in hell he was going to let that happen. "Put your clothes on," he said roughly.

Color swept into her face but, she went right on facing him, the clothes held to her breasts.

"Falco. I beg you. Listen to me—"

"Do you hear me, dammit? Go inside. Get dressed. Pack. There'll be someone here soon to fly you to Los Angeles."

"Fly me…? No! I won't go. If you're going to be so—so pigheaded, I'll stay. I'm not leaving you."

His mouth twisted as he moved past her, into the coolness of the house.

"I'm not giving you a choice, Bissette."

"Wait a minute. Wait just one damned minute!" Elle rushed after him, grabbed his arm. Tears of anger and frustration streaked her face. Looking at her made his throat constrict.

"I love you," she said. "Do you understand? I love you! I'm not going to let you do this. I love you. And you—and you love—"

His heart turned over. She was right about part of that. He loved her. Why deny the truth to himself? He loved her with every fiber of his being and that made it all the more imperative to get her out of here. He could not do what he had to do if he worried about her stepfather somehow getting past him and putting his filthy hands on her.

There was only one way to make sure she left, and he took it.

"You're wrong," he said, fighting to keep his emotions from showing. "You don't love me."

"Dammit, Orsini, do not tell me what—"

"And I sure as hell don't love you. You're beautiful and desirable and sexy but wanting you isn't loving you."

Her face paled. "Falco. You don't mean—"

"You needed a knight errant. And there I was, riding in to save you."

Elle shook her head. "That's not how it was. It was more than that. It was—"

"It was sex," he said bluntly. "Great sex." She tried to look away from him. He caught hold of her and forced her to meet his cool gaze. "Yeah, we made love. But making love isn't the same as being in love."

A moan escaped her lips. He knew he would never forget this moment just as he knew that at least part of what he'd told her was true. She didn't love him. For all her sophistication, his Elle was an innocent. She'd never loved a man, never lain in a man's arms, and she'd damned well never had a man do battle to save her.

Add it all up, she was confusing gratitude with love. He knew it and, once she got a little distance from what had happened, so would she.

"So…" She paused. "So, you were just doing your job?"

"And it isn't over."

She nodded. "But we are," she whispered.

Falco shrugged his shoulders. "You've got it."

She took a step back. Her nose was running; she swiped at it with the clothing balled in her hand. She had forgotten she was naked and he let his eyes sweep over her one last time.

She thought she saw something flash in those eyes…until he simply turned and walked away.

Then she knew, for sure, what they'd had—what she'd let herself believe they'd had—was finished.

CHAPTER THIRTEEN

JACK, THE Maui guy, showed up.

Falco introduced him to Elle. Elle said nothing. Not to his old pal, not to him. Well, sure. What was there left to say after you'd said it all?

Elle got into Jack's car and they left for the airport. Falco had chartered a plane to take them to L.A. He watched until the car was just a spot of dust. His heart was heavy but he knew Elle would be safe. Back in the day, he and Jack had trusted each other with their lives. They still did.

It was time to prepare for Willy Joe Johnson's arrival.

He checked the house, its perimeter, touched up a couple of refinements he'd made to the security system. An hour later, Rick, the L.A. guy, phoned. Willy Joe's plane had taken off on time. Elle's stepfather was on his way to Maui.

Falco ate a light meal. Checked his weapon. He looked at his watch, set it for midnight, lay down on a bed—not the one he'd shared with Elle—and slept. He woke a minute before the watch beeped, threw cold water on his face, went into the dark living room and settled in to wait.

Jack phoned. He and Elle were in L.A., in the suite Falco had reserved at the Four Seasons. Everything was fine, except Elle still wasn't talking to him.

That made Falco smile. What a tough lady she was.

Midnight came and went…one a.m., two a.m. Still nothing. Time was dragging.

He thought back over the last few days, thought about Elle. Sending her away had been the right thing, the only thing. She'd fallen in love with the idea of love, not with him.

And he—he would forget. The taste of her mouth. The warmth of her in his arms. The exquisite feel of her closing around him as they'd made love for the very last time.

That had been wrong. Terribly wrong. He'd known that even as he'd slipped deep inside her, but having her that one last time had been as vital as drawing breath….

The lights on the silent alarm console blinked to life. Falco felt his pulse start to race.

Elle's stepfather had arrived.

In the end, much of Falco's planning hadn't been worth a damn.

He'd expected a stealthy attack. The rear door. The front door. The door to the atrium.

Instead, there was a horrendous crash.

Johnson, evidently not given to subtlety, had smashed his way into the atrium. Moonlight illuminated him, six feet six inches of lard laid over prison-honed muscle.

He had a knife in his hand.

"Where is she?" Willy Joe shouted. "Where is that heathen bitch whose lies sent me to prison?"

Falco stepped into the atrium, gun drawn.

"She's where you can't hurt her," he said in a low, hard voice. "You're never going to hurt her again."

Willy Joe spat on the terrazzo floor. "She lured me to her. Seduced me. She's a whore, just like her mama." He curved his body forward, spread his feet apart. It was the stance of a man who knew how to use the silvery blade he held. "Now she's your whore, Orsini. But not for long. I'm going to kill you and then I'll kill her." He smiled, the smile of a maniac. "Get ready to meet your maker."

Willy Joe took a shuffling step forward. All Falco had to do was pull the trigger and a bullet traveling at better than 1,000 feet per second would stop this hulking mountain of vile flesh.

Instead, he tossed the gun aside.

He had no knife. No other weapon. What he had was the hot, blazing rage a man can only feel when the woman he loves has been violated.

"Come on and try it, you son of a bitch," he growled, and Willy Joe cackled and came at him.

The stalker was as big as a mountain but Falco was fast. And he was all muscle, no fat laid over it. He lunged to the left, feinted to the right and struck out. The first blow staggered Willy Joe but he shook it off, rushed Falco again and closed his massive arms around him. They wrestled. Struggled. Fell to the glass-strewn floor and rolled. Suddenly, the knife was driving down toward Falco's throat.

"Whore-master," Willy Joe shouted, but all Falco could hear was the sound of Elle weeping, the night she'd told him what she'd endured.

Falco roared. Grabbed his attacker's wrist. Slowly, slowly, grunting with the effort, he forced the hand holding the knife backward, toward Willy Joe.

The blade sank in.

Willy Joe gasped, then froze. And rolled onto his back, dead.

Falco shook his head to clear it, got to his knees and looked down at the stalker.

"Give my regards to the devil," he said hoarsely.

Then he staggered to his feet and took out his cell phone, which was when he realized he'd been cut. It didn't matter.

The monster who had caused the woman he loved years and years of pain was no more.

The police arrived, then a crime scene crew and a pair of detectives.

The detective in charge took Falco's statement, took notes, poked Willy Joe's body with the shiny toe of one black brogue.

"Mean SOB," his partner said. "Checked him on the computer soon as we got the call from the local guys."

Falco nodded. The EMTs had cleaned his wounds. He needed stitches but that could wait.

"So, you were staying here, on vacation, and this mother turned up from out of nowhere?"

Falco nodded again. "He must have figured the house was empty and filled with expensive stuff he could steal."

"Not his M.O.," the first detective said. "Guy was arrested and did time years ago for raping a kid."

"Well," Falco said, "I guess he decided to try something different."

"And you were here, alone. Big place, for one man."

Falco forced a smile. "I had some company for a couple of days," he said, knowing that if they checked, the best anybody would do was give a vague description of a woman.

The second detective cleared his throat. "You know, I mentioned you to my captain, Orsini. Says he knew you, back a ways in the Middle East. Knew of you, anyway. Says you were involved in some nasty stuff, says it's a damned good thing Johnson happened to choose this place to rob, that he'd surely have killed anybody else who'd tried to stop him."

Falco shrugged. "The luck of the draw."

The detectives looked at each other. "Yeah," the one in charge said with a quick smile, "that's what it must have been. The luck of the draw."

* * *

Elle read about it in an L.A. newspaper.

She knew things had gone the way Falco had intended because his friend, Jack, got a call from Falco, smiled and told her she could leave the hotel anytime. He wouldn't say more than that.

It was a small article, just a few lines. An ex-convict had broken into a house on Maui and attacked the vacationer staying there. The vacationer had killed him. No names mentioned; it wasn't an important enough news item for that.

A clear case of self-defense, said the police, but it would be up to the district attorney to make the final decision.

Elle put the paper down. Her hands were trembling.

Her tormenter was dead. Her lover had killed him. The man she loved—because, yes, she loved Falco and always would, despite the fact that he didn't love her—the man she loved had risked his life, even his freedom, for her.

And what had she done for him except run away?

He'd forced her to leave but the truth was, she could have bolted once his friend got her to the airport. What would the man have done about it? Tie her up? Drag her, kicking and screaming, onto the waiting chartered plane? Not hardly.

She had let Falco drive her away because she couldn't bear the thought that he didn't love her, that he would never love her, that she had been a job and sex and nothing more.

But what about all the rest?

He had brought her out of a lifetime of darkness. He had shown her that sex, that making love, could be joyful. He was her knight and he'd slain the dragon—and she'd abandoned him.

What if the D.A. didn't agree with the police? What if he brought Falco up on charges? Surely there could be consequences. Assault? Manslaughter? Murder?

Tears rose in her eyes. All her life, all the past months, she had thought only of herself. Now, it was time to think of someone else. The one man she would always love.

Her dark knight. Her Falco.

Falco sat in his office in the Orsini Brothers building in downtown Manhattan.

He had a stack of papers on his desk; he knew his e-mail box was stuffed. He'd blown off a meeting this morning and he was in no mood for one scheduled for this afternoon, either.

He leaned forward, hit the button on his intercom.

"Yes sir, Mr. Orsini?"

Falco sighed. His P.A. was new. He'd told her, a dozen times, to call him Falco.

"Cancel my three o'clock, please. Make it for next week."

As if anything would change by next week. As if anything would ever change, he thought, and tilted back his chair.

All he could think about was Elle.

He missed her. He ached for her. He thought of her each morning when he woke up, thought of her last thing at night, dreamed of her.

His brothers sensed something was up. They were about as subtle as elephants in a Victorian parlor. He knew they'd been talking about him. Last night, they'd badgered him into having beer and burgers at The Bar, the place they owned in SoHo. He hadn't wanted to go. The last thing he was in the mood for was fun and games but he'd figured it was easier to agree and then cut out early.

Not early enough, as it had turned out. The burgers hadn't even arrived when Raffaele flashed a phony smile and said, "So, Falco, how're things going?"

"They're going fine," he'd replied.

"Because," Dante had said, "well, you know, if anything's wrong…"

"Why would anything be wrong?" he'd said.

He'd changed the subject, talked some inane nonsense about baseball and they'd let him do it but sooner or later, they'd start pushing. And when they did—

"Falco?"

He looked up. Raffaele, Dante and Nicolo had cracked the door. They were peering in at him and, dammit, they had that look, the look they all got, him included, when they were worried about each other.

Well, hell. He didn't want anyone worrying about him.

"Hey, guys," he said, flashing a big smile, "I'd love to hang around and talk but—"

The three of them stepped into his office. Rafe shut the door.

"But what?" Dante said.

"But, I have a three o'clock appointment. And—"

"The hell you do," Rafe said. "You just cancelled."

Falco sighed. "That new P.A. is never going to work out."

Nick cleared his throat. "What's going on? And don't tell us nothing's going on. We know that's not true."

Falco looked from one of his brothers to the other. For one wild second, he almost blurted it out, almost said, *I met the only woman I'll ever love and I destroyed any possible hope she might have cared for me—*

"Whatever it is," he said coolly, "I don't need the Three Musketeers busting into my life."

"Think of us more as the Spanish Inquisition." Rafe grinned. "We have ways of making you talk."

Falco shoved back his chair and rose to his feet. "Okay, gentlemen, that's it. This meeting is—"

"Do your amazingly high spirits have anything to do with that errand our old man laid on you?"

Falco's eyes narrowed. "What'd you do, Nick? Put your ear to the door?"

Nick grinned. "Hey, I wasn't even there. I got tired of waiting and I took off."

"Yeah, well, good for you. Now, if you'll all excuse me—"

"Dammit, Falco," Dante said, "what's happening with you?"

Falco glared at his brothers. "I'll tell you what's happening with me," he snarled. "I met a woman, okay? And I—I got involved. And I told her I didn't give a damn for her. And—and, hell, it was a lie."

His brothers looked at each other. They were almost as shocked as Falco by his admission.

"So," Rafe said, "so, ah, go tell her. Tell her you—"

The intercom buzzed. Falco slapped the talk button. "Dammit," he roared, "what do you want?"

"I just…someone is here to see you, Mr. Orsini. Sir. I told her you were busy but—"

"But," Elle said as she opened the door and stepped into the office, "I told her I'd only take a minute of your time."

Falco blinked. "Elle?"

She nodded, looked around and bit lightly into her bottom lip. "You must be Falco's brothers."

Rafe and Nick and Dante nodded. Introduced themselves. Shook her hand. Looked at Falco, waited for him to say something…

"Go away," he said, and the three of them rushed for the door and shut it behind them.

"Elle." Falco could feel his heart racing. "You look—you look wonderful."

"Thank you. I guess I should have called first…"

"No," he said quickly, "no, I'm—I'm glad to see you."

Elle's mouth had gone dry. This was her Falco. The man

she adored. She wanted to run into his arms but that wasn't why she'd come here.

And it wasn't what he wanted.

She swallowed hard. "I read about—about what happened."

Hell, Falco thought, she'd hated Johnson but who knew how she felt now, knowing that he had killed him.

"The paper didn't say much, just that Willy Joe—that he broke in and—"

"We scuffled. I lucked out."

"He could have killed you!"

"No way," he said with a smile meant to be reassuring, "you know what they say about guys who were born to be hung."

"Falco." Her eyes blurred. She came toward him, lightly touched the small scar above his eyebrow. "Oh," she whispered, "did he—did he—"

"It's nothing." But the cool touch of her hand was almost more than he could bear. He caught her hand and laced his fingers through hers. God, he wanted to take her in his arms…

"The paper said that the police called it self-defense but that the final decision would be up to the district attorney."

"Right. It always is. And—"

"And," Elle said, hurrying the words together, "and if he decided it wasn't, you'll have to stand trial."

"No. I mean, yes, but—"

"I won't let that happen! I'm going to fly to Maui."

"What?"

"I said, I'm going to Maui. I'll tell the D.A. exactly what happened. How—how Willy Joe abused me. How he was sentenced to prison because of me and how he hated me for it and stalked me and—and—"

Falco felt the first flutter of hope. "Why would you do that?" he said softly.

"Because—because it's the right thing to do. I can't let you go to prison because of me."

He reached out and touched her hair. He couldn't help it. The need to stroke those dark strands one last time was too strong.

"I won't go to prison, honey. The D.A. reached a decision a couple of days ago. There won't be any charges."

Elle let out her breath. "Oh, I'm so glad!"

"You'd have done that, for me? Gone to the D.A.? Let your story go public?"

She nodded.

"Because?"

"I told you. It's the right thing to—"

Falco had lived his life taking risks. Now, he took the greatest risk of all.

"Tell me the truth," he said huskily. "Why would you do all that for me?" She didn't answer and he took her in his arms. "Is it because you love me, baby? Because you love me the way I love you?"

Tears spilled from her eyes. "Do you mean it? That you love me? Because I love you, Falco, I adore you. And—and I'd do anything for you, my knight, anything, anything—"

He kissed her. She gave a little cry, rose on her toes and wrapped her arms around his neck.

"Are you sure?" she said, against his lips. "Please be sure!"

"I love you with all my heart," he said huskily. "I love Ellie Janovic and I love Elle Bissette. With all my heart, all my soul. I'll love you until the end of time. Don't you know that by now?"

Elle made a sound that was half laugh, half sob. "You said you didn't. And you said I didn't love you. You said—"

"Hush," Falco said, and kissed her again. "I said a lot of things that day, every one a lie." He smoothed his thumbs over her cheekbones, felt the warmth of her tears against his skin.

"I loved you then. I love you now. I was just afraid you'd fallen for the man you thought I was—"

"I did. I fell for my knight in shining armor."

"I'm no knight, honey. I'm a lot of things but not that."

Elle smiled. "How little you know, Orsini. Of course you're a knight. My knight. And you always will be."

He smiled back at her. "You are one tough broad, Bissette. There's no arguing with you when you're sure you're right, is there?"

"Not about this," she said. "Never about this."

Falco drew her closer. "Still, there are things about me you don't know."

"For instance."

"For instance, your knight's old man is a crime boss."

"You already mentioned that." Elle laid a light kiss on Falco's lips. "So it's a good thing I'm not in love with your old man. What else?"

"Well," he said, straight-faced, "the other thing is even worse. I'm not a bodyguard."

"I sort of figured that when I looked in the Manhattan directory and found the listing for Orsini Brothers."

"Yeah. I'm an investor, along with those three idiots who just stumbled out the door."

"An investor." She smiled. "You're right. Considering everything, that might be even worse." She kissed him again. "But I'm willing to survive it if you can."

"Elle." Falco's expression grew serious. "Elle, will you marry me?"

Her eyes filled with happy tears. "Just try and stop me, Orsini," she said, and Falco reached past her, locked the door and kissed her.

EPILOGUE

THEY were married in the same little church in Greenwich Village that had so recently been the setting for Dante's and Rafe's weddings. Mercifully, no police cars were parked outside and only one photographer showed up. He beat a quick retreat after the Orsini brothers had a little talk with him.

Elle wore ivory silk; she carried a trailing bouquet of white orchids and wore her new mother-in-law's wedding veil, which made Sofia beam with delight. A heart-shaped canary-yellow diamond glittered in the hollow of her throat; another adorned the ring finger of her left hand.

Falco was gorgeous in the same tux he'd worn on what Elle called their first date, back in Hawaii. Isabella, Anna, Chiara and Gabriella were her bridesmaids, all of them beautiful in gowns of pink silk. Her new brothers-in-law kissed her and told her how happy they were to have her in their family.

The reception was held in the conservatory of the Orsini mansion. Everyone laughed, drank champagne, ate lobster and caviar and even managed bites of the huge wedding cake.

By late afternoon, things were getting quiet.

The bride and groom slipped away. They were going to Hawaii, though not to Maui, on their honeymoon. Dante and Gaby left with their son, Daniel, asleep in his daddy's arms.

Rafe and Chiara left, too. Chiara was pregnant, glowing with happiness, as was Rafe.

Nicolo kissed his mother goodbye, avoided his father as he'd done all day. Avoiding Cesare was habit; he didn't like the Don any more than his brothers did and besides, Nick was very aware of the fact that he had, thus far, avoided the talk Cesare had wanted to have with him a few months ago on the day Dante and Gabriella had married.

He and Falco had both been told their father wanted to see them. Falco had gone in first, Nick had waited outside for a few minutes and then he'd though, *Eff this*, which was exactly what he'd said to Felix, his father's *capo*, had put out a hand to stop him from leaving.

"I am not one of the Don's soldiers," Nick had said coldly. "He wants to see me, let him call and make an appointment."

But there'd been no call and Nick had figured he'd escaped his father's latest "after I'm dead" speech.

"Nicolo."

Nick, halfway to the front door of the big house, groaned. He took a deep breath and turned around.

"Father," he said politely.

"We must talk."

"I have an appointment. And you and I have nothing to talk about."

Cesare smiled around the fat, unlit Havana cigar clutched between his teeth.

"But we do. Besides, you owe me a few minutes. Did you think I had forgotten how you slipped out the last time?"

"I didn't 'slip out', Father, I just got tired of cooling my heels like one of your men."

"Exactly. You are not one of my men, you are my son. Surely, you will give me the courtesy of a chat just as your three brothers have done before you."

Nick's jaw tightened. His father was right. Dante, Raffaele and Falco had all gone through the wringer. It was his turn now, and he wasn't a man to walk away from a responsibility.

"Five minutes," he said brusquely. "That's it."

"Of course, Nicolo," Cesare said smoothly. "In my study, *per favore*. Yes?"

Nick strode toward the dark, overfurnished room from which Cesare ruled his empire.

"Whatever speech you've prepared, Father, had better be good."

The Don's *capo*, silent as a cat, stepped out of the shadows. Cesare motioned him aside and followed his son into the study.

"I assure you, Nicolo," he said as he shut the door, "it is."